WAKING UP IN THE LAND OF

glitter

A Crafty Chica Novel

KATHY CANO-MURILLO

GC

GRAND CENTRAL
PUBLISHING

NEW YORK   BOSTON

Grand Central Publishing
Hachette Book Group
237 Park Avenue
New York, NY 10017

HachetteBookGroup.com

Printed in the United States of America

First Edition: March 2010
10   9   8   7   6   5   4   3   2   1

Grand Central Publishing is a division of Hachette Book Group, Inc.
The Grand Central Publishing name and logo is a trademark of Hachette Book Group, Inc.

Library of Congress Cataloging-in-Publication Data

Cano-Murillo, Kathy.
Waking up in the land of glitter : a Crafty Chica novel / Kathy Cano-Murillo.
p. cm.
ISBN 978-0-446-50924-4
1. Hispanic American women—Fiction.   2. Handicraft—Fiction.
3. Craft festivals—Competitions—Fiction.   4. Phoenix (Az.)—Fiction.   I. Title.
PS3603.A556W35 2010
813'.6—dc22
2009020993

The first dedication of this book is for my husband, Patrick Murillo. If it were not for him, I never would have had the courage to come out of the closet as a wannabe artist so many years ago. Seeing potential I could not, he coaxed me into decorating a blank wood box with paint pens, glitter, feathers, and Mexican imagery. Little did we know that action would set our future in motion!

The second dedication is to all the creative individuals out there who have a vision to do something great. Whether it is on a public or private scale, I hope the characters in this book will inspire you to reach your goals. Remember—no idea is too big or too crazy!

The third dedication is to my parents, David and Norma Cano. Thank you for blessing me with your artful spirit and extreme tenacity so I could fulfill my dream of writing and sharing this book!

And last, to Ellen DeGeneres, self-proclaimed disliker of glitter. May she see that there is a type of sparkle for every personality, and that waking up in the land of glitter can be a good thing!

WAKING UP
IN THE LAND OF

glitter

1

Hello, Arizona! Crafty Chloe Chavez here—braving the heat in front of La Pachanga Eatery with your weather update! It's already ninety-eight degrees on this otherwise lovely Phoenix August morning, and it is time to break out the ice cubes, because we'll hit one hundred and ten by this afternoon! Coming up after the break— why was this beloved local business a target of vicious vandals?"

"Um, you can't go on live TV with blood on your arm; our viewers are eating breakfast," the cameraman said, nodding at Star's elbow as he hoisted his equipment up on his shoulder.

"Crap!" Star whispered before she licked her finger and scrubbed off the stain. "I wish it *was* blood," she mumbled, while standing in the parking lot of her parents' restaurant.

"Ah, don't be so nervous. You'll do fine," he said.

"I'm far from fine this morning, but I'll deal. And for the record, it's not blood, just a smidge of spray paint."

"Spray paint?" he repeated, his attention piqued.

"Hey!" Star chirped. "Speaking of blood, by any chance, do you knit?"

Star set aside the current troubles on her mind to enthusiastically explain the blood-to-knitting transition. "See, I've been working on this high-impact art project—the Victims of Violence blanket. It is dedicated to those who have been wrongly hurt all across the world. I want to get as many people as possible to help create a ginormous knitted blanket to represent our unified offerings of comfort and warmth. I feel that if we all just came together in the name of peace and love—"

"I don't knit," he deadpanned, cutting off her passionate plea. "You're live in less than three minutes."

Star shoved her arm into her limited-edition Tokidoki messenger bag that was slung across her chest and fished for her cherry lipstick. "It's totally cool if you don't know how," she said as she retrieved it. She whisked the color across her mouth, and then wiped the sweat from her neck with her other hand. "It's not about technique or even knitting itself. It's about the intention. Each stitch is original and represents that person's energy. That's what makes it *art*. Art that *matters*. Not silly crafts that Crafty Chloe does. The Victims of Violence Blanket project could change the world."

"We're outside, sweating like pigs in a sauna, and you're talking about knitting? At least it's for a good cause. Almost done?"

"Actually...I haven't started. I don't know how to knit either. I'm more of a visionary type." She raised a fist, shrugged, and grinned. "But I have hope! All I need is to find the right person to partner with, and I'm on my way!"

Star mentally congratulated herself for being so perky and positive, despite her current off-color condition, which consisted of a guilt-ridden hangover and eighty-seven minutes of half sleep. Who was she kidding? Every time someone cornered her, she changed the subject to an endearing topic. It served as her cutesy defense mechanism.

The cameraman didn't find her cute. He appeared as if he wished he had taken the evening shift, where they cover stories like trials, riots, murders, and football games—or any combination thereof.

"Live in one minute. Can you harness that hair?" he barked. "Chavez is territorial about her screen time, and your head'll take up more than half the shot."

"Sure. Hey, has anyone ever told you that you look like that actor Ving Rhames?"

He ignored her.

Rude! Star thought. That was a compliment. Ving Rhames rocked. Hello, *Pulp Fiction*? Even if this man knew how to knit, she didn't want his grumpy vibes woven into her blanket. She grabbed a stray lock that hung over her face and used it to tie back her curly mane, which hadn't been tamed since the day before.

Meanwhile, a concerned crowd gathered in the parking lot to witness the damage to the property. Star looked at them and bowed her head. "Oh God, this is really, truly happening." Suddenly the magnitude of last night's crime sank into her gut and, even worse, her conscience. She bit her lip, looked to the sky, and chanted a power prayer seconds before she would lie to thousands of TV viewers across Arizona.

Star kept her knees in locked position as she stood in front of La Pachanga, Phoenix's most-famed Mexican restaurant, adored by art enthusiasts, culture hounds, visiting celebrities, and wealthy folks in Hummers looking for a dash of instant culture.

Chloe's chubby red-haired assistant powdered the reporter's satiny cheeks. She then whipped out a toothbrush, spritzed it with hairspray, and used it to smooth the cone-shaped crown of the reporter's stick-straight frosty blond hair. She then gave her shoulder-length tresses a heavy coat of spray.

The Arizona sun was beyond hard-core. Star had lived in Phoenix all her life and still couldn't adjust to the summer temperatures, which included driver's arm sunburn and the melting of sentimental mementos—most recently a memory stick with all her favorite French pop songs. She inspected Crafty Chloe's flawless appearance and wondered how, even without the touch-up, she could look so fresh in a long-sleeved suit standing in direct sunlight. There wasn't a drop of sweat on her, whereas Star could feel her own T-shirt damp on her back. Then again, Crafty Chloe wasn't the one in the karmic hot seat.

Chloe stepped next to Star and gave her a courtesy smile, trailed by a horrified sneer at her hair. Star bypassed the visual insult and gulped back tears of shame as Chloe began the interview.

"It's a sad day for Phoenix's art community," Chloe stated, somber, as if she were covering war in the Middle East. "In the darkness of the night, vandals ruined the award-winning mosaic mural here at La Pachanga Eatery—with, of all things, spray-painted happy faces. Local artist Theo Duarte garnered national attention when he created an ornate replica of the Sonoran desert. Using only pebbles and river rocks from Arizona locations, the neighborhood-funded project that took more than a year to complete was heartlessly defaced in one night."

Star's head throbbed, cottonmouth set in, and she became dizzy. She focused on a tan Chihuahua across the street, joyously lapping water from a lawn sprinkler. She wished she could be that dog right now.

"I have with me Star Esteban, daughter of La Pachanga's owners," Chloe announced to the viewers of *Wake Up Arizona*. "You look absolutely devastated, Star. What does your family make of this atrocity?" Chloe scrunched her brows together as all dedicated reporters do. She shoved the cordless handheld mic to Star's mouth.

Estrella "Star" Esteban considered herself a worldly girl. But this morning, no goddess, saint, healer, shaman, or even Nana Esteban in heaven could repair the anarchy she had ignited last night. Star cleared her throat, knowing her disappointed parents watched from home. Even worse, Theo had just walked up and stood a few feet away, his art-repair caddy in tow. Several patrons patted him on the back to show their sympathy. He shook their hands and graciously thanked them. Theo must have sensed Star's pain because he offered her a smile and two thumbs-up for support. Poor guy had no idea about the knife sticking out of his back.

Like a pirate on the edge of a plank, Star prepared for the death plunge. She gripped the bottom of her glittered el Corazón shirt, inhaled, and went for it.

"No, Chloe. Unfortunately we have no idea who would have committed such a cruel act. It's such a horrible shame," Star replied with so much false confidence, she almost believed her own lie. "But we are a loving family, and we'll get through it. Regardless, our award-winning menudo is still just one dollar a bowl until noon!"

Chloe paused and tilted her head, confused, then went on.

"As you can see, the crime hasn't even sunk in yet to this emotionally exhausted girl," Chloe said, yanking the microphone away. She appeared irritated by the spontaneous sales plug, though she attempted to cover it with her fake local-TV-reporter sympathy.

"Star, there must be a surveillance tape that shows the perpetrators in action. On behalf of the artist of the mural, the community, and La Pachanga Eatery, of course, you will prosecute, correct?"

"And Art Space," Star blurted. "It's La Pachanga Eatery *and* Art Space. You always leave off the Art Space. Aside from the restaurant, we're a nationally respected gallery."

"Point taken, Star. About the mural, you will prosecute, correct?"

"Well, my father is a firm believer in second chances. It was probably just a silly prank by some kids. At least it was just happy faces and not anything vulgar. Right?" she asked. Star shrugged innocently, then clapped her hands in front of her chest. "Well!

I better go check on that menudo! Thank you, Chloe!" Star took one giant step backward out of the frame, bent down, and blew out a burst of stress.

Chloe pursed her glossy lips and wrapped the segment.

"If anyone has any information about the Happy Face Tagger, please call our station's hotline. And speaking of hot—don't forget to come see me this weekend at the twenty-fifth annual Home and Garden Show! I'll show you how to turn your flowerpots from frumpy to fabulicious! This is Crafty Chloe Chavez, reporting to you from La Pachanga Eatery for KPDM-Channel 11 News. Amy, back to you!"

Chloe held her supersized grin until the camera light went off—then she slapped the mic in the cameraman's hand and ripped out her earpiece. She smoothed her taupe linen suit and approached Star with a glare wicked enough to rival any animated Disney villain.

"Everything okay?" Star asked, batting her eyes, even though one of them twitched uncontrollably from nerves. Why, she didn't know. This was just the silly TV craft lady who took herself way too seriously.

"Something's not right," Chloe accused. "Is this some kind of sick publicity stunt?"

"No! Not at all! How could you even think that?" Star shot back, offended at such a rude claim.

She had never been a fan of Crafty Chloe. She loved channel 11, but changed the TV every time her face came on. Her beat was supposedly the local art scene, yet Chloe had never once covered any of La Pachanga's exhibits. Chloe always discounted the "Art Space" part of La Pachanga's name, just proven on live TV. As PR director of La Pachanga, Star had sent Crafty Chloe numerous press releases for events and shows, none of them featured. But right now, Star represented her parents' business and she would do her best to be professional.

"I'm sorry if I flubbed the interview, I—I—I couldn't think straight. I promise to fill you in if we hear anything."

Chloe took a step closer and lowered her voice. "Look, Miss Esteban, how do I present this without sounding disrespectful... I find it odd that one of our city's most well known public landmarks has been defaced—it happens to be on *your* parents' property—and you're pushing the Sunday menudo special. All we need is to air that surveillance tape so viewers can help identify the culprits. Case solved, right?"

Star clasped her hands behind her back and rocked back and forth on her shabby Converse sneakers. "It's not that cut-and-dry..."

As always, Theo stepped in to defend Star. He set down his caddy and extended his gentle, broad hand to shake Chloe's tense, thin one. "Ms. Chavez, hey. I'm Theo Duarte. It's no big deal. I can remove the paint with turpentine."

Chloe recoiled her hand. Even Theo couldn't soften the crusty exterior of her personality. "That doesn't erase what happened. I'll just wait for the police report," she said.

Star couldn't be polite any longer. This glorified content deliverer made it impossible to be polite.

"What do you care anyway, *Crafty Chloe*?" she snarked. "Isn't there, like, a pastel centerpiece crisis somewhere that needs tending to?"

Just then, the cameraman walked up to Chloe, whispered in her ear, and motioned to his elbow. They both looked Star up and down.

As if Nana Esteban found a way to intervene, Star's iPhone rang from inside her bag, which she had set by her feet. Thank God! A reason to ditch this scene. She flashed Theo an uncomfortable "Thank you" grin, Chloe a sarcastic "Later" one, reached for her cell, and turned to walk away.

"Hey, Star," Chloe called out. "I have one more question."

Star stopped and looked back. "Yah?"

"Is that blood on your arm, or perhaps—*spray paint*?"

Star froze, and then replied, "Speaking of blood—by any chance, do you knit?"

Moments after sneaking away from the circus in front of La Pachanga, Star slipped around to the side of the restaurant's compound to answer her best friend Ofie's call—or rather, to field the barrage of questions about her crafty idol.

"Sweet mother of Martha!" Ofie shrieked. "You met *the* Crafty Chloe face-to-face! She showed how to decorate a water bottle the other day. Did she have it on her? Did she talk about crafts? Is she as pretty in person as she is on TV?"

Star peeked around the corner to ensure Chloe or Theo didn't follow. "Crafty Chloe is pretty, all right, pretty brutal. She totally harassed me, as if *I* were the one who spray painted Theo's mural!"

"But, Star, you *did* spray paint it."

Star dropped her bag to the ground and collapsed against the hot concrete wall. "Ugh. Was it that obvious?"

"You couldn't lie to save your favorite cat-eye sunglasses. Don't worry. Most people won't catch on like me. It's because I know you so well. Oooh, I have an idea to get you off the hook! Why don't you hit another mural tonight? It'll throw everyone off the trail of La Pachanga! There's a brand-new one on the I-10 freeway. It's dark, you can do it as a drive-by, but use a water-based paint so it'll come off easy. I have a 40 percent-off coupon we can use to buy some!"

Star giggled at the thought, even though she knew Ofie was serious. "That's okay, I have my hands full as it is."

"Did you at least get her autograph for me?" Ofie asked. "Lord knows I need a pick-me-up. I think the scrapbook group I just joined is already trying to dump me, and this morning, I had a mishap with the glitter spray and ruined Larry's new suit. Wait. Enough about me, your crisis is much bigger."

"I doubt Chloe is kind enough to give autographs unless it's to endorse a check. Screw the scrapbookers, and try masking tape on the suit. I never should have left the house last night," Star stated as she started to pace back and forth between the side of the building and the thick wall of oleanders.

"Correction. You never should have left with Maria Juana," Ofie lectured. "Every time you get in trouble, she's there. I thought you swore her off after the cockatoo switcheroo snafu last summer?"

"She's my cousin, Ofie. She joined that Roller Derby team. Remember? I told you. Las Bandidas del Fuego. Last night was her first bout and she invited me. I promised my dad I'd try to get along with her. We're the only two kids left in the Esteban bloodline. I meant well."

"Wait," Ofie countered. "If you went to the bout, what happened to the big dinner with Theo? Oh my gosh! The wedding proposal! Did you get engaged?"

Star covered her face with her hand and muffled her mouth. "I bailed."

Ofie sucked in a gallon of air. "No! So you not only trashed his mural, but you ditched him too? Ay, pobrecito, Theo..."

Star's eye caught another paint smudge on her arm, this one green. She rubbed her elbow against her sequin-accented gypsy skirt to remove it. When it didn't come off, she grunted at the guilty residue.

"Ofie, it gets hella worse," Star said into her phone. "The lead jammer from Las Bandidas set me up with this irresistible rocker dude from Ireland. He had gobs of tats, and his accent was so Hollywood. He turned me on to this drink that is supposed to make you see little green fairies. You know I'm not the saucy type, so it just about killed me. I don't remember much else except making out with him in the back of Maria Juana's tacky convertible... He tasted like mint. I guess afterward I went and spray painted the mural, which I only know about because my parents made me watch the surveillance tape this morning. And then they made me come down here to do that segment on *Wake Up Arizona*. What was I supposed to do? Tell the truth? I'd never make it home alive! Now I have Crafty Chloe on my ass and Theo to contend with."

"You know better than to mix cocktails and your cousin, Star."

Star rubbed her head in disbelief, and knew Ofie was doing the same. "You know, I bet Maria Juana set me up. I have no idea. I know I screw up, like, every other day, but this is the worst. How am I going to explain this to Theo? I don't know what he'll be more freaked at: that I'm the one who spray painted his mural, my new tattoo, or the hickey on my neck."

"Tattoo?" Ofie asked.

Just as Star spun around to make double sure Chloe wasn't eavesdropping, she bumped into a buff chest.

Theo's chest.

And the hardened expression on his face confirmed he heard the confession in its entirety.

"Ofie, uh... Theo's right here. I gotta jam. Bye, love you, peace out," Star whispered, turning off her phone and slowly slipping it into her purse.

She opened her hands and raised them to the sides of her face, as if it would help her say the right words. "Theo, from every ounce of my heart and soul, I am so sorry—I can totally, totally, *totally* explain this—"

"No need," he replied. "I'm through with you."

Star's heart sank at the thought of facing Theo. Never once had he let her down, or hurt her feelings. He always had her back, even when he didn't know the full situation, just like earlier with Crafty Chloe.

How did she return the favor?

By not only blowing off his wedding-proposal dinner, but also jacking up the biggest and most personal art piece he had ever created—thousands of pebbles and small rocks arranged into one spectacular mosaic of various Arizona scenes. The multicolored mural sprawled across the twelve-foot-tall front walls of La Pachanga. Titled *Mi Tierra*, its glory was showcased in coffee table art books, on national TV shows, and in magazines. Visitors from Africa to Alabama visited La Pachanga just to take a snapshot of Theo's masterpiece. He considered *Mi Tierra* his visual love poem to the state and vowed to never leave his hometown. And that artful affection added magic to the already enchanting grounds of La Pachanga.

Theo didn't feel that magic this morning. He felt resentment toward Star. After overhearing her conversation with Ofie, he hustled to the front of the restaurant. Star chewed on her thumbnail and mini-jogged at his side to keep up.

Where do I even start? she wondered, watching as he prepped for the emergency restoration. Her heavy black eyes lingered on his baggy khaki shorts, which hung low on his waist, and the thin white tank that stretched tight across his chest. Even with forty extra pounds on his stealth frame, grungy paint-stained clothes, and cheap black flip-flops, charisma oozed from his stance. She cracked her neck right and then left, and went to confront him as the entrance area buzzed with gawkers.

"The wall, the wall. How I love the wall...," pined a weeping poet who couldn't have been older than eight. A frilly black veil dripped from her head and she followed behind Theo, reciting her scribbled verses from a La Pachanga take-out napkin. "Mr. Duarte's wall makes me feel tall...and it, nor I, shall ever fall..."

Star put her hands on the girl's shoulders to comfort her. "I know, m'ija, it's awful what happened, but it'll be back to normal soon, I promise."

The little girl removed her veil and leaned in to Star. "I'm not sad for the mural, really. I'm sad because it hurt Mr. Duarte's feelings. He's nice. He comes to our classroom every year to teach us about Día de los Muertos. I come here with my parents all the time. I see you two. You're his girlfriend, right?"

Star couldn't answer. Instead she watched Theo examine the mural, her throat thick inside from swallowing tears. She hadn't felt this nervous since the first time she met Theo a little more than three years ago.

Thanks to her spiky heel and his worn sneaker, their worlds collided, literally. Twenty-one and fresh out of college with a marketing degree and a plan to be an artist, Star moved into her former bedroom at her parents' house and planned to stay a year at the most.

On an errand for her father, she went to the local thrift store to unload a batch of her dad's clutter—a bulging Hefty bag of tattered Levi's, old college textbooks, and timeworn cassette tapes.

Theo, then twenty-three and a budding civil engineer at the City of Phoenix, had just been promoted to a cushy gig and purchased a gem—a recently foreclosed 1937 Spanish Colonial Revival home in the historic Willo district. He visited the thrift store that day to thin out his own wares after just moving in.

Decked out in her favorite fifties naughty-secretary sweater-dress with patent-leather pumps, Star stood in front of the drop-off bin outside the building. She raised the lumpy load over her head to stuff it in the opening, but lost her balance—and caught it quickly, without losing her dignity. However, one of her three-inch heels pierced into something fleshy. It had poked through the tip of someone's holey sneaker, smack between the big and second toe. Theo's toes. He howled in pain.

Flustered, they bumped noses as they tried to untangle their bodies. He used her waist for leverage, and she did the same with his defined shoulders, while she secretly inhaled the sweet scent of his cologne (she later learned it was Krishna Musk oil). They politely struggled while introducing themselves and comparing their monikers. His parents, fans of *The Cosby Show*, named him after Theodore Huxtable, while her parents went the New Age route with Estrella—Star for short.

Star would later describe the experience to Ofie as an extreme meteor shower of Cupid's arrows that pierced her chest plate.

Star and Theo spent the rest of that day—and night—together. From then on, he chose to call her by her real name, Estrella, instead of the English translation of Star. She liked that her dad and Theo were the only two people in the universe who did that.

Theo had a profound effect on her life. Even though her parents owned one of the valley's top Mexican restaurants, Star nixed anything that didn't come between two slices of nine-grain bread. Not that she disliked Mexican food (she had yet to explore it), but as a second-generation Mexican-American, it irked her that people assumed she spoke Spanish, knew how to make tamales, and smashed piñatas at all her birthday parties. She didn't want to be lumped into those stereotypes. So she rebelled by distancing herself from her culture. That night, Theo told her she should be ashamed, and coaxed—okay, seduced—her into tasting a forkful of green chili. At first she refused, but he scooted close, held the fork to her curvy lips, and she melted inside. Not from the smell of the food, but from his presence. In one slo-mo bite, her life's outlook changed and she wanted more.

After dinner, he took her to a concert in Tempe at La Isla del Encanto, a hot new Latin music club. They downed slushy margaritas and danced for hours to Reggae Sol, a Spanish-language reggae band from Puerto Rico. Star loved each note and lyric of every song. The lead singer—a tall, handsome, dreadlocked man with tamarind candy-colored skin and huge green eyes— smiled at her and Theo, as if he were dedicating each song to them. Theo wrapped his arms around Star's waist from behind and they swayed to the heavy bass beat.

Star felt as though the enchantment of Reggae Sol's music followed them out the door, and not just because she bought their CD. One long light-rail ride home later, and the excitement of the day's adventure caught up with them. They went back to Theo's, played the CD on repeat, danced, kissed, and ultimately consummated their admiration in a drunken, passionate romp, even though they both were involved with other people. Their romance never physically continued past that night because of their then–significant others, but the newfound relationship did evolve into a soul-to-soul friendship.

She admired his quiet and sweet nature, and his intuitive viewpoints on world issues impressed her, as did his charm. He had that effect on folks. His parents and siblings may have moved to Sacramento, California, five years ago, but he sure didn't lack a surrogate family. Without even asking, the nana across the street tended to the plants on his front porch, the office secretary brought him home-cooked meals at least once a week, and his gangbanger neighbors washed his prized '48 Chevy regularly. Even the pigeons that overtook his roof respected his living space. Everyone loved Theo.

But Star jolted his life as well. Soon after they met, she discovered a filled sketch pad in his bedroom, and challenged him to translate it on canvas.

"I'm only doing this to prove you wrong," he joked that afternoon.

He finished his first piece, a Keith Harring–esque portrait of a woman resembling Queen Latifah. Star hung it in the foyer of La Pachanga, and by lunchtime it had sold for five hundred dollars, which he split with her. Star convinced him to hatch a plan to ditch his day job and become a full-time artist. One year later, with Star and La Pachanga's help, he did it. But he didn't stick with paintings. He surfed smoothly through different art genres— punched-tin wall hangings, stained-glass vignettes, jumbo bronzed sculptures, and welded gates. Theo became Theodoro Duarte, one of Arizona's brightest new mixed-media artists.

Within a year of Star and Theo's friendship, they blossomed as respective professionals: he a painter, and she a kamikaze marketer for his work and La Pachanga. He took his job seriously; she took hers for granted. Their lives remained intertwined, just as their feet did at the thrift shop that day. Star took comfort in the unspoken commitment between them; after getting out of their previous relationships, neither had dated anyone else, yet they didn't officially date each other. They knew if they did become an exclusive couple, the relationship would automatically fit into the serious zone thanks to their already hefty friendship. Neither of them were ready for that. They masked the topic by agreeing romance would be a distraction to their careers. However, they both craved a repeat of that first night. And it was Theo who acted on it last Thursday.

That day, he slipped a copy of *El Solitario: Jinete Sin Fronteras*, a racy Mexican romance comic, in Star's purse. The comics had always been a running joke between the two. He loved the illustrations and she giggled at the wacky melodramatic storylines. He had bookmarked the page of a rancher couple making love on a grassy hill under the moon. He claimed it was a silly gag to make her blush, but they both knew it was a clear indication of what was on his mind. Star expected it—he threw out a hint every six months. She couldn't bear to think of life without Theo, and if that meant keeping it platonic, so be it. Therefore she never acted on his hint.

Except for Thursday. After three long years, Reggae Sol had finally returned to perform in Phoenix that night. Star and Theo hadn't seen the band perform since that first evening they met. Just like last time, Star bought Reggae Sol's new CD before she and Theo took the light-rail to his house, where they danced until he kissed her. They couldn't help but repeat the events from their first meeting. Star told herself to go with the moment and savor the experience.

But something unexpected happened during their lovemaking. He whispered, "I love you."

His sultry comment made Star's insides ping. She wanted to reply, but didn't know what to say. Finally she said, "Me too." The next morning, a weird vibe lingered between them. They ate their bowls of Honey Bunches of Oats in front of the TV, made small talk about the genius teaming of Jimmy Stewart and Kim Novak, and Star casually said goodbye and left. She paced around work all day, and couldn't handle the tension. She wanted to get back to their usual chumminess, so she swung by to see him on Friday after work, as if nothing had happened. The sooner they got back on track, the sooner it would blow over. Star had made a few publicity budget mistakes at La Pachanga recently, and was already behind on booking events for the busy fall season. She didn't have time for complications. Theo usually rescued her from stress; he was never the cause of it.

When she stepped into his home, he invited her to sit in the living room while he changed his clothes in the bedroom. Just him saying the word "bedroom" made Star antsy, even if she did enjoy the night. Star bounced down on the firm tan leather sofa, and sorted through the magazines on his coffee table that included *Popular Mechanics, Rolling Stone, Made,* and *Urban Latino.* She picked up the latter, and just as she was about to read the table of contents, a scary surprise fell out—wedding package brochures from various local resorts. She picked them up, confused. Her heart stopped when all of a sudden it clicked.

Theo wanted to get married.

Oh no, no, no, she thought. Star hadn't even begun her *real* life yet. She had plans to bust out of Phoenix someday. To do what, she had no idea, but it would be big and fabulous. Living at her parents' and working at their restaurant was just a placeholder until she found her mission, maybe start on that art career. She didn't have time for a wedding *now.* Sure she loved Theo, but she hadn't even traveled much. How could she already know if he was her soul mate?

Star heard the wood floors squeak in the hallway signaling Theo's return to the living room. She quickly shoved the papers back on the table and slapped a pile of magazines on top of them. He sat down and set his hand on her knee. *Already claiming his property,* she thought.

"Hey, how about a quiet dinner tomorrow night? I have a surprise for you."

Out of the corner of her eye, she saw him reach for her hand. Her *left* hand. Her stomach jiggled under her skin, and she shot up as if she had just sat on a pin.

"Sure! Oh darn, I forgot that my dad is waiting for me at the restaurant right now. I'll be by tomorrow night, then. Bye!" She shook his hand hard, like a proud banker who had just approved his home loan, and left.

And as the hickey on her neck, the tattoo on her arm, and the spray-painted happy faces on his mural proved, she never made it to that dinner.

"Don't look at her. Do *not* let her off easy," Theo said to himself as Star stepped into his personal space. It would be harder than carving marble. He couldn't resist her. Theo didn't only love Star—he was obsessed with the girl.

How the hell did this happen? he thought. Before they met, he effortlessly broke a string of hearts owned by chicas fine enough for a *Sports Illustrated* swimsuit calendar. He used to be a player and proud of it. How did he go from that scene to being whipped? Easy. He fell in love.

Star didn't compare to other women. She came loaded with an arsenal of irresistible quirks. She knew all the Bollywood dance moves, and with her exotic features, she could pass as an Indian or Mexican pop star. He appreciated her clumsy Spanish, her kooky range of vintage outfits, notebooks scribbled full of business ideas, and her never-ending wish list of tasks she wanted to accomplish. Star reminded him of that crazy *Pretty in Pink* chick, chicana style. He teased her about her crazy hair, which she twisted, braided, curled, straightened, and dyed on a regular basis. These days, she rocked two tones: berry red on the top layers and jet black underneath. He fell for all of it. Especially the Jessica Rabbit curves that he'd had access to for two brilliant nights over the past three years.

Star chattered on daily about making the world a better place, living each day as if it were her last, being spontaneous, practicing good karma, and paying it forward. She thought preaching those words meant she had her shit together, but really? She didn't have a clue. Hell, she couldn't even decide on a paint color for her room. Every month she sweet-talked him into helping her coat it with a new shade. Worst of all, her life revolved around the word "someday."

Someday she'd sell artwork she hadn't made. *Someday* she'd break away from La Pachanga to find her own path. Someday was a copout.

At least she had finally told him she loved him, kind of. Which was why he'd invited her over last night. Like a dumbass, he blew two hundred bucks preparing a home-cooked dinner with French wine and candles. Only to dump it all in the trash.

Of all of his girlfriends, Star was the only one his family approved of. She made them laugh by sharing animated stories about her best friend, Ofie, La Pachanga, and her cousin Maria Juana. She played Monopoly with the kids, and sang karaoke with the teenagers. Theo's mom bugged him to bring her to every family event so they could show her off. He planned to invite her to his cousin's house in Sacramento next week for a Duarte reunion. But instead, she had to go and stand him up, leaving him waiting like a pinche pendejo. And then to find out she made out with some tattooed Irish homie? And trashing the mural on top of it?

This was a wake-up call from the Aztec warriors of the past. No self-respecting bachelor should ever let a woman have that much power. "Beat-down" did not exist in Theo's machismo dictionary and it mortified him that he had almost entered that territory. And he had even gained twenty pounds since he met her, thanks to eating at La Pachanga almost every day. No more. Now he realized all Star cared about was herself.

He squatted to untie the string around a rolled-up plastic tarp. She kneeled next to him and put her hand on his shoulder. "Theo, I can explain..."

He brushed her hand away and stood defensively. "I'm done

with you and this place," he said, gesturing toward La Pachanga. He picked up the tarp, snapped apart the first fold, set it down, and reached for the can of turpentine.

"You have every right to hate me. You have no idea how ashamed I am right now," Star said with a pathetic look of desperation on her otherwise cute face. "I'm sorry. It must have been pent-up anxiety. But above everything—we're *friends*. I didn't mean to hurt you. I let my cousin get me wasted."

"You need to brush your teeth. Tequila?" he asked, unscrewing the metal lid from the can, avoiding eye contact.

"Worse. Absinthe." Star sighed guiltily as she scooped a mint from the pocket in her bag and chewed it. She moved in closer until he could feel her breath on his cheek. "I was drunk when I kissed that guy. We didn't do anything more, I swear. He's one of Maria Juana's Roller Derby friends. You know how it is. Every time I hang with her, some kind of drama goes down. This time I was in the middle of it. She's probably laughing her ass off right now."

Theo stepped back. "There you go again, making excuses, Estrella. She didn't put the spray can in your hand, or shove your tongue down that dude's throat. By the way, nice hickey."

Star raised her hand like a stop sign. "Please, don't."

"Oh, I forgot," Theo shouted. "We're *friends*."

"Can you lower your voice?" Star said, her voice cracking. "You know you've been the only one."

He faced her chin to chin. "Whether you like it or not, Estrella, we're more than *friends*, and it's messed up that we act like we're not. So what are we, then?" This was the sliver of an opening he left her to redeem herself.

She paused and he held his breath.

"Why do we have to define it? Putting a label on it lessens it," she whispered, gazing at the ground. A vision of the wedding brochures paraded along the walkway before her. Star shook it off. As much as she cared for him, she didn't want to lead him on until she was sure she wanted to accept his proposal.

He shook his head in disgust. "You are so full of it," Theo cracked as he focused on a section of the wall. He dipped the corner of a rag in the jar of turpentine and began to swiftly scrub at the first happy face she had put there the night before.

"This mural is the exact representation of us," he said, pointing at the wall. "See these pebbles right here? I hiked to the bottom of the Grand Canyon to get them, and had them blessed by a Havasupai elder. I make every action count, no matter what state of mind I'm in. And look what you did to it."

He flicked his finger at a garish orange smiley face that Star had painted over it.

"Everything to you is one big sloppy happy face, Estrella. And the fact that you did this over my artwork is symbolic."

Tears began to stream down Star's cheeks. He was laying it on thick but she knew she deserved it. She sniffled. "I'm sorry."

"Sorry doesn't cut it this time. Unlike you, Estrella," he said, "I want foundation and labels in my life, and I want them now. I don't want to live wondering what is going to come my way. I want to make it happen for myself."

Star used both hands to wipe her face and walked around to his other side. "I want that too. I just need to sort things out. You know me. I'm unpredictable."

Theo made a sour face, as if he didn't buy her explanation.

"Go ahead and roll your eyes. Maybe I want to get out of here, and help make the world a better place. Make a difference in people's lives. Someday the right plan will hit me and I'll be ready. So there."

"Don't you see?" Theo said, raising his voice. "Someday is *now*. When we first met, you bragged about becoming a famous artist, or joining the Peace Corps, and how you'd find a job in another country. If you really wanted any of those lives, you wouldn't be standing here. You've been out of college for three years and you haven't changed anything except your mind."

Star put her hand on her hip and stepped back, offended. "I've changed lots of things!"

"Your hair and clothes don't count."

"Whatever. After all this time, you *really* don't know anything about me."

"No, mujer. For the first time, I see how you *really* are," Theo said, shaking his head. "You have no idea what it's like to suffer and sweat for something you're passionate about. To strain for a goal. You act like a free spirit, but don't take any risks. And you know what? That makes you boring. And predictable."

Star hung her head low, angered by his words. Scared they were true. "What do you want me to say? Tell me how I can fix this."

"Leave me alone for a while."

There. He said the words he never thought would come out of his mouth. He bent down to unpack his supplies from the caddy so she wouldn't see his hands shake from the adrenaline. She touched his arm, and he brushed her off as if her fingertips were toxic. An invisible thought bubble blinked over his head, filled with the image of her kissing some drunk asshole. The passersby noticed the tension and dispersed to allow them to argue in private.

Slowly, Star leaned in to whisper in his ear. He had lied about the bad breath. She smelled delicious, as usual. He wished they were fighting about his brand-new Latin Playboys T-shirt that she'd cut up into a halter top last week. As much as he wanted to hate her, he ached for a kiss.

She used her index finger to tilt his face in her direction and studied his expression, just like he used to do to her. "Give me a little credit, please? I help you with your art, I book all your shows, make all your flyers. No one believes in you more than me. Isn't that worth something?" Her dark eyes glistened under a set of curly black lashes.

Theo dipped his rag in the can again, contemplating his response and its consequences. This was one of those head-versus-the-heart dilemmas. Why did she have to look so damn sexy right now? Even at nine in the morning, with mangled hair, a wrinkled tee, a sequined skirt, and old ratty sneakers he often teased her about? He sucked his lips and shook his head.

"We've run our course, Estrella," he said.

"What do you mean by that?" she asked.

"Exactly what I said. I want to go it alone for a while," he repeated, slow and sharp, as he rubbed the rag over a splotch of green paint on the wall.

"Okay, I understand. Can I ask how long is 'a while'? Like, a day, a week?" she inquired in a soft voice.

He shrugged and still refused to look at her. "I don't know. But I do know if you want to salvage the last thread of patience I have for you, I suggest you start right now."

Star wanted more than anything to fall into his arms and beg for forgiveness, to tell him how sorry she was and how much she loved him. Should she tell him about the wedding brochures and why she'd freaked out? She wished she could press a rewind button and go back to not only last night, but the last few years. Theo knew her too well. Star had no clue what her mission in life was. There were no words that could win back his respect. Star would give him time to cool off, so she could devise a killer plot for redemption.

"Okay. I get the hint," she said as she backed up and held her bag with both hands. "I'd give anything to take it all back. And I *will* make it up to you. Someday."

She waited a second for him to respond, but he didn't. So she stood on one foot, kissed his cheek, turned, and left him alone, just as he wanted.

3

Everything pissed off Chloe Chavez this morning. She drove away from La Pachanga's mural mayhem and went through her mental checklist:

1. Working on a Sunday and not downing her triple shot of Café Bustelo yet.
2. Having her weekly craft segments moved to a prime time slot and her mother not even mentioning congratulations when she called and told her last night.
3. The thought of Ezra, her lazy boyfriend, snoring without her in the California king bed *she* bought in the loft *she* paid for.

Oh, and number four: her brand-new tube of MAC Viva Glam lipstick that had melted on the leather seat of her BMW X3—a result of parking in direct sunlight for the La Pachanga assignment. Chloe wondered why in the world the owners would host such an intricate piece of art on their premises anyway, and then act surprised when it was tagged. That's what happens when you own a business on Grand Avenue.

"Thugs on that stretch of the city are as normal as dollar

stores in South Phoenix. The Estebans should be grateful. The damage could have been far worse than spray-painted smiley faces…," Chloe mumbled. It steamed her that the family obviously knew who did it, thanks to D-level acting by the owner's weirdo daughter.

"Loser," Chloe thought of Star. That centerpiece comment really ticked her off. Didn't she know Chloe was an Emmy-winning journalist and craft celebrity?

Chloe cranked up the air-conditioning and felt her left fake eyelash wilt away from her skin. She rolled her eyes in disgust. The unforgiving August heat was no match for waterproof eyelash adhesive. Rather than remove the felon falsie, she chose to not blink unless absolutely necessary. Her camera-ready face didn't dare come off until the front door of her north Scottsdale loft closed behind her. One more grievance to add to the list, she thought as she cruised down Grand Avenue, ignoring the artful scenery on both sides of the road. Chloe didn't understand the hype about this area. The city government, community groups, and hundreds of local artists strived to revive the crime-ridden street by attempting to turn it into Arizona's version of Greenwich Village.

The first Friday evening of every month, Chloe covered this area for her job as arts reporter for KPDM's evening news. The streets closed for twenty blocks, from 7th Street to 17th Avenue, to make way for thousands of artsy ilk and musicians who weaved in and about dozens of galleries and boutiques, in which La Pachanga Restaurant and Art Space served as the epicenter. To her, the place was nothing more than a typical Mexican restaurant with a glorified art nook connected to it. She wouldn't buy into it and refused to eat there, much less cover any of its so-called "art openings." To her, a serious gallery would not be set up inside a place that served quesadilla appetizers. Chloe didn't have a clue why people swooned over La Pachanga or how it even won awards. What she did know was that every time she reported from Grand Ave., she craved a loofah scrub down.

At the moment, she needed a coffee fix, so she squealed the wheels of her Beemer into the parking lot of the Chi-Chi Coffee Cabana—another one of Grand Avenue's gimmicky avant-garde eateries. Her plan? Tuck and roll to score her liquid fix and exit quickly.

"I'll take a Triple Underwire Sugar-Free Vanilla Latte—or whatever you call it," Chloe requested, tapping her French-manicured fingers on the counter as she tried to decipher the extensive menu. "And, please, I'm in a hurry this morning," she mentioned to the cheerful clerk in the silver lamé apron. In reality, Chloe had all day to kill. The whole "I'm in a hurry" line was just a habit she'd picked up to make others (and herself) see her as important and exclusive. Having completed her shift, Chloe planned to go home, change into a soft Juicy Couture tracksuit, sit at her desk, and outline the next twelve months of her career at KPDM.

"You got it, sugar cube!" the barista sang back. He scribbled the order on a paper cup and surveyed her attire from the shiny black pumps, up her long legs, over her cotton micro-mini suit, and stopping at her hazel eyes.

"Here it comes," she thought. Used to the attention, especially when it came to her meticulous taste in designer attire, she prepared herself for answering the usual fan-friendly questions like "Can I have your autograph?" or "Where do you get your hair done?"

She stiffened her back, proud and ready to field his burning query.

"Hmmm," he said, tapping his chin. "I think you're a push-up kind of girl. Sure you don't want to upgrade to a quad? It's only a quarter more."

Obviously the minimum-wage minion didn't tune in to the

Valley's favorite news station. Regardless, Chloe would have accepted his recommendation but became sidetracked when a muscular dreadlocked man in a crisp red tee and dark slacks stepped in her path. "May I have a small cup of hot tea with honey? According to your menu, I guess that'd be . . . a *handful*?"

If it weren't for his charming Jamaican accent, smooth café-con-leche skin, and emerald eyes, Chloe would have lectured the gentleman on coffeehouse-line etiquette. He lucked out. The comforting aroma of the freshly brewed coffee temporarily diverted her attention. She approved the Push-up and scooted away so Mr. Cool Runnings could have his tea and honey. She picked up a "Work for us" postcard from the countertop and pretended to read the fine print. As if she would really represent a business that named drinks after boobs.

"You just cut this lovely lady off, Rasta-head! This is the Chi-Chi Coffee Cabana! Chi-chis come first!" snapped the server, gesturing his lanky, blotchy arm toward Chloe. The man, embarrassed by his social crime, offered to spring for Chloe's latte when another barista slid it down the counter to her.

"I didn't mean to cut you off, miss," he apologized. "I take it you're a regular here—Miss Underwire Push-up?"

"Excuse me?" she said, offended.

He pointed down to her hand and winked. "Your drink."

Chloe remembered the gist of the joint. "Oh yeah. No. First time." She lifted her cup and sipped. It had a hard bite, just what she needed. She and the dread-locked gentleman reciprocated flirtatious blinks and a cool breeze brushed over her body. She'd never believed in actually *feeling* someone's energy—until now. His presence was strong, regal, kinetic. Warm and soothing, practically glowing. For the first time since she could remember, the normally uptight Chloe relaxed.

He extended his hand for an introduction. "I'm Gustavo Olivera," he said, his gaze connecting with hers. There could have been a massive explosion behind her and she wouldn't have even blinked. She took his hand while her mind surveyed her internal file system of flirty comebacks. There weren't any relating to handsome Caribbean strangers.

"I'm Chloe. Chloe Chavez. I'm a broad."

"Oh really. I've never met one of those before," he kidded.

Chloe felt her cheeks warm up about a thousand degrees. "I've had a rough morning. Let me try that again—I'm a broad*cast* journalist. I'm kind of a celebrity around here," she said right before she winked at the barista. He confirmed her proclamation with an exaggerated hand wave, and handed Gustavo his tea.

"Pleasure to meet you, Chloe," Gustavo said.

She adored the way her name rolled off his full lips, and imagined him repeating it while they rolled around naked, in one-thousand-thread-count Egyptian-cotton sheets. Lust and love—two indulgences her life lacked. At least she had her Under-wire Push-up, which she took a big swig of.

Gustavo motioned for them to step away from the Chi-Chi pick-up counter. He pulled something out of his red, yellow, and green striped messenger bag and handed it to her. Chloe's heart quickened at the mystery gift. She may as well have been a giddy sixteen-year-old accepting a class ring from a varsity quarterback, as opposed to a twenty-eight-year-old professional woman.

"What's this?" Chloe said, not even looking at it. She couldn't remove her focus from Gustavo's island-kissed facial features.

"It's for my band, Reggae Sol."

"Local?" Chloe hoped for an affirmative.

"No, Puerto Rico. We're on tour right now. We're here in Phoenix for a couple of gigs."

"Really? Puerto Rico? I've always wanted to visit, but the opportunity has never presented itself. I'm half. My dad was born there."

He smiled, revealing a set of shiny white teeth that would

make four out of five dentists applaud. "Same here, we have something in common, then."

"I guess we do. My mom is third-generation Italian. What's your other half? I hear some kind of Caribbean accent in there."

He leaned against the wall and sipped from his cup. "Dad is a full-blooded borincano, Mom is Jamaican. She raised me until I graduated; then I joined my father in PR for culinary school. I ended up as lead singer of a reggae band instead."

Chloe strained to contain her enthusiasm. Something with this guy clicked. The type of click a safe cracker hears when he hits the last correct digit. A moment of silence and a childish shrug later, Chloe noticed Gustavo was just as fidgety as she. He pointed to the package in her hand.

"That's our new CD—and a ticket to our show tonight. It's our last of a pair of gigs here, and then we're off to New Mexico. It's our farewell tour. After ten years, we're all going our separate ways."

Chloe read the back of the CD. "Reggae en español? Hmm. Haven't heard that before."

"Well, then, you should come check it out. Maybe we can get an early dinner before the show—or a late snack after."

Chloe ached to jump at the chance. She breathed in to collect herself, to think rationally. How could she consider it? She didn't know this man. Whatever bit of excitement pricked up her neck minutes ago subsided.

Her two-second clinical analysis: Toying with single pretty women from city to city must have been his way to collect groupies. Clever bastard. He probably had some exotic island wife, topless in a tie-dye sarong, waiting for him back home in a secluded beach hut. Chloe passed back the disc and ticket.

"Thank you, but no can do, Gustavo. Gracias for the offer—and the chat. You're a sweet man and I wish you the greatest success with the rest of your tour."

Gustavo replied with a slow blink. "Chloe, what can it hurt to keep the CD? It's good music."

The plan sounded safe enough. "Okay, I'll keep the CD, if you insist." She knew she would never see him again. She politely slid the disc into her Coach purse.

"Well, I'm on my way, Chloe Chavez. Off to soak up this magnificent Arizona sun while I have the chance. Much respect to you and your family." He embraced her with both arms. An unexpected gesture, yet it didn't startle her. Chloe received his hug openly and allowed herself to enjoy the moment. He tapped her nose and said, "Happiness is free like air, Chloe. Allow yourself to indulge once in a while. Goodbye."

She flinched at the intimate moment, not knowing whether to be offended or flattered.

"Goodbye, you bewitching creature," she sighed under her breath, regretting that she let him walk away. The thought dissolved with the upbeat chime of her BlackBerry: the ringtone she had programmed for when Mark Jefferies, CEO of KPDM, rang. She credited him as the fast pass for her career. If it weren't for Mark, Chloe would be just another real estate agent, rather than the Arizona TV queen she had become. She made her way to the farthest, most private table of the coffeehouse to take the call.

Mark never let her forget his favors. There were only two reasons he ever rang: with good news or for bad sex. She had been waiting for his call all week—for the former reason, of course.

"Do you have news about the craft convention?" she asked, sucking in her anticipation.

"As a matter of fact, I do," Mark replied, clearing his throat. "The executive officer of the nineteenth annual International CraftOlympics is in town this weekend. He saw your segment this morning at that Pachanga place. I talked him into having you host the whole thing. Chose you over Betty O'Hara. Consider it your big break. Every other host of the National CraftOlympics has gone on to superstardom in the home décor industry, so congratulations! This is your big break and I made it happen for you."

Chloe eeked out a sly grin and *poof!* Gustavo's smile disappeared from the forefront of her mind.

"Oh. I almost forgot," Mark continued. "The committee wants to know if you can demo a class for residents from the women's shelter on the last day of the convention."

Chloe lowered the volume of her voice. "Will it be on camera?"

"Probably not."

"Skip."

"You are such a cold bitch, I love it," Mark purred.

"Let's just focus on the big picture."

"Done." Mark chuckled. "Now for the other reason I'm calling…"

Chloe slouched half a millimeter. *Here it comes,* she thought.

"What's on your agenda tonight? Can you spare a little Q-time for your boss?"

She rolled her eyes and flinched simultaneously. "What did you have in mind?" she asked, knowing full well what to expect from her tubby, balding superior.

"We can—let's just say—go over the finer details of this hosting job I *single-handedly* scored for you. You can repay the favor like you always do, starting with a back rub. And guess what? I waxed this week! And I even picked up a flick for us. *Kinky Kong*! I taped it from cable. *Grrrr*!"

Chloe bit her tongue so she wouldn't tell this freak to get lost. Someday that time would come, but not now. She could only stomach the relationship one way: He used her for casual sex, and she used him right back for professional advancement. She hoped for the day when she could make it on her own.

She swallowed hard and visualized informing her unenthusiastic family, that she—Chloe Chavez, classic middle child disappointment—landed her own nationwide home décor television show because the executives of the CraftOlympics found her worthy and talented. Even if Mark did help. Her mother and sister didn't have to know every little detail. That information would be another one of Chloe's little secrets.

Chloe lifted her chin and answered like a trooper.

"Fine. Tonight's agenda includes me, you, and a room at the Biltmore."

4

Ninety minutes had passed since Star's brutal conversation with Theo. Ninety crazy, drama-filled minutes.

Thanks to a slow news morning, Crafty Chloe's live on-camera interrogation wasn't the last. All the other local stations followed, each requesting an interview with Star—in front of the mural. It pained her to recite the same fib multiple times while Theo scrubbed her spray-painted doodles from his former masterpiece. Sunday, August 1, was officially the worst day of her life.

As she pulled her '59 Chevy Bel Air sedan into her parents' carport, she winced at the kink in her neck and the bruise on her spirit. Her body ached from the inside out—exhausted physically from last night, and emotionally from today. And it wasn't over. More guilt loomed on the other side of the front door. She paused for a quick prayer before crossing the threshold of her parents' cozy 1930 Willow bungalow. She passed the entryway to the kitchen.

As expected, her folks were in the same spots as when she left this morning.

Al and Dori Esteban sat at the chunky pine kitchen table, hands folded, both wearing resolute expressions, as if their only daughter had betrayed them and they were about to announce her sentence.

Star figured her otherwise peaceful parents had spent the past four hours discussing and dissecting her recent missteps, awaiting her return to reveal their adjudication. In turn, Star planned to propose a complete 360 to start fresh. She would switch jobs from the restaurant's publicity person to merchandise buyer!

She dropped her bag to the floor and reached for the metal barstool her mom had decoupaged with botanical images last summer. Star plopped down and joined her parents at the kitchen table. She took in the details of their environmentally friendly kitchen complete with pressed-bamboo countertops and wheat-board cabinets. They spent so much sparing the planet, maybe they would spare her a verbal beat-down. Still, Star braced for the worst. Her tip-off? Her stomach growled from the yummy scents of her mom's tasty fried soy bacon and organic hash browns. Normally they saved her a breakfast plate, but not today. Not even a crumb from yesterday's batch of honey bran muffins.

Before her father could give his Come to Jesus talk, Star took cuts.

"Mom...Dad...Please don't say anything until I finish. I have no excuse. I was irresponsible. I should have known better than to party with Maria Juana. I apologized to Theo, and he wants nothing to do with me." Star wiped the tears that began to flow and continued her pleading. "It hurts me that I let you down. I love you so much. Please believe that I am so sorry. I'm going to get focused. I mean it this time, I swear. I'm ready for an overhaul."

"We agree," Al said.

"I was thinking I could switch from publicity to merch buyer or maybe set up a life coach program for our shift managers. We can all work on becoming better people together—"

Al interrupted. "You're not coming back to the restaurant."

Star's mouth gaped. She expected them to be harsh, but hippie-parent harsh, not tough-love harsh.

Al slid back in the stained-wood chair and fingered his black buffalo bone necklace, given to him by a Hopi elder years ago. He always rubbed the beads to draw empowerment at times of doubt, which often involved his daughter. "Look at it as a leave of absence until further notice."

Star stood from the barstool and began to pace about the kitchen. "You mean I'm being exiled?"

"Siéntese—*sit*. Come back, and be mature," he shot back.

Star slinked onto the barstool, bowed her head, and shook it in disbelief.

"Look at me, Estrella," he said. "I see a creative, beautiful young woman who lacks confidence and self-discipline. We've been there for you all your life and now it's time for you to venture out on your own."

Star picked at the red pompom fringe that trimmed her seat, sat up straight, and revved up her rebuttal.

"You guys, give me *some* credit! I've devoted my whole life to La Pachanga. I work more than forty hours a week. I've helped turn it into one of the hottest hangouts in Phoenix. Grand Avenue is cool now, thanks to our weekend dance nights and art receptions. The crowds have helped younger businesses in the area. Dad, I found you dedicated employees. *And* it was my idea to build the coffee bar. I...I...I find lucrative sponsorships...I send out sassy press releases to keep us in the limelight. Just because I got drunk and spray painted all over the building doesn't make me Lindsay Lohan on a bender!"

Her folks were not impressed.

"We appreciate your hard work," Dori said, opening her hands in front of her. "It's just that, well, there are deeper issues. We pay you a healthy salary, but you come and go as you please. You leave projects and paperwork unfinished. You don't answer your cell phone. Last month you double booked bands on Sunday night and your father had to settle the commotion. A riot practically broke out. We've given you too much room to grow and your irresponsible antics keep getting tangled up in the business, and even the finances."

First Theo's reprimand, now her parents'.

Star couldn't help the way her mom and dad raised her. She thought back to her childhood and couldn't recall one instance when they forced her to do anything. Her life had been about calm negotiations and free expression. There were no time outs or spankings for bad behavior, only rewards for good. Al and Dori allowed their only child to customize every minute of her day. Even down to her obscure clothing and picky food habits. In fact, Dori still cooked all Star's meals to order. The Estebans embedded in their daughter's mind that the world offered a wealth of golden tickets and she could cash them in to her liking. Star did not know boundaries, only a million choices. They unknowingly groomed her to be a bohemian princess, and now they all paid the price.

Star felt like her whole world had been upended. She was confused and hurt, and that made her angry. She leaned over and snatched up her bag. "Sorry I'm such a loser. Fine. I quit. Happy now? I'll put my notice in for December, and you'll be rid of me," she snapped.

Her dad let out a sarcastic chuckle. "December? Hmmm, I seem to recall last Christmas when you opened La Pachanga in the middle of the night and cooked for all your friends. We didn't have chorizo for the customers in the morning. The next day we sat here discussing this exact topic. You *quit* then too—and put your notice in for August. Dori, what is today's date?"

"August first," she replied.

So much for righteous indignation. Star had to come up with

Plan B, *pronto*. "At least give me time to get something going. Can I stay if I pay rent?"

"How much savings do you have, Star?" Dori asked.

"Thirteen dollars. But that doesn't count the money Nana left me in her will. And I could sell off some of my vintage jewelry. Let me prove myself. I swear I'll make this debacle up to you a thousand times over. Please, Dad."

She could usually read her dad's mind, but not now. She could tell even her mom didn't know what to expect. The next few seconds passed as fast as a turtle on Valium.

"Dori, get me a paper and a pen, please," Al said to his wife. Dori got up, hustled to the kitchen counter, grabbed a notepad and a fine-point Sharpie, and handed them over. Al quickly sketched a makeshift contract.

"This is how it works: You have six months to establish a new career and tie up loose ends of your abandoned projects at the restaurant. In December, if you haven't fulfilled the agreement, you have to pay us three fifty a month for back rent—that's twenty-one hundred dollars, and find a new place to live."

Star fidgeted and bit her thumbnail. He had backed her into a corner and she hated that. Why couldn't he just trust her? "What if I just pay the twenty-one hundred upfront out of Nana's money?"

Al didn't acknowledge the comment, and Dori flashed her daughter a scary scrunched-eyebrow look of disgust. "And what if she does meet the agreement, Al?"

He finished scribbling out the terms without looking up. "She can have her job back if she wants it, keep renting her room—and depending on how she does, I'll move her from employee status to partner." He slid the paper across the table, and Star quickly signed to show her commitment.

Of course she planned to move out *someday*, but not anytime soon. She loved this roomy, historic cottage that her parents bought when she was in second grade. Her bedroom could pass as a studio apartment, and the adjoining guest room came in handy as a walk-in closet for her massive wardrobe collection.

"Sooo...um, what abandoned projects?" Star asked.

"The back house," Al said.

Star groaned.

"Don't make that face, Estrella. You begged us to let you use it as your art studio and now it's nothing but a pigpen."

Ugh, Star thought. They just had to drudge up that stupid back house and rub it in, as if she didn't feel like a loser already. When she finished college, she had come home with a mission to become an artist. Didn't everyone who took fine arts classes? She pleaded with her parents to let her have the back house as her studio. Theo renovated it; Al and Dori bought her hundreds of dollars' worth of art books, classes, and supplies. Star needed to find her signature style, but there were so many techniques and genres to choose from. If she waited, life experience would help. Why rush something so important? No, Star would wait for the perfect time to launch a serious art career. She didn't want to end up in rickrack purgatory like Ofie. All of it overwhelmed her, and as the months passed, the more insecure she became. Instead, she invested her energy in La Pachanga.

These days she despised that ugly back house because she had let it become a shelter for her pop culture souvenirs, impulsive eBay finds, and the restaurant's broken fixtures and signs. The two-bedroom, one-bath space was piled from floor to ceiling with junk. She couldn't bear to look at it, much less open the door, because it was a gruesome reminder of a failed dream.

"Wouldn't it be more cost efficient to level it to make more outdoor seating?" she offered. "I can do that with a single phone call and move on to the next task."

"No. And that's not the only item on this list. What the hell is the CraftOlympics? You signed us on as a sponsor? What does La Pachanga have to do with crafts? I thought you were an *artiste,* too good for glue guns."

She perked up. "Don't worry, this is a good one. It's the National CraftOlympics. It's a ginormous consumer show at the Phoenix Convention Center—think Comic-Con or the South By Southwest Music Fest, except with scrapbook paper and pinking shears! It's supposed to draw more than thirty thousand people. One of the hotel partners is the new Los Saguaros Suites."

Al rubbed his head as if his brain throbbed. "The old Prickly Pear Palace? That place is a dive."

"Dad, it's all been revamped by Starglass Hotels. It's really hip now. Anyway, the shuttle runs right by La Pachanga. Ofie told me about it, so I called the headquarters. They traded us a bronze sponsorship package for us providing handmade centerpieces for the swanky awards dinner. Two hundred of them. It will give us great exposure, because we can hand out coupons and draw gobs-o-customers during the convention. Minnie and Myrna can work overtime to make centerpieces."

This time, Dori chuckled. "Minnie and Myrna are busy managing all of La Pachanga, Star. You can't just assume they can take on a new project like this. This is one more example of—"

"Okay, okay, I'll handle the centerpieces." Star made a mental note to hand this one over to Ofie, who would eat it up.

"That doesn't mean to dump it on Ofie, either. We want *you* to be responsible for them. We want sketches, a budget, and a timeline. No last-minute rush," Dori said.

Star fumed while Al used the pen to count on his fingers. "All right, then. Number one, find a new job. Second, the CraftOlympics, and third, the back house." He crossed his arms and stared into her eyes, as if another plan had been hatched.

"Estrella, whatever happened to your art plan? You were so

excited about it, and your work showed a lot of potential." His voice softened a little as he said this.

Star chewed her pinky nail. She hated this subject. "I'll get around to it. I just want to make sure I'm refined enough to relay a strong message about my views on the world, society, consumerism, and culture. I see people like that Crafty Chloe chick and I loathe how people like her water down what real art is. Even Ofie...I love her to death, but it sucks to see her family struggle to pay the bills and there she is, buying the latest fancy glue for a Shrinky Dink necklace. Not me. I am all about serious art."

"Oh yes," Al replied. "Like your most recent statement to the world—happy faces in aerosol acrylic."

5

The dinner plates were stacked in the dishwasher. Eleven-year-old Anjelica shopped for school supplies with Nana Chata. Husband Larry relaxed in his recliner, ready for a night of reality TV.

Another boring evening in the Fuentes home? Not for Ofie. The twenty-nine-year-old wife and mom savored the quiet time to indulge in her two favorite pastimes: cookies and crafts.

In the conventional oven on the left wall of her 1975 Glendale kitchen, chocolate chip snickerdoodles browned to perfection. To the right, the mini toaster oven cured a dozen brightly colored polymer clay button covers that looked pretty enough to eat.

Sitting on a lopsided turquoise barstool and enjoying the semitoxic aroma swirling throughout the air, Ofie anxiously tapped her chubby fingers on the beige Formica countertop and waited for Star to call at seven p.m. It had been two days since her "incident" and Ofie could already see a change for the better in her friend. Star spent all of Monday applying at different businesses and in the meantime, she took a barista position at the Chi-Chi Coffee Cabana. Tonight they were to discuss forming a craft group to make the centerpieces for the CraftOlympics, and

Ofie couldn't have been more ecstatic. Being the experienced crafter she was, Ofie dreamed about attending the prestigious conference—and this year she'd actually be a professional contributor, thanks to Star and her drunken spray-painting crime spree! She could say that because the two were best friends. No one had ever been kinder to Ofie than Star.

Their iron-grip bond was sealed one evening at La Pachanga when Star was thirteen and doing her algebra homework in the courtyard. Ofie, eighteen and pregnant, had just run off after a heated argument with her soon-to-be mother-in-law, Chata Fuentes. She ended up at the Estebans' eatery, the only place that brought her joy at the time. Within minutes, Ofie found herself helping Star with her math and ultimately spilling her guts to the plucky eighth grader. Wise beyond her years, Star pulled out her cell and had Ofie dial Chata's number and demand an apology. Chata was so in awe at Ofie's cojones, she stammered and stuttered her way through the words "I'm sorry." Star gave Ofie a high five and made her pinky swear never to let anyone make her feel inadequate again. Ever since, the two had been solid sisterfriends.

The clock on the grease-stained microwave flipped to 7:00—no Star. Finally at 7:25, the phone rang. Ofie snatched the handset and couldn't get her words out fast enough. "I-got-an-idea-for-the-centerpieces!"

Star giggled. "I knew you would. Okay, girl, you're on. Let's hear it. But no tin flower arrangements made from soda pop cans like the ones you made for your cousin Marta's wedding. My mom still has a scar on her index finger."

Ofie chuckled as if it were a cute memory, as opposed to one that sent twelve wedding guests to the emergency room. "I had no idea soda pop cans were so sharp after you cut them!"

Star thought it was best to change the subject. "Let's nail down some ideas and then post flyers for volunteers for production. I don't think any real artists will go for this, so we have to get crafters for production. We can hang the posters on La Pachanga's community bulletin board."

"Sounds like a plan! I have gobs of ideas. I thought we should do something that represents the magical desert land of Arizona. How about . . . *tumbleweeds*."

"Tumbleweeds?" Star repeated, baffled. "As in those dry things that float through ghost towns in old Western flicks? Um, I've lived here all my life and have never seen one."

"Neither have I. But can't you envision them at the center of every table? Covered in chunky gold glitter?"

Ofie began to ramble on at warp speed about cheap glitter and how to apply it to objects like tumbleweeds, dream catchers, and chili peppers—all stereotypical gawd-awful southwestern knickknacks. On the other end of the line, Star covered her face with her notebook. Wrangling Ofie in from her kitschy concoctions would be more challenging than actually making the centerpieces. Star couldn't afford one more mistake at this point. These things had to be red-carpet worthy.

"It's all cute, sweetie," Star said, "but this is a formal dinner for industry professionals and using that much glitter is so . . . I don't know, tacky?" The term she wanted to use was "crafty," but she didn't want to offend her friend.

"No, silly." Ofie giggled. "Once the glue dries, it won't be tacky, and we can spray on a sealer so no flakes will fly in the fondue."

Star paused, speechless.

"Why are you against glitter, Star? It's so pretty! The more the better!"

"I'm not against it. I ordered some imported glass glitter for Theo not too long ago. I just feel it is something that should be used in micro-moderation. Like whipped cream. We save it for dessert. If we used it on our dinner salad and entrée, it wouldn't be exciting."

"But ambrosia salad has whipped cream."

Star tossed two Tylenol in her mouth and chugged water from a gallon jug. "Ambrosia salad is a dessert, Ofie. Never mind about the whipped cream. My chunky butt is on trial right now, so let's focus on the centerpieces. No glitter."

"If we really want to make a stunning impact, we should at least leave it on the list," Ofie volleyed back with a crack in her voice.

"Fine. We won't cross it off yet, but maybe we should wait until the craft group is intact so each member will have an opportunity to contribute an option. Martha Stewart is the keynote speaker. These centerpieces have to be beautiful enough to at least make her blink. I don't mean to be all corporate, but I want these to be perfect and finished before the deadline."

"Huh?" Ofie asked. "Is this Star I'm talking to? You sound so . . . so . . . determined."

"I have to be. I'm at the top of everyone's hit list. I've been fired by my parents, dumped by my sort-of-boyfriend, and am one video tape away from Cell Block H. I've said sayonara to my slacker days."

"Wow, it hasn't even been forty-eight hours and you have a new outlook and even a new job. I'm proud of you, Star!" Ofie said. "Tell me about the Chi-Chi today. Did it feel weird working in a new place?"

"I love it! It feels good to be out on my own. I know I should try for something with more pay, but for now, I just need easy, mindless, and yummy. Enough about me. How's the Nana Chata situation?" Star asked.

Right then, Larry walked into the kitchen and rubbed Ofie's back. "Oh, Nana Chata is wonderful!" Ofie sang out. "She was so sweet—she came over and cleaned out Anjelica's room, cooked Larry's favorite dinner, and scrubbed this nasty kitchen until she could see her reflection! I think I'm the envy of all the wives in the world."

Larry kissed her forehead and walked back to the family room. Ofie scrunched down on the linoleum floor and whispered in the receiver, "She's driving me nuts! She color coded all of Anjelica's socks, polished the leaves on my silk plants, and ironed the sheets! With *starch*! Who irons sheets? Oh, I feel a panic attack coming on—change the topic to something happy, quick!" Ofie said, fanning her face with a Chinese takeout menu she grabbed from the countertop.

"The CraftOlympics! Warm chocolate sauce! Glitter!" Star blurted.

Ofie purred. "Ahhh…much better. I can feel my heart rate slowing already…"

The women took notes on their thoughts for the centerpiece committee. Star would outline the agenda, and Ofie agreed to make handbills and hang them to recruit members and offered her house for the meetings. After the business talk, Ofie switched the conversation to Star. A couple days ago the poor thing's life had unraveled like a cheap sweater. Amazingly, Star seemed to handle the pressure well. Ofie sure wouldn't have been able to. One glitch and she'd crumble like dried-out Play-Doh.

There were only a few privileged peeps who knew Star's scandalous secret, and Ofie was honored to be one of them. She would never spill. Wild rabid wolves couldn't drag it out of her. Neither could Ofie's idol, "Crafty Chloe" Chavez. Even if the talented Ms. C. personally rang to offer Ofie a guest spot on her TV segment as barter for the scoop, Ofie would politely hang up. Ofie was loyal with a capital L when it came to Star.

Ofie hollered for Larry to remove the goods in the oven in five minutes so she could finish the phone conversation in the bedroom. She warned him not to eat the clay button covers, but to help himself to the cookies.

"Let's talk about Theo," Ofie said as she fell into her bed with the cordless handset.

"There's nothing to talk about. I'd say he needs about ten years of cooling-off time," Star replied, sounding more bummed than Ofie could ever remember.

"Have faith. Love is a journey, you know. It starts at forever and ends at never..."

"I'm totally freaking. I think he was serious when he said he wanted nothing to do with me," Star said. "He won't answer my calls. I even swung by there today and his neighbor told me she's watching his house because he went to California for the week for a family reunion. He never told me about a family reunion!"

"It'll be fine when he comes home," Ofie reassured. "He's crazy about you. It'll all be fine. The mural looks even better than before. He did a super job fixing it."

"Ofie, I can't stop thinking about him," Star confessed. "I keep replaying our whole relationship in my mind. He's done nothing but make me happy, yet I'm plagued by phobia to move to the next level. Those darned wedding brochures did me in!"

"Star, relax. It's so obvious you two are meant for each other. If you had asked him to wait, I'm sure he would have."

"Ofie, I'm crazy in love with him...," Star said softly. "Why couldn't I see that before Saturday? I mean...it even hurts to breathe when I think of him kissing me. Or worse, never kissing me again. I'm such an idiot for taking him for granted. Do you think it's too late to win his trust back?"

"I would at least wait until the hickey is gone. Use the back of a spoon and rub real hard. But after that, no! It is not too late! Why don't you visit him when he comes home from the trip? Oh, lordy, I have the best idea *ever*!" Ofie declared. She then rolled onto her tummy and kicked her legs in delight. "A shadow box dedicated to your love for him."

"Oh, jeez. You mean like a love shrine? He'll think I'm a stalker!"

"Not if you make it so powerful it speaks what your heart

feels. Then he'll know how much you appreciate and love him. No words necessary." Ofie sighed, as if the year were 1957 and she was daydreaming of Elvis Presley.

"Maybe I could make it inside one of those Romeo y Julieta cigar boxes. Or maybe I could make a photo album and write letters to him all throughout it," Star pondered aloud.

"A scrapbook!"

"No!" Star nearly screamed. "Not a scrapbook. I wouldn't be caught dead making a scrapbook. Never mind, it's too crafty. I don't do crafts. I'm an artist."

Ofie hated when Star dismissed crafts as though they were beneath her. Over the years, scrapping had brought Ofie heaps of joy. A lot of bounced checks too, but so what? Documenting memories was priceless.

"Let me marinate on the idea. Maybe I'll just write an old-school letter."

"Borr*ring*," Ofie sang out.

"Whatever I decide to do, I'll give it to him Saturday, before his show at Sangria. I have no clue what I want out of life, but I do know I want Theo in it."

"Yay! Let me know if you need my help!" said Ofie, pleased at Star's decision.

Star paused. "Let's say hypothetically, maybe, I considered creating an assemblage box, maybe Joseph Cornell meets Frida Kahlo, I think I have a focal-point picture."

"I knew you liked the idea! Continue!"

"Don't laugh, and do not repeat this!" Star couldn't believe she was about to share this, but whom better than with her dear friend? "Last week Theo put a Mexican novella comic in my bag with a nasty page bookmarked. He said he meant it as a joke— but it was more like a hint. That was the night, we, you know…That's the night I want to remind him of. I want us to pick up where we left off."

"Which novella?" Ofie asked.

"Hold on, I'll find it." Ofie heard Star fumble with the phone while rummaging through her stuff. Ofie simultaneously swiped her arm under the mattress to feel for Larry's stash of novella comics. They were his dirty little secret.

"Star, I have a stack right in front of me. Which one is it?"

"No way. You do? Woo-hoo, you and Mr. Larry got it goin' on, huh?" Star chuckled. "It's called *El Solitario*.

"Oooohhhh. *Rider Without Borders*. That's a juicy one. I have it. What page did he mark?"

"The top of thirty-six. What do the speech bubbles say? My Spanish is horrible and I need to decipher the dialogue."

Ofie turned to the page and read the lines out loud. "'Amame, como nunca has amado a nadie, esta noche...sera imposible de olvidar...'Wow. Yup, the boy has the hots for you!"

Star howled on the other end of the line. "Tell me! Tell me!"

"Well, okay. He's a beefcake Mexican cowboy and she is a voluptuous, buxom ranger girl. Her blouse is too small, so her cleavage is busting out. They are at the top of a grassy hill and there is a full moon. He grips her fleshy hips under her skirt with one hand, rips open her shirt with the other, the buttons fly off, she moans in delight, and he devours her chi-chis..."

"Ofie, I have the comic here—I can see all that—what does the speech bubble say? Verbatim."

"Oh. Sorry. Alrighty, let's see. He says he wants her to love him like she has never loved anyone before. And their night together is going to rock! And in the next scene, he opens his mouth, like he is going to lick—"

"Jeez, you're making me blush!" Star laughed. "It's perfect. He won't be able to resist. If—and that is a big *if*—I decide to make something. It has to be high art or the deal's off." Tomorrow's first task on Star's agenda—go to the library and check out Joseph Cornell books.

"Whoops, something's going on!" Ofie announced. Both women heard Larry cuss and shout from across the house. Ofie dashed to the kitchen and stopped. She raised the cordless receiver to her ear and tried not to laugh.

"Oh sweet baby Jesus in a manger," she said. "Star, I gotta go. Larry tried to eat a button cover. He thought it was a cookie."

From: myrna@lapachanga.com
To: estrellafeliz@lapachanga.com
Date: August 4, 2010, 8:30 a.m.
Subject: Glitter

I have 350 pounds of glitter here with your name on it. Explain.

From: estrellafeliz@lapachanga.com
To: myrna@lapachanga.com
Date: August 4, 2010, 8:33 a.m.
Subject: RE: Glitter

LOL! Not me, sister. I'm frightened by the stuff!

From: myrna@lapachanga.com
To: estrellafeliz@lapachanga.com
Date: August 4, 2010, 8:40 a.m.
Subject: RE: Glitter

I'm serious. 58 boxes of glitter were delivered here, all addressed to you. Sender is Udell Industries based out of Hamburg, Germany. Is this an error? Invoice is $4,985.99 and was charged to the publicity account on your corporate card. How would you like me to proceed?

From: estrellafeliz@lapachanga.com
To: myrna@lapachanga.com
Date: August 4, 2010, 8:50 a.m.
Subject: RE: Glitter

Myrna, I placed an order on July 10th for 3.50 pounds of vintage glass glitter that was on clearance from Udell Industries. I e-mailed them the order and distinctly remember typing in 3.50 pounds. I provided payment information by phone and all I can think of is that something was lost in language translation. The order was for Theodoro Duarte's upcoming installation. I calculated the cost to be approximately $50, including shipping. This is a mistake on Udell Industries' part. I will call and get it straightened out. I apologize for the trouble!

Chalk it up to another "Star-aster"! LOL!

From: myrna@lapachanga.com
To: estrellafeliz@lapachanga.com
Date: August 4, 2010, 9:15 a.m.
Subject: RE: Glitter

I just tried to call the number on the packing slip and it has been disconnected. The Web site says the business has closed and all orders have been shipped.

Star, I've worked for your parents for years because they are good, honest, hard-working people whom I respect greatly. In case you haven't noticed, business is down. Ever since the graffiti incident, we've heard many customers are reluctant to visit because they are worried about crime. The glitter situation is far from an "LOL" matter. This mistake of yours has cost La Pachanga

$5,000, not to mention the outrageous contract for the CraftOlympics sponsorship. Simply put, we do not have enough money in the marketing budget to cover all of it. Unless these funds are replaced in the near future, we will have to cancel the annual Día de Los Muertos festivities this year. In the interest of your parents, La Pachanga, and the sugar skull–loving community, I sincerely hope you remedy this problem immediately.

P.S. And as your former childhood babysitter, I feel it is my duty to tell you to get your act together!

From: estrellafeliz@lapachanga.com
To: myrna@lapachanga.com
Date: August 4, 2010, 9:17 a.m.
Subject: RE: Glitter

Do not worry. I'm on it. All I ask (beg) is the following:

1. Please do not tell my parents.
2. Please have maintenance move the boxes inside the back house.
3. Please let me know when the credit card bill arrives and I will pay it.
4. PLEASE DELETE THESE E-MAILS & EMPTY THE TRASH FOLDER TOO!

Thank you, and again I am so sorry. Call me on my cell for any further questions, I promise to answer on the first ring!

6

Every week for the past two years, "Crafty Chloe" Chavez has presented a new handmade idea on KPDM's lunchtime newscast. It became the most popular segment with the show's mostly female audience and elevated her status from field reporter to "Crafty Chloe," the ultimate creative guru of the city.

Chloe predicted that with the help of Mark Jefferies she'd become a beloved national figure within a couple years—an international do-it-yourself personality with a daily show, best-selling books, and product lines galore. Chloe planned to follow in the footsteps of Betty O'Hara, aka "Betty Oh!," a former local morning-show host who went on to fame and fortune thanks to her morning craft segments.

Today, inside the fifteen-story high-rise on 16th Street and Camelback Road, Chloe paced up and down the carpet aisle way outside her cubicle to burn off nervous energy.

At last, the timid voice she was waiting for.

"Hi…Ms. Chavez?"

Chloe arched one of her thin eyebrows. Her savior had arrived: Frances, resident introverted office clerk. The insecure girl was a sight to behold. Frances' bright red hair hung limp and stringy down her round cheeks, except for the crooked baby bangs that cut across her forehead. And then that body—a plump, fleshy torso propped up by a set of toothpick-thin legs. However, this unassuming paper stapler had a few tricks up her sleeve, including enough decorative concepts to fill a *Mission: Impossible* movie script. And as Chloe's dedicated unofficial personal assistant, those brainstorms came in handy every week for Chloe's live craft segment. Frances Turner was the TV personality's secret to success in a twisted Cyrano de Bergerac sort of way. But rather than hand over romantic verses, Frances supplied her boss with resourceful and decorative ideas. *Original* ideas.

Chloe popped her head above the surrounding gray portable walls to scout for witnesses. "Coast is clear. Have a seat and let's do this," Chloe dictated, still ticked off from having to wait two more minutes than usual.

Frances rested her booty at the edge of the navy blue office chair as her thick freckled hands gently passed a lumpy brown bag over to Chloe, who grabbed it and ripped off the paper.

Frances' left eye blinked uncontrollably as Chloe let out a sexy whistle of approval. "*Frances*, you've outdone yourself this time. It's magnificent," she said about the handsome lamp that had a shade meticulously covered with silk leaves and gold micro stars.

"Oh, it's nothing," Frances mumbled through a half smile. Her beefy finger pushed up her black horn-rimmed glasses as she kicked her scuffed-up mary jane creeper into the tile. "People are crafting for September, so I wanted to do something related to fall."

Chloe shoved the fixture out of her way and ran her soft, slender hands across her suede taupe desk blotter and took a deep breath.

"I have big news, Frances. You know how the CraftOlympics is going to be held here in Phoenix this year? Well, get this: The executives selected *me* as the official host of the entire three-day event. Not only that, I actually beat out Betty O'Hara—and she has a best-selling book and a top-rated show! This is big-time. Martha is the keynote speaker!"

The strained look on Frances' face stunned Chloe. "What's with the stare? Are you choking on your Nicorette again?"

Frances relaxed her face and neck muscles. "I've never understood...well...how you...*you know*...," she whispered, as if she was frightened to unleash her thoughts.

"How what?" Chloe asked, raising her chin in self-defense.

Frances chewed on the inside of her cheek and twisted a lock of hair. "Um...How you call yourself Crafty Chloe when...you know...you *hate* crafts. The only time you touch a glue gun is when the camera is on."

Chloe chortled and jerked back to serious mode. "Don't even go there, Frances. All you need to know is that I'll always take care of you. But right now I need you to help me prep. Did you know every host for the past five years has gone on to national fame? Now it's my turn and I want to be spot-on."

Frances rubbed her stubbly chin. "Word on the clothesline is this year's CraftOlympics will be the biggest ever. Red alert, Ms. Chavez. It's almost eleven. You'd better get on set..."

Frances' warning was supported by a hefty cameraman, who hollered from across the newsroom.

"Chavez—you're on in ONE minute, thirty-four! They bumped up your tease." He signaled the media princess over while gripping the mic over his mouth and jogged her way. He apologized for shouting and introduced himself as Larry Fuentes, her newly assigned in-studio cameraman. Chloe would have given him the icy treatment, maybe even complained to her boss, except he mentioned that his wife, Ofelia, was a Crafty Chloe groupie and even kept a VHS library of all her segments.

Chloe bounced up from her chair and headed toward Stage One, right on Larry's heels.

"Tell the Mrs. I said gracias." She clipped her mic pack to the back of her skirt and threaded the cord up the front of her silk tan and white Pucci blouse and clipped it at the neckline. She smoothed back a bright chunk of yellow hair and shouted another assignment to her handy assistant.

"Frances, come with me to La Pachanga this afternoon. I'm staging a mini ambush to find out more on the Happy Face Tagger."

"Today?" Frances said, clicking around on her BlackBerry. "You have three appointments: teeth whitening, hair relaxer, and your therapist. You won't be done until at least five."

"Reschedule the last two."

Her dutiful assistant took note, and ran up to shove the finished lamp in Chloe's arms. "I already set up the cook table with the step-outs of the project. As always, everything is sorted and ready to go. Just plug in the lamp so viewers can see it glow," Frances said.

Chloe noticed the camera crew snickering and flashed them a dirty look. "Good girl, Frances," she said before sprinting down the tile hallway. Her feet screeched when she reached the cook table on the set. She set down the lamp and plugged it in. "Dim the lights!" she ordered.

"Five, four," Larry said as he held the floor camera with one arm and counted down with his fingers stretched out in front of him with the other.

She quickly composed her facial posture. For a brief moment, a flashback of hiking up her black pencil skirt to bang Mark Jefferies on that very table bobbed in her head. She shook it off and concentrated.

"Three, two...," signaled Larry. He relayed "one" by pointing his finger like a gun at Chloe.

A true professional, she unleashed a supersized Crest White-strips smile. "Hey there, Phoenix, Crafty Chloe here! It's only the first week of August and we're already thinking of September. I'm going to show you a craft that screams fall..."

She glazed her hands over the front of the lamp, looking as sultry as a *Price Is Right* model.

"Here is a lovely light fixture to celebrate the upcoming cooler temperatures," she said, hamming up each word. She raised the back of her hand to her forehead. "People, I sweated over this baby for you! Stay tuned until after this commercial break, because I'm going to show you how I made it!"

Star, decimated after Myrna's jarring e-spank, baked a tray of gooey chocolate chip brownies, saturated them in fudge sauce, and sprinkled smashed Oreos over every inch. Sitting on the cold wood floor of her bedroom she used a tablespoon to scoop up mouthful upon mouthful of the shameless dessert until every crumb had been consumed. She then desperately scraped each corner, as if in search of a prize. She relented, yawned, and rested her heavy head against the wall... a sense of dizziness overtook her physique... her vision blurred, and she slipped into a sugar-induced nap.

The combination of the week's firestorms, plus the crash from the brownies set her subconscious to swirl with Tim Burton–esque nightmares. She found herself immersed in a pit of emerald glitter—just like quicksand, but sparklier. She squirmed and fought to stay afloat, but the micro-granules sucked her down fast until only her head protruded above the ground.

"Thank God! Save me!" she pleaded, when her parents showed up. With them stood Theo, Ofie, Myrna, and all of the La Pachanga waitstaff. Star used all her might to drag her arms up and out of the glitter vortex to reach for their help. But her beloved friends and family only watched her struggle.

"You brought this upon yourself, Estrella," her dad said. "We can't help you anymore. You must find your own way out so we don't drown with you."

"I can't!" Star cried out, as she sank deeper. The glitter began to cover her mouth, and then her nose. Right before it reached her bottom lashes, she lurched for air and woke up.

Star never intended to spend the rest of that Friday night attempting to unload 350 pounds of vintage German glass glitter on eBay.

"No bidders! What the heck?" she whisper-whined as she über-flicked her Mac keyboard in frustration. Her auction had been up for a day and a half—and nothing. Even Maker's Marketplace, the largest arts and crafts supply outlet in Phoenix, didn't want the glistening cargo. They did take five pounds, but that was a thimble out of the swimming pool.

Star's stomach growled and her head throbbed. Except for her brownie binge, she hadn't eaten real food since last night. She munched on a bag of her mom's fancy granola mix and reflected about Theo, the mural, the glitter, and her parents. She had to extinguish this lighted wick before it triggered any new explosives.

Squirming in her silver vinyl office chair, she raised the volume on her stereo and half smiled at the bay window area that Theo and Ofie had covered in thousands of mini mirrors as a sci-fi surprise for her birthday last year. It offset Star's inspiration wall: A nine-by-twenty-foot spread where she meticulously created a mosaic of tacked-up magazine pictures, headlines, quotes, photos, vintage Hollywood lobby cards, poems, book pages, fabric swatches, and anything else that made her happy. And then her bed! Every night she slept under a sequined teal and fuchsia sari that draped from the ceiling to the floor. The cheery décor didn't even lift her mood.

Star lamented her current state of loneliness until she spotted the Romeo y Julieta cigar box resting on the upper corner of her desk. Ofie had brought it over earlier in the day to pressure Star into making that silly love shrine for Theo. She considered it for a millisecond, but the more she weighed the possible outcome, the more she ruled against it. Too big of a gamble. And then she recalled Theo's scolding.

"You don't take any risks..."

Star sucked her teeth and reached for the box. It didn't mean she would make the love shrine though. She took a deep breath, opened the lid, and pulled out the novella comic. She turned the square five-inch page of *El Solitario* to view the full-on nookie fiesta on page thirty-six. The same page Theo bookmarked for her.

"God, this is *so* vulgar. Sexist. Obscene. Beyond filthy. I love it!" She chuckled, and then imagined she and Theo naked, on top of that grassy hill, all lusty under the full moon, admiring the romantic dimensional artwork she made for him. Chills raced up her arms as she envisioned the next scene, but a rap on the door busted the fantasy.

"Estrella, please...take it down a bit," her dad shouted over the wild Latin electronica track that pumped from her iPod speakers. He could be so hip one moment, and a crusty curmudgeon the next. At forty-five, those gray hairs affected more than just his sideburns and beard. Regardless, her face always lit up when he dropped in unexpectedly.

She loved that her dad, Alfonso Ortega Esteban—Al for short—was the classic Mexican-American machismo father figure—with a twist. After going through the Chicano activist era with his parents in the seventies, and then on his own in the eighties and nineties, he took a trip to Jamaica in 2000 and fell in love with reggae music. Therefore, Star called him El Rasta Chicano.

She admired both him and her mom, for their strong "one

love/one world" outlook. They raised her in a colorful house of truth, righteousness, and holistic healing. For the most part, Star followed the basics of the New Age lifestyle, except for eating meat and the random illegal mishap.

Al tugged his tie-dyed tank over his head. "I'm all for new grooves, but not when it knocks the pictures off the bookcase in my bedroom." His comment tapered off as he stepped to the center of the bedroom and scoped out the scenery. "This room is one wild piece of work, all right. You definitely have your own style."

Star stretched out her hands and palmed her knees. "Why, thanks!" Maybe the whole contract nonsense would blow over.

"And I expect the same energy from you for the back house."

Eh, maybe not.

"How's the Chi-Chi coffeehouse gig going?"

Star swiped a mechanical pencil from her desk and used it to scratch her scalp under the hot-pink scarf wrapped around her head. "I . . . kinda quit today."

"After less than a week? Ay, mujer!" Al sneered, rubbing his forehead in irritation.

She slipped the writing utensil behind her ear and shrugged. "They had me grind coffee beans all day, and the lamé apron made me sweat. I'd rather work freelance and write press releases for Phoenix's indie-business community. I'm going to the offices of Local First Arizona on Monday. Please, let me do my thing."

"Fine—for the next six months," he said, giving her a good night kiss for the first time in seven days. "I'm going back to bed. Turn down the music, por favor."

Star felt herself relax as she closed her door behind him. She clasped her hands behind her back and sauntered to her jumbo custom-built wall unit that housed an iPod sound system, a Sony flat screen, DVDs, books, and a bottom row of drawers where she stashed secret treasures. She knelt, opened the first drawer, and retrieved a heavy, crumpled, black shopping bag. She got up, locked her door, and then sat at her desk and removed the items from the bag one by one. A set of craft paints, decorative-edge scissors, two types of glues, ribbon, scrapbook paper, crystals, beads, and a hot-glue gun. With all her preaching about art versus craft, Star couldn't be caught dead with these items. Originally she bought them for Ofie, but now Star contemplated using them. If she did, it would be only once, and she would never breathe a word of it to anyone. Besides, if Frida Kahlo lived in this era, perhaps she would use curvy scissors now and then. It wouldn't diminish the seriousness of *her* work.

The clock hands moved to the midnight hour, and Star remained restless. Why not burn off some anxious energy by giving Ofie's love shrine idea a try? If it sucked, Star would trash it. If it rocked, she'd offer it to Theo as a truce. As soon as she made the decision, she grabbed the box and couldn't wait to start.

Two hours later, Star still slaved away on the shrine. The week of solitude renewed her spirit, as did the thought of a fresh start. Gathering the items for the art piece was the only remedy that would keep her sane. Maybe her dad was right and she hadn't given herself enough credit for her artistic flair.

To her surprise, she actually enjoyed the process of sketching the layout and then affixing each memento in its place. She moved her body in swift mini circles to the bumping reggaeton beat from her stereo. She whistled in rhythm and reached for the zigzag scrapbook scissors to cut out the scene of the couple in their glorious moment. Hunched like a crafty surgeon about to perform a double-collage bypass, she snipped just below the couple's interlocked arms, letting the rest of their nude ink-drawn bodies float to the floor. She affixed the picture to a piece of thick red glittered foam board mounted inside the cigar box. The side panels glistened with the vintage glass glitter and the border's edges shimmered from two rows of ruby crystals.

The final touch was a papier-mâché banner that Theo had sculpted and painted for her last year declaring his love. It said simply "Te amo."

The next time she looked at the clock, it read two a.m. Groggy and spent, she inhaled the air of personal satisfaction. Mission accomplished. This was a breathtaking, astounding art piece. The composition? Flawless. It exuded emotion and dizzying levels of devotion. The way the light gleamed from it had a mesmerizing, almost hypnotic effect. Star swore she saw a halo of light beaming around the edges; then again, the marathon craft session blurred her vision. She couldn't believe something so beautiful came from her hands. Her imagination. Her heart. Could she really have what it took to be a real artist?

She clenched the box. The thought of Theo seeing it was excruciating, but she had to control her elation. By this time tomorrow, hopefully he'd forgive her so they could start a new relationship, this time as official boyfriend and girlfriend.

Star scooped up the supplies, shoved them back in the bag, and returned it to the drawer. She cleared her desk of any crafty evidence and then set the artwork on her nightstand and heard her mother's light footsteps creek on the hallway's hardwood floor. Dori entered, holding a cup of something steamy and delicious smelling. She sat down and patted the mattress for Star to join her.

"I made you a cup of green tea. I can't believe you are still up. What are you doing?"

Star kicked off her polka-dotted Dr. Scholl's and sat. "It's so stupid and totally off base for me, but...I made a shadow box for Theo to say I'm sorry." She gestured her arms to the nightstand.

Dori leaned over Star to inspect the finished piece. "M'ija, it's lovely. It certainly has the shine."

"The shine?" Star asked, rubbing her eyes.

"Yes. The love shine. When something is full of so much positive energy, it glows—and practically levitates with joy. Like a mother who has just given birth, or love at first sight, or making something beautiful with your two hands."

"You don't think it looks too crafty?" Star asked.

"Love it. It's fantastic."

"Thanks, Mom," Star said before she yawned, faced her mother, and took the cup. The sun would be out soon. The thought made her giddy. It meant her plan for Theo was only sixteen hours away.

"M'ija," Dori said. "I want to give you something to go with your cajita. It's a poem your father wrote for me on the night of our first date. We spent a summer at the Omega Institute and went to this tiny vegan café for a poetry night all about apartheid. That was before it was abolished of course. Ah…it was such a romantic night."

Star smiled. She had never heard the story of her parents' first date. "The Omega Institute? Isn't that like a holistic hippie retreat back East or something?"

"Yes. In the grassy woods of Rhinebeck, New York," Dori said, gazing dreamily at the ceiling as if there were beautiful butterflies floating about. "Next month is our twenty-fifth anniversary. Maybe I'll surprise your father and take him back there…"

"Tell me about this poem," Star said after taking a sip and resting her chin on her mom's shoulder. Dori kissed her cheek and slipped away. When she came back, she put on her geek-chic granny glasses and reached in her hemp terry-cloth bathrobe pocket. She unfolded an aged piece of stationery and read the verses slow and soft. It was the most enchanting prose ever to grace Star's multipierced ears.

"Wow. Daddy sure had a way with words. I'm going to write that poem on the back of my shrine."

Dori grasped Star's dark-skinned hands and lowered her head in prayer. Star made a quizzical face and didn't budge.

"Dear goddesses of the universe, Aztec Warrior Angels and Lord almighty—hear my call. Please watch over my happy star. Protect her, guide her, let this warm summer night be remarkable, amazing, and fantastical. Let the beautiful shrine bring power to all who admire it. Let it bring respect, truth, and above all, eternal love."

It was too much for Star. She threw her arms around her mom's body. "I love you. Thank you."

"Many blessings with Theo, it will all go well," Dori said as she approached the doorway to leave. She stopped, raised her fist in the air, which caused her stack of Guatemalan friendship bracelets to slide down her thin arm. "If not, your father and I will kick his ass."

8

"Another stupid craft fair down the drain," Ofie whined, loading her rejected, misunderstood crafts in the van. She calculated the investment: a fifty-dollar entry fee, one hundred and fifty dollars for the eight-week ceramics course, and another forty dollars in supplies—all for a bunch of bird-brained shoppers to mistake her terra-cotta luminarias for pineapple paperweights. One guy had the nerve to ask if preschoolers made them!

Ofie sat up straight and recited one of her favorite Ralph Waldo Emerson quotes to lift her spirits. "What lies behind us, and what lies before us, are tiny matters compared to what lies within us."

There. Now she felt all better.

She started the ignition and accepted her next mission: to spend her last fifty dollars on groceries, and somehow make it look like one hundred dollars' worth.

"It'll be fine," Ofie rationalized in her minivan, which she affectionately called the Craftmobile. With the faded hula girl air freshener as her witness, Ofie reasoned aloud while driving to the store. Her life would improve once the craft group formed. Being around other creative people would kick-start her luck, as would her important role in the upcoming CraftOlympics.

Combined with her talent, it would lead to more family income and Larry, Anjelica, and even her mother-in-law, Nana Chata, would deem her a hero.

Ofie didn't crave a fat bank account, but she did pine for respect. Heck, not even that. Just to be acknowledged would be a blessing. At five-ten and 270 pounds, she felt more invisible than a sheet of Cling Wrap. She counteracted the internal torture with external graciousness. Aside from Larry, and Anjelica, Ofie's delight came from making and sharing handcrafted gifts. Craftiness provided inner peace, most of all, on sweaty Saturdays like this.

"Mother Mary of Mosaics, it's bulk trash collection week! Pickup must be Monday!"

Bulk trash collection occurred four times a year and consisted of homeowners unloading their unwanted wares at the edge of the curb. But before the local garbage truck came to whisk it away, desperate Dumpster divers or the artistically enabled rummaged through to pick off the good stuff. Ofie considered herself among the latter.

She smacked her lips, cruised the blocks like a salivating T. rex at a meat factory, and within twenty minutes scored a large wood box and nesting tables. The grand finale appeared on Butler Avenue, where she spotted a duo of steel garden chairs on an empty driveway.

"They're practically brand-new. Some people are so wasteful!" she whispered in amazement. She parked on the curb with the motor running and snuck out of the van. Even though most folks knew the bulk trash goodies were free for the taking, she did a quick courtesy scan while opening the back hatch. The hefty housewife shape-shifted into a sleek ninja as she tiptoed to the chairs, grabbed one in each hand, and sprinted to the Craftmobile like a cat burglar.

"STOP! Thief!" yelled a heavyset woman with a smoker's

voice. "That Mexican Sasquatch woman is stealing my Kathy Ireland lawn furniture!"

Ofie had committed the ultimate bulk trash sin. The chairs weren't *technically* on the curb. In the peak of her conquest, she had overlooked that minor detail. She approached the woman to gracefully apologize. The lady must have been in her sixties. She reeked of cigars and sported a head of wiry gray hair secured in a loose bun with a large blue crochet hook.

"Oh, ma'am, please excuse me. I am so, so sorry. I thought these were for bulk trash," she said to the lady with the red-alert attitude and upper arms that reminded Ofie of honey-roasted hams.

The lady practically pressed her nose up to Ofie's. There would be no forgiving. "The only bulk trash around here is you, you stealin' señorita. I know how your people work, wantin' everything for free. Stay right there. I'm calling the cops! For your sake, I hope you have papers!"

Papers? Ofie thought. *What papers? Newspapers? Car registration papers? Neighborhood papers?* Fear and confusion sent a spasm attack on Ofie's chin. How would she explain *this* to Larry?

The woman turned to yell for someone else in the house. "Henry, call 911! We got us a thief!"

Ofie chucked the chairs on the driveway and darted for the Craftmobile. She hopped in, floored it, and peeled out. The back door flapped and the nesting tables spilled out on the blistering summer street in a cloud of dust. She was gone in much less than sixty seconds.

The rush made Ofie forget the groceries, and she remembered as she approached her home and saw the car parked in front of the house. It represented something more nerve-racking than getting busted for stealing garden furniture: Nana Chata, domestic-critic-at-large. Next to playing with her granddaughter, Anjelica, Nana Chata's favorite activity was offering advice.

Ofie pulled into the driveway and whispered a quick prayer. "Please God, let Anjelica have put her dirty underwear in the hamper. Please let her have picked up the dog poop in the entry-way. Or at least let her be clever enough to have covered for me..."

Anjelica opened the door that was covered with five years' worth of dirty fingerprint smudges and greeted her mother with a tight embrace. Right behind her, Nana Chata stepped out and planted a confrontational stance in her daughter-in-law's path, launching quickly into a tirade about time, food, and sorting socks.

"Why are you sweating and why is your makeup smeared? You look like a lucha libre victim. Where is the food?" Nana Chata asked as if she were speaking to a child who came home late from school.

Ofie needed to think of an answer, fast. "Today is what us Fuentes chicas call Girls' Time Out," she offered sheepishly, tug-ging down her size 2X T-shirt to cover her hips. Her self-esteem shrank even further when she peered over her mother-in-law's shoulder at the spotless kitchen sink. Nana Chata had washed three days' worth of dishes and dirty pans.

Nana Chata tilted her head, obviously conducting a lie detec-tor test via mother-in-law ESP.

"Yeah, Nana Chata! It's Girls' Time Out," Anjelica blurted. "We always eat out on Saturdays, and shop on Sundays. Right, Mommy?"

Anjelica's burst of authority shattered Nana Chata's interro-gation. The unflinchable fifty-eight-year-old actually flinched. She bent down and squeezed the girl into her meaty chest. "Que linda! Whatever mi reina says, goes!"

Thanks to Anjelica, Ofie was off the hook from Nana Chata, but she still couldn't shake the feeling of failure. What kind of a mother allows *trash* to lure her away from buying food for her child?

Disgraceful, Nana Chata thought, looking at Ofie. And yet she had compassion for her daughter-in-law. She used to take Jazzercise with Ofie's aunt a long time ago and knew the family was eccentric but kindhearted. Ofie followed suit, with a dash of ditzy added on for good measure. Nana Chata's stomach soured when Larry married her and she swore to have patience. But on days like this, she couldn't help but scold her scatter-minded daughter-in-law. Especially when it came to Ofie's obsession with crafts—and spending Larry's humble earnings on pricey kits. It wouldn't be so bad if the woman had a lick of talent, but she didn't. It was a secret friends and family kept from Ofie throughout the years. None of them had the courage to admit her projects looked as attractive as a hairless dog with pimples.

The family's fourteen-hundred-square-foot house consisted of low-income basics: modest furniture, used appliances, and the hideous home décor concoctions Ofie churned out. Aside from its being unkempt and neglected, there were garish wall stencils of geckos, cacti, dancing mice, unfinished mosaic tables, and unraveled stitched couch covers. To Ofie, the projects were treasures; to everyone else they triggered nightmares.

But Larry and Anjelica adored Ofie, and dealt with the tics, such as the occasional premenstrual meltdowns that could only be tamed with tempera, a sponge brush, and a clean chunk of wall space.

Ofie's crafty compulsive disorder emerged shortly after Anjelica's birth. The baby entered the world four weeks early due to a bad case of toxemia, which resulted in an emergency C-section for Ofie. That trauma stunted the lactation process and Ofie could not feed her newborn. As with everything, Nana Chata came to the rescue with a Gerber paradise of bottles, nipples, thermometers, baby Motrin, and cases of formula. Her actions not only nursed Anjelica into a healthy girl, but also contributed to Ofie's insecurities as a maternal reject.

Six months later, Ofie hadn't yet surfaced from her postpartum pit. Daily naps stretched into medicated chunks of slumber, shielding her from Anjelica's colicky glass-shattering shrieks. Nana Chata and Larry consulted with doctors and read stacks of self-help books at the library to find a way to bring Ofie back.

Healing finally arrived sixteen months later in the form of children's finger paints. Ofie bought a set at the dollar store for Anjelica, and from then on spent every day making crafts with her daughter. By third grade, Anjelica lost interest, and Ofie took over the hobby for herself. At last she had found a calling and adopted it. Ofie smiled and laughed again, which pleased Larry. He set up a craft area in the corner of the family room to encourage her, but little did the family know Ofie's addiction would consume their property and finances. Therefore, Nana Chata made it her life duty to be the family's safety net whether it was by cash, cooking, or cariños.

On this sweltering August afternoon, Ofie erased the day's misadventures and couldn't wait to spend quality time with her daughter. They'd spend that last fifty dollars at La Pachanga by indulging in a spicy combination platter, chat about silly sixth-grade gossip, and then pass out flyers for the craft group, a task Ofie had been eager to complete all week.

"Knock, knock…what's going on in that ping-pong little head of yours…?" Nana Chata asked, snapping her fingers before Ofie's eyes.

The first plan of action would be to send Nana Chata on her way. How could she do that delicately?

"Oh! Um, yes! Girls' Time Out it is, sweetie!" Ofie said to Anjelica as she detached her from Nana Chata's side.

"Well, Nana Chata, we're getting ready to leave now. Thank you for all your help today!" Ofie said, giving her mother-in-law a warm "See ya!" snuggle hug.

Nana Chata froze like a manufactured burrito. "You tryin' to get rid of me?"

"Nana Chata, why don't you come with us?" Anjelica offered in her perky tone.

Ofie clapped her hands, but inside she wanted to cry. So much for a lighthearted lunch. "Of course! I was just about to ask you myself!"

Nana Chata crossed her arms and a wide grin stretched across her tan, weathered face. "Aw, all right, since you really want me to. I'm starved. Where we going?"

9

Ofie, Anjelica, and Nana Chata sat at the best table at La Pachanga, thanks to Dori, who welcomed them at the entrance.

"Are you really going to make us eat here?" complained Nana Chata. "The walls...*Ay!* They give me a headache." She pressed a finger in the center of her forehead and rubbed.

Ofie wondered why Nana Chata couldn't loosen up for once and enjoy the atmosphere. Practically everyone in the southwest gobbled this place up like a salted cheese crisp, but not her mother-in-law.

In English "la pachanga" meant "rowdy celebration" and the restaurant certainly lived up to its name: three thousand square feet of ultimate party pleasure for the senses. It was a certified five-star dining establishment, but also the champ of Best of Phoenix awards for quirky categories like "Best Place to Tango on a Tuesday," "Best Midnight Chorizo" and Ofie's favorite, "Best Place to Spark Your Creative Spirit."

Even walking through the door was an event worth scrap-booking. Most guests arrived through the front to see Theo's mural. But Ofie preferred the back entrance. It took more effort to park, but the scenery made it worth it. Her pulse always quickened when she walked up the brilliant mosaic pathway that divided two rows of majestic oleanders, and doubled when she crossed the painted terra-cotta archway that led to the garden patio. Ofie loved to come at night even, to tip her head back and view the hundreds of crisscrossed strands of white mini lights that twinkled high above. Al and Dori never promoted the rear patio entrance because of the shabby shack back there. Ofie didn't care. It added character. Plus, that patio was where Larry asked her to marry him years ago when they found out Anjelica was on the way.

But on this late afternoon with her mom-in-law and daughter, Ofie explored the crowd from her table while the sexy DJ Brazilia spun infectious latintronica dance tunes. At the back of the restaurant, she saw snobby espresso experts clustered at a light table making hash marks on photo contact sheets with a China marker. And then she stared out the side window and admired the lowrider enthusiasts polishing the hoods and wheels to their shiny muscle machines.

The place was an artist's haven. Food, coffeehouse, and nightclub aside, La Pachanga served as an experience for all the senses. Ofie often daydreamed that she owned La Pachanga. Sometimes when she made her crafts, she imagined herself in a sparkling miniskirt, winking at the dancers below while rocking out as the lead singer of Las Feministas, La Pachanga's all-girl house band that performed on Friday and Saturday nights on the patio balcony.

"Greetings, ladies!" chirped Dori with their meals, causing Ofie to rejoin the living. She adored Dori and wished Nana Chata could be more playful like her.

"Ofie, did Star tell you the surprise we have planned for her father?" Dori asked, eyes glistening with delight.

"No, but you're going to tell us, aren't you?" Nana Chata said.

Ofie scowled in her mother-in-law's direction before replying to Star's mom. "The trip?"

"Yes! Our twenty-fifth wedding anniversary is coming up and I booked a romantic getaway at the Omega Institute—the place where we met—for three weeks. After seeing Star's glorious shrine for Theo last night, it reminded me of when Al first told me he loved me."

Ofie sprinkled her red chili enchilada with salt. "That's just awesome, Dori. You know what they say: Love is what's left in a relationship after all the selfishness has been removed. I'm so happy Star embraced her crafty side!"

Dori nodded and then kneeled down and slid her arm over Ofie's chair. "Would you mind keeping an eye on our girl while we're gone? She's going through a bit of a rough patch."

"Of course! Friends are the flowers of heaven, right, Nana Chata?" Ofie asked.

Nana Chata didn't hear. She was too busy scarfing a chunk of a blue corn tamale. She moaned with pleasure, and together the Fuentes trio devoured every morsel on their plates. Del Tambor Africana, an African drumming circle, took center stage and Ofie and Anjelica ordered a chocolate quesadilla for dessert. To their surprise, Nana Chata requested a kiwi margarita on the rocks.

The goblet hadn't even grazed the tablecloth when Nana Chata grabbed it. She cupped the glass with both hands and sucked on the skinny straws until half the drink had entered her body. She put it down and shivered. Her thin lips glistened with the green liquid until her tongue flicked out and cleaned them.

Please let her be okay, Ofie silently prayed. *That's all I need—Nana Chata tipsy.*

Nana Chata picked up the glass again and finished the cocktail. "I love this music...," she affectionately sang out. "It reminds me of the African vacation my Juanito—God rest his soul—

took me on for our honeymoon. He was such a good man. Did you know 'jambo' is the Swahili term for hello?"

"You went to Africa?" Ofie asked, slapping her chest from laughing and choking on a piece of chocolate-covered fried tortilla at the same time. The twinkle in Nana Chata's eyes confirmed she was buzzed. Oh well, it had become Girls' Time Out after all, thanks to the charm of La Pachanga.

"Sí," she said as she dropped her elbow on the table and then parked her head in her palm. She grinned, her eyes moist with happy tears. "There are a lot of things you don't know about me. If Juanito were still alive and sitting here now, he would be up there drumming. We loved this music," Nana Chata explained right before bouncing her shoulders frontward and backward in tribal unison with Del Tambor Africana.

"You know what they say, Nana Chata: A love song is just a caress set to music!" Ofie chimed.

"Ofie...," Nana Chata said, still engrossed in the music. "You should stop with the craft nonsense and learn to crochet. It's cheap, less messy, and I can teach you in an afternoon."

Ofie frowned.

Nana Chata finished suctioning what was left of her margarita, but stopped when she spotted a local celebrity. "Hey, look everyone—it's Craft Bimbo! Someone go ask her if she puts that makeup on with a trowel...heh-heh!"

Ofie's face blushed as if she had just won the lottery. "Oh. My. Glue gun! It's Chloe Chavez! Nana Chata, she isn't a bimbo! She is high-gloss royalty."

Anjelica held up a torn piece of butcher paper from the table covering and waved it toward her mom. Written in crayon it read, "HANG FLYERS!!!!"

Ofie winked at her daughter and prepared to slink away. "I'll be right back, I have to go to the bathroom. Anjelica, stay here with Nana Chata."

Ofie approached the board and hung her first sign, hurrying so maybe Crafty Chloe would see it before she left.

WANTED: Creative people to join a local arts and crafts collective. All skill levels welcome. We'll make table centerpieces for the CraftOlympics to be held in December and share glitterific ideas, eat snacks, and best of all, build new friendships & have craftalicious fun. Serious chicas only. Call (623) 555-8750. Glendale area.

Ofie folded her arms and congratulated herself. A stunning job indeed. The craft group may have been initiated on Star's behalf, but Ofie would contribute the most.

"Mommy, I want you to meet my new friend," Ofie heard her daughter say from behind.

Wait, wasn't Anjelica supposed to be with Nana Chata at the table? Ofie turned to scold her, but made an exaggerated "Wow!" face instead. Attached to Anjelica's hand was Crafty Chloe in the flesh. Ofie soaked up this once-in-a-lifetime moment and wondered what Chloe's clever mind was cooking up today. She probably had a ruler and mini scrapbook cropping station in that big bag that her assistant was carrying. It ticked Ofie off that many viewers, even Star, referred to Chloe as Craft Bimbo. They were just jealous of Chloe's natural beauty and expertise.

"Mommy, this is Ms. Chavez. Ms. Chavez, this is my mom, Ofelia Fuentes. She's a groupie of yours. And my dad is Larry Fuentes. He's a cameraman at your studio!"

"What a small world," Chloe replied, about to direct her attention elsewhere. She would have walked away, except Anjelica's concrete grip prevented it.

"Mommy, I told Ms. Chavez about your new craft group and she wants to join."

Chloe scowled, as if the notion was beneath her, but attempted to appear as friendly as possible. "Excuse me?"

"You want to help my mom make the award-dinner center-pieces for the CraftOlympics? It's a very high-profile job, lots of glory. Martha is gonna be there! The meetings are at our house in Glendale." Anjelica spouted off the details like an experienced car saleswoman in the body of an eleven-year-old.

Anjelica's maturity stunned her mother. How could anyone turn down that kind of offer?

"Oh, bummer. I don't do the west side unless I'm on the clock. I live in Scottsdale..." Right then, Chloe's plump assistant appeared and whispered in her ear. Chloe listened while bobbing her head, blinking fast, and giving Ofie a once-over. Whatever the girl said changed Chloe's mind in an instant.

"Actually, count me in. Great speech, chiquita," Chloe said, winking at Anjelica and then turning to Ofie, who hopped up and down and clapped her hands.

"You're saying yes? *You* really want to join *my* craft group?"

"Of course," Chloe replied through a tight, beauty-pageant smile.

Chloe's assistant fumbled through her bag until she retrieved a bright purple electronic organizer and used her thumbs to type away. A few seconds later, she shoved her glasses up her nose, hunched over the electronic data gadget once more, and looked up. "She can do Wednesdays, or Fridays after three p.m."

"Can you plan around that?" Chloe asked with a polite "take it or leave it" attitude.

Ofie took it. Her first craft group member, Crafty Chloe! It would take a bit to win Star over, after the La Pachanga TV interview tousle, but Ofie would deal with that later.

A song blared from Chloe's leather hobo bag. She pried her hand free from Anjelica's to answer her phone.

"Tonight at Sangria? It's my night off. What do I get out of it?" argued Chloe.

Anjelica and Ofie's eyes bulged with exhilaration.

Chloe caved. "It's a deal only if it runs prime time." Without so much as a goodbye, Chloe pressed a button on the phone and shoved it in the pocket of her cream tapered blazer that covered a lacy v-neck camisole. Ofie wondered what her life would be like if she had a sexy body and silky clothes like Chloe's. Maybe she'd be the one on TV with her crafts.

"Frances, did you get that?" Chloe commanded.

"Already on it, Ms. Chavez. Sangria on 5th Avenue and Main Street in Scottsdale. Reception starts in three hours. Sangria is that new dig in town. They are trying to get Saturdays going for the younger crowds with weekend art receptions. At ten the place turns into a club. Kinda like a La Pachanga knockoff. The Theo Duarte art show is kicking the whole thing off tonight."

"We know Theo Duarte!" Anjelica offered.

"You do? He's why we're here. I can't believe how fast he fixed that mural. Anyone hear about who did it yet?" Chloe asked.

Ofie and Anjelica kept straight faces. "Nope," they said in unison.

Chloe shrugged and handed Ofie a business card. "Call Frances, my assistant, when you get everything set up. Have a nice weekend, ladies."

Ofie and Anjelica spun around, slapped a mid-air high five, and headed back to the table. Ofie would have called Star to give her a heads-up about Chloe and Sangria, but she forgot as soon as she noticed Nana Chata's empty chair. Ofie and Anjelica looked up to the stage and couldn't believe what they saw—or rather whom.

Nana Chata! Behind a set of metallic teal bongos, drumming in perfect synch with the band. Atop her salt-and-pepper hair rested a tilted kofia mud-cloth hat. She raised her brows at the girls and then tossed her arms in the air and unleashed a wild Mexi-Africano grito: "Ay ay ay! Jambo Jambo!"

Ofie grasped her daughter's hand and the two ran to the dance floor to join in the fun, thrilled that at last Nana Chata had let La Pachanga cast its spell.

10

Even Star's car felt the pain of Theo's absence.

He helped her pick out the 1958 Chevy Bel Air two years ago, and assisted with the upkeep. He instructed her on how to maintain and troubleshoot it. From changing the oil, spark plugs, and tires, he had it covered. They reupholstered and refurbished the vintage auto inside and out until it became a visual sweet spot around town.

But now, after only a week alone, the brake lights went out and Star noticed a hot engine smell. She cursed herself for not paying closer attention to Theo's tutorials. How could she take so many things in her life for granted? As a Band-Aid solution, she gave her car a pep talk and promised to take it to her dad's mechanic on Monday. That is, on the condition it delivered her to Sangria on time.

By 7:45 p.m. on Saturday, all systems were go for Operation Love Shrine.

Star whispered thank you and pulled her Chevy Bel Air into one of the few parking spots left at Sangria, turned off the ignition, buried her face in her hands, and then sat up straight.

"I can do this," she thought. As each day passed without Theo, she grew more and more aware that the last three years were a gift she had taken for granted. Even to the point of hurting him. But she would make it up to him, no matter what it took.

Between her planned speech and the shadow box, how could he resist? She even wore an ensemble of his past gifts: the flowy lime peasant dress from their day trip to Nogales; the chunky coral beaded choker from Christmas; the canvas tote he painted when her wisdom teeth were pulled. For the final touch, she wore two long, thick braids weaved with red satin ribbons—the same hairdo as when he painted her portrait two years ago. If that combination didn't say devoted, nothing did.

Star couldn't wait to be near him again, to take in his scent. His aroma intoxicated her—she would smoke it in a hookah if she had the chance. She would can it as air freshener, or maybe put it in a spritz bottle and douse her pillow every night. A Theo air freshener for her car! Bath bombs, so she could have his scent all over her skin after a long soak in the tub. First she had to find him.

She entered Sangria and marveled at its beauty. Overall, the place could pass as La Pachanga, Version 2.0, only with a modern industrial touch. While chunky wood and thick wrought-iron accessories trimmed her mom and dad's outlet, Sangria possessed a slick, sexy energy of polished steel and embossed silver. And as the new corporate-owned Latin hot spot, pricey details punctuated every corner with accessories her parents couldn't afford: scores of masculine leather barstools, a lit dance floor, and vaulted ceilings. Any other time, she would have jotted down notes in her superspy competitor notebook.

Star clutched her bag as if it were the last life preserver on the *Titanic* and stepped into the pristine gallery. Her eyes widened in amazement at Theo's evocative two-color abstract paintings that adorned the gunmetal walls. A stark departure from his work for La Pachanga. Dark. Heavy. Definitely more serious.

There he stood, across the room, and the vision refreshed her thirsty soul. He glanced up, and their eyes connected as he shook hands with a patron and sifted through the crowd her way. He wore patent-leather creepers, pleated charcoal slacks, a snug gray knit pullover, and appeared all shiny and groomed. He even looked thinner.

Dusty Springfield's "The Look of Love" piped through the gallery speakers, one of his favorite songs to sing a cappella. She took it as a good sign. Star held her breath as the billow of his Krishna Musk oil swirled two steps in front of him and she inhaled to capture every microfiber of his being. Overall, Theo's makeover scored a ten, a solid step up from his usual khakis, tees, sneakers, and wraparound sunglasses that he often wore indoors and at night.

"Hey," he said, as if she were the last person he wanted there.

Rather than reciprocate the greeting like a normal person, Star's jitters overtook her and she mechanically shot out, "Hi, hi, hi, hi, hi, hi…" like a trigger-happy machine gun.

"What's up?" he asked. Obviously his mini vacation had done nothing to lessen his anger.

She gulped to regain composure. "Can I talk to you alone?"

"Estrella, it's my first reception at this gallery. Please, not tonight."

"It's really important. It's something exciting, I swear," she coaxed.

He gestured to the steel double doors at the back of the gallery and walked ahead of her, as if it were a chore to slow his pace. When a tall blonde in a slinky cocktail dress and mile-high heels glided in front of him and smiled, he replied with a sly grin. Star's stomach churned at the concept of Theo flirting with someone other than herself.

They entered the outdoor courtyard, and the sharp scent of the fresh-cut grass taunted her allergies. Otherwise, the setting couldn't have been any more romantic: the sun had set over the towering oak trees that blinked with mini lights. They passed a humungous talavera mosaic water fountain in the center. The setting rivaled a Lifetime Valentine movie on steroids.

"This is good. Go ahead," he said.

"Perfect!" she said, facing him. She bluffed chipperness, when really she wanted to shake that snide, barbed tone out of him. "So, how was your week?"

Star hoped to hear that he'd been dead lonely without her, but Theo never had a chance to respond. A hot breeze blew their way, and it entered with the aroma of expensive designer perfume.

"Theo? Theodoro Duarte?" said a sultry, husky Demi Moore– like voice.

Star couldn't believe it—Craft Bimbo extraordinaire, Chloe Chavez! She floated in rocking a Bumpit in her hair, looking skinnier than embroidery thread, her eyes more hazel than brown and her face masked by thick, albeit flawless, Hollywood makeup. Her skin sparkled with Jared jewelry and she donned a sleek black low-cut number that would have been better suited for the Academy Awards red carpet than a small-time Scottsdale art event.

In princesslike fashion, Chloe stretched out her malnourished arm to Theo. "Pleasure to see you again, Theo. This is a much better scene than last week, wouldn't you say? I'm really impressed at how quickly you repaired the mural."

"It really wasn't a big deal," Theo said.

"Well, congratulations. I just heard the news that Sangria is your new home."

What did than imply? Star wondered. It sounded like a dis on La Pachanga. She expected the homeboy to come out in Theo, and that he would set Craft Bimbo straight. She knew Theo despised Chloe as much as she did, because of the jokes they'd crack when watching her craft segments on TV. The projects were cool, but her delivery of them sucked, as if she was a spokesperson who knew nil about the product.

Instead, he shook Chloe's hand.

A sour twang flinched in Star's stomach while a spicy vignette flashed in her mind: Star shoving the media hag into the fountain, dragging Theo to his car, forcing the shrine in his face, and blessing him with one thousand mini kisses all over his Schickshaved cheeks. Star released a shaky breath and summoned positive thoughts.

She's a reporter, just doing a story. He has to charm her; that's his job tonight. The press will be great for him. After we are officially "together," I'll become his manager and handle this stuff. Why did I decide on braids and a frumpy green dress? Oh God, I feel sick.

"Theo, I'd like to do a feature package on you about your art, as well as being a victim of vandalism," she said.

He must have sensed Star's repulsion. "Ms. Chavez, this is Star Esteban, remember you interviewed her for the mural? Her parents own La Pachanga."

"Oh," Chloe said, pursing her collagen-filled lips. "I'm sorry, of course, Star Esteban. I didn't even recognize you with the braids. You look so *different*. As a matter of fact, I visited La Pachanga today to inquire about the Happy Face Tagger. Your parents haven't filed a police report."

Star tapped her fingers against her thighs to restrain her anger, shifted her weight to her other leg, and just as she opened her mouth, Theo cut in. "Actually, we were in the middle of a personal conversation. Would you mind if we finish up?"

Chloe threw out a Renée Zellweger squint-smile. "Sure, I'll wait inside."

Star watched the vixen swivel on her hoochie heels and sashay back to the gallery. The name Craft Bimbo didn't do Chloe Chavez justice, but Crafty Bitch sure did.

Theo touched the small of Star's back and guided her to a fili-gree bench in a secluded corner. This was it. Her parents' lec-ture, Ofie, the *El Solitario* comic, using THEODUARTE as her computer password—it was all for this moment. She teetered so close on the cliff of anticipation; she could feel the shrine heat-ing up her leg from inside her purse.

"So, what's up?" he asked. She sat down. He didn't.

Star crossed her feet for good luck, and prayed for the best. "I have something for you." She reached into her bag for the shrine, which she had meticulously wrapped in hot-pink tissue and sealed with a red velvet ribbon. The blissful moment to come would be even better than the steamy, carefree night they spent together on their first date. Better than his hands on her waist that first day at the thrift store.

As she pulled out her artwork, the ribbon caught on the zip-per of the bag and the shrine tumbled to the ground. Star scram-bled to pick it up and offered it to him slowly and cautiously, as if it were a precious artifact she had risked her life to retrieve.

He didn't even touch it. "What's that?"

She ripped away the ribbon, exposing the front of the cigar box shrine. He took one glimpse and stepped away. "Estrella, don't do this."

She could have slugged him. Didn't he know how hard she had worked on that gift? She rose from the bench for a stare-down. "Just look at it? I made it for you—it's my art. It's a love shrine that celebrates every facet of our friendship. That's what I came to tell you tonight, that I truly love you and want to be with you."

He got up, took a couple steps, and ran his hand over his head. Star noticed a chunky silver bracelet on his wrist. Since when did he wear accessories? Why didn't he say anything?

"Theo, I'm going to tell you the truth about last weekend, okay?" She drew in a heavy breath. "Remember the last Friday morning when I came over and you were changing your clothes in the other room? Well, I kinda found the wedding brochures under your magazines on your coffee table."

"You searched through my things?" he asked, offended.

Star spoke faster; his cold attitude made her uneasy. "No, I picked up *Urban Latino* magazine because it was the issue with Manu Chao on the cover. The brochures were under that. And then when you asked me to dinner and said you had a surprise...I connected the dots...I knew you were going to pop the question and I wigged out. I do want us to go to the next level, maybe not marriage, but at least...Look, everything I'm wearing are gifts you gave me! I'm here to tell you I'm serious now! I've matured so much this past week."

Theo checked out her outfit, cocked his head back, and laughed sarcastically. "Back up. You thought I was going to ask you to marry me? Don't flatter yourself, Estrella. Those wedding brochures were for a bridal shop. The owner wants a wedding mural on the side of her building." Theo looked away and shook his head. "So that's why you assaulted my mural."

Now it was Star's turn to be speechless.

"I've told you all along, I'm never getting married," Theo stated. "My parents have been divorced twice. What the hell gave you the impression I wanted to settle down with you anyway?"

Star had never been more humiliated in her entire life. Even more than the day she left the house in a bra and jeans and didn't notice until a motor cop pulled her over for a broken taillight.

Theo turned to face her. "Estrella, didn't we agree to go our separate ways? It hasn't even been...what? A week?"

Star choked back tears. Why did he turn into such a jerk? What happened to him? She coveted that spark they used to share, the way he used to rest his head on her shoulder when they watched old movies, when he'd ask her to make him her special blend of champurrado. She had all of it for three glorious years, overflowing in her arms, and now it all slipped through her fingers like sand. Gone. She didn't recognize this alien jock before her, and wished for a way to draw out one teeny thread of the old Theo.

"It's just that...," she whispered. "I want us to be friends again."

"To be your friend comes with a price."

She wished he would comfort her, hug her like old times. Instead he put his hands in his pockets. "I can't give you any more of myself. You sucked me dry. I need simple. I invested so much in your life; it's time for me to focus on mine. I want to erase the past three years so I can move forward."

"Are you saying you regret ever meeting me?" she asked, astonished at his biting attitude.

He paused. "I'm saying I regret allowing myself to fall in love with you."

She leaped off the bench, grabbed his tense face, and kissed his lips with all her might, as if it were all she had left to offer. He received it willingly and for half a moment she felt electricity between them. When she finished, her heart pounded a million times a second as she searched his expression for a clue of what would come next. He gently pushed her away.

"Go do your thing, and I'll do mine."

"But—"

"Let me go, Estrella. Please."

Star's chest caved and her face tingled as if a thousand needles pricked her skin. She felt her stomach crumple like a ball of used tinfoil. The setting around her became a blur. Her plan had just been crushed. Annihilated into bitter, toxic, invisible dust.

"Theo, are you two done yet?" Chloe crooned from the back door.

"Yes, we're done. Come on out," he hollered in a friendly tone, which made Star even more appalled.

"Good luck with your new life," Star said, sharp as a cactus needle. She marched into the gallery and reached the main entrance door. From the corner of her eye she saw Theo lounging next to a relaxed Gwyneth Paltrow–esque Chloe on the bench, engaged in pretentious chitchat as if nothing had happened.

She reached the foyer and took one last look behind at the carnage of her night: Theo still yakking at Chloe, but oddly, Chloe watching her.

In need of a place to unload her fury, Star turned to a young waiter. "This cookie-cutter shithole stinks. It will never be as good as La Pachanga! Tell that to your corporate honchos!"

Star shoved Theo's cigar box shrine in the tall rubber garbage bin. As she fled, she saw the waiter from the corner of her eye. He tossed a stack of empty food trays in the same container, raised his leg, and shoved his foot down hard to make room for more trash.

The shrine, just like her heart, had been demolished beyond repair.

11

"Oh shit! Chloe, get over here, you'll never freakin' believe this. No, God, no, please! Don't let this be happening!" panicked Ezra Mendoza, Chloe's live-in boyfriend.

Rather than leap to his rescue, Chloe remained unbothered, sprawled belly down on the taupe leather chaise that rested on her taupe floor rug in the center of her spacious taupe mod living room. Chloe loved her some taupe.

Her fingers traipsed through the new *Martha Stewart Living*, while she offered imaginary concern. "What is it this time? You got another crease in one of your vintage anime comics?"

Ezra's lanky body sprinted across the generous concrete floor in nothing but boxers, plaid socks, and Buddy Holly glasses. He slid to a halt when he reached her. "Worse! I lost a collector's edition anime DVD!"

"Lemme guess—it was *Robotechiyaki of the Astro Boy and the White Lion Sushi Something Something…*"

"No, Volume One of *Neon Genesis Evangelion*. Why are we so bitchy this morning?" he said while clutching his hip bones. "Oh. I know. The sun has risen on this otherwise happy Monday morning. That means Mommie Dearest called with her daily dose of guilt trips."

Chloe removed her frameless Prada eyeglasses and squinted. "*What* did you just say about my mother?"

"Hold on, that was uncalled for. I apologize." He blinked at her with despair, as if he were a spoiled child in search of his lost nanny. "I heard you arguing and I knew it was her. Didn't you tell her about scoring the CraftOlympics gig? She should be proud."

Chloe turned her face back toward her magazine so Ezra couldn't read her expression. "She still doesn't get it."

"What do you expect, doll? All your family knows you hate crafts and you're trying to claw, steal, bribe, and cheat your way into the industry."

Chloe deleted that despicable comment from the air, even though he was right.

"Anyway, I need your help. That DVD is valuable!"

"I brought it from work for you. It was *free*, Ezra. For God's sake, your dad is practically the Bill Gates of the lampshade industry. Ask him to order you a new copy from Amazon," Chloe snarked, reluctantly closing her magazine and tossing it on the imported Parisian wood coffee table.

She sighed, bored. "There is a disc on top of the DVD player in your 'media room,'" Chloe said, flicking her fingers for air quotes. Ezra's "media room" consisted of a utility closet where he operated his Web design business that consisted of three clients—including her. "I saw it there yesterday when I printed out my new head shots."

Detached from the crisis, she sat up, slid on her taupe satin slippers, and headed for the kitchen. He trailed, holding an invisible box in his hands. "Great, you probably used up all the ink in the cartridges. Now I'll have to buy new ones."

"Wrong. *I'll* have to buy new ones, because God forbid you pay for anything," she shouted as she switched on the coffee grinder. "And I wouldn't have used it if you would have completed the task in the first place. I told you I needed fifteen press kits for my boss to send to the CraftOlympics executive committee and guess what? Once again, I had to handle it myself. So until you pitch in around here, I can print out rainbow wallpaper if I want."

"Why didn't you ask Frances?"

Chloe flashed him a death stare. "How many times do I have to explain? Frances handles *local*. You handle *national*, remember?"

It didn't take much to set Ezra straight. They both knew who drove the sugar mama gravy train and he would be an idiot to jump off. Ezra, a self-proclaimed snooty slacker, created Web sites for a living. Correction: *Part-time* living. His penny-pinching ways were insane considering his father became a millionaire by inventing a line of cheesy lampshades that rotated and displayed silhouettes across the room. He literally handed over tens of thousands of dollars for his son to launch his own business, not to mention a trust fund. Yet the antiestablishment Ezra refused to spend any of it because "he couldn't be bought." Although he didn't seem to mind Chloe earning the cush so they both could enjoy a lavish existence in a trendy north Scottsdale loft.

"Oh, kitten. Forgive me. Don't worry, I'll find something soon. A buddy of mine is launching a Web site to sell kick-ass *World of Warcraft* LARP memorabilia. High quality. I told him I'd go in with him. Hey, can I grind a scoop of French Roast when you're done?"

"As long as you tell me how you define 'LARP memorabilia,'" Chloe inquired smugly. "I'm intrigued."

A wild sparkle danced in Ezra's blue eyes as he sat up on the kitchen counter to explain. "Live Action Role Play. Cool shit—you know, like costumes the characters wear in the game—metal plate armor, chain mail for dudes, bikini mail for chicks, pewter swords of Azreoth. You can't even find stash like that on eBay. Slick, huh?"

Oh yeah, ladies would be crashing their computers for a bathing suit made from jump rings. Chloe didn't need his money, but she was tired of him living off of hers.

"Good for you," she said, tightening the belt on her crisp taupe linen robe. She ignored him and went to work on her guilty pleasure piece of machinery: a fifteen-hundred-dollar Jura Capresso Impressa S9 One Touch Automatic Coffee and Espresso Center. One of the few items under her roof that was not taupe. She didn't smoke, rarely partied, had no time to enjoy the thrill of a shopping spree, and her sex life compared to the excitement of the Sunday-night lineup on the Weather Channel. A high-maintenance girl needed some kind of joy. Hers was one hour at the gym every day and custom gourmet coffee. She chugged espresso like pirates drink rum.

Ten minutes later, Chloe sat at her vanity bedroom throne and activated the daily two-hour primping process of transforming her face from "reality natural" to "camera-ready natural."

"I found it," Ezra muttered from the doorway.

"Found what?" she said, tapping $110-per-ounce Crème de la Mer skin cream on her cheeks.

"My DVD. It was just where you said it was. I don't know why I doubt you. Thanks!"

Chloe replied through the reflection in the mirror. "You're welcome. I can't talk now. I need to get ready for work."

"Why are you so negative? Aren't you excited for your new gig? All the networks will be covering it and you're the main star. Betty O'Hara must be crying in her craft room right about now."

Chloe stopped with the face cream. "Ezra, I guarantee, Betty Oh! is not crying. You know why? She is still the national spokesperson for the craft industry association. She doesn't even need the CraftOlympics anymore. She's outgrown it. Plus, she's married to a great guy and they have two beautiful kids. Everything else to her is icing on the cake. The woman is happy; therefore everything I grasp and sweat for plops in her lap like a cherry on a banana split. She could trade in her glue guns for stuffed porcupines and she'd still be the be-all, end-all to the public. If I could have one ounce of her career—"

"Chloe, you're hosting the National CraftOlympics. Again, it's a big deal. Can't you be happy for once? You weren't like this when we met. As soon as you decided to conquer the craft world, it was like you forgot how to have fun. Come to think of it, I haven't heard you laugh since...I can't even remember."

"You know why I don't like to laugh."

Ezra whipped out his iPhone to check for new e-mail. "So what if you snort? It's cute. All I'm asking is for you to lighten up a bit before those frown lines set in."

"I'm fine," she said, allowing half a smile.

Really, she wasn't fine. The exhilaration of the hosting job wore off knowing it came by way of putting out for Mark Jefferies. The thought of that man naked made her shudder. She had to do it though; otherwise she would be stuck at KPDM forever.

Ezra removed his specs and cleaned them with the bottom of the "Karma: It's your choice" T-shirt he'd thrown on over a pair of jeans. "I can go update your iPod if you want. Make you a new playlist? The Pinker Tones have a new disc out. Can't you at least try to be upbeat?"

"No, really. I'm fine. Go do whatever it is you do while I'm gone."

"Thanks! Love ya," he said. He attempted to kiss her mouth, but Chloe pointed at the hair removal cream above her lip.

He shoved one hand in the pocket of his wrinkled jeans and the other he used to graze his greasy black faux hawk. "Hey, um.

Do you mind if I take the Beemer tonight? Me and the boys, we're gonna go down some Bronsons at the bar, and check out what's on the clothesline. Do you mind?"

"Can you speak English?" Chloe asked.

"I'm going with friends to drink beer and gossip."

No wonder he couldn't function as a credible adult. "Nah, go on ahead, have fun with your *Bronsons*. But you better fill the gas tank."

Raised in the upper crust of Los Angeles, Chloe had one younger sister, an intrusive mother, and a workaholic lawyer father who died from a heart attack at fifty. As valedictorian and sorority queen of her graduating class, Chloe sparkled as the jewel in her mother's society crown. Especially when Clive Diaz, a noted California Realtor, fell loco in love with Chloe. No sooner had she opened her diploma for her master's in journalism than he asked for her to take his name. She accepted, because that's what girls like her did. But eventually she ditched her rich fiancé for an entry-level field reporter's position in Phoenix. Add in a mooch for a live-in boyfriend and mamita went on a rampage.

Every morning, Chloe woke to a call from her mother, begging her to move home and give Clive another chance. And every morning, Chloe hung up pissed and depressed that her mother refused to take an interest in her profession, much less her feelings.

Truth was, Chloe regretted Ezra moving in, even if he did somewhat help build her reputation. Two years back, Chloe featured his father's invention on the news and he introduced the two. Ezra pitched the seemingly limitless opportunities of the booming home décor industry and Chloe took the bait. She actually hated crafts and anything D-I-Y. She preferred to B-U-Y. The motivation was strictly career-oriented, her mission was to be the Rachael Ray of *something* by age thirty. If crafts paved the way, so be it.

Her muse came in the form of Betty O'Hara, a former KPDM morning anchor, busy mom, and "a crafty Heloise for the now generation" according to the press. Early in her career at the station, Betty fit daily craft demonstrations into her morning newscasts. From pumpkins to pillows, the frugal mom worked her magic. Within months, her popularity surged among viewers—young, old, male, female, rich, and not so rich. She preached the gospel of crafts as a way to not only save money, but also to inspire individuals to express their creativity. Thanks to her clever, classy, but never costly, design ideas, her fans did as they were told. They adored the way she punctuated the end of every segment with "Oh!," which led to her nickname of Betty Oh! That catchy moniker, combined with her comical personality, landed her a book deal and national TV show. As soon as Chloe learned arts and crafts raked in thirty billion dollars a year, she absorbed every aspect of Betty O'Hara's success to use as a platform for her own.

With the help of Mark Jefferies; her inventive assistant, Frances; and a weekly segment, Crafty Chloe emerged—ready to follow in Betty's embossed footprints and conquer the universe one rhinestone at a time, likely with Ezra tagging along for the ride.

She wished he could be more like that musician she met at that coffeehouse, or Theodoro Duarte, the artist she interviewed Saturday. Both exhibited kindness, honesty, strength, and even a dash of sexy mystery. It was refreshing to talk with men who weren't whiny wimpsters, like Ezra. That night with Theo was the most insightful conversation Chloe'd had in months. She dabbed her foundation on her makeup sponge, and as she smoothed it over her skin, she replayed the memory from two nights ago:

The last patron had left Sangria. Chloe didn't intend to stay the entire evening, but so many prominent local arts figure attended, she used the time to network and toot her horn about hosting the CraftOlympics. Next thing she knew, the place had cleared out. She and Theo collapsed on the remaining upright chairs as the crew cleaned around them. His paintings were a hit, no surprise. Chilled from the alcohol, for once she turned off her work mode and allowed herself to have informal dialogue with another human being. Not for a story, not for her career, not for any reason other than camaraderie. Their small talk began with chuckles about some of the guests and their off-the-mark interpretations of Theo's work, and the discussion soon weaved into more meaningful subjects.

"I can tell you love your job," Theo said, removing a silver bracelet from his wrist.

Chloe shrugged and crossed her legs. "You want to know the truth? I don't. It's a difficult business. I'm only twenty-eight and they treat me like I'm forty. It's a requirement to look like a camera-ready Jennifer, twenty-four/seven."

"Jennifer?" he asked, confused.

"You betcha. Lopez, Aniston, or Garner. For a woman like me to succeed, it's all about a wrinkle-free forehead, lots of sass, ganas, and mucho overtime. I'm not even thirty, and I already have Botox brochures in my desk." It was supposed to be a joke, but Theo didn't laugh.

"Why do you stay?"

Chloe removed her necklace, opened her evening bag, and dropped it in. "Because I know I'm good," she said, snapping the clutch closed. "When I'm in front of that camera, a rush hits me because I morph into someone people admire. I know in my heart I deserve something big. My dad even saw it in a dream when I was in high school. He told me I was on every television set in the country and people loved me. I laughed about it until he passed away on my nineteenth birthday. Now that I look at the big picture, I guess you could say I'm trying to make his dream come true." Chloe felt a strange tingle in her nose and sniffled.

"I'm sure he's proud of you. You've accomplish more than a lot of other people I know," Theo said.

Now that Chloe had started, she couldn't stop. "I've put up with so much bullshit. I've made blunders and now I'm on a quest to do it right and do it fast. I've been asked to host this huge craft convention that is coming to Phoenix. My life is going to upgrade and it won't come a moment too soon." Chloe kicked off her heels, walked to the buffet table aftermath, and half filled two cups from a straggler champagne bottle. She handed one to Theo and downed the other.

"Do you know they call me Craft Bimbo?"

"Who?"

"Everyone! They whisper it behind my back at work, people on the street, craft haters everywhere. That's why I need to prove myself. To make them all eat their words."

"I'll admit I've rolled me eyes at TV people before."

"Ha! You mean at me, don't you? I can tell by the polite expression on your face. You are an awful liar."

"There's something about media people. They seem so phony, like they have to overdramatize every emotion and it comes off as fake. But I promise I won't roll my eyes anymore. At you."

"Gee, thanks," she kidded.

She walked back to the bottle and gulped what was left of the bubbly.

"So here is where Craft Bimbo came from. It started the summer before I graduated from college, when I worked at the station as an intern. There was this wild annual holiday party, everyone acting like fools, you know? I was young and shit-faced stupid. I got drunk and screwed the CEO of the station. We didn't even go to a hotel. We did it right there on the cook table on the main set! Get this—the *same* table where I demo my craft segment each week. Can you believe that? And now, every week when I stand there and affix ribbon to colored card stock, I relive that night in my mind. It's revolting. He's bald and fat now." She refused to share that she still slept with the ogre on occasion.

"So what happened?" Theo asked, as he watched her mope back to her chair.

"Of course, word leaked out. I moved home to L.A. with my mom and made wedding plans with an egomaniacal realtor who had big bucks. All I wanted was for my mom to be proud of me. To her, catching a man with a bottomless bank account equaled success. I couldn't go through with it. On the day of my wedding, out of the blue, Mark—that's the CEO—called my cell and offered me a job at the station. I took it as a sign from the universe. So instead of walking down the aisle, I bolted for the airport. Because of my dad's dream, you know?"

Theo nodded. "That's cool."

She shook her finger at him. "Hold on, guy—it wasn't any easier when I came back. Everyone at the station knew the truth. When Mark promoted me three months later, they assumed it was my 'cook table connection' and not my talent. First it was 'News Bimbo.' And when the crafts came, well…here I am, the resident Craft Bimbo. Hey, can I have the last sip of your champagne?"

"You don't need it. You're driving home, right?" Theo crumbled the cup, aimed for the trash, threw it, and missed. "People are cruel. They'll latch on to gossip so quick, it's not fair. It makes them forget their own shit. Don't you have any friends to hang with?"

"No. But I did join a committee to help me prep for the CraftOlympics. I was chosen as the host of the whole event."

"Hey, congrats!"

Chloe smirked out of one side of her mouth and noticed that

his cup landed near the same trash bin where Star stood before storming off.

"Hey, Theo . . . what was up with your amiga tonight? The La Pachanga girl. What is her story?"

"Estrella."

"I thought her name was Star."

"It is, but I call her by her real name, Estrella," he said. "Yeah, you walked in on a pretty intense moment. We used to be tight, now we're not. It's complicated."

"She's an odd one. Reminds me of that chick in *Ghost World*, always trying to stand out," Chloe said acerbically. "I wanted to grill her about the Happy Face Tagger ordeal, but I kinda felt sorry for her."

Theo stood up abruptly, pulled his keys out his front pocket, and swung them around his finger. "She's the most genuine person you'll ever meet. Listen, it's been nice to get to know you, Chloe. Best of luck with your career."

They shook hands and Theo left for home.

Chloe couldn't get Star out of her brain. What did this nice guy say to her to make her lose it like that? And what did she throw in the trash? Chloe investigated the scene in true reporter fashion. Despite her glamorous outfit, she grabbed a fork from the table and used it to sift through the sticky plastic cups, lipstick-stained napkins, and soggy remains from the fruit trays. Beneath a cake-smeared Chinet plate, she spotted a red velvet ribbon stuck to pink tissue paper wrapped around a boxy container.

"Hey, do you guys have a bag and clean napkin I can use?" she shouted to the workers.

A chubby teenage boy with bad acne and a tight white uniform jogged over and offered a paper bag with handles. Chloe squinched her face in disgust and carefully lifted the item from the stinky trash. She slid it into the bag and headed home, late, and in pain, due to the snakeskin stilettos that had mutilated the tops of her pinky toes.

"The box!" Chloe said, her mind snapping back to the present as she tapped on light beige concealer under her eyes. She forgot that Saturday night, she came home, exhausted, and tossed the bag on the top laundry shelf. And that's exactly where it would stay until she figured out what to do with it.

12

The fourth day crawled by since the latest expiration of Star's relationship with Theo. Feeling as secure as an amputee without a table to lean on, she checked herself into a bedroom pity-party lockdown. No Theo on her schedule and no eBay bids on her glitter.

Sunday she slept. Monday she sobbed. Tuesday she wept. Today she did all three. Why? Because she regretted picking up that copy of *Urban Latino* from Theo's coffee table that day, seeing the wedding brochures, and thinking they were for her. And the mural, of course. But even more so, she hated that she had listened to Ofie and made that stupid love shrine. Could Theo have crushed her any harder than to not even look at it? The scene replayed continuously in Star's head. The humiliation made her want to grab her hair and scream.

This morning, Star rose like a shackled prisoner and went straight to her movie collection, and snatched up specific flicks. She grudgingly set up her video camera, tripod, and laptop, and then created a fifty-minute movie reel that she then burned to a disc. She curled up on her bed with a box of Puffs Plus with Lotion and watched it over and over.

Al busted through the door midafternoon and clicked on the

light. "Estrella, up. Now." He stopped and tilted his head, confused. "Are you watching *The Way We Were?*"

Star didn't move from under the tent she had created with her sheets. "Just the last four minutes. I made a DVD of all the endings to movies with doomed love stories."

Al backed up slowly to check out the DVD cases strewn across the red and green striped area rug. *Splendor in the Grass. Moulin Rouge. West Side Story. Titanic. Romeo and Juliet. A Place in the Sun. The Notebook. Casablanca.*

"What? Are you trying to kill yourself by clogging your tear ducts?"

Wearing her favorite sleep clothes—high school gym shorts and an "I am a fictional character" XXL tee, Star climbed across the mattress and perched on the edge of her bed. She watched the screen, blew her nose on a ratty tissue, and tossed it on the floor with the others.

"I don't feel as alone this way," she explained. "Care to join me?" she asked, holding up the tissues.

Al took the box, set it on the bed, and reached for his daughter's hand. She grasped it and climbed off the mattress to face him.

"Estrella, I know you miss Theo, but all this crying isn't going to bring him back."

Star collapsed into her father's inviting arms. He held her tight and patted the dirty hair she hadn't washed in days. She loved him so intensely that, for one instant since Saturday night, she actually felt a peg better. His hugs always had that effect on her.

"Dad," she whispered, resting her head against his chest. "Theo is half of me. I thought I was half of him. But I'm not. You should have seen all the people at his reception at Sangria. He's doing great without me. And La Pachanga—it's doing fine without me too. I'm like junk food. Empty calories. I'm always saying I want to make my mark, yet I could vanish right now and there would be no trace that I existed."

"Keep yourself busy and you'll find your stride," he said firmly. "And quit the self-pity. We taught you better than that."

She pulled away and clasped her hands in front of her chest. "Please just let me come back to La Pachanga in my old job. I don't have one ounce of creativity in even a single cell of my body. Dad, I want to have *hope*...but it's impossible right now."

Her father shook his head, disappointed. "Why do you quit so easy? Do not give in. Have faith—which is better—because to have hope means to have doubt."

"I'll try," she said, hugging him tightly again. He cleared his throat, indicating an announcement would follow. Star braced. It could be anything from firing someone at La Pachanga to needing her primo closet for storage. "Estrella, we have a family guest staying with us for a while."

A guest? They rarely had guests, except visiting family now and then. "Who? When?"

He cleared his throat again. "Since Sunday. I'm asking you to keep an open mind, especially since all that's happened."

"Sunday? That long? Why didn't anyone tell me?" Star said, realizing she had been a hermit for the past week. She paced a couple steps and came to a gruff halt and smacked her head in disbelief. "Oh God, Dad. I know. Please, no. I can't deal with—"

"Maria Juana," he said, tying his dreads into a ponytail.

Star dove on her bed and shoved her face into the pillow. At the same moment, piercing screams shot out from the television, as the ill-fated *Titanic* had just cracked in half. "Just suffocate me now, por favor," Star ordered, muffled by the fiber-filled cushion. Her inept-but-cunning chola cousin who had infamously been named after two aunts—Maria and Juana—was not what she needed these days.

"Star, be mature. You have no idea the rough life that girl has been through. You're Paris Hilton compared to her. She is stay-ing in the guest room."

Star rolled over. "As in—my walk-in closet?"

"I told you all along you could use it to store your racks of clothes until we needed it for something else. Maria Juana is the something else. She's been evicted from her apartment and needs a temporary home. We're doing it for Auntie Carol. Maria Juana is going to help around La Pachanga until she finds a job and gets back on her feet. How did you put it on the news?" Al made air quotes with his fingers. "'We are a family that believes in second chances.'"

"You let *her* work there, but not *me*?" Star whined. "It's not fair. Why can't she go back home with Auntie?"

"It's complicated drama. Auntie Carol is getting married to her new boyfriend. She's worried about Maria Juana being too...friendly...I guess you would call it."

"You mean she knows Maria Juana will tap his trunk. She's right. You know how she is!" Star sat down on the edge of her bed and counted off Maria Juana's flaws. "Last time she stayed here, she hit on Theo. She swiped my jewelry. She told Mom I hated her organic tamales."

"But you do hate her organic tamales."

"But I didn't want Mom to know that. I always eat one in front of her, because I love her and want to make her feel good. Maria Juana is a gangbanger-Roller-Derby-hoochie-mama freak."

"She is also family. She has no place to sleep. It's a done deal. And by the way, how are the centerpieces coming along?"

Star rolled over on her back and stared at the ceiling. "We're meeting today for the first time. God help me."

Her dad left the room and Star almost went back to her mopey movie marathon to burn time until heading to Ofie's for the craft group—until she caught a glimpse of herself in the TV screen. Did she really look that crusty? Her hair, which normally hung in tiers of ringlets, stuck out in a ratted, matted mess. She sniffed under her armpit and caught a DEFCON 4 whiff of BO.

"Gross!" she shrieked. Actually, it wasn't so bad. Boycotting personal hygiene would go with her new "screw the world" introverted, woman-scorned lifestyle. However, it would have to wait. She had the first meeting for the goofy CraftOlympics centerpieces. She didn't work at La Pachanga anymore, but she still served as a representative and had to make good on her promise to her dad.

Even more so, to herself.

13

Chloe knew joining the CraftOlympics Centerpiece Committee would impress the organizers of the convention. Not that she needed to. The news of her recent success spread to California, proof of which came in the form of a job offer from a top-rated Los Angeles station. She turned it down. The CraftOlympics was in December and last year's host signed an endorsement contract by January. Chloe expected the same time frame for herself, at least by February. First, though, Chloe had to survive the next few months of preparing for the gala by serving time with these glue gun geeks.

"It's three eleven. I canceled Pilates for this?" Chloe sniveled to Ofie's front door—a brown and orange stenciled monstrosity. Its ugliness fueled the TV reporter's intolerance. The inaugural gathering was set for three p.m., *sharp*, but the shabby little shack appeared abandoned.

Chloe paced about the faded Astroturf that lined the compact porch's entryway, and surveyed the clumsy landscape: overgrown bougainvillea, neglected cat claw vines, and scattered wilting cacti imprisoned in dusty terra-cotta pots. She held her finger under her nose to prevent a sneeze. It didn't work.

"Ahhh-choo!" she screeched in a high Mariah Carey octave. Chloe sniffled and checked her wristwatch: 3:20. "What a waste of a Wednesday afternoon...," she barked, digging through her taupe Prada hobo bag for her car keys.

"Are you *the* Crafty Chloe?" asked a young voice from behind her.

Chloe clenched her teeth and pivoted, graceful, like a swimsuit model. For a perky TV personality, there was nothing worse than to be busted in a bitch fit. She could handle it though. By the time she faced the mystery greeter, she had morphed back to shiny happy Crafty Chloe Chavez, professional roving reporter and pretend ruler of all paper crafters across the land.

Before her stood a teen boy, with one dimple and pop star good looks.

"You *are* Crafty Chloe! Thrilled to meet you!" he said with a warm, inviting smile that shone underneath a bar of black peach fuzz. "I'm Benecio. Oh! You smell as scrumptious as you look. Divine! Is that the new Bvlgari?" he asked, gripping the strap to the black leather satchel across his chest and sniffing in her direction.

Chloe adored her fans; they were the closest she'd come to genuine affection. She blushed and clasped his hand with both of hers. Maybe she could hold on a few more minutes for the crazy craft lady.

"Likewise, Benecio. Thank you," she replied.

Screech! A car backed into the driveway. Chloe and Benecio locked eyes in anticipation and darted to the wrought-iron gate that separated the porch from the front lawn. They stood in the open entryway and glared at the pimped-out black PT Cruiser with a red bumper sticker that read: "Honk if you mix your own masa!"

A burly salt-and-pepper-haired woman in sneakers, a visor,

a knee-length green jersey, and denim capri pants leaped from the car holding bongos under one arm and a young girl at the end of the other. She eyed Chloe and Benecio for a moment before turning her attention to another woman hustling up the brick walkway that divided the lawn.

"Hi, Nana Chata! Hi, Anjelica! These are the people for our centerpiece committee," said the young woman as she gestured to where Chloe and Benecio stood.

Chloe recognized her: Star Esteban from La Pachanga, in yet another wild outfit. This time it was a black ensemble of a men's guayabera shirt, Bermuda shorts, Chinese slippers, and three plastic baby barrettes in her wild mane of hair.

Chloe mumbled softly under her breath as Nana Chata silently shot her the evil eye.

Benecio folded his arms and shook his head at the roof. "This is weird. I should have listened to Alice and stayed in my own dysfunctional home."

"Nana Chata," Star pleaded. "We need to let them in, please. Ofie is running late."

"Fine!" Nana Chata said, opening the gate and then unlocking the front door. She looked like she thought they would rob the place, Chloe thought. Not that Chloe could imagine who would want to steal anything from here.

Star guided them into the house with a welcome swing of her arm. She turned to Benecio. "Hi, I'm Star. Ofie should be here soon."

Chloe expected Star to give her the brush-off, but instead she offered a dry smile. Chloe would have reciprocated if it weren't for the stench of stale coffee, microwave popcorn, and Febreze that lingered in the air, causing her to grimace instead.

Immediately Star's expression hardened. She shot Chloe an icy look and returned her attention to Benecio. "Come this way to the Arizona room. That's where she wants us to gather," instructed Star.

Chloe stopped and thought of the holding power of her hair and makeup. "The Arizona room? As in, screened-in porch? It's August. It's one hundred and thirteen degrees outside."

"Remember me?" Anjelica said as she took Chloe's elbow and escorted her across the threshold. "Don't worry, it's enclosed and we have a swamp cooler and spray bottles if it gets too hot."

Benecio stayed close by Chloe's side and together they zig-zagged through the house, taking in the painted plastic plants, mice-and-mushroom stenciled floors, and the glittered popcorn ceiling. It was obvious they shared identical impressions—*Ofie's House: When Bad Crafts Attack.* Chloe made a mental note to consider Ofie's digs for an upcoming Decorating 911 segment, but first she would have to call in a clean-up crew. She was try-ing to figure out if they could air the show in time for sweeps when another commotion took place.

"Ofie!" Star squealed. "Your hair—I mean, you're here!"

The woman of the hour had arrived, her auburn hair a curly, gelled bob, slightly pointed like a tee-pee on top and lopsided on the sides. Her high-pitched voice sang out as she apologized repeatedly.

"Please, please forgive me for being late to our first meeting—at my house! I'm Ofelia Fuentes, but you can call me Ofie for short. That is Nana Chata, my husband's mother. And, Benecio, you're the only one who hasn't met Anjelica; she's my daughter." She studied the faces of her new friends and rubbed her heart. "Won-derful! Happy is as happy does! Please, sit down, make your-selves comfortable, and I'll go get the treats. I hope everyone likes gourmet mochas!"

The guests swapped questionable glares as they sat on mis-matched chairs arranged around a rickety buffet table lined with a tattered disposable tablecloth. In the center rested three dented metal baking pans piled with crusty glue bottles, old paints, glitter jars, kid scissors, and splintered chopsticks. Chloe felt her MAC studio foundation melting on her face from the heat. So much for the swamp cooler.

"Hello, Star. How are you?" Chloe asked as she smoothed the tablecloth in front of her. The silence was as stifling as the heat. Chloe was willing to do anything to soften the awkward moment.

"Fine, thanks," Star replied, picking at a chunk of dried paint on the back of her chair. Maybe she seemed rude, but thanks to the TV segment and the Sangria debacle, Star would forever associate Crafty Chloe with Theo heartache.

All too familiar with the hidden tension of arguing adults, Benecio ignored both of them, whipped out a journal from his satchel, and sketched. Chloe abandoned her attempt at chitchat and checked her e-mail on her BlackBerry. Star removed an elastic tie from her wrist, created an instant beehive look with her hair, and tapped her fingers on the table. All of a sudden, a loud clanging noise came from the kitchen.

"I think I'll go help Ofie with those drinks," Star said as she headed into the kitchen, Nana Chata and Anjelica on her heels.

Chloe had never felt more uncomfortable and out of place. She would rather be on Grand Ave. in the seediest art house than spend another minute in the tacky little house. She contemplated making up an excuse to leave, and would have, except Benecio waved her over by the window to the kitchen.

"I think she had a panic attack," Benecio stated, gawking through a slat in the blinds. "She must be really nervous to have us here."

Chloe hunched below Benecio and peeked. Star tended to Ofie, who rested on a barstool, breathing into a paper bag, tears streaming, while Nana Chata rubbed her back.

On the other side of the wall, Star rested her forehead on her friend's. "What happened, chica?"

"I got attacked by two dozen uncured resin bracelet pieces last night. Somehow they got stuck in my hair before I went to bed. This morning, the resin had hardened. I had to chop it all off. Another blunder," Ofie said. She dropped the paper bag, hung her heavy head in the direction of the kitchen's harvest-gold linoleum floor, and blew her nose in a three-ply Brawny. She examined Star from the toes up. "Cheese and rice. Why do you look like you're going to a funeral?"

Star wagged her thumb over her shoulder. "Why didn't you warn me that Craft Bimbo joined our group? How did that happen? She is, like, my least favorite person in the world."

"Hey, now," Nana Chata broke in, nodding her head toward Anjelica to remind the women she was in the room, "let's get on these snacks, ladies. We have company." Star and Ofie each grabbed a plastic plate of crackers and headed for the back patio.

Ofie entered first, and came to a cold stop.

Star poked her head from behind and let out a silent scream and then rushed to the table, set down the plate, and threw her hands over her face, as if to hide.

There on the floor of the enclosed patio, in plain view of the nervous guests, were the family Chihuahuas, Lola and Rocco, snarling and playing tug-of-war with a pair of Ofie's size-22 lime-green floral granny panties. The oldest pair in her collection, as shown by the large hole in the crotch and a loose piece of wavy elastic that trailed behind.

Chloe slapped her hands over Benecio's eyes. Nana Chata pushed Ofie and Star—who still had her hands on her face—out of the way and snatched the panties from the dogs and stuffed them in her bra. "Hee-hee, these *perritos* love them some *chonies*!" she said as she scooped up the dogs, opened the screen door, and tossed them in the backyard.

Anjelica giggled and, as always, the sound of her daughter's laughter made Ofie feel like everything would be okay. She set the plate on the table and sat in a chair, still a little shell-shocked. She frowned for an instant, and then smiled proudly. "Ladies, and little gentleman, thank you for coming. Before we start I want us all to remember one thing: The work of the hands brings forth the spirit of the heart!"

"Okay," they all said, silently agreeing to pretend they hadn't just witnessed two tiny dogs fighting over an enormous pair of women's underpants.

"Well, I guess now is a good time for introductions before we get into the serious convention stuff. I'll go first. I'm a proud craftaholic!" Ofie proclaimed.

Star placed her hand gently on Ofie's arm. "Can I start, sweetie?" This project had to be streamlined and precise, and Star needed to take control before Ofie led them down the twisted side road of Glittered Dream Catcher Lane.

"Thank you for participating in what will be an exciting and rewarding experience for all of us," Star said, using her best business voice. "As you know, the nineteenth annual CraftOlympics will be held in Phoenix the first week of December. La Pachanga Eatery and Art Space"—Star emphasized the last part just for Chloe—"is one of the sponsors. We are responsible for creating two hundred boutique-worthy centerpieces for the awards gala dinner. In return, we will be provided VIP badges for the entire show, each of our names will be featured in the program, we'll receive two comp booths, a mention at the awards, as well as a letter of recommendation, if we should ever need one for our respective careers."

Chloe had to admit, Star impressed her, as did the deal perks.

"We will need to meet at least once a week for seventeen weeks, and we will finish twelve centerpieces a week. I'm confident the four of us can handle it. That said, let's open this meeting with introductions, and then go into brainstorming. Ofie, take it away..." Star nudged her friend.

"Wow, Star, that was good!" Ofie cheered.

"Really? Thanks! I rehearsed it on the drive over," she whispered back to her friend and chuckled for the first time in four days.

Ofie then turned her attention back to the group. "Well, I make lots and lots of really neat stuff, as you can see," she said, pointing to the various crooked, indiscernible objects around the room. "I am one-half Mexican-American, one-quarter African-American, and one-quarter Native-American. My mother-in-law says I'm a quarter short of a dollar! Ha!" Ofie laughed, and then paused with a puzzled look on her face.

Nana Chata crunched into a pork rind.

"Anyway," Ofie continued, "my talent is a gift that has been passed on by my ancestors. I live to create and inspire. To me, crafting is like a big, warm, gooey fudge brownie. It makes me feel good and I love to share. I'm not the best housekeeper or cook, but when I craft, I feel like a superstar. And speaking of superstars—I am so thrilled to have the remarkable Crafty Chloe here. I still can't believe you are sitting right here in my house! I love everything you do, and your ideas are the best I've ever seen!"

Star wanted to stick her finger down her throat, but refrained.

Chloe's eyes wandered to a hanging knotted object made from plastic lacing and fluorescent-pink pony beads. She blinked a few times and focused her attention back on Ofie. "Thanks," she responded coolly, as she sipped from the watery liquid that was supposed to be an iced mocha. "Um. Wow. Is this Folgers?"

"No, no, no...it's flavored instant—the expensive gourmet stuff. I splurged for you gals," Ofie bragged. "It's Vanilla Nut and I used two heaping tablespoons per glass, like the package says. I can go get the can, if you want it stronger."

More than anything, Chloe wanted to spit out the vile concoction before she gagged on its grittiness. Unfortunately, that was not an option. "It's fine, thanks. As for my introduction, you already know—I'm Crafty Chloe Chavez. I'm an award-winning broadcast journalist, I cover the local arts scene, and, as you all know, I'm what you call a craft-lebrity. I'm very pleased to share with you that I've been selected as the host of the CraftOlympics. I've worked so hard to get where I am. I deserve this break. It will lead to bigger and better connections for me. Star, I know you must have your hands full with your parents' eatery *and art space*, so if you would like me to take over this project, I'll be more than happy to. Once we choose our design, just send the supplies my way and I'll make sure they are made to spec and delivered on time."

Chloe came up with a genius idea on the fly. She would stall the brainstorming meeting, have Frances make the prototype and finals, pass them off as Chloe's, and promote them at the show. *Voilà!* She just found a way to add a licensing deal to her national platform.

As Chloe mentally calculated her future net worth, Star shot up in her seat. "No, that won't be necessary. My father assigned me to oversee this directly. But before we discuss that any further, we have two more intros. I guess I'll go next." She snatched a paintbrush from the box, inspected its bristles, and slouched. She wanted to sound as polished as Chloe, but it just wasn't her style.

"Honestly? I'm here because I blew my dad's money on this sponsorship. He's keeping a close eye, so I'm kinda in the hot seat. So if I sound like a craft Nazi, that's why."

Chloe perked up in her chair. "Oh, a centerpiece crisis! I guess I'm at the right place then, right, Star?"

"Ha. Ha," Star fired back. Secretly she was a little impressed that Chloe remembered her comment. As much as she wanted to tell Chloe her services weren't needed, she knew her credentials would elevate the status of the project, and Ofie would be five-hanky sad if Chloe left. "Here's another confession to deal with—I'm not a crafter. I'm an artist."

Benecio raised his hand. "What is the difference between the two?"

Star twisted the thick silver ring on her thumb. "Art is something you make only once, that someone else cannot replicate. Crafts are when a lot of people make things that look alike."

Chloe raised her hand. "Therefore, Ofie's work is art, because I know I couldn't replicate that...cute...knot thingy hanging up there."

Ofie's eyes twinkled at the compliment from her idol. "It's a plastic macramé birdfeeder! Wow, I never thought of it as art. I guess I'm an artist too—like you, Star!"

Star squirmed. "Not exactly, because art is also something that relays a statement or message, something profound that forces people to reexamine their views on that particular topic."

"Oh," Ofie replied. "Well, my statement is to make people happy. Does that count?"

Star didn't have time to answer because Chloe jumped in. "I didn't know you were an artist," she baited. "What do you make, Star? Does it involve spray paint?"

"I'm currently exploring all genres..."

"Star made a love shrine last week!" Ofie announced.

Chloe's eyes widened. So that's what the box was—a love shrine. If only Star knew it now resided in the reporter's laundry room.

Crunch, crunch, crunch. The group turned to Nana Chata, who feasted on her chiccarones. "I want to know what Chacho is here for," she said, aiming a half-eaten pork rind at Benecio.

Chloe felt a sibling connection to the kid and playfully ran her fingers through his hair. "You are so dang gorgeous. Like a Latino Issac Mizrahi if he got zapped with a shrink gun."

"Actually, I prefer to think of myself as Narciso Rodriguez, but thanks," he said. Benecio wore pressed slacks, patent-leather loafers, and a sky-blue polo. A dark head of combed-back ringlets and mature green eyes offset his unblemished caramel skin. This kid had won the gene pool lotto. Chloe thought this pint-sized chap had more style in his left earlobe than Ezra had in his whole skeletal body.

"My name is Benecio Javier Valencia II. I'm fourteen, I'm a handbag designer, and I live in Scottsdale. I'm here to help so I can score a badge and have a booth to show off my bags. I'm quite handy with a sketchbook and sewing machine."

"I don't know about this, Benecio," Ofie said. "I'm thinking we need permission from your..."

"Parents? They couldn't care less. All they worry about is making money. Our house manager, Alice, keep tabs on me. She's the one who told me about this group. She stops by La Pachanga every day to pick up my dad's pan dulce. And she's my ride, too." He slid a black leather binder across the table. Chloe took it and opened the cover. Star jumped up and ran over to see, as did Ofie and Nana Chata. Each plastic-protected page contained an eight-by-ten glossy of a gorgeous handmade purse. The designs ranged from slick and skinny embossed-velvet clutches to fluffy feather drawstring hobos. The women were captivated.

"My parents think I'm at basketball practice. Alice covers for me, and they don't ask questions. As long as I don't intrude on their work schedules, I can do whatever I like—except design women's accessories. They don't appreciate my sensibility for fashion. Narciso Rodriguez was just like me. His parents wanted him to be a doctor or a lawyer. Now look at him: Salma Hayek, Sarah Jessica Parker, and Michelle Obama bow to his talent."

"What do your parents do for a living?" Star asked with the

interest of a news reporter. Even Lola and Rocco picked up their heads to listen.

"They own Valencia Variety, the largest Hispanic entertainment agency in the southwest."

"Shut up!" Star exclaimed. "As in *the* Valencia Variety? My parents' ultimate dream is to someday be able to afford them to run our Día de los Muertos event. Wow, and here you are!"

Chloe knew all about Valencia Variety. She had met the owners once, and often saw them at affluent Latino networking events. She never recalled them mentioning a son as incredible as Benecio.

"Still, Benecio, it's just not right," repeated Ofie. "I know who your parents are. I see them at La Pachanga every so often. Maybe I can talk to them."

"Ah, leave him alone," Nana Chata said, licking her fingertips one at a time and tapping her short legs against the footrest of the patio chair. "He's got the maid, and you all can watch over him. Kid, you're in," Nana Chata said.

The group—specifically Ofie—spent the next thirty minutes presenting ideas for the centerpieces. She dragged her daughter's old Playschool flip chart into the room and shared (in detail) her renderings—and all included dizzying amounts of glitter. From cowboy boot planters and upside-down lampshades to cross-stitch angel dolls and mannequin heads, the committee members sat dumbfounded. Chloe planned to assign Frances to the task first thing in the morning. There is no way the award-winning Crafty Chloe Chavez could be associated with a glittered cowboy boot planter.

"I say we call it a day. I'm exhausted from the office, and then all this craftista talk," remarked Chloe.

"Craftista! That's a cool name," said Star. The excited remark slipped from her mouth before she could remember she didn't like Chloe and her ideas.

"We should adopt it for our group. You know, to give this project more of a family feel," Ofie suggested.

No one objected. Star asked them to return Friday to present samples, and then meet every Wednesday thereafter.

Before they could say their goodbyes, Nana Chata—who had disappeared sometime between the lampshade and the doll head—entered with a dish of steamy flautas, salsa, guacamole, and a Mexican glass pitcher of strawberry margaritas to celebrate a very productive first meeting.

From: EstrellaFeliz@lapachanga.com
To: rastachicano60@lapachanga.com
Date: September 3, 2010
Subject: Hi, Pops!

Hi, Dad!

How is Rhinebeck?

Hope you and Mom are having a blast at your impromptu holistic honeymoon! Were you surprised that we pulled it off without you having a clue?

Even though Mom told me not to, I peeked in at the shop last week. Myrna and Minnie are holding down the fort just fine. You have nothing to worry about. Maria Juana is still here. She bleached her hair platinum blond. That's all I really know of her these days. She's gone a lot, so we don't have time to say more than "Hi." At least we're on civil terms, right?

Our centerpiece committee is off to a slow start. We met a couple times but couldn't agree on what to make. Get this—I dropped by Ofie's the other day and discovered she was about to make glittered tumbleweeds for the centerpieces. Where does one find tumbleweeds? Well, I'll inform you. She constructed a model from *chopsticks* she swiped from Pei Wei restaurant! Thank God I caught her. Can you imagine two hundred chopstick tumble-weeds covered in glitter to represent La Pachanga? I immediately e-mailed everyone and we are meeting this weekend to finalize, no matter what.

Guess what? I picked up three new clients to write press releases for. A Scottsdale bakery, a paint-on-pottery studio, and Wag 'n' Wash, that wild pet store on 7th Avenue. Things are coming together!

I just realized you might not be checking your e-mail up there. In that case, I'm signing off. Besides, I hear Maria Juana coming up the hallway and I want to hide. Whoops! Did I just type that?

Love you!! Give Mom a kiss and a hug for me! Write me back!

XOXO, peace out,

Estrella

14

Haaaay, gurl," coaxed Maria Juana as she entered Star's bedroom.

Hiding in the closet, Star held in a sneeze brought on by her cousin's cheap body spray and peeked through a crack in the door.

Maria Juana ruffled through the papers on Star's desk before she relaxed into the sparkly office chair. She tapped her bare toes on the carpet and spun around to soak up a full view of the atmosphere. She released a hissy whistle through her front teeth, one of which was silver due to a double date gone bad.

"Dang, esa, why does it feel so dead in here? It feels all lonely or something. Wass up with that? What happened to mi loca artista?" she said, as she skimmed her hands on her ribbed black tank to adjust her breasts for maximum cleavage. "Why you in the closet?"

Star surrendered, exited, and put the final touches on today's outfit: pointy black flats, dark camouflage capris, and a black and gray striped T-shirt.

Maria Juana fingered one of her several gigantic door-knocker earrings and blathered on in her husky chola speak while Star stood in front of the full-length mirror, parted her hair, and spun two chunks into tight micro buns at the crown of her head.

"Damn!" Maria Juana said, after popping her Bubble Yum between her over-outlined lips. "Make that mi artista de la muerta! You still hurtin' about losin' your ruco?"

"He was never my ruco; he was my friend," Star said as she checked her face for zits. "And this is the new me. I'm going through a dark phase. It says 'back off.'"

"It doesn't say 'back off,' prima. It says, 'Get away from my face before I throw down!'"

"Good. That's kinda what I'm going for."

"Hey. You should wear vampire teeth." Maria Juana rubbed her fingertips down the sides of her chin and cackled. "Get some fake blood drippin' down or something. Go to La Pachanga, and scare the waiters... ha! Now that's some funny shit."

"Whatever. Now, please... back off, por favor?" Star replied, unamused.

It's too bad Maria Juana lived up to the tacky Latina stereotype. She had such a pretty face and Star wondered why she gunked it up with that awful chola pancake makeup and those pitiful hoochie clothes.

"You're so pretty, Star, why do you have to mess your face up with that pancake makeup and those butchy clothes? Sheesh... you look like Donna the Dead. No wonder your man don't want you."

Star's jaw dropped—no way could she be sharing a thought with her cousin. She quickly snapped her mouth shut, along with the closet door. "Are you done now? I need to be alone. My favorite show is about to start."

"I've seen him around, girl. He looks fine as wine," Maria Juana said before she romantically kissed the air. "Did you know he has a novia now? I heard she is real pretty too, pero—muy chiquita, like a dainty little doll."

Star ran to her cousin and swiveled the chair front and center. "No! Are you serious?" No wonder he blew her off so cold that night at Sangria!

"Ehhh, psych. I'm just messin'," Maria Juana said as she licked her pinky and smoothed a floss-thin brow. "Don't be ashamed of your love, esa. What happened between you two, anyway? He prolly dumped you 'cause of the wall, huh? Damn, I'll never forget that night! Viva la Bandida Estrella!" Maria Juana hooted, while spinning in faster circles in the chair. She stopped, rolled her head back, and tapped her way-too-long glossy red nails on the armrests. "Ay. This chair gives good buzz."

"Hey, watch it. I paid a lot of money for that! It's vintage. And for the record—I was never his girlfriend. We were good friends, and we drifted apart. No big deal."

"Woooo...that *is* the reason! I tried to stop you, cuz. You were all like—'Gimme another shot!' 'Where can we score spray paint in the middle of the night?' Hey, cuz—do you know why you did it?"

"Did what?" Star asked innocently.

"Whaddya mean, did what? Hell—tag Theo's mural, that's what! I know why you did it. You told me that night—"

Star covered her ears. "Shut up, I'm serious! Like I said, I'm over it!"

"You lie, Star. Your mom said he stabbed an arrow through your corazón. I got an idea. Want me to give him the homie background check? I got friends who can find out *ev-er-ree* thing!"

Star flinched and put her fingers in her ears. "Stop, *please*. I told you, I'm over it." Maria Juana loved to dig up dirt on seemingly nice people, especially local Latinos. Hand her a full name and the city that person is from and she'd come back with a family tree color-coded with scandals.

"Okay, okay," Maria Juana relented. "Let's have some coldies out back. It'll get your mind off him."

Any other time, Star would have kicked her cousin's lowlife chola butt out the door. She had hours of convention duties ahead of her for the day and besides, she hadn't sipped the sauce since *that* night. Drinking beer with her slacker cousin was not an entry in her brand-new empty day planner. At least, it shouldn't be.

"Aw, hell. Why not?" Star answered. "Let's go in the backyard."

Two hours later, on purple plastic lawn chairs under the shady oak tree, Rick James tunes bounced from the boom box. Star and Maria Juana had slurped and stuffed the afternoon away. Maria Juana downed one St. Ides forty-ouncer, and Star, mojitos. A whole pitcher. Star downed the last sip from her mug.

"Oh! I love this song," she gushed when the "Mary Jane" track came on.

"Me too! It's about mota, man." Maria Juana hopped off her chair to bump and grind to the groove. She twirled her hands over her head and swayed her hips like a topless dancer.

Star howled like a hyena.

"Hey, lady, don't you laugh at me! Come show me what you got. You're an Esteban too. You gotta have some soul somewhere in that stiff-ass body. Get up here!"

"Ha! I do too have soul!" Star argued, jumping in place next to her cousin. The girls danced and knocked hips in time to shout-sing to Rick's chorus:

I'm in love with Mary Jane!
Shhhhe's my main thang!

The song ended and their limp bodies fell to the soft grass like giant sacks of potatoes. Maria Juana pulled herself up, dusted the grass off her chest, flopped in the chair, and lit a ciggie.

Out of nowhere, Star began to giggle. She laughed softly at first, but her laughter soon grew into loud cackles, before erupting in a full-on, hysterical laugh riot. She rolled around on the grass and clenched her stomach in pain.

"Damn, girl, can't you control your ass? Remind me never to take you to a party in the hood," Maria Juana said, leaning back in her chair so it rocked on its hind legs. She slid on her black Mad Dog sunglasses.

Star sat up, shaking her hands in front of her face, which now had blue mascara smudged on her cheeks. "Wanna know what I did?" She giggled again, but took several deep breaths to calm down "I...accidentally...ordered...three hundred fifty friggin' pounds of glitter. And I don't know what I'm gonna do with it!" She let her body fall backward, flailed her arms about, and laughed some more. "I'm so screwed. It cost my parents five thousand dollars and they don't even know yet."

"Duhhh, girl. Hawk it," Maria Juana said, irritated.

"I tried! I put it up on eBay and I didn't even get one bid." Star began to sober up. The glitter secret had been burning a hole in her conscience, and it felt good to confide in someone. Even if it was her whacked-out cousin. "It's premium vintage glass glitter imported from Germany. I bought it on clearance for thirteen dollars a pound."

Maria Juana hissed. "Damn, woman. Thirteen bucks a pound, and you can't even catch a buzz from it? What a waste!"

"Believe me, Ofie would get a huge buzz just from being within one yard of it. It's gorgeous. Worth every penny, hold on, I'll show you," Star said.

Star hopped up, sprinted inside the house, and within fifteen seconds emerged with a brown shoe box. She ripped open the plastic shrink-wrap with her teeth and lifted the lid just below Maria Juana's heavily stenciled eyes.

"Wow, that's pretty, Star. You should be able to score mucho coin for that. Treat it like weed. Throw together some four-finger bags and hit up the parking lots at First Fridays. I bet you'd make a killing."

Star considered approaching local paper arts stores, but maybe she could give the arts crowd a try. Those mojitos must have worked some magic, because she had a vision of counting stacks of cash by the night's end.

"You know, I like that idea. Why didn't I think of First Fridays? The streets are packed with thousands of artists. Oh my God, that's the ticket! I'm doing it! I'll take a shower and then get to work. It's almost three now, so I have about four hours to prep."

"I'll help you," Maria Juana offered. "My friend Little Rick, his cuz, Big Rick, has a scale I can use. Go sleep off your buzz. You're all borracha right now, thanks to all these mojitos. I'll weigh it, sort it, and roll it for you. Where's the stash?"

"It's in the back house at La Pachanga. Ask Myrna for some small cello bags and a roll of satin ribbon. Make them cute but elegant. Think Martha style. Take my car and load them in my trunk. Thanks!"

Star got up to head into the house. Hesitating, she turned back to face her cousin. "Do you really think we can do this?"

Maria Juana gripped Star's face. "You are gonna kick ass." She slouched back in her chair and removed her sunglasses. "I'll be back by six thirty."

15

In other parts of the country, the September coolness crept in and beckoned knitted scarves, hot apple cider, and leaves-a-plenty. But not in Phoenix. Residents sported swimsuits, sunglasses, and they could still see the shimmer of heat rising from the blacktop. Star didn't mind one more month of sweat. She had survived the worst of summer and welcomed the new energy of fall. Starting with tonight.

She made her way to the First Friday art walk, which by seven p.m. had already lured a couple thousand enthusiasts to Roosevelt Street. Crowds checked out the latest receptions, admired the local creations, and networked. And Star was right there with them, making sure 250 of those patrons would leave the scene with an eight-ounce bag of gourmet green glass glitter purchased for a mere twenty bucks. Not only would the bill be paid before her parents returned from their vacation, but she would also have half of the glitter to donate to the arts community in La Pachanga's name. Her dad would be so proud! Star would also give a special stash to Ofie, who practically ate the stuff. At least 75 percent of Ofie's crafts involved some type of glitter: brush-on, spray-on, squeeze-on, sprinkle-on, even paper and paints embedded with it. Ofie's obsession was the main reason Star didn't spill about the shiny surplus. She figured it would be like telling Joan Rivers a plastic surgeon moved in next door.

Star wanted to look as graceful as the imported glitter she would be peddling. She arrived decked out in a money-green cocktail dress, spiky heels, and a slick Audrey Hepburn updo, toting a large ebony doctor bag. Inside were fifty rolled Baggies of the glitter. At first she panicked because Maria Juana didn't use the pretty cello bags and satin ribbon, but Star proceeded with the game plan anyway.

It worked. Within the first hour of visiting a few galleries, she earned a little over nine hundred dollars. Using 100 percent enthusiastic desperation, she explained how the glitter came from finely crushed European glass ornaments, and how it traveled to Phoenix direct from Hamburg. Her excitement transferred to anyone who would listen. Many scooped up a bag as a souvenir, while others invested in several, including a performance artist, the owner of a hair salon called Bedazzled Beauty, a shadow box artist, and even a hunky fireman who bought five bags for his German-born crafty mom. Star made sure to give them all her cell phone number, just in case they wanted more.

Feeling more confident than ever, she made an executive decision to bypass one-by-one introductions and devise a broader method. Down the street in a parking lot, she noticed a man with a megaphone surrounded by a large crowd.

Amplification! Excellent! she thought. She'd just worm her way into the middle of the action, borrow his equipment, unload some of the sparkly, and wrap up the night early. A proud smile spread across her face as she strutted down the sidewalk, seamlessly weaving in and out of the oncoming crowd. Every few seconds she heard thuds and crashes, which grew louder the closer she got. She reached the area and excused her way to the front. The shouting artist strutted before a line of rowdy people who took turns hitting a yellow Hummer with their choice of tools: sledgehammer, crowbar, spray paint, or electric saw.

"This is what I call Frustration Art!" the artist shouted to the onlookers. "Down with mass consumerism! Free yourself! Exchange one of your possessions for some stress busting by beating on this gas-guzzling beast!"

The crowd hooted and shouted, and Star joined them. Three bodybuilder types handed over their cowboy hats and each picked up a weapon of choice. While they had their way with the Hummer, Star explained her situation to the artist and handed over forty dollars in return for two minutes on his megaphone. He took the bills, stuffed them in his pocket, and handed her the bull horn.

"Come closer, people," she said, waving her arms in the air and summoning her inner ringleader. "Mr. Hummerman Artist is taking a quick break to replenish his fluids. Until then I'm here with an important commercial break." Star watched as the crowd grew thicker. "Are you tired of living in the dark, never allowing yourself to let in the light of your dreams?" She began to pace back and forth in front of the Hummer, à la Tony Robbins at a self-empowerment convention. "What if I told you I had something to help you see that light—and that it was only twenty dollars?"

People inched forward, and goose bumps raced up Star's back. "Ladies and gentlemen, you've heard of angel dust, right? Well, let me introduce you to the healing properties of *Star*dust!"

Star set down the bullhorn, planted her feet firmly on the asphalt, and held the top edges of a Baggie of glitter over her head, letting it roll down. She reached in, retrieved a handful of the powder, and spread it across the air, like a seasoned shaman releasing a magical mist. The crowd ooohed and ahhhed at the dazzling display of twinkles floating to the ground. Star felt a hard tap on her arm. She peeked over her shoulder and wondered who in the heck would have the nerve to interrupt this almighty moment?

Two cops, that's who.

"Ruh-roh," she mumbled as one of them snatched the Baggie from her hands. That's all it took for the parking lot to clear.

"Miss, you wouldn't be selling illegal substances, would you?"

"No!" Star pleaded. "It's imported glass glitter, I swear—look—" she said, pointing to the Baggie. The officer unfolded the sandwich Baggie, smelled the contents, licked his finger, and stuck it in the coarse powder.

Star tried to grab it away, but the other cop gripped both her arms from behind. "No! It's made of crushed glass! And don't waste it, it's imported! I paid thirteen dollars a pound." However, he lifted his finger to dab it on his tongue anyway.

She envisioned herself crouched in a cold jail cell corner, chanting, "It was only glitter! It was only glitter!" She held her breath, anticipating the officer's next move.

"I'm not tasting this. She's right, it's glass glitter...it's really pretty too. I could see my wife using this at Christmas."

"Regardless, miss. You need a permit to sell. We could give you a ticket."

"Officers," said a female voice from behind Star. "Would you really want to do that when across the street there is a band playing in a flatbed truck in a residential neighborhood—a clear violation of Noise Ordinance Sec. 23–11?"

Craft Bimbo! Star remembered that she covered First Fridays every month for KPDM. Never in a gazillion years did Star think she would be happy to see Chloe and her annoying crease-free business outfits, this time a smart—surprise!—taupe linen suit. The cops, obviously fans, were delighted. Chloe gave them both a warm handshake and even flirted until they relented and returned Star's glitter. Star felt so relieved, she told them to keep it, and even gave the other cop a bag for his wife. The two patrollers walked away admiring their gifts.

Chloe stepped in front of Star and crossed her arms over her chest. "Okay, do tell."

Star didn't just tell, she showed. She told Chloe to follow her in her car to La Pachanga. They approached the front of the restaurant to find the parking lot filled to capacity, thanks to Las Feministas, an all-girl band that performed outside on the balcony to a crowd of partiers below. Star waved and pointed to behind the property.

They turned off their headlights, left their vehicles, and snuck around to the back house. Star unlocked the side door and opened a box of the glitter, letting Chloe in on the secret sparkle stash—all remaining 325 pounds of it. Chloe backed up from the room with caution, as if the cargo was hissing cobras, not craft embellishments. She didn't need to see any more, and steered Star to La Pachanga's coffee bar to discuss the situation. Plus, she needed a shot of French Roast right about now.

As they walked into La Pachanga, Chloe couldn't pinpoint why she had helped Star out with the cops earlier. Perhaps because every time she encountered the girl, some kind of tornado swirled about. Chloe noted the good deed in her favor scorebook and knew she'd cash it in at a later date.

"Let me make this clear: I despise glitter," Chloe informed Star, while adding a squirt of liquid sugar into her cappuccino. "It's the most tacky substance ever invented. It makes me break out in hives—the thought of those micro-plastic pieces stuck on my clothing or, ew, my skin." Chloe shivered. "Can't you dispose of it? Have you tried Craigslist or eBay?"

Star noted the new folk duo playing in the coffee area as she gripped her striped mug of decaf and listed all her efforts up until tonight. She even confided about trying to prove herself to her parents, and how this mishap would set her back to square one.

They would likely cancel the centerpiece project altogether and make her move out. Even worse, lose all faith in her. Star missed her job at La Pachanga, wanted it back, and the centerpieces were her only connection. Chloe listened to Star's dilemma, finished her coffee, and pushed the cup in front of her.

"What is the budget for this project?"

"Three grand, but I made nine hundred dollars tonight."

"Star." Chloe sighed as she set her mug on the counter. "I know you're thinking what I'm thinking. As much as it repulses me to say this, we have to use the glitter on the centerpieces so you can tell your parents you ordered it on purpose. To offset the cost, we'll curb expenses on the remaining supplies. We have two hundred of these to complete. You can't spend all your time hustling on street corners. We'll have to find something and cover it in glitter to use it up." Chloe already regretted what she had just presented. *Ugh. Gliter*, she thought.

Star let out a reluctant groan. "Yah, I know, I've been thinking of that too. It goes against my glitter philosophy—I'm from the 'less is more' school—but to hell with that. I have to get rid of it!"

Chloe rubbed her diamond stud earring and flashed her eyes toward the ceiling, "Oh my God..."

"What?" Star asked.

Chloe leaned back on her barstool. "You know Ofie is going to push that horrendous glittered cowboy boot idea on us. I can't be a part of this if it is not up to par with my other creations. I have a reputation to uphold. We'll have to be firm with her and not let her take over. No matter how excited she is."

Star nodded in full agreement and slid her mug to the side. "True. I can't afford any mistakes either. But we have to be delicate. Ofie is a binge-crafter. She has self-esteem issues and she crafts to make herself feel better. You saw her stuff. I love her, but she has no artistic skills whatsoever. Crafts are her life. She's a basket case when it comes to any kind of confrontation."

"Well, perhaps it's time she toughens up," Chloe said, as compassionate as a prison warden. "If an honest craft critique is the worst of her problems..."

"She is borderline bipolar!" Star said just as the duo's song ended. She lowered her voice. "We can't do anything to hurt her. If you're gonna call her out, you can't be in the group." Star glared into Chloe's eyes to assure she meant business.

Chloe reminded herself about her professional motives. "Fine. Then let's make it look like her idea. I'll have Frances draw up some ideas tomorrow."

Star tilted her head. "Your assistant Frances? Why her?"

"What I mean is, Frances has a list of all my ideas. I can have her organize them."

"Let's just save time and come up with something right now. Like, I don't know, we are in the southwest, we have hundreds of pounds of green glitter, how about a cactus garden? Flower pots are only a buck or so, and we can pick up some faux cacti at Maker's Marketplace."

Chloe hooked her fingers around her mug and raised it to Star. "Problem solved. Truce—to get through this?"

Star relaxed, eeked out a grin of ease, and clinked her mug with Chloe's. "Truce. To get us through."

"Now all we have to do is convince Ofie that our classy glittered cactus garden is her idea."

"No sweat," Star said. "Just follow my lead."

16

The following Wednesday, the group met at Ofie's, determined to set the centerpiece project in motion.

"Out of all the treasures in the world, there is nothing more precious than giving someone a piece of your heart, and that is why I made these necklaces for you," Ofie said to the group, holding three small boxes. "They are a piece of my heart that I'm giving to you for being my new friends."

One by one she hugged Chloe, Star, and Benecio and handed them her gift. They opened the boxes to find an odd-shaped lump of silver hanging from a ball-chain necklace. Benecio, elated, slipped it over his head. Star and Chloe gave warm thanks and each put the gift in their respective purses.

"It's supercute, Ofie," Star assured her friend. She, Chloe, and Benecio were on the committee only for professional gain, but Ofie embraced it as a deeper commitment. For years Ofie had joined other craft groups—beaders, scrapbookers, and even mixed-media collectives where anything counted as "art." They always ended the same way: By the third meeting, they conveniently broke up only to re-form later without her. Even though Star dreaded the upcoming centerpiece production, she was happy to give Ofie what she wanted most—company.

"Now let's get down to business," Star said. "The more I think of it, Ofie, the more I like your glitter idea. Don't you agree, Chloe?"

"Yes," Chloe recited just as she and Star had rehearsed.

Ofie clapped in joy. "Let's do a rainbow-striped glittered cowboy boot with balloons coming out of the top! I can hand draw a horseshoe on each one with gold metallic puffy paint!"

"Hmmm," Chloe said, swallowing hard. "But maybe something that represents desert life, since this is the first time the CraftOlympics has ever been in Arizona. What is a well-known desert motif that we can cover in glitter?"

"My tumbleweed idea! Or no...a desert rock—a red rock of Sedona!" Ofie said.

Star silently winced at the thought of two hundred red glittered rocks as centerpieces. "Something green! Think botanical!" Star coaxed.

Chloe served her last dish of patience. "Something prickly, Ofie. Something that has *sharp little needles* all over it. Want me to draw you a picture?"

Star kicked Chloe's foot under the table for being cold. Benecio, mature for his age, caught on and joined in. "Something with sharp little needles that hurts your butt when you sit on it!"

The three of them leaned in Ofie's direction as she rubbed her chin, squinted her eyes, and concentrated. "I got it!" she said, raising her index finger. "A cactus! Let's glitter cactuses!"

"Love it!" Star cried out in relief. "Let's do it!"

Ofie clenched her fists and pumped them in the air as if her favorite quarterback had just scored the winning touchdown. "Don't move—I'll be right back!"

Sweaty from the swamp cooler's humidity, the craft committee members fanned themselves in the humid Arizona room while Ofie raced into her house. A series of tumbling noises followed and she returned with an armful of terra-cotta flowerpots and plastic cacti.

Star smiled and blinked hard. "Why am I not surprised that you happen to have an abundance of plastic cacti?"

"I bought them a few years ago on clearance," Ofie explained, while admiring the odd-shaped objects. "I don't have a green thumb, so I was going to plant them in front to make our yard look pretty. I forgot about them until now!"

"Wait—this is amazing!" Star dramatically brought her hand to her forehead, as if suddenly struck by a thought. "I have a trunk full of green glitter! It's like fate!"

"What?" Ofie's eyes grew wide with shock. "You bought glitter and didn't tell me? What kind is it? Where did you get it? How much do you have? Why is it in your trunk?"

Star stood up. "It's no biggie. I found it in the storage room at my parents' place. I think it was leftover from a project or something. I'll be right back with it." She ran to her car to bring in the goods, pleased that the meeting had gone even better than planned. At this rate, she estimated those centerpieces would be finished in a flash.

Back in the Arizona room, Ofie passed out the pots and pricklies.

"Chloe, do you think you could please jot down a materials list? I don't seem to have a free hand right now..."

Chloe's posture stiffened. "No, but I'll let you use my pen so you can write it yourself." Crafty Chloe didn't write lists. People wrote lists for *her*. Embarrassed, Ofie apologized to the local TV celebrity, set down the items, and took the pen.

Star reentered balancing two sealed shoe boxes over her head. She carefully slid them onto the table. She used her car key to slice one open and removed two palm-sized plastic bags. "This is very expensive crushed-glass glitter from Germany—a little goes a long way. I'll share this between the four of us so we can each make our first centerpiece. It'll be plenty, but if you need more, let me know."

Ofie shoved Star out of the way, practically knocking her over so she could stick her hand in the box and grab a separate bag. She bit the corner of the plastic with her teeth, and swirled her fingers through the granules. "This is the most beautiful glitter I've ever seen in my life, Star. I can't believe you've been holding out on me. You know how much I love glitter! Please can I have this bag? How much? Can you take a post-dated check? I'll buy it from you!"

Star knew Ofie didn't have money to spare. The Fuentes family survived on one income because Larry insisted Ofie work as a stay-at-home mom for Anjelica's sake. Star could never accept money from Ofie, so she told her to keep the glitter as a gift and split up the remaining amount between herself, Chloe, and Benecio.

"Well then," Star said, standing at the front of the table. "We have our supplies to make our first batch today. Let's make these really artsy. If you don't mind, I'm going to work in private in Ofie's family room craft corner to make mine. I need peace and quiet to create."

Benecio grabbed a TV tray and set up a workstation on the other side of the room. He then went in and out of the house to search for specific objects. Ofie slid on reading glasses she had decorated with nail polish and rounded up the must-haves for her piece.

Chloe arranged and rearranged her materials to kill time. She would take them home and have Frances make a centerpiece model tomorrow. She removed an Aquafina bottle from her bag and watched as Ofie prepped for her soon-to-be wacky creation. Chloe had never paid much attention to the woman, but now her curiosity bubbled. She wondered why the eager-to-please Ofie seemed to spend more time crafting with strangers than bonding with her daughter.

"Ofie, your girl is so sweet. Does she ever craft with you?"

"She used to, but I don't know, around third grade, she lost interest. Now she's too busy with dance, gymnastics, chorus, and theater. But she does love for me to make her things."

"How do you juggle her schedule and still have time for all of this?" Chloe gestured around the room with her hand.

"Nana Chata," Ofie said with a hint of discontent. "She enrolled Anjelica in all those classes and takes her to every one of them. She said it's good for kids to have extracurricular activities. She raised Larry and he's the kindest man I've ever met, so she knows her stuff. She cooks for us almost every night too. And does our laundry."

"Do you *want* her to do those things?" Chloe asked.

Ofie squirted purple paint on a paper plate and swirled her foam brush in it. "She does them so well, and I want the best for Larry and Anjelica. I can't do any of those things as perfect as Nana Chata. I don't want to rock the boat by messing things up, which is what happens every time I try."

Chloe's heart softened and she almost felt rueful for the earlier pen comment. She handed Ofie the flowerpot to paint. "Larry speaks very highly of you at work. I can tell he loves you very much." In reality, Chloe never conversed more than a few words with Larry, but the small lie made Ofie's face light up.

Ofie smiled triumphantly just before loading the pot up with a glob of paint. She poured the glitter onto a paper plate and rolled the pot around to pick up the flakes. The method left random bald spots all over the surface—even counterfeit-crafter Chloe knew that was not a successful application. But Ofie admired it as if it were a fifty-carat diamond. "Gorgeous," she said.

Chloe peeked across the room to check on Benecio, who appeared immersed in his project. "Ofie, I'll be back in a bit. I'm going to check on our little man over there."

*   *   *

An hour later, Star came into the room to present her master-piece. Excited, Ofie swept the creation away from Star and set it next to hers and Chloe's. Nana Chata and Anjelica came out with great interest to see the final prototypes.

Nana Chata put her hands on her hips and snorted. "What the heck happened here?"

Star flinched in disgust. "What do you mean? Mine is a wake-up call to what is happening in the world! See, I used a metallic paint pen to write Bob Marley lyrics all over the base of the pot. And then I affixed images of starving children all over the cactus. I want each centerpiece to be more than just a deco-rative accessory that is used only to fill the gap in the middle of an eating station. This is art."

"Where is the glitter, Star?" Chloe asked, annoyed.

"Whoops! Forgot it, heh-heh," Star joked. She picked up a pinch from the bag on the table and sprinkled it on top, like nuts on a sundae. "There."

"Look at mine!" Ofie said, pointing to hers. "My statement is that we all need more sparkle in our lives. Therefore, I coated the entire centerpiece in the glitter—the pot *and* the cactus! People will see these from a mile away."

Benecio bent over and touched it. "Cool, it looks like it's moving…"

Star joined him. "I think it *is* moving. It looks like the glitter is sliding off the cactus. Maybe you used too much glue, Ofie. Either that or glass glitter is superheavy."

"And what about this one?" Anjelica asked, pointing to Chloe's, which hadn't even been made.

"I didn't make one. I hate glitter. I just had a manicure and I need gloves."

Dead silence.

"You're Crafty Chloe. Out of all of us, you should have made the best one!" Star beefed. Nana Chata playfully elbowed Chloe.

"Why are you all staring at me? I need proper tools and for God's sake, air-conditioning. I'll make mine at home and e-mail you a picture. Honestly, I don't see any potential with any of these designs. Maybe we should hire eager design students and be done with it. Where in the contract does it state that *we* have to make each and every one?"

"Oh, please don't get mad, Chloe," Ofie begged. "We think it will mean a lot that we, Arizona craftistas, created them. We'll find the right pattern. If not, there is always my tumbleweed idea…"

"I hate to say it, but Nana Chata is right," Star said, ignoring her friend. "What the heck happened? Look at these samples! They suck harder than Paris Hilton singing the 'Star-Spangled Banner.' We can't do this! We have to pull out before they throw us out! I might as well move out of my parents' house before they get home. These centerpieces are a joke." Star marched to her bag and slung it over her shoulder to leave.

"Wait, you didn't see mine yet," said Benecio. "It just so happens we are covering desert life in science class right now. I used red paint for the lip of the flowerpot and purple for the base. I inserted floral foam, then coated the cactus with decoupage medium and poured the glitter all over it. I lodged it inside and covered the surface with gravel from Ofie's lawn. Last, I found a toy hummingbird on the ground, cleaned him up, and glued him to one of the branches of the cactus."

The women hugged him, except Nana Chata, who put him in a happy headlock. Benecio then provided a step-by-step list of directions for each member. "Vern Yip says that the most important element of design is to always keep the client in mind. These centerpieces are not about us. They are about the guests at the awards dinner."

"I hereby nominate Benecio as project manager," Star said. She cursed herself for wanting to give up—the exact flaw she was trying to overcome. She couldn't let her doubts take over. "Tell me what you need, any hour of the day, and I'll make sure you have it. Consider me your loyal assistant!"

Just as Star began to relax, her iPhone rang. She didn't recognize the number and thought it might be her parents in Rhinebeck. She excused herself and walked inside to Ofie's family room. A few minutes later she emerged, her face flushed.

"Is everything all right?" Ofie asked, concerned.

"I just got asked out for a drink by a totally hot fireman I met last Friday night," she replied, dazed. "And I think I said yes."

17

After the meeting, Star thought of every reason under the blaring Arizona sun to bail on Harrison Delta. At First Fridays he bought a lot of glitter from her for his mom. He called during the centerpiece meeting to not only ask to buy more, but also to invite Star for a drink that night at George & Dragon, an English pub on Central Avenue.

Star still pined for Theo—when she woke up every morning, when she drove in her car, in between writing press releases for her clients, with every chew of her food. If she dwelled on the subject too long, tears flowed. One month had passed since she last saw him and the pain had yet to subside. She hoped a new guy friend would give her a break from the chronic heartache.

She arrived five minutes early to find Harrison, a husky and tall muscleman with a short brown crew cut, waiting for her outside the front door. Not at all her type, but why would that matter if she only wanted to hang out? As it was, she only vaguely remembered him from First Fridays because she'd had glitter to hawk and had perceived every person as a walking dollar sign.

"Nice blouse, did you make that?" he asked, his warm brown eyes centered on hers.

Star bashfully half-smiled and pinched her Mexican peasant top at the waist. "No . . . it's from Ensenada. I just like the colors. Thanks!"

He opened the heavy door and The Smiths' *"Heaven Knows I'm Miserable Now"* blared from the jukebox. Tiny tables lit by small candles were sprinkled throughout the small club, surrounded by sixties-era red vinyl couches.

They sat in a private booth away from the tunes, and ordered drinks. After one bottle of Sam Smith Pale Ale, Star loved that she felt relaxed with him. She explained all the gory details of the Great Glitter Fiasco. After the second bottle, she reenacted the popo busting her for illegally soliciting glitter in the parking lot. A chucklefest broke out over the Lucy-esque episodes, and settled down once the waitress brought over their plate of sausage rolls. Harrison slowed down the mood with his tragic tale of a cheating wife in Chicago. He explained the details of the betrayal and ultimate divorce, and how in the end, he threw a dart at a map and—hello, Arizona! He even traded in his career as an accountant to become a fireman. Engaged by his storytelling, Star didn't notice two hours had passed. The conversation flowed with ease and for the first time in weeks, she felt like maybe, just maybe, she would be okay.

Still, when Harrison reached for her hand, Star's nerves got the best of her.

"Yikes! What time is it?" she said, reaching for her purse to check her phone.

Harrison accepted the hint. "I didn't mean to move too fast," he said, clasping his fingers behind his head. "I just think you are the most adorable woman I've met in a long time. Do you mind if I ask if you're seeing anyone?"

Star took a sip from her water, set down the glass, and let her head rest heavy in her hands. "Trust me, Harrison, you don't want to date me. Everywhere I go, I set off car wrecks and explosions behind me."

"I don't believe that. Maybe because you are so sweet, they're in awe..."

"Sweet rots teeth," Star said as she spun the straw around in the glass. "And trust me, there are a few toothless folks wandering around in a daze, thanks to me."

Harrison cracked up with laughter.

"Don't get me wrong," Star continued. "You seem awesome, but I need to get my act together. I know the glitter ordeal sounds like something from an old *Ugly Betty* episode, but it's serious. My parents' business is at stake because of me, and I have to fix it. In fact, I should probably be getting back home," she said, doing her best to make a polite exit.

"It's cool. Friends it is. No pressure." Harrison paid the bill, and helped Star out of her seat. They chatted on their way to the exit, and he opened the door for her.

Star looked down and combed her long curls behind her ears before stepping out.

"Estrella?"

Her head, ears, chest, face, and spirit all perked up at the same time. "Theo?"

Theo eyed Harrison and then Star. "How's it going? I haven't seen you around. What's up, girl? Everything okay?"

Star couldn't believe his question. After the way he severed her heart from her soul at Sangria that night, did he really expect to see her around? Of course everything was not okay!

"Sure! Everything's great," she said with a forced, megawatt smile.

The three of them moved to the outside entryway, and Star's pulse raced just to see Theo's facial features up close again. She stared at his full lips and wondered if they had kissed anyone lately. She pretended not to notice his new chiseled physique. Not only had he lost weight since moving on, but he also must have picked up Billy Blanks as a new friend. He rubbed his hand over his head. "Yeah, I'm meeting some friends here for a drink. Hey, I've been meaning to call you to say thanks."

Star shrugged. "For what?"

"That day we were on the morning news, you know—the mural..." he said in a hushed tone. "Well, an art agent from New Mexico was in town, and he saw my work on TV, checked out my Web site, and signed me. I officially have an art agent now. I'm moving to Santa Fe by the end of the year."

Star shoved her hands in her jean pockets to anchor herself from the thought of him physically being out of her life forever. No more worrying—or hoping—she might bump into him around town.

"You're welcome, I guess? Glad something good came out of that mess. Congrats."

"So what's new with you?" he asked, sliding his gaze quickly toward Harrison. "You look cheery. I remember that blouse. We bought it—"

"I'm *very* cheery!" she interrupted. "I've been doing freelance PR. I'm organizing stuff for the CraftOlympics...and...I have my debut solo exhibit! At La Pachanga! On November fifth!"

Theo leaned back and stroked his chin, just like he always did when he was surprised. They hadn't seen each other in a while, but she could still read his expressions like a children's alphabet book. "Well, check *you* out, Estrella Feliz. I'll have to come see it."

"Sure. Well, take care and good luck," she said. He passed through the entrance and saluted her. She waited for the door to close and then collapsed against it.

"I didn't know you made art," Harrison said.

"Neither did I." She giggled. "But I better get on it!"

From: rastachicano60@lapachanga.com
To: EstrellaFeliz@lapachanga.com
Date: September 12, 2010
Subject: Checking in

Hello, mi reina, how goes it? Your mother and I are enjoying our time here at Omega. In the mornings we start the day with tai chi, followed by meditation. Then we work in the garden, prepping the veggies for meals. In the afternoon we volunteer in the library.

Off the record, I'm craving a beer and am bored out of my mind, but at least I've lost weight!

Your mother, meanwhile, has taken up with a renegade beading posse and she has cranked out some incredible jewelry using healing stones, crystals, and African trading beads. I'm using the time to chill, although I do help in the kitchen now and then. They have an incredible chef who is sharing his recipes for me to use at the restaurant. New Age Mexican food—what do you think?

I'm happy to hear the centerpieces are going so well. Thanks for sending the picture. I think you should make a few extra that we can put in the restaurant. Have Myrna cut you a check for the extra supplies.

As far as the gallery for your exhibit—are you serious? If you can confirm enough pieces for a show, you can have the space. Opening reception will be Friday, November 5th. We booked the room for the Día de los Muertos children's artist installations, but we can mix it up this year and put those in the atrium. Please send me pictures of what you plan to show. Have Myrna print up the postcards immediately. Can we hire you to write the press release for your own event? (Just kidding).

I'm very proud of you, m'ija.

If you need us, call Omega's main office and they will get us. As you know, cell phones don't work out here. We'll be home soon.

Love to you,
Dad

18

Thanks to 50-percent-off coupons in the newspaper, Wednesday afternoons at Maker's Marketplace rivaled any designer-store clearance sale. The sixty-five-year-old retail outlet spanned ten thousand square feet of every type of bead, elastic, glitter, plastic flower, and every other notion invented. The business attracted more than just local crafters hooked on wholesale prices. It also drew in wedding coordinators, interior decorators, kitschy collectors for the array of vintage findings, school teachers, art directors, and prop masters. No chain store in the country could compete with the treasures at Maker's Marketplace.

Coupons in hand, Ofie, Chloe, Star, and Benecio counted and plucked the plastic cacti from the shelves and dropped them into the basket. A bit of attitude lingered. After two weeks, the craftista honeymoon had worn out its welcome as the members dreaded the chore ahead of them. Even the stock boy pricing the silk ivy vines noticed the tension, and hurried to get out of their way.

In the past two meetings, the group had produced only eight centerpieces, much less than the quota Star asked of them. The women began to grate on each other's nerves. Chloe blamed Ofie for taking up precious time with the show-and-tell of her heinous craft projects. Star resented Chloe for being a so-called "expert," yet never helping to get a system down to create the cactus gardens. Ofie complained at dinner every night about both Star's and Chloe's lack of enthusiasm, and tried to round up the group other days of the week. But no one besides Benecio would agree to it. The momentum faded further as Chloe's work schedule doubled due to the fall arts season and the launch of Hispanic Heritage Month events; Ofie came down with strep; and Star spent all her free time researching emerging art trends for her upcoming exhibit. The only committed CraftOlympian turned out to be Benecio. In between algebra and government class this morning, he text-scolded all the women to meet for the buying trip, and then he begged Alice for a lift.

Star, embarrassed a fourteen-year-old cracked the whip instead of her, used the day to hop on task. She called Maker's Marketplace to ensure they carried the necessary centerpiece ingredients, and then measured out the balance of the glitter needed. Between eBay, Craigslist, local paper arts stores, and Harrison's mom's craft group, twenty boxes remained for the centerpieces out of the original fifty-eight. Her parents were due home in a few days and the five thousand dollars had been replaced in their bank account. As soon as Star cleared the hurdle of her exhibit, she planned to take Myrna out for a lobster dinner to thank her for keeping the ordeal under wraps.

"Can you believe the CraftOlympics is only a couple months away?" Star sang out in an attempt to spark conversation.

"Please don't stress me out right now, Star. I know time is short. We'll get them done," Chloe snapped. Meanwhile, Ofie wandered off to the fabric section.

"Ofie," Chloe hollered down the main walkway of the store. "Please don't shop now. Come back here with us. We need you."

"Oh, I'm sorry. Sure thing!" said the pudgy housewife, hustling over while adjusting her bra strap under a black tee decorated with hand-drawn hearts. Chloe sighed. Her involvement with the committee incited a new set of problems—Ofie's unnecessary splurging. At the first meeting she presented everyone with necklaces she made with precious-metal clay. The next day, Larry came into the station, distressed. He confessed to Chloe that after buying the kiln and all the tools with her Maker's Marketplace credit card, Ofie had spent almost five hundred dollars, and he would have to take on extra hours to pay for it. He said Ofie swore to make back the investment with sales of the necklaces, but both Larry and Chloe knew that was as likely as snow in the summer. Chloe didn't want to become anyone's personal counselor, but she did feel worried for the Fuentes family, mainly Anjelica. Therefore, she agreed to derail Ofie from spending money if the opportunity arose.

The saddest part?

None of the group members could identify what Ofie's handmade pendants were supposed to be. Benecio thought they were avocados, Star figured they were eggs. Chloe lost hers. If she'd known it cost $166, she would have taken better care of it.

Star pointed out the adhesive aisle to Chloe, and together they swept up twenty-four jars. Chloe despised every second. Not only did she loathe crafts, but the scores of rabid shoppers mixed with the cheap scent of potpourri that permeated the air made her nauseous. Not to mention getting stopped every few minutes for autographs. She wished she could go home and slither out of her work clothes, which today consisted of a slinky thyme-colored Carolina Herrera cotton dress with elegant white topstitching, and a four-inch-high pair of taupe death wedges. Her body and spirit ached. She had spent the past six hours at the office in strategy meetings, one of which consisted of a disgusting quickie in the oft-empty nursing lounge with Mark Jefferies. This time he wagged a bit part in a blockbuster movie shooting in downtown Phoenix next year. The role called for a

TV reporter. Chloe cursed herself for accepting the bribe, but couldn't pass on the film credit to her already blooming résumé.

"Chloe...Chloe...are you okay?" asked Ofie.

The reporter patted her own face to pay attention. "Sorry, it's so clammy in here, I lost track for a second. Did you ask me something?"

"Do you think I should sign up for the Scissor Smackdown?" Ofie asked as they made their way through the adhesives area. "They have entry forms on the bulletin boards up front. I wanted to use a scrapbook as my base..."

Chloe, Star, and Benecio read each other's minds. Next to Speed Crochet and the Speed Knitting, the Scissor Smackdown was the biggest event of the CraftOlympics. Noted artists from all over the world competed in a race of skill and creativity in front of a team of evil, nitpicky judges. Only the bravest of enthusiasts signed up—and they often left the event traumatized. It was the WWE of crafting, sans the ropes. Chloe and Benecio had yet to witness one of Ofie's craft-related meltdowns, but Star had. The thought of Ofie gracing the stage to complete one of her klutzy paper concoctions in front a rabid panel of judges—and a heckling audience of thousands—would likely send her over the glue-stick edge.

"Nah, don't waste your money. It's all a scam. It's all tied to product endorsements," Chloe remarked as she pushed the shopping cart up the narrow aisle of glitter, sequins, and buttons.

"And creativity shouldn't involve competition," Star added. "Aren't scrapbooks supposed to be about preserving precious memories? Do you really want to succumb yours to possible ridicule?"

Ofie trailed behind and continued to champion for her cause. "But I love to scrapbook and with all my expertise, shouldn't I be involved somehow? I'm really good. They have cash prizes. Maybe I can win one for my family."

"I don't think so, and here's why...," Star said as she put her arm around Ofie and led her ahead of the cart. Chloe felt a micro trace of jealousy. These women had each other's backs, no matter what the drama.

Normally, Chloe wouldn't waste energy dissecting the friendship. As much they grated on her nerves now and then, they were two of the kindest people she had ever met. Star had created a list of talented local artists for Chloe to look into for profiles, along with links to Web sites. She also provided a list of creative story angles for First Fridays, and wanted nothing in return except for Chloe to encourage the community to visit the city's many galleries. Star may not have been certain what she wanted in life, but she sure helped those who were. Ofie didn't have as many connections, but her enthusiasm exceeded anything Chloe had seen. If she were to ever launch an official fan club, she wanted Ofie as the president. Chloe wondered what Star, Ofie, and even little Benecio thought of her.

Shaking her head, Chloe pushed the thought aside. She couldn't let herself become emotionally attached. This event was far too critical to get sidetracked. She needed to work every angle and person in order to elevate her personal brand to national status. More so, because this afternoon she declared she would never, *ever* sleep with the slimy Mark Jefferies again. She had to work to succeed on her own merit. Hosting the CraftOlympics would seal the deal.

Chloe pushed the cart past the trims and fringe aisle and heard a familiar voice.

"Hmmm. Black pleather or black lace...?"

Planted on the floor in the middle of one of Maker's Marketplace's many rows, Frances sat with a pile of dark fabrics on her lap.

"Hello, Frances."

Frances jerked her face up to see her boss, Chloe Chavez. Or rather "Crappy Chloe" as Frances often mumbled under her breath. She scooped up the goods and rose to her feet, her arms spilling over with an array of textured materials.

"Hello, Ms. Chavez. These are for a personal project I've been working on."

"You dropped your fake leather fringe." Chloe bent down to retrieve it, but Frances seized it off the warehouse's concrete floor and slapped it under her arm. It appeared to Frances that Ms. Chavez and her craft buddies were on a field trip today. A difficult concept to grasp. The local craft queen who hated crafts? Who didn't even know how to work an embossing gun? Why would she spend her free time here? Frances thought sarcastically.

"Frances, don't forget I need something for next week's segment. You're a day late."

The shy assistant shoved her glasses up the bridge of her nose. "Ms. Chavez, I know this is not the appropriate time or place, but I was informed this afternoon that you declined my request for a promotion. Is this true?"

Chloe motioned Frances to come close. "Yes. Our plan, remember? We both know I'm going to be the next Betty Oh!—I'll be moving up and out from this hole soon and you're coming with me. That will be bigger than any promotion the station can offer. Can't you hold out a bit longer until after the CraftOlympics?"

"I guess."

"Thanks!" Chloe said as she waved bye and rejoined her friends.

The corner of Frances' lip curled and her jaw protruded, like an angry ape that had lost her last banana. She slapped the fringe over her shoulder and headed to the checkout line.

With her items now bagged and paid for, she hid until Ms.

Chavez's BMW was out of sight and it was safe to enter the parking lot. The less she saw of Crappy Chloe, the better.

"You dropped your *fringe…*" she said in a high voice as she flounced to her car, mocking her arrogant supervisor. "One of these days Ms. *Cha-vez*, I'm gonna show you what I'm made of!"

Frances slammed her plastic Maker's Marketplace shopping bag on the roof of her tomato red 1995 Chrysler LeBaron convertible that had seen better days. Her three yards of shiny black faux leather fringe slid across and landed on the hot asphalt. Every time Chloe went on air with one of Frances' ideas, the girl went home and downed a triple pepperoni pizza drenched in ranch dressing. She'd gained fifty pounds since becoming Chloe's sequined slave. As a result, Frances resented Chloe and felt the woman didn't deserve to even touch a glue gun, much less use it on live television. She dreamed of the day when the phony Ms. Chavez would leave KPDM so she could take over the craft segments. Crafty Chloe assumed Frances would follow her to national, but heck no. Frances aimed to escape from Crafty Chloe's shadow and forge her own career, which is why she had applied for a recently opened production position. She should have known Chloe would find out and kill it.

But Frances wielded a wild card. She knew—and could name—every skeleton in her boss's closet: the repulsion of homemade items, using the craft group to her advantage, boning Mark Jefferies, not knowing *any* of the techniques she demoed—and a few other juicy tidbits.

Chloe didn't know it, but Frances had a secret of her own.

Just then her flip phone buzzed with a new message. From Chloe.

It's time to step it up. I will need five weeks' worth of projects by Monday. Thank you!

Frances whipped off her chunky black Buddy Holly glasses.

"That's *it*! I hate her!" She clenched her fists to the air above. "Bitch is going down!"

From: EstrellaFeliz@lapachanga.com
To: rastachicano60@lapachanga.com
Date: September 24, 2010
Subject: Here here

Hi Dad!

I just got the word you are staying an extra week! You know how much I miss you two (especially mom's cooking), so I'm warning you, this will be a long letter.

I've done nothing but sleep, eat, and experiment with all kinds of art techniques like a crazy woman. Remember the catastrophic love shrine I made for Theo? Bottom line? That has been my favorite, even if I did throw it away. In the last week, I've made assemblage boxes inside any kind of container I could get my hands on: silverware trays, glass jars, a fish aquarium (don't worry, I bought a new one), candy tins, and these cute little cigarette cases I found at the thrift store.

I even invaded the garden shed and made a funky shrine out of Mom's old shovel! I also nabbed your old black loafers and made little collages in the foot openings and then I mounted them to a piece of wood and added a picture of when you first wore them to my sixth-grade violin recital— and then I framed it all in Plexiglas. Hope you don't mind. You don't wear them anymore, so I thought I might as well make them into a memory box. I'm using glitter as a theme to tie all these pieces together, like my signature touch. Even though I've been going through paint and glue like Mom goes through wheatgrass and tofu, I don't have anything for the show yet. I'm trying to think of a topic for a cohesive collection. The trouble is, it has to come from my heart and I don't know what that is yet. I feel like I'm still in my self-discovery phase (so corny, I know). Every night I pray the magic will come to me.

Okay, what else—ahh, the craft group! Centerpieces are coming along! Excited for you to see them!

Love you,

Estrella

P.S. I started clearing out the back house too!

P.P.S. I have a new friend I've been hanging out with. His name is Harrison and he is a fireman. Again, he is a friend, so don't go all twenty-questions on me. More details when you come home, promise!

P.P.P.S. I will have some cold beers ready for you!

19

Chloe's alarm clock buzzer went off as usual at 6:30 a.m. She removed the satin mask from her eyes, yawned, and peeked at Ezra's side of the bed. Empty. Likely because it was October 13—her twenty-ninth birthday.

She figured he spent the morning cooking up a surprise breakfast, just like last year. Sure enough, the rustle of whisking and pans clanging filtered upstairs. Maybe Ezra didn't exactly make her heart flutter, but at least she could count on him.

She stood up and slipped on her robe and grinned. The day would bring more than birthday candles. Today's craft segment could lead to a hefty promotion at her station's parent company, the Hadwick Corporation. The CEOs and their wives, all dedicated gourmet crafters, were to visit the station and Mark had invited them as guests on her segment.

The best part? He didn't even ask Chloe to sleep with him. She felt empowered that he took the hint after weeks of brush-offs. These days on her scale of personal growth, self-worth outweighed desperation.

It had been two months since she met Ofie and Star, and day by day, being around them made her feel not so angry at the world. The situation with her family hadn't improved. Her mother still phoned nearly every day, disappointed with her for shacking up with Ezra, but at least now with Ofie and Star around, Chloe had more of a social life to cushion her anger. Hanging out with those two chicas exercised her conscience muscle.

All of it pushed Chloe to examine her life.

The idea clicked the other day when Star invited her to attend a seminar, Boomerang Boost: How to Attract Good Karma. In the six-hour session, Chloe took in lectures, workshops, and indepth tests that detailed her decision-making methods and the motivation behind them. In the final minutes, Chloe tallied up her figures and the correlating profile summaries. She just about squawked in shame, and shoved them in her purse so Star wouldn't see. The result? According to the Bommerang Boost theory, Chloe's actions earned her a fireball of bad karma.

During the long drive home, Chloe analyzed her life and swore to make changes to ward off negative energy. As soon as she entered her house, Chloe didn't even set down her purse before shoving the papers through the shredder. She curled up on the couch, nibbled a rice cake, and gazed at a talking head on the television. She recalled one of the Boomerang Boost speakers and their suggestion of a "vision board" project. At first Chloe banished the concept. It sounded hokey, like something Star's woo-woo mom would do. Then again, Chloe thought, Dori always sounded pretty dang happy.

Chloe leaped off the couch and gathered all the paper supplies available in her office—plus scissors, glue sticks, and magazines. Hello, vision board! She'd make a collage of all the people and events she wanted to attract into her life. One problem, she couldn't find an inspiring background surface. Chloe tapped her bare foot, scratched her head, and let her eyes roam about her work area. And then she saw *it*.

Above her computer hutch hung a four-foot-tall glamour shot

of Crafty Chloe in all her on-screen glory, fuzzy lens and all. She climbed on top of her desk and ripped it from the wall. She hopped down, set it on the floor facedown, and removed the backing and the poster-size photo. There! That would be the foundation.

For the next two hours, she lay on her belly, propped up, to cut and paste. In the corners she added the words "love," "beauty," "inspiration," and "respect." She then went online to visit the Web sites of Oprah, Betty O'Hara, and the CraftOlympics, printed out several pictures, and used those too. She grabbed a jumbo red marker and drew a crown on her head. To tie it all together, she took a blank sheet of typing paper and wrote down her father's dream, just as he told it to her. She kissed it and affixed it over her heart on the photo. Just when she thought the piece was done, she paused, as if the collage needed one more accent. She jumped up and sprinted to her stereo, grabbed the Reggae Sol CD, and brought it back. She took a deep breath, snipped out Gustavo's head from the glossy sleeve, and applied it too. She then reassembled the frame and returned it to its spot on the wall.

If that didn't show commitment to change, she didn't know what would.

What better day to exercise her new outlook than the anniversary of her birth? First up, Frances.

Yesterday Larry informed Chloe that her assistant complained to coworkers about her job. At first Chloe went into silent hysterics, worried that Frances had spilled their secret, but Larry described it as more of a "grumbling under her breath" situation. Frances had been on vacation for a week and was set to return today, just in time for the important segment. Despite her verbal discontent, Chloe knew Frances would always come through. Chloe made a note to pick up a batch of fresh calla lilies on her way into work, tie them with a taupe satin bow, and give them to her assistant as a gesture of appreciation. She would then talk to Mark about giving the girl a raise, and then she would take her to lunch—maybe even a shopping spree for a makeover. *How's that for karma?* she thought.

"A new year, a new outlook on life!" Chloe whispered as she jogged down the stainless-steel stairs of her loft, excited to see what Ezra had cooked up. But when she reached the bottom of the stairs, she inhaled.

"Happy twenty-nine!" shouted Ofie and Star in unison. They stood at the bottom of the stairs and posed as waitresses with plates of scrambled eggs, pancakes, and hash browns stacked upon their arms.

"You got me! How did you pull this off? Did Ezra put you up to this?" she asked, scanning the room, waiting for him to jump out.

"He left the key under the mat for us. He had to take off early," Star explained. "He said he had a top-secret surprise for you today. Hurry and come down here, these trays are heavy!"

Ofie carefully made her way to the outdoor patio, still balancing the dishes. "Maybe he'll propose! He had a very sneaky look on his face...," she sing-shouted.

"I need a double cappuccino! Quick!" Chloe blurted, running to the expensive espresso machine for a thick dose of Illy, shaking her head to dissolve the horrifying thought. In fact, she planned to ask the bum to move out this weekend. The relationship had become strictly convenience, no respect or companionship. She suspected Ezra had a second girlfriend—typical signs of late nights, hushed phone conversations, new lingo. Chloe didn't mind. In fact, it made her life easier to have him out of her lightened tresses. She needed to purge the dead weight to make room for all the exciting opportunities that would pour in after the CraftOlympics.

Maybe even love.

Not Ezra-love, but Ofie and Larry-love. Their bank account may have been dryer than brittle bones, but they were rich in every other way.

Twenty minutes later the ladies sat outside on Chloe's high-rise patio to soak up the first tolerable Arizona morning of the season. Between them, they scarfed down a dozen heart-shaped banana-pecan pancakes—a recipe from Ofie's "Chubby Girl Delights" file. Ofie and Star cleared the table, sang "Happy Birthday," and handed over their gifts.

From the brown paper gift bag from Ofie, Chloe pulled out a set of black Converse sneakers Ofie had decorated using a bleach pen. One shoe had a neat series of dots and dashes, but the other was smeared beyond recognition. Chloe immediately kicked off her slippers and put them on.

"I had a sneeze fit while I made the right one; that's why it's fuzzy," Ofie confessed, crouching over to see how they looked on Chloe's feet. "Otherwise, aren't they as sweet as honey on apple pie? Oh, and there are cotton panties to match! Nana Chata bought them at Wal-Mart for me, but they're too small. I thought they'd fit you. I used the bleach pen to write CC all over them. For Crafty Chloe!"

Chloe gripped the undies to her chest and scooted over to give Ofie a pat on the shoulder. In Chloe body language, that equaled a bear hug.

Star set a pretty black, white, and taupe box on the glass tabletop and pushed it with her purple-polished fingertips. Chloe opened it to find the book *52 Projects: Random Acts of Everyday Creativity* by Jeffrey Yamaguchi, a black-and-white mud-cloth journal, and a CD wrapped in pretty origami paper.

Star, a desert native, reached for her turquoise silk shawl and put it over her shoulders to calm her shivers from the sixty-nine-degree temperature. "I know you are Crafty Chloe, queen of all things creative, but I thought you might like this book. Just when you think your left brain is tapped, peek at any page. It has all kinds of random art adventures to try. And the journal is from my mom. She made it at the Omega Institute and mailed it to me just for you. That mud cloth was given to her by a beautiful Nigerian healer. Mom says it has good energy."

Tears sprang to Chloe's eyes, and she thought of the beautiful box Star had so lovingly made for Theo. The old Chloe had rescued it from the garbage for selfish reasons, and the new Chloe regretted being so thoughtless.

"No need to cry! Wait, there is one more gift," Star said.

Chloe slid her manicured finger under the clear tape so she wouldn't rip the paper. She held the package upside down and slid out the CD. "No way!" she said in the most gleeful tone Star or Chloe had ever heard from her.

"It's reggae en Español," Star said. "The band is called—"

"Reggae Sol, I've heard of them," Chloe said, hoping she didn't blush too much. "I actually met the lead singer at that silly Chi-Chi coffeehouse on Grand Avenue. Nice guy."

"Oh my God. The lead singer from Reggae Sol had coffee at the Chi-Chi Coffee Cabana? I worked there for one day. I feel honored now! If they ever come back here for a concert, we are so going. You gotta hear them live. Consider it the rest of your birthday gift!"

If only she could find a way to return the favor to Star. Chloe didn't feel she deserved these friends. She had lied for months and yearned to make it up to them.

"Thank you," Chloe said, her voice almost cracking. "No one has ever done anything like this for me." She rose to set the gifts inside the house, came back, and walked to the edge of the patio to face the crisp blue skyline.

"Our craft meeting is at La Pachanga today, right?" she asked. She wanted to come clean with her friends about her lies. But first she had to get through the day.

"Oh yah, it was Star's idea, because Nana Chata has drumming practice at the house. Same time though. Fourish?" Ofie said. "You okay, sweetie? Your face is flushed. I hope we haven't embarrassed you. We're just proud of you. You're so classy. People don't think crafting is as nerdy because of you. You're a sexy vixen who sews."

"Don't forget that she's a role model for artistic Latinas, too," Star added. "You've made a career doing what you love, working hard, and aiming high."

Ofie jumped in again. "Oh! Oh! Like Les Brown, that motivational speaker, once said—it's better to aim high and miss, than to aim low and hit."

"I aim high because of my middle-child syndrome." Chloe laughed. "Trying to get a bit of recognition."

"You know? Come to think of it—I don't aim at anything," Star concluded. "I go with the flow and live each minute to the fullest. The journey is more surprising and entertaining that way! Eh, unfortunately, it's also my downfall."

"I'm a low-aimer who wants to be a high-aimer," Ofie announced. "And that's why you enlighten me so much, Chloe. You aren't afraid to go after what you want. You're the real deal."

Chloe, ashamed, returned to her chair. "All right—*now* you're embarrassing me. I'm changing the subject. Star? Can I ask you something personal? We know each other well enough, right?"

Star put her hand on Chloe's. "Of course, silly. You can ask me anything. Except physics stuff. I'm bad with that."

Chloe looked into Star's eyes. "Who is the Happy Face Tagger? You can trust me. I'd never breathe a word about it." No sooner had the words left her mouth than Chloe swore she saw Ofie choke on her drink.

Star cleared her throat, blinked, and stared back at Chloe with a sincere expression.

"Honestly, we never found out. It's over with."

"I'm sorry I was so rude to you that day," Chloe said with sincerity.

An uncomfortable silence invaded their otherwise happy conversation, but then Chloe quickly changed the subject. "So, lady, what's up with Harrison? I noticed he's picked you up from our meetings for the past three weeks."

Star stretched her arms up and folded them on top of her head. "Yes, he has…but it's not what you think. You know that English pub on Central Avenue, the George & Dragon? We hang out there Wednesday nights. They have fish 'n' chip specials and he is in their dart tournament. That's all there is to it."

Chloe play-punched Star in the arm. "Oh, please. He's hot and he loves Brit rock. In my book, that is irresistible."

"Okay, I know. He *is* superhot. My eyes love him, but I haven't felt the tingle yet. Or like my mom says, the love shine. Plus, everywhere we go, chicks hit on him. He's out of my league. But then he is supersweet and goes out of his way to call me. So, I don't know…we'll see. It's good the way it is."

"Whatever. Have you tested his fire hose yet?" Ofie asked. "Does it have any kinks?"

Chloe cackled and gave Ofie a big high five.

"Ofie!" Star whimpered.

"Come on, we have a wager on this. I say yes, Ofie says no," Chloe said as she slapped her hand on the table and picked up her coffee cup, took a big gulp, and raised her brows.

"It's not always about sex. Jeez!" Star replied.

Chloe and Ofie tilted their heads together and chimed, "Nope, she hasn't."

"Don't tell me it's because of Theo," Ofie said. "He broke all our hearts when he busted yours. But we've all moved on. You can't let that stop you from a decent kowabunga. Especially with a fireman!"

Chloe snorted and almost spit out her coffee in laughter. "Kowabunga? What the hell is that? I think I know, but I just want to hear you say it, Ofie."

Ofie squirmed and waved her hands in the air. "It's when you know ... *it* happens *down there* and you yell: 'Kowabunga!'"

"TMI, Ofie," Chloe remarked with a dry chuckle.

"I wouldn't know about kowabungas anymore," Star said, thinking of Theo.

Chloe sensed Star's dip in emotion and immediately steered the conversation up again. There would be no boyfriend drama on her birthday!

"Join the club!" Chloe laughed. "Well, ladies, it's been lovely, but I have to get to the flower shop to buy a gift for my assistant."

"Frances? Why?" Star asked.

Ofie rubbed Chloe's shoulder. "Larry told me how Frances has been a brat lately. That girl has a lot of nerve after all you do for her! I wonder if she knows how many people would kill to be your assistant, all the things they could learn from you! She's lucky you don't fire her!" Ofie angrily tossed her spoon down on the table.

Chloe stood up and began to clear the table. "It's not that bad, really. It's a very demanding job. I just want to tell her thanks, which I've rarely done in the past. In other words, I want to be a nicer person. Being a bitch is exhausting!"

Star raised her mug as if to say "Cheers!" "Chloe, my dad always says when you admit your flaws out loud, it sends a message to the universe. I believe it. Like Sam Cooke would say, 'Change is a comin'.'"

20

No better form of satisfaction existed than to create art as a gift, and have the recipient adore it. And that is precisely what happened at Chloe's birthday breakfast. As Ofie drove away in the Craftmobile from Chloe's Scottsdale loft, she danced and sang along to Beyoncé's "Survivor" on the CD player. She had spent two hours last night on those sneakers, and the joy on Chloe's face when she opened the box was worth every minute. Ofie wanted to continue that joy. She would make sneakers for Anjelica and, yes, Nana Chata, too, and surprise them. Instead of attending her Wednesday-morning paper-making class, Ofie directed the van toward her Glendale house, excited to repeat her bleach-pen magic.

Ofie entered the carport, stepped out of the car, toe tapped in a circle, and closed the door with a swing of her hip. She day-dreamed about fabric markers and shoelaces and the bliss they'd bring to her family. All of a sudden, she froze. A thunderous voice came from inside the house, which should have been empty. Ofie quietly stepped back and reached into her purse for her cell to call 911.

Holding her breath so as not to make a peep, Ofie listened closer and heard a familiar voice.

Aw, it's only Nana Chata, she thought. *Maybe she stubbed her toe on the tie-dye tub again.*

But no, Nana Chata scolded someone on the phone—half in English, half in Spanish, and her angry tone echoed off the linoleum floors. A bewildered Ofie peeked through the crack in the door and witnessed Nana Chata arguing into the cordless handset that Ofie had covered in glued-on buttons.

"Ofelia's with the craft group again! This time at the crack of dawn! I'm sorry to tell you, m'ijo. But your wife needs help. Did you know she sent Anjelica to school today with a one-hundred-and-two-degree fever? Thank God you changed the emergency contact number to me, instead of her. It's nine, and I've been trying to call her since seven thirty. Her cell has been off all morning!"

Ofie, astonished, nervously bounced on her leg and wondered if she should leave. She didn't.

"I know, Larry. I know. You don't have to explain. I don't mind giving you the money for the mortgage. Don't worry about paying me back. You know I'd do anything for my son and grandchild. But you have to do something about your wife. Anjelica can't grow up in this environment. And how will you ever save for her college? Last I heard, Arizona State University doesn't accept cans of varnish as payment! Ofelia needs to get a job like everyone else, instead of spending your hard-earned money on that craft crap. Anjelica still has nightmares over that awful mural in her bedroom. I keep shoving the dresser in front of it, but your wife can't take the hint and moves it away. Even her friends know she has no talent. You have to talk to her. Tell her to try crochet, something safe."

Nana Chata paused, Ofie presumed, to listen to Larry.

"Yes. I swear to God, they do! They talk about her when she leaves the room. They're worried about her too. Look, I have beans in the Crock-Pot. I'm going to go write a letter to Dr. Phil about this. Maybe he can do an intervention. I'm taking Anjelica home with me and I'll clear my schedule today to stay with her. You deal with your wife tonight. Call me in the morning."

Ofie ran to her van, devastated that Nana Chata would say such awful things about her to Larry. And Anjelica did not have a fever before school. Ofie knew she was far from a perfect mother, but she did give 100 percent to her only child.

"Don't I?" Ofie asked aloud. And how horrible of Nana Chata to say her friends felt the same way. As far as Ofie was concerned they were the only people who truly understood her. Ofie held back a sob, turned on the ignition, and sped away as fast as she could.

21

Chloe yanked open one of the tall glass doors of the office building and checked her watch as she entered the lobby. It was 10:45 a.m. already! She should have arrived by ten, but her surprise birthday breakfast ran long. She flashed her badge to the security guard and hopped in the mirrored mosaic elevator, only to find Mark Jefferies inside.

"Sweet. There's the sexy lady I've been dreaming about. Happy birthday," he said, wearing a fancy suit and standing inside in the lift. "Looks like we have the space to ourselves."

Chloe greeted him with a professional head nod, attempting to keep a straight face. She refused to demean herself any longer by giving into this slimeball's advances. She turned to the mirrored back wall to fix her hair with one hand, while balancing her purse and Frances' flowers with the other. She almost fell backward when Mark suddenly shoved his chubby hand down the front of her silk blouse and squeezed her breast like a bike horn. She lifted her foot and, with all her force, smashed her heel into his loafer. The move backfired, as he grabbed her other breast to catch his balance. Furious, Chloe was just about to elbow him when—

Ding! The elevator doors opened to reveal Frances, standing firm with her arms crossed.

"I heard you had arrived," Frances deadpanned.

"Hello, Frances!" Chloe squeaked as she detangled herself from Mark, shooting him a you-are-so-gonna pay-for-this glare. "Can you please book an appointment for me with Human Resources today? I have a sexual harassment complaint to file."

Frances did not react. She remained stiff as a surfboard, and used her middle finger to push up her glasses. "Happy Birthday, Ms. Chavez. You're late. Everything is set up and ready to go. Did you memorize the directions I wrote for today's projects?"

"Chavez, you're on in ten minutes!" a producer hollered, as Frances coldly hooked up Chloe's mic pack and adjusted her clothes.

"Yes, I did memorize the directions, thank you. And it's not what you think, Frances. Jefferies has been blackmailing me for years. I won't take it anymore."

"So he uses you, just like you use me, Ms. Chavez?" Frances asked.

Chloe did a double take. "I owe you the biggest apology in the world, Frances. These flowers are for you." She blinked twice and presented them as a humble commoner would to a queen. Frances accepted them, and her face softened for an instant, but hardened again as her eyes turned to a cold stare that sent a chill up Chloe's neck.

"Chavez! We're waiting!" the producer hollered.

The station's craft queen hustled through the newsroom and onto the set. Frances deserved more than flowers. Chloe knew she deserved a better job. Just as promised, the crafts were laid out in perfect order for the do-it-yourself spa segment. There were three: bubble bath confetti eggs for the kids, peppermint lotion, and the grand finale—fizzy bath bombs.

"Hey there, Crafty Chloe," Mark said, cooler than a polar bear in a Coke commercial. By his side was his wife, along with two executives from the Hadwick Corporation and their wives.

"As I mentioned before," Mark explained, "our wives will join you for the spa segment. They're here for the Celebrity Fight Night Fundraiser this weekend, so we'd like to give them a big welcome to the valley." He held out his arm to three trophy wives, all mic'd and ready to go.

"Fun!" Chloe said. "Come this way, ladies." They followed and took their places at the waist-high display table. Chloe scanned over the notes, and assigned one woman to each project. The floor director held up two fingers.

Chloe took a deep breath and revealed her regional Emmy Award–winning smile.

The red light flashed.

"Hi! Crafty Chloe here! Isn't the weather absolutely gorgeous? On a day like this, who wants to work?" Chloe asked, reading the lines on the teleprompter. "Why not take some time to pamper yourself and indulge in some *lavish* spa treatments? I'm here with Mary, Karla, and Taymah, and we're going to share three easy recipes for relaxation."

The women waited with excitement as Chloe continued feeding the camera.

"First of all, I'd like for all of you to know—as always, I personally dreamed up and created these very special samples I'm about to share. They came from my heart and I hope you enjoy whipping them up just as much as I did! So let's get crafty!"

Mary stepped close to Chloe and rubbed her hands in anticipation.

Chloe lifted a brown egg from a wicker basket and raised it as if it were gold. "First, I'm going to show you how to fill these darling faux eggs with luxurious bath salts. Here's how I did it... ," Chloe said, recalling Frances' notes.

"Simply poke a small hole in the bottom and pour in the dry mixture like this...cover it with a small piece of tissue paper and glue. When you get in the tub, just crunch the egg between your palms, and let the salts go to work in the water! The faux eggshell dissolves. Go ahead, Mary. Try this one that I made earlier . . . ," Chloe urged as she handed Mary the egg and a small water bowl. "Let's get a close-up of this, so our viewers at home can see how pretty it looks!"

Mary smashed the egg between her hands over the bowl. The cameraman zoomed in.

"Ew! It's a real egg," Mary cried. Startled, she jumped and knocked the water bowl down the front of her blouse.

"What? It can't be! Who put that there?" Chloe asked, confused and turning her head back and forth across the table. She picked up an egg from the basket and smashed it between her hands. "Oh, you're right. These are real eggs!" She faced the camera, and tee-heed for a moment. "And that's what we call a craftastrophe! But the fun of crafting is that when things go wrong—you simply try again. Mary, go ahead and rinse your hands off over there . . ."

Chloe wiped her own slimy palms on her brand-new Stella McCartney skirt and went in for Round Two.

"Always a surprise around here . . . Let's move on to this delectable hand cream I created by blending baby oil, mint leaves, and silky white lotion. Karla, it's your turn, babe."

Karla took a deep breath and surrendered her palms to the so-called expert.

"Oh, what pretty hands you have! They'll feel even softer after this lotion goes to work!" Chloe calmly squirted the mixture on Karla's slender manicured fingers.

"Wooo, tingly," Karla cooed. "I like it."

Thank God, Chloe whispered without moving her lips.

"Wooooo . . . this is *very* tingly." Karla held out her hands to the camera. "Actually. It's kinda hot. It burns. Oh my God! My hands, they sting!" Karla wailed.

"Wait over here, dear," Chloe said as she used her non–egg drenched wrists to swiftly maneuver her guest off the set.

The red light still shining, the floor director signaled for Chloe to continue. Chloe could not understand why they didn't cut to a commercial. She clapped her hands together and playfully nudged the next victim.

"Whaddaya say, Taymah? Up for some fizzy bath bombs?"

"No." Taymah did an about-face and exited the stage.

Chloe lifted a jar that said "citric acid," let out a weak grin, and turned to the camera, with a bold grin.

"Well, Phoenix! You've been Punk'd!" She beat her hands on the craft table and pointed to the audience, just like her favorite game show host. "This was my little way of spicing things up around here. Did we getcha? Okay, now to Brian for weather!"

The red light went off, and Chloe dropped her head onto the table while the crew rushed her from every angle.

"What the hell, Chavez?" Mark scolded. "Are you trying to get out of your contract early?"

"Here's the first-aid kit for the burned hands!" someone else yelled.

"How do you get egg out of linen?" another voice said. "Does the station pay for wardrobe damages?"

Her face plastered to the table in a comatose state, Chloe caught a glimpse of a manila envelope that said: *Read me, Craft Bitch.*

"What's this? Who left this?" she asked as she propped herself up on her elbows and opened the flap. The crew gathered behind her to see.

She slid out a glossy eight-by-ten from the envelope and squinted her eyes to zero in on the image. The photo showed Frances and Ezra nude with their arms entwined. The packet also contained a file folder with a notarized cover letter from Frances, printed e-mails, and microcassettes. Chloe fanned through the stack to discover that each paper was addressed to

Mark Jefferies, as well as the executives from the Hadwick Corporation—and the CraftOlympics too!

"Brilliant. Brilliant. Brilliant," commented a snarky intern with a peacock-blue pompadour and rockabilly clothing.

Chloe marched with Terminator-style force to her assistant's desk. When she reached it she found Frances, without her glasses, face flushed and clenching the calla lily bouquet. She whacked it hard in her boss's chest. Chloe, startled, frightened, and offended, staggered back and caught her balance.

"Ms. Chavez, after all you've put me through, the way you've treated me, a bouquet of flowers will not suffice. I do not accept your apology, as I do not feel it is sincere, yet only an exploit on your own behalf."

Chloe stood, speechless, along with all of her coworkers.

Frances put on her glasses, picked up her purse, and began to breathe very heavily. She turned sideways to walk down the aisle and then swung her head toward her former boss. "And one more thing. No matter how hard you try, you will never be Betty O'Hara! Betty O'Hara is nice. And funny. And friendly! I do not feel one ounce of guilt for what I did to you out there. You do not deserve to be a part of the craft community, nor the craft industry, because you *hate crafts*!" Frances stood on her toes, pointed at Chloe, and screamed at the top of her lungs like a wild woman, "I repeat. Crafty Chloe hates crafts!"

Chloe felt the sting of all eyes on her, yet she kept her composure and watched Frances stomp out of the room, Ezra at her side.

A tap on her shoulder startled her. There waited Mark Jefferies, holding Frances' manila envelope in his hand. "Chavez, follow me to my office, please."

The karma gods had come to collect.

22

The spirits of the dead had already arrived at La Pachanga two weeks before el Día de los Muertos—the Day of the Dead. The place bubbled with anticipation in this world and the next. In the gift shop, the clerks bumped into one another as they struggled to keep up with the frenzy of customers on the hunt for ofrenda—altar—accessories. In high demand were sugar skull molds, prayer candles, papel picado tissue banners, papier-mâché skeletons, copal incense, and small Mexican toys.

The restaurant business doubled and guests waited at least twenty minutes for a table. To pass the time, Al set up stations out front with art supplies so customers could make tissue-paper flowers to be used at the upcoming festivities.

After the Nana Chata phone rage earlier that morning, Ofie refused to return to an empty house. So she arrived six hours early for the meeting, centerpiece supplies in tow. She scored a corner booth in the coffee area and planned to stay all afternoon. La Pachanga's festive surroundings were just what she needed to lift her spirits.

Benecio, as promised, showed up at two thirty to teach her to crochet before Chloe and Star arrived at four. Larry called once and didn't mention his conversation with Nana Chata, but did share some awful news about Chloe that Ofie did not believe. Chloe would never steal craft ideas, or use sex to get ahead in her job! As soon as Chloe arrived, she would clear it all up. For now, Ofie wanted to forget about all of it, which would come easy once everyone arrived to work on the centerpieces.

But first, crochet lessons. Benecio demonstrated how to tie a slipknot around the hook and start the first row, and although Ofie worked furiously, she couldn't seem to get the hang of it. An hour later, Christina Aguilera's "Beautiful" chimed from the high-tech phone on Benecio's waistband.

"Don't give up, Ofie, you can do it...keep going," Benecio encouraged as he read the name on the caller ID. "Yikes. It's Mom. I have to take this outside. She thinks I'm shooting hoops at school until six. Star promised to get me home in time because Alice is off today."

Ofie watched him exit through La Pachanga's bright purple and green doors and stretched her arms across the Spanish-newsprint decoupaged table of her booth. She inhaled the sweet aroma of freshly ground coffee beans, removed the skeins of yarn from the bag, and lifted them to the tip of her nose. She smelled them, inspected the fibers, and lovingly squeezed them while she imagined owning her own Scottsdale yarn store and waiting on celebrity knitters like Felicity Huffman and Court-eney Cox. When Ofie crafted, the world was perfect.

But from one second to the next, a wave of sadness rushed over her thinking about what Nana Chata had said. Her friends would not do that to her. Her mother-in-law hated to see her happy and likely made it up to turn Larry against her.

Benecio jogged back in and slid into the fruity oilcloth-covered booth across from Ofie.

"Does this look good to you?" she asked, raising a lumpy, knotted, holey, but still technically crocheted rectangle.

"It's a good start. Keep practicing!" Benecio said.

Ofie skimmed the bottom of her cheek with her shoulder and eyeballed a framed portrait of Frida Kahlo across the room. She thought again about what she had heard Nana Chata tell Larry on the phone.

"Benecio, we need to talk."

"About the centerpieces? I know, we need to work faster!"

"No. something else. You've become like a son to me and a brother to Anjelica. I'm going to talk to you the same way I do to Anjelica. I'm going to ask you something and I want you to tell me the truth."

Benecio agreed by blinking through his long lashes.

"Do Star and Chloe talk behind my back?"

Benecio smiled nervously. "Ofie, we still have seventy-five centerpieces left to make. We should really get busy."

She slammed her hand on the table. "It's true, then. Nana Chata was right," Ofie said, stuffing the yarn back into the bag and reaching for the semi-crocheted rectangle. "I need to hear this. Please, Benecio, tell me. I won't mention your name."

It bothered Benecio when Star and Chloe made mean remarks about Ofie's crafts. And the way they always ended it with "Oh, but we love her!" to make themselves feel better. But he wouldn't dare repeat that to Ofie.

"Please, Benecio."

Why did they have to put him in the middle? Benecio thought. He bowed his head. "Star told us to like everything you make because you're a basket case and you'll have a meltdown."

"Really? Go on," she said, as she placed the project in her lap and clumsily weaved the hook in and out.

"Sometimes when you leave the room, they crack jokes."

"Um-hmm, and..." Ofie's hand moved faster—up and down in circular motions, almost as quick as her elevated heartbeat.

"The glitter from the centerpieces? Well, Star had three

hundred and fifty pounds of it that she ordered by accident. She hid it from you. It was expensive German glass glitter and she thought you would want it all and then just waste it."

"Star wouldn't do that. She's my best friend. And by the way, I don't have meltdowns. I'm just sensitive. Just so you know, okay. What else?" Ofie said.

Benecio pushed up the sleeves of his charcoal sweater and drew in a big breath. "Last week Chloe told us that your husband is worried because he has to work a lot of extra hours to pay for your craft supplies. Anjelica is sad because she thinks you like crafting more than her. And Chloe said your iced mochas feel like Drano surging through her intestines. She empties the cup in the backyard when you aren't looking. They hated your glittered boot centerpiece idea, so Star and Chloe had an emergency meeting to come up with the glittered cactus and then made it look like it was your idea. And—"

"That's enough! I got it, thanks, Benecio!" Ofie concluded. She closed her eyes and counted to ten to ward off an oncoming panic attack.

"Um, it's four o'clock already, Ofie. Chloe's here," Benecio whispered with his head lowered.

A disheveled Chloe stumbled in wearing her usual five-star newscaster clothes, except today her blouse, stained and wrinkled, hung untucked from her skirt, which had shifted so that the zipper lined up with her hip instead of her back. "Hey, crafty peeps. I have some shit news to unload, a confession, I guess you could say," she said as she slid two chairs to the end of the booth.

"I'm coming!" Star said, holding a handful of birthday balloons and skipping her way between the tables wearing red pin-up girl pumps and a slinky dress made from T-shirts that draped perfectly over her curves. Her dark twirled ringlets sported fresh chunky blond strands that framed her happy-go-lucky face. She plopped in the seat at the end of the table and handed the balloons to Chloe.

"Happy birthday again! Ooh, you guys are crocheting! I'm feeling frisky. I want to learn! Ofie, break out the sequin yarn we bought the other day. I've been dreaming about it!"

Ofie didn't answer. She wondered why Star hadn't bought the sequin yarn for herself that day, instead of encouraging Ofie to splurge on it. Ofie grabbed the sparkling skein and shoved it in Star's direction.

Star drew back her head, concerned. "Qué pasa, amiga? You all right?" She then gave Chloe a once-over. "For being your birthday, you don't appear to be very cheery. Didn't they celebrate it at the station?"

"Funny you should mention that." Chloe rubbed the top of her legs with her hands, as if to warm up her courage. "I need to come clean about some things..."

"I heard all about it. Larry told me." Ofie grimaced, as she gripped her work-in-progress. "You stole craft designs from your assistant and passed them off as your own. You hate crafts and used us to get in good with the CraftOlympics people. And you sleep with your boss. No wonder they call you Craft Bimbo."

"Ofie! Stop it! You don't sound like yourself today!" Star blurted. "What are you talking about?"

Chloe put her hand up. "My boss is none of your business. Otherwise, she's right. For the past three years, I've used Frances' designs for my craft segments. Crafty Chloe was an act to further my career in television. But that's not how it is now..."

"What? It's true? So all this? The group? Our friendship? It was just a front to further your career?" Star asked, gesturing to herself, Ofie, and Benecio.

"Please calm down so I can explain. You guys mean everything to me. At first I hated the group, but now it's all I look forward to. Let's talk about it," Chloe said.

"I should have known you were a fake when you tried to use hot glue on terra cotta," Ofie growled.

"It's all making sense," Star calculated. "That's why you're so secretive about sharing your ideas. You don't have any!"

"No! I mean *yes*. I mean *no*. It was, but it's not anymore. I don't know," Chloe said, nervously fiddling with her long, loopy chain-link necklace. "I joined under false pretenses, yes. I wanted to get on the good side of the CraftOlympics committee. But now I'm here for different reasons. Remember this morning I said I wanted to change my life? That's because of you guys. Star, Ofie...you have families who love and support you. Mine only sees my mistakes. My dad had a dream that I was this huge television icon, and then he passed away. I was so desperate to fulfill his dream that, once I started, I got sucked into a sneaky downward spiral, and I couldn't stop. One lie tangled into another and another..."

An invisible wall of defense rose up around Star. "You should have told us the truth earlier. We would have been on your side. Withholding something is just like lying. It's totally messed up."

Ofie stopped her crochet project long enough to pop up her head and proclaim, "Star is the Happy Face Tagger." She then lowered her head and resumed her stitches.

The group hollered out, "What?"

Star evoked the spirit of *The Exorcist* and twisted her head toward Ofie. "You didn't just say that."

"You?" Chloe asked, jolting her head back in disbelief as she slid out of the booth. "No way! You lied to my face all this time, and I believed you! Even this morning! What a hypocrite!"

With the interrogation spotlight pointed at her, Star fidgeted. "It's not what you think. I didn't mean to spray paint that mural. I had good reason."

"She got drunk with her *puta* cousin that night," Ofie remarked.

Star stomped her foot. "Ofie, I can't believe you just did that!"

Chloe slung her bag over her arm. "Look, Star, maybe what I did was wrong and I may lack creative talent, but at least I have specific ambition and drive. I don't have parents who allow me time to find myself. Give me a damn break! I'd bet all the scrapbook paper in the world that you don't even go through with your art show. As soon as something gets hard, you ditch it."

"Nice to know what you really think of me," Star replied.

"So much for a happy birthday." Chloe sighed. "I woke up this morning intending to make peace with the universe, and it's been the worst day of my life. Regardless, I don't have time for this craft crap anymore. Happy, Ofie?"

"Don't you dare be mean to her!" Star warned Chloe.

"Don't you dare be rude to me! I haven't done anything but open my home to you!" Ofie barked.

Chloe switched her weight to the other leg and balled up her fists at her sides. "Fine, Ofie. Go home to your loving husband who sacrifices his free hours to work overtime to pay for your craft habit. And your beautiful daughter who wishes you would take the time to braid her hair, instead of making stupid butterfly ponytail holders that she is embarrassed to wear. And together, you and your little familia can laugh about me over the tasty enchilada dinner your mother-in-law makes that you hate, but you eat it anyway because you can't stand up to her."

Chloe shot Ofie and Star a prissy smile, spun around, and click-clacked her heels the heck out of there, just like a bitchy supermodel working the runway.

Benecio sprinted after her. "What about the centerpieces? We still have to finish!"

Chloe stopped, pushed her saucer sunglasses over her eyes, and turned to face him. "I'm sorry, Benecio. I never wanted to disappoint you. But it's not my problem anymore. If you were smart, you'd split too. I'll see if I can score you a media pass to CraftOlympics without your parents knowing.

"Take care, kid," Chloe said to Benecio. And with that, she split.

"We'll get them done, B," Star offered, as she put her arm around him for reassurance. "But we'll talk later. Why don't you wait outside for me so you don't have to hear any more of this?"

Before he could move, Ofie spoke up. "Star, what is the real reason you didn't want me to enter the Scissor Smackdown? And why didn't you tell me—your best friend—about all that glitter?" Ofie's tears began to fall like raindrops on her yarn. "Is...it...true, Star? Is it because you think my crafts are ugly?"

Star thrust her hands over the table to comfort Ofie. "Who told you that?"

"Do you think my crafts are ugly? Yes or no?" Ofie prodded.

"Ofie, don't be silly!" Star answered.

Ofie jerked away. "So it *is* true. You think my crafts are ugly," she said as her thick fingers gripped the metal hook and jabbed it into the red worsted-weight yarn. The next moment she put it down and used the table as leverage to heave her heavy body from the tight space. She began to breathe heavily and fast.

"Oh no," Star mumbled. "Ofie, sit down," she advised, gently touching her best friend's arm. "Let's do the yoga breathing exercises my mom taught us."

Ofie pounded her fist on the table, causing the silverware and condiments to rattle.

"You are nothing but a spoiled, self-centered brat, Star! And I'm tired of listening to you complain about your life. You have no idea how good you have it! You have no direction; you're like a leaf in the wind, blowing any which way. Chloe is right. You get drunk and vandalize your parents' property, and all they do is give you more space to *find yourself*? Boo. Fucking. Hoo. You don't know what it's like to struggle."

"Not true, Ofie!" Star countered. "I've struggled. I just don't tell you."

"What? Like Theo hurting your feelings, only after you hurt his first? Flirting with a fireman? Living with your parents? Try thinking what it's like for people like me and Larry to get pregnant and married at eighteen. Try feeling like a failed mother and wife. Try having your electricity turned off because you spent more money on beads than bills. Try eating dinner with a mother-in-law who thinks you're useless. How dare you mock my dreams, when you don't have the guts to follow your own. I agree with Chloe. I'd bet all the scrapbook paper *and* all your stupid glitter that you don't go through with your show. You'll probably use this as an excuse to cancel it."

Star choked at her friend's biting remarks.

Ofie panted as she stuffed herself back into the booth, picked up her crochet needles, and resumed her power hooking.

Star slipped from the booth and stood next to her friend. "You are the last person I would ever want to hurt."

Ofie wouldn't look up at her. "That's what you told Theo too. Now I know what he felt like. There is nothing you can say to change things, Star." Ofie's voice cracked, thinking how the phrase "stitch 'n' bitch" had literally come to life. "Crafting was the *one* thing I enjoyed. I was so excited for the CraftOlympics, and you have spoiled it for me. Once again, I'm an outcast and a fool. I'm glad Theo got away from you. You don't deserve him."

Star clenched her chest and kneeled on the floor at Ofie's side. "I'm sorry. I only meant to protect you. I didn't want anyone to hurt your feelings. I didn't realize I was doing the same thing."

Ofie wouldn't meet Star's gaze. As far as she was concerned, their friendship was over.

"Veté!" Ofie ordered without a window of negotiation. "Go!"

"Please, Ofie," Star said, her chin quivering. Ofie ignored her.

Star rose and placed her hand on Benecio's back to guide him out, their frowns just about dragging on the floor.

"Peace out, Ofie. I love you," Star said.

Benecio broke away, ran to Ofie, threw his arms around her neck, and sobbed. She remained in her stiff crochet-induced trance.

"I never, ever, *ever* said anything bad about you," he pleaded. "Everything you do is beautiful. Look..." He pulled a chain out from under his shirt. "It's the avocado necklace you made me. I haven't taken it off. It's my good luck charm."

Ofie didn't budge. "It's supposed to be a heart." A teardrop fell from her eye, rolled down her cheek, and plopped on what was now beginning to look like a bright red baby blanket.

"It's an *avocado* heart, and I love it. I wish... *I wish so bad*... my mom could be like you."

"Go home to your family, Benecio. You're better off without any of us," she replied in a hushed tone. He kissed her cheek and did as she said, wiping his eyes as he left.

23

Not much later, the Valley of the Sun fell victim to a massive thunderstorm that Star believed was brought on by the many souls shaken that afternoon.

Her eyes swelled from hours of nonstop crying. She didn't care about the centerpieces, Chloe, or even Benecio. All Star wanted was for Ofie to feel better. After the La Pachanga verbal bloodbath, Star dropped Benecio off and went home to find her parents giggling together while sharing jokes from their extended anniversary getaway. Star brewed a pot of Green Mountain coffee, sat them down, and explained everything. Dori agreed to go over to Ofie's with Star to straighten the mess out.

Before they left, Star wanted to make a gift for Ofie as a peace offering. A gift that expressed her gratitude and loyalty, and that Ofie would really love: a friendship shrine. Star bolted upstairs to her room and worked feverishly to complete the art piece as fast as she could, stopping only to blow her nose every few minutes.

From her dresser she grabbed a lumpy mosaic-tiled jewelry box she used to hold her brooch collection. She dumped the pins on her bed. Ofie had made the box for Star's last birthday and now it would serve as the foundation of the shrine. Star used the bottom of her T-shirt dress to remove the dust from inside the box and then went to work. Her iPhone buzzed several times, probably Harrison, but she ignored it. She didn't have time to explain, and he wouldn't understand anyway. Star languished over Ofie's feelings. Her mind reeled at all the negative thoughts and wisecracks she'd ever made.

Losing Theo she could deal with, but losing Ofie? Unacceptable.

"Please, you have to let us in, Larry. I'm begging you. I have to talk to Ofie," Star pleaded through a loud crash of thunder, as she tried to force her way through the Fuentes' front door.

Larry braced the entrance to keep her at bay. "I'm sorry, ladies, not tonight. Star, Dori—come on now. My poor wife has been through enough, don't you think?"

Though Larry's tone was polite, right now he couldn't care less about these women. Who did they think they were? Egoísta! Selfish! They trotted over here every damn week, made their mess, and left. To them, the craft group served as a time filler. To Ofie, it meant the world! Larry thought of how many times he wanted to say "Enough!" at the dinner table when Ofie would go into her forty-minute recap of the meeting and everyone's lives. Now even Anjelica wanted to host an afterschool craft group. And it had all come down to this—Star making fun of Ofie behind her back, which sent Ofie into her worst breakdown ever.

Dori attempted an intervention. "It's a misunderstanding. We want to help Ofie. We love her. Please can we come in?"

Larry stepped out onto the front porch and inhaled the fragrance of dampened marigolds from the flowerbed. He wished the current mood could be as pleasing. He rested his palm on his forehead and delivered the bad news. "This craft group isn't a good idea anymore. I should have never encouraged Ofie with this. Please—if you really care about her, don't call. Don't come by. She needs her family right now."

"I'm her family too. You know that, Larry. Look at how long we've known each other," Star sobbed while a web of lightning flickered across the sky. "Please can you give her this? It's a gift I made for her tonight—a friendship shrine."

Larry looked down at the box and took it. "Go home before the roads get too flooded. This storm doesn't look like it's going to stop any time soon."

Star stepped up to his face and clenched her thin camel-colored sweater at her chest. A strong gust of cold wind blew from the side and made her teeth chatter. "Wh-at are you saying-ing-ing?"

Larry moved back toward the door. "I'll tell Ofie you came by. G'night."

"Take care of her and tell her we all love her," Dori said as she took Star's hand to lead her back to the car.

"Star," Larry called out against another loud clap of thunder.

Star rushed back in his direction. "Yes? Can I come in?"

"Of all people, I never expected *you* to hurt her this way."

Star opened her mouth, but no words escaped. She turned and ran to her car. Larry waited until he heard Dori's footsteps trot down the concrete pathway, past the plastic Malibu lights that Ofie had covered in turquoise fleck stone. After they drove away, Larry wondered if he had done the right thing.

He stepped inside the house, turned off the front porch light, and locked the door. A lump formed in his throat, and his body panged. He put the box on the top shelf of the wall unit and then knelt down to pick up the legs that had been broken off a painted plant stand. He held one piece in each hand and walked forward to clean up the remainder of Ofie's rampage.

*   *   *

After a few hours of sweeping and straightening, Larry tiptoed to his wife's side where she lay in bed, passed out from exhaustion.

When Larry had arrived home from work at eight thirty that night, the house appeared as though a gang of drunken thieves had visited. The art and handmade decorations that once graced the walls, dressers, and countertops were broken and scattered all over the floor. Black marker covered the family tree wall painting that Ofie spent three months on last summer. Same with the mural in Anjelica's bedroom. All of Ofie's favorite pieces were smashed to bits in every nook and cranny of the house.

Petrified, and assuming the worst, he sprinted to Anjelica's room, snagged a softball bat from her closet, and snuck through the house, ready to swing at the heartless intruder.

When he reached the bedroom, he heard Ofie weeping, but couldn't see her.

"Ofie! Mi amor, are you hurt? Did you call the police?"

"The police? What happened?" she asked in a little-girl voice.

"Someone broke into the house! Where are you, honey?"

"In the closet. They must have come after I destroyed all my ugly work. I must not have heard them because I've been in here."

Larry opened the door to the walk-in closet and found Ofie sitting in the back corner, curled up on top of a massive pile of dirty laundry. Ofie always sacrificed laundry time for craft time. He set down the bat and kneeled at her side. "Wait. You did this? Tore up the house?"

"Oh. Yeah. I did," she said, clenching her fuzzy pink bathrobe to her neck.

"Why?" he asked.

"Because I found out today that my crafts are…are…*ugly* and

no one likes them. They all think I'm a fool, Star, Chloe, and...
your mother." She let out a wail of pain. "I'm such an idiot!"

She spent the next half hour recounting the entire ordeal. The
more Larry learned, the more furious he became with Star and
the other women. He brought Ofie a Tylenol PM, a glass of
water, led her to bed, and rocked her to sleep.

He had thought of all this while he swept up the mess and
thanked the Lord neither his mom nor Anjelica saw any of this.
It was a stroke of good luck his little girl was staying with her
grandmother tonight. What if they had been here? He sweated
while he worked, not from the physical exertion, but because he
had no idea what the outcome would be. Would he need to ask
for time off from work to care for Ofie, which may cost him his
recent promotion, which would lead to less income for the family? Would she need medical attention?

At 12:30 a.m., Larry checked on Ofie. She snored loudly, her
mouth wide open. He fixed her flannel nightgown and pulled the
covers up to her chin. He noticed something poking out from
under her crossed arms: a red blanket connected to a ball of yarn.
Larry carefully slid it away and set it on the nightstand.

"Larry...," she said groggily. "Where's Anjelica?"

"She's with Nana Chata. It's all good, mi amor, relax."

"Do they know?"

"No. They don't and I'll never tell. Now get some more sleep."

"Please forgive me, Larry."

"There is nothing to forgive. You had some tension to release
there, didn't you?" he joked, stroking her frizzy box-dyed auburn
hair. "Please forgive me for letting it get to this point without
intervening."

"I wanted to get rid of the mess I made of this house," Ofie
said as she dragged her heavy body up, rested her head against
the wall, and gulped down the last of the water, which seemed
to refresh her.

"I can take the truth, Larry. I realized it when I came home. It all looks so cheesy. Why couldn't I see that? Something came over me and I just wanted it all to go away. I don't think I ever want to see another stencil or rubber stamp as long as I live."

Larry peered at the yarn that she had been cuddling minutes ago.

"Well, except yarn." She laughed. "Before Star sent me over the waterfall of humiliation today, Benecio taught me how to hook! Or crochet, I mean."

"You made that entire thing *today*?" Larry reached over and retrieved the project to examine it. "My God, you're like Speedy Gonzales. My nana used to make blankets all day long and it took days to get that far."

"Here, give!" She reached her hand out for the yarn and scrunched her fingers in and out like a baby grabbing for candy. Larry smiled and passed the yarn and crochet hook to her. Ofie returned his smile and went back to work on her blanket. The same stitch over and over. It was as if she had been doing it her whole life. She could even carry on a conversation while she looped her way down the row and up again.

"See? I can do it. I was so upset at La Pachanga after everyone left and my brain just sort of shifted to the yarn," she said in a matter-of-fact manner as she continued her work. "Einstein once said, 'In the middle of every difficulty lies opportunity.'"

Larry couldn't believe how sweet his wife was—or how fast her hands churned. And she was supposed to be sedated!

Ofie stopped and stroked her husband's razor-stubbled cheek. "Larry, can I ask a favor, and if you say no, I'll never mention it again?"

He closed his eyes and savored her caress. "My love, I'd do anything for you."

"Is it okay if Nana Chata doesn't help us out so much every day? Like shopping for Anjelica's clothes, and cooking, even the laundry? I know she means well, and she loves us, but I want to try doing those things myself. I've never spoken up about it because I didn't want to be disrespectful. I want really badly to show you that I can be a good mother and wife. I know I can. Chloe hurt me today with what she said, but inside I knew it was true. I can do much better."

Larry kissed her hands. "My mom loves you a lot. She's told me. She means well. But I understand. Consider it done. Except her menudo. I can't live without that."

"Deal." Ofie's whole face lit up. "And I'm going to get a job too, and pay her back every penny she ever gave us. Just wait and see. Now you go to bed. I'm going to keep on crocheting for a bit. It relaxes me."

Larry covered her hands with his, lifted her chin with his nose, and pecked her forehead, her nose, and her lips. "Tomorrow we begin with a clean slate: our house and our minds."

Ofie squirmed her hands free and continued with her new favorite hobby. "Let's redo Anjelica's room first, before she comes home."

Larry agreed, climbed off the bed, and removed his clothes down to his polka-dotted boxers and black ankle socks.

"Did Star call?" Ofie asked nonchalantly.

He sighed, not knowing what to say. "Why? Would you like to talk to her?"

"Yes, of course. But... not just yet. I want some alone time. This will all blow over, I know it will. Many so-called friends have walked in and out of my life, but Star is the only one who has left footprints on my heart. She's my best friend."

"Well, take all the time you need, mi amor." He loaded a CD into the boom box on the nightstand, pushed a button, and turned up the volume knob. "You feeling better?"

"Lots."

"Good enough to dance with me? It's Buena Vista Social Club, our wedding music."

Ofie laughed. "Larry, after the day I've had? Look at me. I'm a mess! And I need lipstick!"

He stood at her bedside and held out his palm. "To me, you are as beautiful as the first day I met you."

Ofie set down her yarn, rose from the bed, and gave him a long kiss. The two embraced, and swayed in unison to the Cuban love ballad "Dos Gardenias."

The song ended, and Larry escorted his wife back to bed to tuck her in.

An hour later, Larry was the one blowing the z's into the air while Ofie crocheted. The Energizer Bunny had nothing on her. She kept going and going and going.

All through the night, Ofie immersed herself in a one-woman hook-a-thon. A switch of some sort had been turned to high, making her a lean gazelle in the process of stitching in, over, and through. She could easily see her work was flawless—not a lump or hole in sight. Even her rows were even. She only knew one stitch—the double crochet—but she worked it like Fergie in front of a microphone. Ofie found the process soothing. Every time she wrapped the yarn around the hook, she erased a nugget of self-doubt.

Ofie not only finished that tear-soaked baby blanket she'd begun earlier in the day at La Pachanga, but she also began another and there were still a few hours until daylight. At one point, she ran out of yarn so she searched the house for substitutes. She found expensive chenille, cheap craft yarn, scrapbooking fiber embellishments, and even embroidery thread. She scoured Larry's toolshed and retrieved kite string and neon orange twine. When she couldn't find any more, she took old sweaters from the closet and unraveled them to add to her new blanket in progress.

Larry awoke at eight a.m. to a crocheted bonanza. He sat up and rubbed his eyes in awe. Ofie was three-quarters finished with a crazy afghan.

Unfazed, he watched his wife sleep in peace, clutching that first red blanket to her chest.

Any other husband would have called the mental ward to deliver a straitjacket. But not Larry. He knew this was a sign of good things to come.

Ofie had *finally* found her craft.

24

The next day, Chloe rested on a chaise longue on her loft's balcony. Wrapped in a thin shawl that Benecio had knitted for her birthday, she turned off the ringers on her phones for peace of mind. As she swirled a glass of chardonnay, she gazed at the decadent Phoenix sunset. Despite four hours and four hundred dollars spent at the Biltmore Resort and Spa today, she still felt like Satan's semi had plowed over her several times.

But if there was one thing Chloe had picked up from her short time with the craft group, it was to find positive in the negative—a practice she had subconsciously been working on these past few months. However, this situation presented a challenge. She set down her wineglass and created a mental checklist.

Friends: As of yesterday, nada.
Love life: Buh-bye, Ezra! Hello, single girl in the city.
Job: Transferred to KPDM's dinky sister station in Tucson, following her unpaid leave of absence.
Career: Forget it.

Last night after La Pachanga, she phoned the CraftOlympics head office to inquire about her spot as host. An administrative

assistant returned her call this morning to inform her of a misunderstanding. Apparently, there had been a change in plans and
Betty O'Hara was offered, and had accepted, the job months ago.
Chloe hung up in a stupor. She didn't know what to make of it.
She left multiple voice and e-mails for Mark Jefferies and he didn't
return any of them. Did he scam her for sex? Would he really be
so evil? Did the CraftOlympics executives change their minds in
the last twenty-four hours? She couldn't relax until she heard the
truth. Since Mark wouldn't answer her messages, she'd have to
escalate the case to *Fatal Attraction* status and call his home.

Chloe opened her leather address book, punched in the code
to block her number, and then dialed Mark's home number.

"Jefferies' residence," Mark said in a chipper voice.

"It's me."

"This is highly inappropriate."

"I just called the CraftOlympics headquarters and they claim
Betty O'Hara was chosen as the host. They said she had the gig
months ago. You lied to me."

Mark began to speak in a sneaky whisper. "I never *technically*
said you had the job..."

"Yes, you did."

"Well, it's too late now. They would have dropped you anyway. Your career is done. Our viewers think you're a joke, not to
mention the station staff and arts community. But maybe I can
pull a few strings in your favor. My family's away for the weekend. Come over here and we'll figure something out. I'll chill
some wine for us, just like old times."

Chloe slammed the phone on the receiver.

It didn't matter. She'd decided last night that her crafty days—
maybe even her TV ones—were over. No more centerpieces to
worry about, people to impress, or meetings to attend. Those
women just doused her life with mushy sentimental nonsense,

distracting her from her goal of climbing the network ranks. And what did she get out it? Knowledge about high-gloss varnish versus matte.

She sighed, finished off the contents of her glass, and fell back in her chaise longue, buzzed. All of that hokey art stuff was in the past. She would use her non-paid suspension time and lounge in Cabo San Lucas as a "cooling down period" as Mark put it. When she returned, she would work in Tucson until she could hook up a new gig in L.A.

Already, she dreaded facing her mother to hear the "I told you so" speech.

Chloe went into the kitchen and fired up her stereo, which pumped out the honeyed island sounds of Reggae Sol. After she met Gustavo that day, she came home and immediately bought both of the band's albums online. Now she owned their latest disc too, thanks to Star. His soulful lead vocals comforted her, and made him feel somehow close to her heart, bringing her a sense of peace.

Happiness is free like air... he had told her. Yeah, right. She wished it were that attainable. Maybe in Puerto Rico, but not in Arizona.

She tightened the belt on her robe, let her head fall back to soak up the music, and then swallowed two diet pills to boost her energy. Her to-do list covered a whole piece of notebook paper. Bills to be paid, e-mails answered, laundry washed and packed before she left for the airport...But before she prepared for her unexpected vacation, she would dispose of Ezra's leftovers. As she changed into a gray turtleneck and black capri exercise pants and slipped on a headband, the Reggae Sol mix ended and the Brazilian bossa nova sounds of Bebel Gilberto began. Chloe got down to business.

She found an old microwave box in the garage and set it on the dining room table. One by one, she sorted through Ezra's travel and design magazines, his anime comics and DVD boxed sets of *The Hills* and *90210*. Chloe imagined him and Frances reenacting the melodramatic musings of vintage Lauren Conrad.

"I wish them well," she muttered with sarcasm as she taped up the flaps. Just then she heard a chime from her office. Incoming e-mail.

From Ofie, perhaps? One of her corny send-this-to-five-people-for-good-luck chain letters? Or she hoped maybe Star or Benecio...

She dropped the packing tape gun, raced to her laptop, and clicked on her in-box. Ezra.

> Sorry, Chloe. It wasn't jiving between us and I didn't know how to tell you. Frances says sorry too. We're in love. She gets me. Between your pseudocareer, mood swings, and banging your boss, you never had time for me anyway. Wish you well, candyface. Take care.
>
> —E.

If she had been a weak person, Chloe would have chucked her Dell laptop across the room. Why should she expect that Ezra, Star, or Ofie be concerned for her? Why would KPDM want her back at the station? But it was she who had made herself so disposable. Chloe never had the intention of leaving a lasting impact on anyone. She expected others to serve her needs, end of story. She led a shallow life on purpose, and this was the result. No ties. It was better this way. So why did she feel so hurt and...useless?

The heck with positivity, Chloe thought as she sauntered her way to Ezra's "studio." She paused at the kitchen to shove an entire Dunkin' Donut in her mouth (more Ezra leftovers), and returned to her mission. She entered her ex-boyfriend's cramped art space under the stairs, grabbed an ugly gray suitcase of his, and stuffed it with his junk. She lugged it to the kitchen, where she scarfed another doughnut. With her mouth freckled with icing, she tugged open the fridge's door to take a quaff of skim milk straight from the gallon jug, leaving a lipstick imprint behind.

Chloe went back to the studio for the books. Ezra had so much World of Warcraft junk, all funded by her. She loaded it in the cartons and shoved them in the laundry room. Once she returned from her trip, she would make sure to donate everything to a children's shelter. There. That was her good deed in all of this.

She pulled the light cord in the laundry room and just as the room went dark, a sparkle from the top shelf caught her attention. She paused and pulled it again.

Star's orphaned love shrine for Theo. Chloe figured she should just toss it and cut the ties with these locas, but her curiosity got the best of her. She just had to peek. Chloe would never forget the first night at Sangria when she saw Star shove it in the trash.

Chloe entered Ezra's studio again, this time with the shrine. She situated herself at the table, tugged at the lamp chain for extra light, and examined it. She found the art piece extraordinary. It had dice for feet, all kinds of shiny knickknacks glued on it, and the contents consisted of mementos that relayed pasión. Star really did have talent. Such a shame she didn't show it off more. Chloe would give up her local fame just to be able to have an artistic bone in the tip of her finger. In the center of the box rested a 3D novella picture of a hunky Mexican man about to devour the neck of a woman with big black hair and a thick, heaving bosom. The speech bubble was in Spanish and it read, *Amame, como nunca has amado a nadie*. In English it meant *Love me like you've never loved anyone before*. Different kinds of glitter covered the outer edges and at the top was a white papier-mâché banner that said "Te amo." I love you.

Chloe turned the box over to find a message:

Theo,
If the sun should lose its fire,
And the moon should lose its glow,
If the stars that shine should never be seen again,
That wouldn't diminish my love for you.
I would relight the sun so it would shine on your day.
I would rekindle the moon to illuminate your way.
I would harness the stars
And place them back in the heavens to say—
You are the love of my life and the heart of my soul.
I love you always and in all ways,
Estrella Feliz

Star's love poem did Chloe in. She wiped her tears off on her sleeve. Twice. She cried partly on Star's behalf, and the remaining sobs for herself. She wished she had that kind of love for someone, or even crazier, that someone would ache enough for her to make a romance shrine.

"Theo needs to see this again," Chloe affirmed. She found a piece of purple art paper from Ezra's desk and covered the box. She scribbled a note on one of her handmade greeting cards and slipped it under the ribbon. When she returned from her trip, she would give it to him.

When she finished, Chloe went into her office and retrieved two pieces of handmade paper with matching envelopes that Benecio had given her last month. She sat at her desk, pulled out a pen, and wrote the first one to Star.

Dear Star
*   I'm leaving for a mini vacation to wrap my head around*
all that has happened. I hope to return a better person,
someone like you, who is not afraid to hold out for what she

*loves. I am so sorry for the mean-spirited words I said to you.
It was a sick way to deflect from my own inexcusable actions.
I truly believe that good things come to those who work hard
and play fair—that means you, Star. I know we won't see
each other much anymore (I've been reassigned to Tucson),
but I hope a bit of your infectious, artistic energy has rubbed
off on me. You are an incredibly gifted woman and I know
you will become the strong Latina artist you were meant to
be. Best of luck with your art show. I know it will be a
success. Everything you touch turns to gold—no, make that
glitter.*

As you always say, "Peace out!"
Chloe

Setting the note aside, she began a second for Ofie.

Dearest Ofie,

*I'm sitting at my kitchen table, tears streaming down my
face, crying like a crazy woman. I wish I had the guts to call
and apologize for my behavior at La Pachanga. By no means
did you deserve such a fierce confrontation. Every week you
graciously open your lovely home to me and stretch yourself to
the limit to make sure I'm comfortable and happy. I've never
had anyone do that for me, and I probably never will again.
I'm cringing right now thinking about the horrible things I
said. In fact, the minutes replay in my brain and it feels like
I'm floating in the air, looking down at my body and I can't
believe the ugly, hateful person I see below. I don't want to be
that person anymore. I want to be like you, Ofie. Someone
who sees beauty in imperfection. You have a beautiful family
that loves you very much, and that is the sign of a truly classy
and successful woman. We all have so much to learn from*

*you. I hope someday you can find it in your heart to forgive
me and we can be friends again.*
    Blessings to you and yours,
    Chloe

*I never thought I'd say this, but I really do miss your iced
mochas!*

She sealed and addressed them, then went back to packing.
She boxed up all of Ezra's remnants and left them on the curb
for bulk trash collection. She gathered her luggage, her sunglasses, iPod, but not her cell phone, turned off the lights, locked
up, and left for the airport. On the way out, she would mail the
letters.

And that would mark the end of Crafty Chloe.

FRIDAY, NOVEMBER 5TH
DEBUT EXHIBIT
·L·O·V·E· ·S·H·R·I·N·E·S·
VISUAL STORIES OF PASSION

**As presented by
Estrella Feliz Esteban**

Inspired by Ofelia Fuentes

25

"Well, that's it. The last one. What do you think?" Star asked her dad right after she hung the final art piece in La Pachanga's gallery space. At last, the morning of her debut art exhibit had arrived, and she couldn't be more prepared. She rubbed her eyes, which stung from working through the night to paint the walls bright orange and barn red and apply a sheen of pink glitter glaze over all of them.

"M'ija, they are beautiful. *You* are beautiful," Al replied, scratching his chest over his Reggae Sunsplash T-shirt and stepping back to absorb the entire collection in one view. "Last month you were in a panic to find your niche and here we have twenty-four intricate creations. I am impressed."

"Thank you," Star said, as she curtsied. No drug in the universe could make her feel as high as she did right now. And to think she had made the multidimensional pieces in less than two weeks.

Al clasped his hands behind his back and leaned his head to the side. "So why'd you go with love shrines instead of Día de los Muertos? Something going on with Harrison that you want to share?"

Star, wearing overalls splattered with paint, hopped on a tall teal barstool trimmed in yellow fringe and inhaled the scent of pork and beef chorizo that was being prepared in the kitchen. That meant it was almost seven a.m. and the usual breakfast crowd would be arriving any minute. As her stomach growled it dawned on her that she hadn't eaten since lunch yesterday. She also realized how much she missed working at her family's business.

"Earth to Estrella," Al said, clapping his hands twice in front of her face.

"Sorry...My love shrines aren't *that* kind of love, Dad. They are about *universal* love. And friendship. The things that make us happy and give us the 'love shine,' like mom always says. When our craft group busted up is when this show was conceived. That night I cried so hard for Ofie. I felt so crappy for the way I'd judged her because I thought crafty stuff was cheap and senseless. I couldn't sleep, so I went to Mom's craft room to try and make something. Next thing I knew, I was playing with her paper punches, working her sewing machine, testing all her glues, and I think I went through, like, fifty pounds of glitter! I made Ofie another friendship shrine, and then one for Chloe and Benecio too. From there, I thought about all the things and people I love. I had a revelation. All these years, I put myself in this rigid box thinking that to be an artist you have to have a serious message. I wouldn't allow myself to create until I thought I had a worthy statement, when all along I did—we all do, it's love!"

Al strolled along the gallery walls, inspecting each love shrine and taking in his daughter's spontaneous dissertation.

"Making these love shrines," she continued, "has taught me that art is about transferring something you are passionate about into something for the senses. That's it, plain and simple. As soon as I let go of my stigma about crafts, the creativity rushed in. I hope Mom knows I'm going to take over her craft room."

Al laughed as he pictured mother and daughter in a tug-of-war over a glue gun. "My daughter is finally a true artist."

"No, I'm not. I'm just Star Esteban, who had to cram for this show. The real artist is Ofie. She's made hundreds of one-of-a-kind pieces and no one appreciated them. Who knows if she will ever make anything again? I wish I'd had my epiphany sooner. I can't change the past so that's why I dedicated this show to her, to let the world know she inspired me. I'm also donating half of tonight's proceeds to Fresh Start Women's Foundation in her honor. Who knows, maybe I'll teach workshops there!"

"Even better, maybe you can empower them to make their own love shrine," he recommended. Dad could always top an idea.

"I wish Ofie, Chloe, and Benecio would come tonight." Star sighed.

"You know Chloe is out of touch, Benecio said he'd come, and Ofie is home with Anjelica. Poor kid has the flu," Al said.

Star slumped on the barstool, propped her arms up on her knees, and rested her head in her hands. "I think Ofie is making up Anjelica's flu just to avoid me."

Al didn't want to see his girl sink back into sadness. He quickly changed the subject. "So, did you make one of these for Harrison?"

"Of course!" she said, trying to pep herself up for her dad's sake if not for her own. She pointed across the room to a fireman's hard hat. "I made it inside his old helmet. It's lined with gravel from the parking lot at George & Dragon. But this shrine is not like the one I made for Theo. I was living on another planet back then. This one is cute and light. Not so desperate."

Al strolled over to the art piece and chuckled. "You are something else, Estrella. Very creative. But tell me honestly, are you and Harrison getting serious?"

Star batted her eyes. "I wouldn't say serious, but we are hanging out more. He's cool. He doesn't overanalyze every move I make. At least *he's* coming tonight. He doesn't know anything about Día de los Muertos, so I'm going to be his personal tour guide."

"Sounds like you have it all under control. How are the centerpieces coming along?"

Star gulped. The centerpieces did not fall in the "under control" category. Since the group's demise, neither Ofie, Chloe, nor Star had spoken to one another. She had received a nice letter from Chloe, but when Star tried to call, all she got was an outdated message. And Star called Larry every day to check on Ofie, but he had asked Star not to visit just yet. Regardless, she sent each member of the group an invite anyway and prayed they would come. Not for the sake of the CraftOlympics, but because she missed them. Thank God at least Benecio stayed in contact, bless his little handbag-making heart.

Just as Star opened her mouth to explain that she and Benecio would handle it, she saw her mother enter the gallery.

"For you, Star!" Dori said, presenting her daughter with a lush bouquet of long-stemmed red roses. "They were sitting outside our front door this morning!"

Star jumped off the barstool and her dad followed. Roses always helped a girl regain her energy. She closed her eyes and inserted her face into the flowers to let the soft petals skim her cheeks. "Read the card, Dad! Read the card!"

Al opened the envelope, pulled out a little cream-colored card with scalloped edges, and read it aloud.

"To Estrella Feliz—my favorite happy star. Congratulations on your show. I never had a doubt."

"See what I mean, Dad? About Harrison?" she said, now holding a rose between her teeth and twirling about the floor.

Al flicked the card with his finger. "They're not from Harrison. They're from Theo."

26

La Pachanga always delivered the biggest Día de los Muertos celebration in the state with week-long festivities. Each year, more than ten thousand people filtered through the plaza, restaurant, gallery, and bakery throughout the grand finale three-day weekend. Busloads of educational tours, art collectors, and families arrived all throughout the weekend, beginning that Friday afternoon. Al and Dori always opened the fiesta with a blessing from Father O'Grady from the Sacred Heart church, and closed on Sunday at dusk with a community candlelight vigil.

Most of the crowd consisted of chicos and chicas who came to scarf carne asada burritos, flirt, and shoot the breeze with their homies. They hung out all day for a variety of activities: to contribute to the community Day of the Dead altar that Star assembled, to watch the Aztec dance performers, to decorate sugar skulls with icing, and to party the night away to the house band, Las Feministas.

The community recognized Star as the pretty daughter of the owners who orchestrated the entire event in past years, but not this weekend. This year her only contribution was her collection of hand-crafted love shrines on display in La Pachanga's gallery.

Star's heart quickened when she saw the KPDM-13 news van pull into the media cove. It would be nice if a miracle happened and Chloe showed up to report live from the event. Holding her breath, she watched as a different reporter climbed out of the vehicle, amazed at the amount of attendees. No miracles tonight.

"Well, hello there, la fina artista," Harrison said as he stood behind Star and placed his hands on her shoulders. She loved that Harrison was trying to learn Spanish, even if his progress was slow. The handsome couple stood on the sidewalk in front of La Pachanga's entrance doors. The sun had just set, which triggered a crisp and chilly November evening.

Star led Harrison into the gallery to see her work, and before they entered, a little girl no older than ten stopped them. She hopped up and down with excitement, and smiled up at Star. "Your picture boxes are supercool. Did you make them all by yourself?"

Star bent over and offered her hand for a shake. The girl stared at it, entranced by Star's clunky junk drawer charm bracelet and the multiple rings on her fingers. "Hi! Thank you for liking them. And yes, I sure did, all by myself in my mom's craft room at home."

"Will you show me how to make one?" the girl asked.

"Sure, I'd love to!" Star stood up, put her arm around the child, and invited her mother and father to leave their contact information with Minnie at La Pachanga's front counter. "If you can bring her some afternoon, I'd be glad to teach her," Star said.

"We really appreciate that. We just purchased two of your pieces," the girl's father said. "*El Perrito* and that big one inside the heart box, I think it is called..."

"*La Chica Tormenta*!" Star blurted, thrilled that they actually spent their hard-earned money on her artwork. "I personally wood-burned all those phrases around the outside of it. My arm is still sore!"

"Well, we love it. You have such a flair for combining colors and textures. Who would have thought to paint on sandpaper? And the crystals—it must have taken forever to put them all over those edges," said the mom. "And your themes are so humorous, but warm too. We're going to hang these boxes in our entryway. Good luck with the show, and thank you for keeping the prices affordable. Also—I *adore* your dress; it really suits your style."

Star thanked her with an embrace and took the compliment as good luck. She had meticulously prepared her clothing ensemble for her debut show. Choosing what to wear turned out to be more difficult than creating the shrines. Her first plan involved a slinky slip dress in honor of Elizabeth Taylor in *Cat on a Hot Tin Roof.* But then Star remembered the fiesta was more of a cultural family event, so she thought about wearing a teal Eastern Indian beaded tunic over a matching pencil skirt. Fifteen minutes before she left for the show, Star ripped off the pieces and settled on what she really wanted to wear in the first place: a sleeveless crimson linen cocktail dress, offset with a shimmery olive-green cashmere wrap around her arms. As with all her ensembles, the dress perfectly accentuated her hourglass figure and had that colorful boho spirit. She positioned a red rose behind her ear, dusted fairy glitter on her eyelids, and slipped on zebra-striped pointy heels that added that final zingy Star Esteban detail. She then clipped on a set of vintage Mayan-inspired silver medallions that were embedded with chunks of coral.

Star and Harrison entered the gallery room and traded "do-you-see-what-I-see?" head tilts. Dozens of men, women, teens, college students, and kids wandered about the space to admire her love shrines. To the left of the room, Star thought she saw Benecio. She stood on her tippy toes, propped her hand across her forehead like a seaman, and searched the gallery.

Margot, a server, stepped in their way. "Hi, Star. Would you like some *star* fruit?" she asked, holding a beautiful spread of the fruity treats.

Star let out a big "Awwwww!" and rubbed Harrison's arm in excitement.

"This is so sweet! Whose idea was this?" Star asked while lifting a toothpick and poking it into a slice.

"His," Margot said, raising her chin to where Benecio stood.

"...And now...if you will step over here, please, this piece is called *Las Craftistas Amigas* and it is *not* for sale because it is priceless. Star was going through great strife in her life with her personal friendships, and used that tragic sorrow as a catalyst for—*oh!* Look, people!" Benecio announced with a broad, toothy smile while waving his arm in Star's direction. "It's Star—the woman of the evening! She's here!"

Before Star could speak, the crowd rushed in to take turns meeting her and asking about her decorated assemblage art pieces.

An hour later, the gallery gawkers were still going strong. They lingered at each art piece, dissected the components, discussed the titles, and made their conclusion of the artist's motivation. Star tuned in to as many conversations as possible, awed that strangers would devote so much attention to her creations. At one point, all the talking made her throat dry so she and Harrison snuck away for a fresh air break. They went outside to the main plaza area of La Pachanga and marveled at the twinkling white lights that Al had strung between the main rows of the vendor booths. The couple sipped on icy margaritas and toured the attractions of the fiesta. On behalf of her parents and La Pachanga, Star stopped to personally thank each vendor for taking part in the event. Harrison moved aside so a skeleton stilt walker could pass.

"So, tell me more about Dee-ya Day Los Mare-toes," Harrison said in the cutest white-boy dialect. She smiled lovingly and faced him.

"First, repeat after me: El. Día. De. Los. Muertos... It means Day of the Dead. It's a three-thousand-year-old Mexican holiday. It's when we honor our loved ones who have passed away. It's believed the spirits return home for one night, and their families prepare for the visit by building altars with yummy scents and foods they liked while they were alive."

"But why are there so many skeletons? For Halloween?" he asked.

"No, no, no... ," Star said. She hated when people connected the two traditions. "It has nothing to do with Halloween. The skeletons represent death, but not in a frightening way. They are happy because they get to hang out with their friends and family again. You will *never* see a scary skeleton when it comes to Día de Los Muertos. Remember that. It's all about embracing the cycle of life and honoring our ancestors and loved ones who have died."

He sighed hard and bowed his head. "Cool. Makes me think of a couple buddies our unit lost last year. Real good guys."

"We're going to light a candle for them. Follow me." She slipped her arm through his and led him through the crowd to the main ofrenda, a shrine she built in honor of both sets of her grandparents, Nana and Tata Esteban and Nana and Tata Ortega. Before they reached the altar, Harrison turned her around and tugged her close. She felt the roughness of his skin against hers when he slid his palm behind her neck and planted a tender kiss on her matte cherry-red lips. He then leaned back and held her chin in his hands.

"This friend shtick is killing me. What does it take for a guy to get an official date around here?"

Star cupped her hands around his. "Name the time and place."

27

Five art booths away from the La Pachanga community Day of the Dead altar, Theo witnessed Harrison plant a kiss on Star's lips. Seeing her with another man made his veins swell. Theo may have lived in an affluent area for the past ten years and had graduated at the top of his class, but this brought out his inner homeboy from when he grew up in Los Cuatro Milpas, a sleepy little barrio just south of downtown Phoenix.

Star's life had changed dramatically in the past few months, and so had his. But not for the better. True, his popularity increased tenfold after the mural incident in August. It introduced a gaggle of new customers, including a well-known Santa Fe art rep, and Theo's client list doubled again since his presence at Sangria.

But none of it sparked his spirit. The euphoria of playing with paint, grout, clay, and glass used to be inspired by his muse, Star. Now his efforts were nothing more than perfected-yet-uninspired techniques delivered in made-to-order pieces for corporate clients and wealthy collectors. He mustered through his projects solely to collect the paychecks that rolled in fat and often. He hankered for Star, and regretted fibbing about the Santa Fe relocation. The offer had just been made the day he bumped into her at George & Dragon. Theo's announcement fell out of his mouth, when he hadn't even made the decision.

He had a deadline of November 8th to answer, three days away. If he accepted, he'd join a roster of nationally celebrated artists. Before he decided, he wanted to discuss it with Star, make amends, and start all over. This time on a serious level. If she agreed, he would stay in Phoenix and grow a life with her any way she pleased.

But seeing her in the moment—happy, gorgeous, successful, and on the arm of another man—he wondered if he had done her a favor. Maybe for the past three years, *he* had held *her* back, rather than the other way around.

Stacey, a longtime La Pachanga waitress, wandered by with a tray of Coronas and Hornitos shots.

"Hey, Theo, Mr. Big-Time Gallery Superstar, what's up?" she said loud enough to be heard over the strolling mariachis. "Where've you been hiding out?"

He drew out a few bills from the front pocket of his slacks and dropped them on her tray. "Two shots, one cerveza, please," he said as he grabbed a folding wood chair and sat on it backward. He downed the first shot, sucked a lemon wedge, let out a dry cough, grabbed the beer, and chugged it. "How are those love shrines going over?"

"Great. It's barely after nine and I heard they've all sold. We're all so dang happy for Star. What a turnaround, wouldn't you say? Who knew she had so much talent? Those assemblage thingies are wicked slick."

"I'm not surprised at all," he slurred.

"The cheapest one is two hundred and fifty dollars and the highest was over a grand. And she is donating half the proceeds to charity."

Theo slurped another mouthful of tequila and downed a chaser beer in one uninterrupted motion. "Uno mas."

"Here, it's on the house," she said, plucking the last shot from her tray. "Hey, don't you have a show in Scottsdale tonight? Star told all of us to go check it out and cheer you on."

"I'm not going. There's nothing worthy to see anyway..." He downed the sauce without lemon or salt, began to sway, and blathered on about his last show at Sangria.

Stacey snuck away in search of Al so he could tend to the guy, but Star arrived first. When she saw Theo from where she stood with Harrison, she immediately grabbed her iPhone and texted Theo's cousin, Victor, who lived in the neighborhood. Then she marched over to Theo.

"Theo, you're a mess. You know better than to go past three shots! Come sit down inside. You need to eat."

He tried to straighten himself up, but staggered instead. He overadjusted the invisible tie around his neck, licked his hand, and sloppily smoothed the front of his grown-out hair. His glassy eyes fluttered. "Estrella...you are like a refreshing, soothing, frosty, savory, delicious soda pop in the desert...and I'm Mr. Thirsty!" He stepped forward and reached his arms out to hug her like old times, but Harrison stepped in.

"Let me help you out there, buddy. Grab my arm...steady now...," he said as he gripped Theo's wrists.

"No." Theo retracted his hands from Harrison's and thrashed them about. "I don't want you. I want *her*!" and he pointed to Star. "*Her!* Right there. Let me have her...*please*...let me have her..."

Harrison neared Star, as if to protect her. Bewildered beyond belief, Star didn't know what to do. She had never seen Theo this wasted. Her initial instinct was to leave the party, take him home, and sober him up.

She placed her hand gently on Harrison's shoulder. "He's a good friend. I can handle this on my own...," she said.

Al entered the scene and motioned for Star to stand back. "He's a grown man. Let him be."

Theo smiled at Star, and fell to one knee. He slapped his hand over his heart and with all his soul, belted out Lola Beltran's Mexican angsty love ballad, "Paloma Negra."

"*Ya...me canso...de llorar...y no amanece...*"

The mariachis, who had paused for the commotion, now followed Theo's drunken, wailing cue and began to accompany him. Theo's head tottered as he went on with the powerful tear-jerker of a song. A small crowd gathered and laughed with endearment, including Theo's cousins Frank and Victor, who had just arrived. When the sodden solo concluded, the audience clapped as Theo's cousins bowed for him and then carried him off to the car, heckling him all the way.

"Let me guess," Harrison said to Star. "Former flame?"

Larry had two habits when nervous: tapping the wedding ring on his finger against any surface hard enough to make an annoying noise and bouncing his leg up and down on the ball of his foot. He did both while at his work desk, holding the handset, waiting for Ofie to answer the phone at home. He had the most frightening, exciting, urgent news to share, but couldn't unless she lifted the receiver.

His wife's breakthrough had only been recent, but the rise in her confidence rivaled years of counseling sessions. Together with Anjelica, they invaded the house one room at a time and pitched everything, except the furniture and window coverings. Ofie collected all her handmade horrors, dumped them in U-Haul boxes, and dropped them off at Goodwill. Just yesterday the Fuentes family chose a light beige paint to christen the walls of their newly unblemished house. To all of them, the empty abode signified a clean slate.

However, Ofie's crochet addiction fascinated Larry. For all practical purposes, that shouldn't have been the case. He couldn't tell the difference between one yarn and the next, but he knew that his wife was on to something big. Big as in *The Guinness Book of World Records* big!

Expect a Miracle

Earlier that day, he had Googled "speed crochet" and discovered it was an actual term for a subculture of those like Ofie, who were the Dale Earnhardt Jr.'s of the craft scene. Not only that, but there was one site that advertised a Speed Crochet race at the upcoming CraftOlympics—the same one that Ofie and Star were making those centerpieces for. From what he witnessed, Ofie could smoke the competition. Larry thought of this and his heart raced as he attempted another call home.

But Ofie couldn't answer at the moment because she was busy with another call.

"Mrs. Fuentes? This is Nurse Cannarella from Cactus Runner Elementary. Your daughter is ill with a sour stomach. She's fine, but needs to skip after-school dance class today."

Ofie pointed her finger to the mobile handset, as if the nurse could see her. "So help me, if it's Turkey Chunk Pie day, we're suing," she mumbled as she darted to the laundry room to put a new load in the washer and dryer. Since leaving her crafts in the dust, Ofie had become a whole new woman—a domestic diva in training who saved her passion for yarn for after her family went to sleep.

She shoved her blanket supplies in her tote, stumbled into her fuzzy slippers, grabbed her keys, and bolted for the garage. The phone rang again. Ofie screeched to a halt, turned, and slid across the kitchen floor for the cordless handset. It was Larry and he was in a panic.

"Honey, it's me, where have you been?"

"Sorry! I'm on my way out the door to get Anjelica. She's sick with a sour stomach. Can it wait?"

"A sour stomach at school? It better not be Turkey Chunk Pie day again!" Larry threatened. "Anyway, mi amor, listen: I Googled speed crochet."

"Speed crochet?" Ofie asked, confused. "Is that a drug?"

"It's for people who crochet lightning fast, like you. There's a contest at the CraftOlympics thing. You should try it."

Ofie dismissed the idea. "Please don't remind me about that. It's still a raw spot in my heart. Oh! Your mom sent me another bouquet of gladiolas and another apology letter. She's been so nice to me since all of this."

"I'm not done, mujer! Hush for a second, please," he said, raising his voice. "The grand prize is free yarn for a year, a national TV spot—AND a free room makeover from one of those fancy HGTV shows!"

Ofie took a deep breath.

"Ofie? You there, sweetie?"

"I can't do it. I've given up crafts and I'm sure as heck not going to the CraftOlympics after all that's happened. What if Star or Chloe are there without me? I won't be able to handle that, Larry, I won't."

"We'll go with you." Larry paused, then spoke his next words in a gentle tone. "It's up to you, mi amor. You have a talent and you belong in that contest. I believe in you."

Tears filled Ofie's large brown eyes. "What if I'm really not as good as you think and I get crushed up there? I thought you, of all people, wanted to keep me away from that."

"I can't explain it, but I feel really good about this. Besides...if I'm right, we'd score new furniture."

Ofie began to laugh along with her husband. "Okay. I'm game. If I lose, be ready to pay for a lifetime of therapy!"

29

After picking up Anjelica from the nurse's office, Ofie reached over from the driver's side to feel her daughter's forehead, which was cool. "Honey, do you feel well enough for Mommy to make a quick stop at Maker's Marketplace? If you don't, I won't be upset."

"Maker's Marketplace? I thought you didn't like that place anymore."

As Ofie explained the contest to Anjelica, the clock on the dark blue dashboard screamed 3:22 p.m. Maker's Marketplace closed at four. Larry had mentioned final applications were due by then.

"Right on, Mom. Let's do it," Anjelica replied with a sweet but crooked smile.

"Thank you, sweetie. Whatever is meant to be, I won't be sad if we don't make it in time, but at least we can try," Ofie said, smiling back at her daughter. "Oh sniveling snickerdoodles! We don't have much time!" The store was thirty miles away, so Ofie made an executive decision to fly down the Loop 202 freeway for a shortcut across town.

Wrong idea. There would be no flying. More like crawling. Major construction blocked all but one lane.

"Oh, darn!" Ofie said as the car glided down the on ramp.

A road worker waved a flag in front of her to move to the far right.

"Crap!" Ofie said sharply when she learned the next few exits were closed. The Craftmobile was stuck in place as the traffic trickled forward as fast as the last drop of glue from an empty bottle.

"Pray, Anjelica!" she ordered her daughter. Ofie envisioned herself waving the trophy over her head, just like Cha Cha DiGregorio in *Grease*, when she won the dance-off with Danny Zuko. Ofie wanted this bad. No. She *needed* this.

She honked the horn three times as tears began to fall from her eyes. "Damn it, why now? Can't anything nice happen for me? Can someone up there give a lady a break?"

Ofie smacked the steering wheel with her fist. They were trapped in bumper-to-bumper gridlock, and now the gas light lit up.

"Are you praying, sweetie?" she asked, whipping her head around every which way for an escape.

"I am, Mom! Ew, my stomach is gurgling again."

Three thirty-five. The Craftmobile finally reached an open exit, but now Ofie was faced with another dilemma: Pull over to get gas, and eat up five minutes, or take a chance and go directly to Maker's Marketplace. Ofie chose to skip the gas station, because Maker's Marketplace was so close. But if they ran out beforehand, that would be it.

"Shit! We're not gonna make it. We're gonna run out of gas. And my damn cell phone is out of juice, too. You're sure you're praying, Anjelica?" she asked.

"I'm trying!" Anjelica said, clenching her hands together under her chin. "But every time I start, you swear and I have to start all over!"

Ofie smacked her own head with her palm and relaxed her back. "I'm so sorry. You're sick. I should take you home. I need to be a good mother." She chanted her recent mantra: "Family before crafts. Family before crafts. Family before crafts."

"I'm fine! Please! Just keep driving. I see the sign right there!" Anjelica begged, pointing across the street.

"Swear on your new unpainted Skechers not to tell Nana Chata about this!"

"I won't, Mom! Just hurry!"

They swerved into Maker's Marketplace's parking lot like Starsky and Hutch and ran inside. There, at the main cash register, stood a long line of eager customers, all holding numbers to submit their contest applications for the convention.

Ofie sighed and took her place at the end of the queue that weaved around three marker posts. *This is a sign. I shouldn't be here*, she thought. *What would Nana Chata think? She'd take back her apology and curse me to Davy Jones' locker. Lord, give me a sign…*

Ofie took a look-see at Anjelica, whose face appeared paler than the neutral paint they had just bought for the house. "Sweetie, let's go home. You're sick. This is selfish of me. I refuse to travel down this path again."

"I can take some of you over here," offered a clerk with bright purple streaks in her hair, wearing a Maker's Marketplace golf shirt.

Anjelica ignored her comments and pointed to the new line. "I'm okay. I've seen you crochet. Dad's right. I want you to win so I can keep the trophy in my room. Do it for me, Mom!"

They shifted into the next lane, right behind a burly woman in a navy blue sweater covered in white pet hair. A greasy gray bun sat atop her plump head. She could have passed for an elderly sumo wrestler. And she smelled foul and fried, like she'd she just emerged from working the grill at a hamburger joint.

Anjelica motioned her index finger for her mom to come close. "Scary lady!" Anjelica whispered.

"*Very* scary lady," Ofie giggled back.

Scary Lady turned around, one bushy eyebrow arched like a comic book villain. Her face revealed a road map of moles, half of which sprouted coarse black and gray whiskers. She glared and then sucked her teeth when she saw the crochet hook and entry form protruding from Ofie's tote.

"Well, well, well. You again. The stealin' señorita," said Scary Lady.

"Huh?" Ofie and Anjelica asked in unison. "I would never steal anything!"

"You—the one who tried to swipe my new lawn chairs last summer. In broad daylight, right from my driveway! Thief!"

"Oh. Those... I thought they were bulk trash," Ofie said as she recalled that afternoon. That was the same day she met Chloe at La Pachanga. A wave of sadness swept over her. She yearned for her craftistas, and wanted more than anything to tell them all about her new talent. Would they ever speak again? Ofie hoped so, but didn't have the courage to break the ice.

"So now you wanna be a crochet champion? Don't you have a quinceañera dress to sew for your little muchacha there?" Scary Lady said with a sneer as she adjusted the heavy, stained canvas bag that hung across her torso.

"My husband and daughter seem to think I'm pretty fast. But I have a long way to go," Ofie joked nervously. Treat others as you want to be treated is what she always preached to Anjelica.

"I'm old school," Scary Lady announced. "Disciplined. Have you heard of those weirdoes out there these days? Knittin' and crochetin' bikinis and lingerie? I'd never wear one. Disgrace. Takes the class right out of it. What is this world coming to?"

"I think that's kinda cool," Ofie muttered under her breath as she crouched down to tie Anjelica's shoe. She squirmed when she saw Scary Lady's ashy cracked heels resting inside a stinky pair of Birkenstocks that, by the look of them, should have been incinerated years ago.

"What's yer SPM anyway? I'm at thirty-five DC's. I'm sure I'm the fastest in the state. I won second place last year at the CO. Lost to a freaky punk-rock girl from Japan. She's a thirty-six. But I got great publicity out of it. I was on local TV and got six months' worth of free yarn from the Cat's Meow Yarn Company. I was supposed to be pictured in their new brochure, but for some reason they changed plans."

"Oh, that's too bad," Ofie said as she scooted back to feel Anjelica's forehead again.

"So? What *is* it?" Scary Lady asked. "What is yer SPM?"

"I don't know what that is," Ofie confessed.

"Stitches per minute!"

Ofie found this woman to be arrogant and snooty, but for Anjelica's sake, she retained a sense of politeness. "I'm not familiar with the jargon, but I only learned how to crochet a couple weeks ago, and I've finished a few dozen blankets since then."

"And she only crochets at night!" Anjelica snapped, with a "take that" attitude.

Scary Lady roared with laughter, and the others in line turned to see. "Did you hear that, everyone? She made a few dozen blankets in two weeks. Give this lady a ribbon!" She jabbed her hands on her hips and stuck her face in Ofie's.

"What kind of yarn and what kind of stitches we talkin' about?"

Ofie backed away from Scary Lady's bad breath. "The regular stuff, but when I run out, I use kite string and twine. I only know the double stitch—is that what it's called?"

"Goody-goody for you. Don't mean to offend, but you may as

well get your lumpy jalapeño rump outta here, because I'm gettin' that Numero Uno spot this time at the CO."

"CO?" Ofie asked, again unfamiliar with her lingo.

"The CraftOlympics! Ding-dong, anyone home? I ain't losin' to no Japanese girl with pigtails and I sure as heck ain't losin' to a one-stitch newbie. Just some words of advice to save you some dough: This ain't your place."

Ofie had never been the type to fight back, but obviously this bully felt threatened, and that was a thick enough thread of pride for Ofie to hang on to. Only two more people in line ahead of them and then she could take her baby home and pamper her.

"Ugh, Mom...I'm not feeling too good," Anjelica said, her eyelids drooping. "I think I have to throw up."

"Can we hurry up here? This kid's gonna lose her afternoon snack!" Scary Lady shrilled to the cashier.

Ofie grabbed Anjelica's hand. "Honey, come on, let's get out of here!" Ofie reached up on the tips of her toes to seek the easiest route, but before she spotted it, a chill shot up the back of her neck. She turned in slow motion, just in time to see Anjelica, who had two fingers over her lips and was shaking her head as if to say *Can't. Hold. It...*

Ofie covered her eyes right as Chunky Turkey Pie rained down in a waterfall of cubed meat, gravy, and canned vegetables. But it didn't hit the floor because Scary Lady's booty intercepted.

That was it. The sign Ofie needed. This was *not* meant to be, she thought, before hustling Anjelica out of line.

A salesclerk held back a gag and picked up the phone receiver at her station. "Cleanup at customer service, please! Urgent!"

The store manager dressed in jeans and a bright lime golf shirt busted out of his office with paper towels to assist Ofie with

Anjelica, and then escorted them to the bathroom to clean up. He invited Scary Lady too, but she refused to leave her space in line.

"Wow. I feel 100 percent better, Mom!" Anjelica beamed.

"Thank you so much for your kindness and generosity," Ofie said to the manager, hugging her daughter.

"Don't worry about it. We see you here all the time," the manager replied. "Did you have an application to submit for the CO? I'll be glad to process that for you."

Twenty minutes later, Ofie and Anjelica practically skipped out of the store. Ofie concluded she would pack a lunch for Anjelica on Chunky Turkey Pie day from now on. The two of them reached the Craftmobile, but were startled by a figure that stepped out in front of them.

"Hey, loca luchadora, think I'm not on to you?" It was Scary Lady. She had been waiting for them by the Craftmobile, which she must have remembered from the lawn chair incident.

"If you don't leave I'm calling the police," Ofie warned while she fished for her juiceless cell phone in her bag.

"Don't mess with us, lady. My mom will double stitch circles around you!" Anjelica snapped like an angry, territorial Chihuahua.

"Hey, little chicle, ask yer mamacita if she wants to throw down," Scary Lady taunted.

Ofie laughed. That crazy woman just called Anjelica a piece of gum.

The last of Maker's Marketplace's customers filtered out to the parking lot and gathered around the commotion. "Do you need help?" one of them offered to Ofie. "I'll get the manager!" another hollered before running inside.

Scary Lady whipped out a gold crochet hook from her bag. She gripped it in one hand, and her current project in the other, as if she had just whipped them out of hip holsters. "You and me. Let's have a race, right here, right now. It's for your own good, to see what you are up against. If you can crochet faster than me then you're worthy enough to be up on that stage at the competition."

Ofie unlocked the car door. "I don't have time for this. I don't care that much about the contest. You can have your silly trophy. I just wanted the room makeover."

Anjelica blocked her from getting in the Craftmobile. "Mommy! Come on! You can take her!" she encouraged, before turning to Scary Lady and sassily snapping her fingers in the shape of a Z. With the Chunky Turkey Pie now out of her system, Anjelica appeared to have made a full recovery. "We're on! Mom, get your hook and yarn! Show her what you're made of."

Ofie's hands trembled as she opened her bag and pulled out her one-and-only crochet hook and the purple variegated yarn attached to the blanket she had been working on. Was she being a good role model for her daughter right now? Or a bad one?

Then again, if this lady really had won other speed crochet races, and Ofie beat her, that would mean...

Ofie cleared her throat. She couldn't believe what she was about to say. "Double stitches only. Three rows. Last one to finish buys the other a full tank of gas across the street."

"You got it. Lady, I'm gonna smash you like a piñata."

They each let the ball of yarn drop to the asphalt and gripped their hooks and work-in-progress blankets in front of them.

"Uh...everything okay out here, ladies?" asked the store manager as he hustled up to the action. "Oh gosh, what do we have here?"

"It's a rumble, only with yarn," an onlooker blurted.

"Anyone have a phone with video? Record it!" said another bystander.

Before he could stop them, two other spectators blocked him. "Let them at it. This will be good," one of them proclaimed.

Little Anjelica took a giant step between the women and raised her skinny arms over her head, just like Cha Cha DiGregorio from *Grease* when the car race was about to start! She, like her mom, loved that movie.

"Ready!"

"Set!"

"Crochet!" Anjelica screamed as her arms slapped to her sides.

A gathering cheered and whistled, all for Ofie. It ended too fast, with the loser hissing and stomping.

Ofie and Anjelica made it home by six thirty. Larry sat at the kitchen table and had just cut into his Salisbury steak TV dinner. "It's about time, ladies, what's up?"

Anjelica ran across the room and threw her arms around her dad's neck. "Guess what, Dad? I threw up at the craft store, Mommy was in a crochet race, and we won a free tank of gas!"

From: BenecioAZ@cmail.com
To: craftersdelite@tox.net.com
Date: November 15, 2010
Subject: Please help!

hey, ofie!

miss u!! i hope u r feelin better. have u talked to NE1? i haven't. bummer our group split up ☹ hey, can u bring the centerpiece junk over 2 my house? no one else is gonna make them, so my mom said she would help me finish them cause they r due next monday and there are still 75 left 2 make. That's how I'm getting a free booth at the show. may b u can stay & hang out! i can finish showing u how to crochet! i still wear my necklace!

i heart you,

b

From: craftersdelite@tox.net.com
To: BenecioAZ@cmail.com
Date: November 15, 2010
Subject: Re: Please help!

Howdy, Benecio!!!!!
I REALLY miss you too!! When I saw your name on my
e-mail, it made me super happy. Anjelica, Nana Chata, and
I will come by this Saturday at 6 to help you and your mom
finish the centerpieces. I can't believe all the other chicas
bailed on this project. I didn't think they were like that.
If I were still talking to Star, I would scold her! Anyhoo,
see you Saturday. I have exciting news to tell you about
my crochet!
Love you!
Ofie

P.S. I'm so excited to see you again and also to meet
your parents (finally!). I'm glad you told them about the
group and your design project! Good for you for being
strong!
P.P.S. Nana Chata is here and she says she will bring
menudo for us!

From: BenecioAZ@cmail.com
To: EstrellaFeliz@lapachanga.com
Date: November 15, 2010
Subject: Please help!

hey star!
miss u!! i hope u r feelin better. have u talked to NE1? i
haven't. bummer our group split up ☹ hey, can u help me

finish the centerpieces? ofie came and dropped everything off. no one else is gonna make them, so my mom said she would help me finish them 'cause they r due next monday and there are still 75 left 2 make. that's how I'm getting a free booth at the show. may b u can stay & hang out! Can u come saturday at 6?

i heart u,

b

From: EstrellaFeliz@lapachanga.com
To: BenecioAZ@cmail.com
Date: November 15, 2010
Subject: Please help!

OH MY GOD!!! Benecio—I am so sorry I dropped the ball on this!! I swear I did not forget!! My mom was supposed to call Ofie and pick everything up so we could finish them this weekend at La Pachanga!! I didn't know you had everything over there!! I'll come and bring my mom, and we will crank them out in no time at all, even if I have to bring my sleeping bag!!! Kudos for coming clean with the parental units! See you Saturday at 6!!

Heart you back!! Peace out, my little man!
Star

P.S. Thank you again for all your help at my show. I loved the star fruit idea, so clever! Pick a place you want to go for lunch. My treat. ☺

From: BenecioAZ@cmail.com
To: chloechavez@aol.com
Date: November 15, 2010
Subject: Please help!

hey chloe!
miss u!! i hope u r feelin better. have u talked to NE1? i
haven't. bummer our group split up ☹ hey, can u help me
finish the centerpieces? Ofie came and dropped everything off. no one else is gonna make them, so my mom
said she would help me finish them 'cause they r due next
monday and there are still 75 left 2 make. that's how I'm
getting a free booth at the show. may b u can stay & hang
out! saturday at 6:00?
i heart u,
b

From: chloechavez@aol.com
To: BenecioAZ@cmail.com
Date: November 16, 2010
Subject: Please help!

I'll do anything to help you become the success you
deserve to be. I'll even give you tips of what NOT to do.
See you at 6 on Saturday. Send me directions to your
house (I'm dying to see it!).
xoxo,
Chloe

30

Benecio Javier Valencia II's parents were "officially" separated, "technically" married, and "conveniently" living together under the same roof.

It surely wasn't for their son's sake.

The power couple had met in junior high, dated in high school, and married right after college. Somewhere between the birth of their son and their first million, the couple made an unconscious decision to sacrifice love for financial success. Fourteen years later they had each invested equal amounts of sweat, equity, and cash in their entertainment agency. Neither would give it up for something as silly and costly as a divorce. Their most important employee had to be their live-in house manager, Alice. She tended to all domestic duties, which included caring for Benecio. He could do without his parents' attention; he fended for himself in every way. The junior designer's checklist included two things: Acquire the necessary high school diploma; move to New York City and attend Parsons School of Design. But first, he had to survive this excruciating requirement called adolescence.

Benecio and Alice dragged the living room couches into the game room and set up three six-foot-long buffet tables. When the doorbell rang at six sharp, Benecio devilishly slunk across the marble tile to the front door. His sneaky scheme had clicked into action!

When Benecio learned his parents would be in New York this weekend at a social-networking conference, he used the opportunity as a way to reunite the group. Alice helped him streamline a plan.

When he'd met the women for the first time—*forget it*! Star reminded him of those frustrated emo chicks in art class who drew on their arms; Ofie could have passed for a deranged kindergarten teacher, and Chloe may as well have been the stuck-up student-body president. He didn't think he'd ever wind up needing them like he did. They became his absentee parents, filling the space in his life that his selfish mom and dad did not. Benecio would deny it to his grave, but ever since the group busted up, he often wept himself to sleep from loneliness. No one at school related to him. All the other kids were into partying, sports, or studying. Not obsessed with fashion and accessory design like he was. If Star, Ofie, and Chloe were too bigheaded to make up on their own, he would be the one to bring them together. He missed them more than he missed his sewing machine when it broke last summer. This nonsense had to stop, if anything, at least for the centerpieces and his free pass into the CraftOlympics.

"You came!" Benecio sang out as soon as he saw Ofie's and Anjelica's smiles across the threshold.

Ofie planted a wet mommy kiss on his cheek. "Benecio! M'ijo, your house is…*gorgeous; it's like a *mansion*!" she said as she lugged in a heavy box of centerpiece supplies and marveled at the bronze mosaic water fountain in the center of the foyer.

"Your parental units certainly do have pimpin' style, B," Anjelica broadcasted as she scratched at the textured faux-finished wall with her finger.

"So, where are your parents?" echoed Ofie's voice from the other room.

"Gone until Monday night because—" Benecio began to explain, but Nana Chata's boisterous entrance cut him off. She busted in with an industrial-sized soup pot.

"Move your nalgas, people! Menudo patrol coming through…Which way to la cocina fina?" she demanded as she hunted down the kitchen. He would have helped Nana Chata, but just then another guest arrived. Make that *two* guests.

"What the hell is going on, Benecio? I thought you said everyone bailed on you?" Chloe said, gripping the strap of her black messenger bag so tightly, the whites of her knuckles showed.

Benecio had never seen her make such a blah entrance. The Chloe Chavez he knew never left the house without camera-ready foundation, lashes, perfectly teased hair at the crown of her head, and a ridiculously expensive outfit that she modeled as if she were on a catwalk. But here she stood with limp hair, in a faded brown peasant skirt, ballet flats, and a tiny tank covered by a baggy denim jacket.

Feeling no regret for his ploy, Benecio clenched his sweaty fists inside the pockets of his Ecko jeans and hoped she would stay and forgive him for his white lie.

"That little cabron set us up!" Star exclaimed, whipping off her crisp black navy pea coat and examining the olive and tan painted palace. Her mother followed close behind. Star walked up to Benecio and kissed his cheek. "And I'm glad he did!"

One of the elements Benecio missed about Star's personality was her crazy sense of style. He forgot how much he anticipated her arrivals so he could soak up her genius clothing concoctions. Tonight she seemed more radiant than usual in black velvet flats, black leggings that ended just above her ankles, a red-and-teal-striped satin fitted top, chunky gold hoop earrings, and a knitted skull cap over her long black curls. Even Ofie had spent time on her outfit. Instead of her usual jeans and Ed Hardy knockoff T-shirt combo, she wore a bright red cotton dress, which brightened up her face. Aside from Chloe, everyone appeared happy and healthy.

Benecio held his breath as Ofie came back into the room to find Chloe and Star standing next to each other, but not speaking. Benecio wondered who would drop the first word and what it would be.

"Thanks for the letter," Star said to Chloe.

Ofie cleared her throat and tilted her head. "Thank you for my letter, too, Chloe."

To give them privacy, Dori guided Anjelica into the kitchen to help Nana Chata chop the lemon, green onion, and cilantro for the menudo.

Chloe clenched her purse strap tighter and glowered up at the vaulted ceiling. The emotions were too strong and she couldn't hold back her tears. "I apologize that I lied. I didn't mean for things to go down the way they did." She lowered her gaze to the cream-colored floor and went on. "Seeing there is plenty of help here, I'm taking off. Just so you know, today was my last day with Hadwick. I'm done with TV. I quit. I'm moving back to L.A. and getting my real estate license. My loft goes up for sale next week. As soon as it sells, I'm gone. Best of luck to you and the CraftOlympics. Thank you for being so kind to me." She turned to exit as Star, Ofie, and Benecio gawked and mouthed "No way!"

Ofie stepped into Chloe's path. "L.A.? Why? You're not going back with him, are you? The guy you ditched at the altar?" she asked in a stern, maternal tone. "Please tell me no, Chloe. We all know you're too smart for that. You don't love him. If you go back, this time you'll be lying to yourself!"

Chloe closed her eyes and stepped around Ofie toward the

front door. "It's for the best. I'm done here. I have to break ground on my new life, and he'll give me a good head start. We've been talking every night by phone. He doesn't seem like so much of a jerk anymore. And considering I've been nothing but a liar, a bitch, and a thief these past few years, I should be happy someone wants this mess."

Star leaped in the way and braced her arms against the sculpted molding so Chloe couldn't pass. "You are *so* not getting out of here, deary. When are you going to get it through your brain that you don't need *anyone* to give you a head start? You can do whatever you want, totally on your own!" Star put her hand on Chloe's cheek and wiped the tear that fell from her friend's eye.

"I can't." Chloe's voice cracked. She stared directly into Star's misty eyes. "I don't have it in me anymore."

Star wouldn't listen. "Like that silly quote Ofie told us on your birthday—you aimed high and missed. Big deal. You're not leaving. Not until you come and sit down with us and spill, so we can talk you out of it. You with me on this, Ofie?" Star asked.

Ofie agreed. In a split second she and Star embodied two New York City bouncers, and refused to let their friend pass. Ofie thrust her arm on Chloe's shoulder to block her from moving forward. "Chloe, didn't you hear about what happened at KPDM last week? Your boss was tossed out by his belt straps!"

"What?" asked Chloe. "No. I haven't been back to the station."

"Yah! Larry told me! That Frances girl didn't only bring you down; she ratted out that Mark Jefferies guy too. I guess after you left, he tried to pull the same horrible crap on her. He played both of you."

Chloe sniffled, and allowed a weary smirk to escape. She had a new-found respect for Frances. "Okay, in some sick, unexplainable way, that makes me feel a heck of a lot better." She paused. "I'll stay on one condition."

"What's that?" Star asked.

"You ladies have to tell me every detail of what you've done since I saw you last."

Star cocked her head side to side and broke into a broad smile. "I had my art show! It was a hit! I donated half the money to Fresh Start Women's Foundation."

"I know," Chloe said. "I snuck in when you weren't looking. I couldn't resist. I bought the one called *Starry Sunrise* to remind me that tomorrow is always a new opportunity to start all over."

Ofie chimed in next. "I was there on your opening night too, Star. Anjelica was sick, but I did sneak out to go peek. I laid low because I didn't want to distract you. I'm so proud of you; you did it! And thank you for the beautiful one you made for me, and for putting my name on the poster!"

Star put her fingers on her eyes to hold back happy tears.

"Ofie, did you see Theo sing?" Chloe laughed. "Star, how did he explain that?"

"He was stinking drunk! I called him the next day and he didn't even have the balls to call me back. I left it at that."

"Good for you, Star!" Ofie said. She rushed to her friends and threw her arms around them. Benecio joined in, then guided them into the living room–turned–centerpiece factory.

Bowls of glitter, bottles of paints, cups of brushes, scissors, paper plates, glue, and varnish were evenly spaced down the center of the long tables. To keep the night grooving, Benecio created a house-mix playlist of his favorite divas: Lady Gaga, Amy Winehouse, Britney Spears, Leona Lewis, Adele, Beyoncé, Christina Aguilera, Madonna, and Kanye.

It worked. Three hours later, production was in full swing. At the first table, Nana Chata prepped the supplies and picked off price stickers. Chloe painted each flowerpot with purple and red acrylics, and passed them off to Benecio, who varnished them, and then Alice stuffed in the floral foam. Star sat at the second table and covered each plastic prickly pear with glue, followed by a thick layer of glitter, which she poured on using a tablespoon. Ofie then carefully inserted the sparkling succulent into the foam. Dori added the final touch— moss—and set them on the last table to dry, while Anjelica inspected each one to ensure perfection.

Throughout the process, each craftista took turns sharing in-depth self-reflections about their upbringing, dysfunctional relationships, and lost loves. When those conversations ran dry, they shared ghost stories, went on to frightful hospital encounters, and then gossiped about coworkers (in Benecio and Anjelica's case, schoolmates). As they finished up the last five masterpieces, silence settled in the air.

Star was the first to speak up. "I have a confession. I have fallen in love with glitter. The more I use it, the more I want to go home and cover everything in it."

"Please don't," Dori countered, glaring over her polka-dot spectacles.

"Believe it or not, Star, but I'm the opposite," Ofie said. "Sitting here making all of these, I enjoy it, but it's the end of an era for me. I think I crafted a lifetime's worth of projects in a few short years."

Chloe swooshed a band of paint around the final planter and looked at it wishfully, as if it were a photo of a long-lost twin she'd never met. "This is going to sound really stupid coming from me," she said, lifting up the pot to her face. "But crafting is very relaxing. I should do this more often."

"Ha!" Star said. She crumpled up a paper towel and tossed it in Chloe's direction. "Well, you think, missy? After two years of teaching crafts on live TV every week, you've finally realized that?"

Chloe swatted the ball with her elbow and giggled. "Seriously, I like the feeling of getting lost in the process. It clears my head and allows my mind to wander, to fantasize. I never do that! It's very healing to cover a drab surface with color. Metaphorical. To think that I have the power to give a makeover, and all it takes is a paintbrush! No wonder crafting is so popular! It's a beautiful concept! It's...it's...*craftastic*!" She sat up tall and smiled proudly.

Not sure how else to react to their friend's eleventh-hour mindblowing revelation, everyone politely bobbed their heads in unison. Except Nana Chata.

"I think we need to move Ms. Craftastic away from Benecio's varnish."

31

Motivated by the craftista reunion, the next day Star decided to tackle the last chore on her list: the back house.

"Tell me again why we're rushin'?" Maria Juana asked Star, who worked the paint roller on the front walls of La Pachanga's adobe-style back house as if she had just downed a double crack cappuccino.

"Because I want this over with so I can get back to making new love shrines."

"Check it out. Now that this place is all clean and empty," Maria Juana noted, "it'd make a kick-ass pad."

"Well, we've been at it for eight hours straight, so it better look kick-ass," Star replied, out of breath. She continued to move her arm up and down faster and faster until she abruptly stopped and released the paint roller from her hand. Enough was enough.

Star let herself collapse on the walkway, panting from her round of speed painting. "How could a lovable color like hot pink take three excruciating coats just to cover white stucco? And as an artist addicted to said color, why did I not know that?"

Maria Juana kept painting. "I tried to tell you at the store."

"I know, but it's worth the effort. I love it. Especially the name: Fantasia Fuschia Fiesta!" Star rolled onto her side and watched her cousin push the paint roller back and forth over the final spot on the wall. "Thanks for helping me, cuz. I can't believe we actually emptied out all that junk, *and* finished the paint job."

Maria Juana yanked Star up from the floor. They dragged their worn-out feet inside the small house and stood back-to-back in the center of the room to admire every inch of their hard work. Clearing the space to its spotless condition was the last duty on Star's list from her dad. Once she finished, her debt would be paid for defacing her parents' business property. She could go back to work at La Pachanga, and do her art too.

"What's your dad gonna do with this casita?" Maria Juana asked, gathering up rags from the floor.

"I don't have a clue. Maybe extra seating or a mini gallery?"

Star stretched out her arms like Julie Andrews in *The Sound of Music* and twirled about the room as a celebratory gesture of her freedom.

Wearing baggy jeans and a plaid flannel shirt, Maria Juana spun around the room too, only faster, and less ladylike. "Whoa, do it superfast, and it's better than—"

"Please don't ruin the moment," Star cracked.

Maria Juana took off her flannel to reveal a black tank with cheap lace trim, and sat on the floor against the wall. Star, in faded Levi's and Theo's Ozomatli T-shirt with the sleeves whacked off, dropped her butt down too.

"Tell your dad to give you this place for your craft cronies."

"What do you mean?" Star asked, as she yanked a Converse sneaker off and massaged her foot.

"You know, like Las Bandidas have."

Star looked down at her arm and examined her tattoo—a skull underneath a set of roller skates and the words "La Bandida Estrella." "How exactly are Chloe and Ofie like Las Bandidas?"

"Well, I mean it's—okay you know La Shorty, the new blocker-in-training? Her uncle Papi owns the roller rink, and he lets us use it as our home base. It's real cool. We always go there to hang out whenever we want. We work on our uniforms, plan our rink strategies, organize our cupcake sales..."

"You guys sell cupcakes?" Star asked in surprise as she removed her shoe.

"Yah, girl! That's how we make some of our cash!"

"I like that. You should come sell them here on Friday nights. I'm sure my dad would love that—a fleet of sexy chicks on wheels with cake icing? It would be great publicity!"

"Focus, chica! I'm trying to give you an idea!"

"Sorry, I don't get the correlation..."

Maria Juana folded her arms against her beefy cleavage. "Cuz, you could do that here and, like, sell pretty papers and crap. Open it to the public so people can get on the Internet and talk about ideas and stuff. You could call it The Glittered Cactus after your centerpieces or something."

Star couldn't believe what she had just heard from her cousin. *Why didn't I think of that?* she mentally chided herself.

Quickly Star began to plan. She could trick out the whole place in the leftover glitter, and high-gloss varnish. It would bring fresh customers to La Pachanga—people could buy espresso brownies *and* a bottle of Tacky Glue. Star envisioned midnight scrapbook-making parties. She could teach love shrine workshops, and Ofie, crochet classes. Genius. She couldn't wait to ask her dad. In the agreement he drew up in August, he mentioned making her a partner in the business, but maybe he would go for this instead. She could even make an offer to buy the small space from him so she'd have her own little stake in the world. She had enough for a down payment and would probably need to score a bank loan—still, it could work.

"That's a fabulous idea! Would you help me run it?" Star asked before second guessing herself.

"Eh, maybe. Depends on how busy I am with my bouts. I got promoted to lead jammer, and they want me to recruit and train some new chicks. Hey, interested in Roller Derby?"

"Hmmm...how about I decorate your outfits instead? Me and my craft cronies?"

"Ha. Maybe." Maria Juana began to pick at her already-peeling nail polish—a sure sign that Star's normally outspoken cousin had something unpleasant on her mind.

"Go ahead. What's your next topic?" Star baited, even though she knew it.

Maria Juana took a deep breath and scratched her scalp. "You ain't gonna like it."

"Go ahead...," Star said in a just-get-it-over-with tone.

"That Harrison dude is crunk. I know everyone is all crazy 'bout him 'cause he's a fireman, but I swear I've seen him at the strip joints lately. You should go back with your real ruco, Theo."

"You go to strip clubs?" Star giggled.

"They have cheap drinks! Besides, sometimes we recruit new members there," Maria Juana said, puffing out her chest.

"Hey, I'm not judging," Star offered, holding her hand in the air.

"Don't you act all high-'n'-mighty. You were at Binki's Cabaret showing your stuff!"

"What are you smoking, cuz? I wouldn't step foot in one of those filthy joints. Gross. You could probably catch an STD just from the hand stamp alone." Star slid down onto her back and began to make invisible snow angels on the shiny saltillo tile floor. Her cousin was totally, utterly insane at times.

Maria Juana slid down too, and poked Star in the arm. "Oh yeah? Let me refresh your memory, prima. That night you jacked up the mural, where do you think you got all borracha? At Binki's! I'm telling you, they have *cheap* drinks. Anyway..."

Star's face froze in a horrified pose. She didn't recall any of it, and didn't want to hear the details.

But Maria Juana continued to reveal events from that fateful night.

"So after the bout—in which we totally whooped their butts, by the way—you told the team that you'd never been to a strip club. You *begged* us to take you. Then once we got in, you kept saying 'Gimme a shot of tequila! Gimme a shot of tequila!' You said you wanted to work up the nerve to tell Theo you loved him, 'cause ya chickened out the night before, and needed liquid vitamins. I tried to tell you no, but you shoved me to the floor and climbed up onstage. You took off your top, and we all saw your old-fashioned super-pointy bra. They were playin' 'Back in Black' on the stereo, and you tried to swing around the pole like the dancers."

"Was I any good?"

"You sucked."

"Oh my God. And the bra? What happened to the bra?" Star asked.

Maria Juana broke out in a homegirl gigglefit. "Nothing. You left it on. But shit . . . then you hit your head on the pole and fell on your ass. We all saw your purple chonies because that ugly old-lady skirt of yours flew up. You got us kicked out of Binki's! So we walk out, right? And what'd you do? You went next door to the Naked Iguana and got that tat."

Star sat up. "No way. When you're drunk, they make you pay and then wait until the next day to get a tattoo. You lie!"

"Naw-aw. Sister Chunky—she's our raddest Bandida blocker—well, her brother's roommate works there, and he did it for free. He thought you were cute."

Star rubbed her fingers over the tattoo on her arm. She had actually come to like it. "You can stop now, Maria Juana. I think I get it. I was shit-faced," Star deadpanned.

"Wait! It gets better. Listen to me. You need to know why you spray painted on Theo's mural!" Maria Juana sat up and hunched her head over, as if she were about to deliver the twist ending to a campfire ghost story. "You're all cryin' from the pain, so we took you to Circle K for Tylenol and water. Also because I didn't want Uncle Al and Auntie Dori hatin' on me for bringing you home all wasted. But instead of the Tylenol you bought frickin' Boone's Farm and slammed it like Gatorade. You paid Prissy—another blocker on our squad—fifty bucks to drive you to her house for spray paint. She needed rent money real bad, so she said sure. Then you paid her twenty more to drive you to the mural, so you could write 'I love you, Theo' on the wall, and surprise him."

"No way! I did? But then where did the happy faces come in?" Star asked, 100 percent enthralled, as if she were listening to Maria Juana explain a complicated movie, rather than hearing about her own exploits.

"When we got there, I guess you chickened out, and made those stupid smiley faces instead. I ended up having to drag your heavy ass to your bedroom. You cut me deep, mujer. You messed up my night with my homegirls, *and* you made out with the Japanese vato I was crushin' on."

"Japanese?" Star repeated, believing her cousin was mistaken. "No, dude, he was from Ireland."

"Nah...the guy who inked your arm was from *England*. The hombre who gave you the hickey was from Japan. Or maybe it was Thailand. Someplace over there. He kinda looks like Theo. That's probably why you forced yourself on him. Anyway, he cleans up the rink after the bouts, and you dragged him along."

Star stuck out her bottom lip. "Ugh. I'm so sorry."

Maria Juana swatted her hand in front of her face. "Eh, I'm over it. He was a real dog, but still. That's what went down."

"Wow. Thank you for that *Mi Vida Loca* play-by-play."

Maria Juana stood up and flicked a dried piece of paint across the room. "You have brains and all these amigas, and familia who loves you. Damn, my mom chooses her men over me all the time. I'd give anything to get what you got."

Star stared sincerely into her cousin's eyes, which were heavy with black liner and clumpy mascara. "You don't give yourself enough credit. You're smart, funny, and a hell of an athlete. And I'm sorry. Really, I owe you big-time."

"Nah, it's cool. Just dump Scary Harry."

Star giggled. "You call Harrison Scary Harry?"

Lying on the empty saltillo tile floor, Star twirled a paint stirrer like a baton in between her fingers. "Theo is moving out of state. I blew that relationship out of the water. I don't want to make the same mistake."

Maria Juana leaned back, whistled through her teeth, and stabbed her fist in the air. "Don't settle, esa! Pull yourself together and go dump his ass! Like my parole officer always says—two wrongs don't make a right. And I think Scary Harry's got a little sumpin'-sumpin' happenin' on the side. I swear on my skates, he goes to Binki's. And not just for the cheap drinks."

A second wind clicked in and Star and Maria Juana cleaned up the last of the mess, then drove home for dinner and to offer the pitch. Star couldn't stop planning for the store. The craft group had already agreed to keep meeting after the CraftOlympics, but Ofie had requested a new location. The store would be perfect!

When Star and Maria Juana arrived at the house, adrenaline pumped through Star's system. She skipped into the house and found her parents up and about, chatting about the new kitchen appliances and blending a batch of wheat-grass refreshments.

Star long-jumped into the room and tossed her keys on the table while Maria Juana elbowed her way around her cousin, opened the fridge, and grabbed a Coke. Before Dori could try and persuade her niece to opt for an organic beverage instead, Star spoke up.

"Dad, I have a proposition to make about the back house, which is totally spotless, I might add."

"You finished early? You never cease to surprise, do you?" Al put his hands on his hips and smiled brightly at his daughter.

"Remember when you said I could become a partner if I completed all the items in your contract? Well, I'd like to go one better. I would like to make an offer to buy the back house and turn it into a boutique art shop. I'm talking supplies, handmade art, book signings, workshops, parties, small art shows, and other events. I can give you a down payment and file all the proper paperwork. I'll still do my press release business on the side to make sure I always have income. Maria Juana gave me the idea of calling it The Glittered Cactus. I swear, this is my calling. I've never felt more sure about anything else. I want to inspire people to use crafts to better their lives!"

Al folded his arms, bit his inner cheek, and bobbed his head as if to consider every angle. Star chewed her blue-painted thumbnail, anticipating his response.

"M'ija," he began slowly, punctuating the word with a dramatic pause, "I think it's a great idea! We can even set up a stereo system, and install a little coffee and tea area too. Someday when it gets going, we can add all kinds of other little touches."

"Not someday, Dad," Star clarified. "I'm talking *today.*"

32

The next evening, Star's face beamed with self-content as she drove across town to Harrison's home in the northwest valley for their first official date. Theo's face belting out that horrible song invaded her head, kicking off a fit of laughter. Someday, decades down the road, if they ever met for a beer, she would certainly tease him about it. She forced his image out of her brain, remembering that he would soon move to Santa Fe. As much as it crushed her, at least she wouldn't have to worry about seeing him around town. Eventually he'd find a woman who had her act together and the two would settle down, have kids, etc. And Star would cry into her German glass glitter, which she still had way too much of.

She concentrated on Harrison. He had proved to be the steadfast, put-together partner her life needed. She didn't quite experience the love shine yet, but it would come. He was even-tempered, nonjudgmental, handsome, giving, predictable, and—best of all—safe. Yup, every girl's dream guy. Star wouldn't dare screw up her first serious adult relationship based on a suspicious accusation from her cousin.

Star glimpsed out the window as she cruised past Arrowhead Mall on Bell Road and 75th Avenue. She lowered the window to let the crisp sweet-smelling November air filter through her Chevy Bel Air interior. As she drove, she noted how Bell Road streets resembled the Las Vegas strip: Instead of hip casinos, there were scores of corporate-owned eateries like Mimi's Café, Olive Garden, and a new branch of Sangria. She would never admit it to Harrison, but his stomping grounds didn't thrill her. She preferred her hood of Central Phoenix, where mom-and-pop-owned businesses like La Pachanga offered guests a sense of individuality and culture.

Singing along to Lila Downs' sultry version of "La Cucaracha," Star pulled into Harrison's driveway in Peoria. His home consisted of a humdrum stucco cookie-cutter foundation in a bland neighborhood where every block appeared identical. Quite a contrast from where she lived. She turned off the ignition, got out of the car, and walked to the front door.

"Where do you think you're goin'?" said Harrison from a distance. Stunned, Star turned to see him sitting on the bumper of his monster Dodge Ram truck across the street.

"Oh my God! I'm at the wrong house again, aren't I?" she acknowledged as she climbed back in her car and crossed the asphalt. This time she hopped out and jumped on him, piggyback style.

"What should we do for our first official date? Want to go see a band on Grand Avenue? Or we can ride the light-rail back and forth and take pictures of weird people with our cell phones!"

Harrison carried her to the front door, where he set her down and opened her black fur-trimmed velvet coat. His eyes traced the roundness of her curves, showcased by a square, low-cut purple Lycra top.

"Look up here, cowboy," Star said, lifting his chin.

He smiled, using only one side of his mouth, and ran his fingers over the six-strand emerald beaded necklace that rested across her dark-skinned chest, and then drew an imaginary line down the middle of her body, ending at the green crocheted hem of her black skirt. He whistled at her legs, which were graced with a tall pair of patent-leather go-go boots.

"I like those," he said.

Star leaned back and kicked one leg up. "Me too! Buffalo Exchange, forty bucks! They're a bitch to walk in, but beauty is pain, right? So where are we going? Have you ever been Latin dancing?"

"I like what the boots are attached to. You look good enough to eat."

She dismissed the uncomfortable innuendo and reached for the door handle. "Stop it! I have so much to tell you about Ofie and Chloe. You'll never believe this—Ofie crochets so fast that she entered the CraftOlympics race, and I'm going to launch a new business—"

He put his finger over her mouth to shush her. "No talk about your friends tonight. Follow me. I have a surprise. But first, close your eyes." He led her through the entryway and down the hallway.

An uneasy feeling crept over Star's skin. The last time a guy offered to "surprise" her, she embarked on a crime spree and woke up with a skull tattoo.

"Harrison…this is a little weird…what's up?" she sang out jokingly, noticing the extreme scent of cucumber candles that were lit throughout the route. Not exactly her perception of their first date. She preferred cucumbers in a salad.

They turned two right corners and stopped. "Look."

Just as she suspected, they had reached his bedroom. She'd never seen it before—eggshell-white walls with a black-lacquered, gold-trimmed California king waterbed in the center and a dresser and nightstand to match.

Ew.

Suddenly Star didn't want a first date anymore. Harrison

made for the perfect companion—as long they were throwing darts or downing British beers. But the seductive act made her uncomfortable.

Harrison stepped in front of a mauve three-panel partition that was arranged by the window. "This is for you." He picked up the partition and leaned it against the wall behind him.

With hesitation, Star tiptoed over to find a tall, brand-new wood easel with a big red bow on top. Next to it sat a stack of thick canvases, pads of paper, and an art desk cluttered with supplies.

"It's a work area for when you come over and make your art."

"A work space in your bedroom?" she asked. She supposed the gesture was nice, if a bit odd. "Um-hum. How…convenient. One glitch: I haven't learned to paint yet. I'm still doing shadow boxes, remember?" She turned to face him, but he had vanished.

"Where'd you go, David Blaine?" Star joked.

"It's never too early to learn," he called from the bed. Nude. Posed like a Grecian statue. A well-endowed and extremely freckled Grecian statue. "I want you to paint me," he said with total confidence and not even a hint of irony.

Star's eyes widened. "You don't want me to paint you. I'm horrible with stiff life. I mean *still* life."

In one swift Wonder Woman motion, she veered around the bed and shuffled backward toward the door, buttoning up her coat. "Hey, do you knit? I just realized I need to get going on my Victims of Violence blanket for starving children…I'll be back!"

She bolted out of the room and hustled down the hallway, reached the front door, and stopped. She couldn't run away. Harrison had been a loyal friend and deserved respect. Even if in her gut she had a feeling Maria Juana may have been correct. Harrison had a saucy side, all right.

"Harrison? You there?" Star called out across the large, empty entryway.

He emerged from his room, jeans on, with a steeled expression. "What's wrong with you? Haven't we had fun?"

"Yes, totally. I loved all of it and I'm so grateful for you being there for me these past few months. And—"

"You're not into this, are you?" he asked, softening up.

She sucked in her lips and shook her head. She pressed her back against the off-white front door. "I wanted to be, though."

"I knew all along. Guys can sense it. Pardon my wishful thinking back there."

"It's okay. Very creative. You definitely get props for that."

"Would you consider one night of secret sex with a good friend?"

Star raised her eyebrow, as if he needed to be disciplined. She envisioned him stuffing dollars in strippers' G-strings at Binki's. She owed her cuz a drink for calling it out.

"Trust me," Star said. "I've been there before, and it doesn't end well."

Like a true (shirtless) gentleman, he escorted her out and to her car.

33

Even though Harrison wasn't quite the man she thought, Star was still pleased she handled the situation like an adult. Driving home from his house, Star craved the familiar vibe of La Pachanga. She decided to check in on her cousin at the coffee bar to see if she needed help. Likely not, since Monday nights were usually slow, but Star went anyway.

"Hi, Maria Juana. You can go if you want. I'll take over from here," Star called out as she removed her coat and walked behind the coffee bar counter. There was her cousin, wearing a legitimate barista apron tied tightly over jeans and a cropped top.

"It's M.J. at work," she shouted over the espresso machine while steaming milk inside a small silver pitcher.

"M.J.?" Star asked, slipping on an apron and tying it around her waist.

"Yeah, that's my handle now. Got a problem with it?"

"No, it's cute. I like it better. It sounds less…illegal?" Star joked. She had been proud of her cousin. According to Al, Maria Juana proved herself a loyal employee during Star's exile from the business. Not only did she become the empress of all caffeine-related beverage services, she also devised and implemented theme nights such as Machismo Mondays, Roller Derby Wednesdays, and Flirt

Fest Fridays, to bring in more evening business. Star would never underestimate her again.

"Damn, girl," Maria Juana chided, acknowledging Star's sexy boots. "You can't work here dressed like that. You ain't serving these cinnamon buns in the red-light district."

Look who's talking, Star thought. "Go easy on me. I just came from a date gone bad."

"Scary Harry?" M.J. said. "What happened?"

"He asked me to paint him. Naked. You're right. He is scary! I bolted."

Maria Juana wagged her tongue and fake gagged as her square purple lacquered nails squeezed a perfect pyramid of whipped cream on top of a cappuccino. She drizzled on a swirl of chocolate sauce and presented the buzzy confection to a drooling customer.

"Can I get some of that, prima?" Star practically crawled across the counter to offer her finger. That chocolate sauce looked pretty therapeutic right now.

"Seriously girl, you look like one of those chicas from *Lowrider* magazine. You should show it off! I'm hittin' a club later with Las Bandidas. La Isla del Encanto. There's some band from Puerto Rico that sings in Spanish."

Star perked up. "Reggae Sol?"

"I think so. Come with us. We can celebrate your freedom from Scary Harry. I'm closing up here in a few minutes."

It had to be a message from the universe. The last two times Star partied at a Reggae Sol show, it was with Theo. This would be her closure. Plus, she knew exactly who to invite as her date—or rather—dates.

"Let me make a couple phone calls," Star chirped. "And then let's roll!"

Chloe entered the club and spotted Star across the room, sipping a fruity martini. The dethroned craft queen spliced her way through the elbow-to-elbow crowd that included everyone from rainbow-shirt-wearing hippies to sexed-up couples in Latin-longue attire.

Chloe could see why Star had deemed La Isla del Encanto her favorite nightclub, even over Friday nights at La Pachanga. Chloe compared the Caribbean club to a tropical oasis planted in the middle of the Arizona concrete jungle. Tall palm trees lined the entire perimeter, and out front, shrubs planted in gigantic red, yellow, and green pots led up to the entrance, which was trimmed in strands of rope lights. Inside, murals, paintings, masks, and magazine clippings cluttered the walls and tables, making Chloe feel as though she were in another city, another time, and another body.

She finally made her way to Star's table near the stage and was met with a tight, tipsy hug. Star cleared her throat to shout over the reggae jams that thumped through the subwoofers throughout the club.

"Thanks for coming! I thought you could stop me from doing anything stupid, and we could party at the same time. Dang, you look fan-friggin-tastic!" Star commented, impressed that Chloe had come fashionably back to life since Saturday at Benecio's.

Chloe rocked a gold clingy halter dress with a courageous neckline that just about hit the top of her belly button. "Thank God for bitty boobs and double-stick tape," she answered, holding her petite hand to the side of her mouth and talking into Star's ear. "I haven't been out since, like, forever. I feel like I need to interview people, and I keep wanting to check on the cameraman."

"Chill and enjoy. Larry and Ofie are coming too!" Star said.

"Believe me, I'm ready to enjoy!" Chloe shouted over the house music.

"Here! Finish this," Star said, shoving her mystery martini to Chloe. "Tonight we drop our guard. Someday we'll be wrinkly and have fat butts, so we may as well live it up now, no? By the way? I'm lovin' the double XL lashes and tight ponytail. They make you look like a mod model from the sixties!"

"Thanks! Oh—there's Ofie."

Star and Chloe lifted their napkins above their heads to wave down the third craftista amiga and her husband, who had just entered the club and were getting their hands stamped by the doorman. Larry took note, but Ofie was too busy asking a guy about his long multicolored dreadlocks.

By the time they made it to the table, two fresh rum punches had just been delivered for them. Larry used his car key to tap the side of his glass and announced "Salud!" Ofie cuddled with him and picked up her glass.

Chloe lifted her second martini to the center of the tall round table. "Here's to my independence from Crafty Chloe, KPDM, Ezra, and all the baggage that came with it. To all of you, the best friends I've ever had—and to finding a man who doesn't give me any lip unless it's for pleasure purposes only!"

Ofie hooted and slapped the table hallelujah style. She then wiggled to make room as if she were a keynote speaker about to address a room full of professionals. "Here's to my crochet hook and my family and friends who support me, bad crafts and all! I love you so much!"

"Awwww, we love you too!" Star said, feeling a bit loopy from her two drinks. "Here's to you guys, of course. But also to the CraftOlympics in two weeks—woo-hoo!—the centerpieces, which are finished and fabulous; to me cutting Harrison loose tonight; and to only having thirty pounds of glitter left!"

Chloe scrunched her face, holding back her astonishment. "You cut *what* from Harrison?"

They all broke out into hysterics—the kind that only come between cocktail-sipping women at a nightclub. Chloe dabbed the tears from her cheeks with her pinkies. As she did so, her blurred vision came into focus.

"Oh. My. God!" Chloe blurted. Beyond Star's shoulder stood a striking island-looking guy with long dreadlocks. Could it be? Yes! Gustavo from the coffeehouse. The musician who made her thighs tango just by shaking her hand.

Star tapped Ofie's finger and then gave Chloe the sly eye. Her plan had worked. "Guess who's playing tonight, missy. Reggae Sol. I told you I'd treat you."

Chloe didn't hear a single syllable. Her gaze locked into Gustavo's, inciting a Tony and Maria *West Side Story* moment. The bouncing background music seemed to muffle and the lights dimmed. He touched the tip of his nose and smiled. *It must be a reggae signal for hi*, she thought. Chloe touched the tip of her nose and bashfully blinked and then threw out a flirty smile.

Star whistled in front of Chloe's face. "Red alert to Chloe! Snot bubble, left nostril!"

"Huh?" Chloe asked, without breaking her locked gaze with

the Rasta hunk. And then Star's words registered and she snapped back to reality.

"Snot bubble? Me? No, it can't be!" She grabbed a napkin, put it over her nostrils, and darted for the bathroom. But running in a dangerous dress and heels isn't the easiest feat after a high-octane cocktail. Inches away from the ladies' room door, her knees buckled, causing her to glide through the air until she landed flat on her backside on the acid-stained concrete floor. She jumped up on her feet, just like a seasoned acrobat, and plowed through the swinging door to the ladies' room, where several dance-floor princesses rushed to her aid.

"Please, God," Chloe begged to the ceiling. "Please don't let him have seen that."

"Honey, everybody saw that one," said a friendly black woman with a gorgeous face and a long shiny mane. "Hold on a few. Go fix your stuff in the mirror, and then prance back out there like you *own* the place. By the way—you okay? That was a nasty crash."

Chloe gave two thumbs-up and then reached for the woman's necklace, which had seven little pictures of Queen Nefertiti of Egypt all linked together. "Wow. Did you make that?"

"Sure did."

"Image transfer on clay! I learned about it from my friend Ofie! It's polymer clay that is clear and squeezable!" Chloe boasted, amazed at her crafty knowledge.

Now calmer and in better spirits, Chloe powdered her face, applied a fresh coat of gloss, and counted to three in Spanish before heading out. Borrowing the regal spirit of Queen Nefertiti from the necklace, she pushed open the swinging door and found Gustavo waiting for her.

"Are you all right?" he asked, concern creasing his eyes.

"Yes. Thanks. The damn tiles here, they're so slick. How's a girl supposed to have a drink and then make it in stilettos all the way to the ladies' room?"

He chuckled and extended his hand. "How fortunate to see you again, Chloe. I hoped you would come."

She took his hand. Large, masculine, secure, with a warm grip. Chloe couldn't let go. She let him slip away before but would not make that mistake again. Gustavo's energy was magical and powerful.

"I'm happy to be here."

"I'm glad you made it. It's our last show. Last-minute booking. To tell the truth, the only reason I had our manager take the gig was because I hoped to see you," he said, skimming his fingers down her bare arm.

Chloe smiled brightly at his words. "I'm here with my friends." She pointed to the table where Star chummily clinked martini glasses with some of her cousin's Roller Derby friends. Chloe looked around the club for Larry and Ofie and spotted them on the dance floor. Still holding her hand, Gustavo led her to the table where Star and Maria Juana were now arm wrestling. He pulled out Chloe's chair for her.

"I don't feel so silly now that I kept tabs on you. I have all your CDs. I love them. I've thought about you every day since we met," she admitted bashfully, not only to him, but to herself.

Gustavo whispered in Chloe's ear, "Let's go out after the show, yes?"

"Sure," she said, nervously reaching for a drink that wasn't there. "I'll be right here, waiting."

35

While Chloe floated on cloud nine, mesmerized by Gustavo and his celebrity status, Star received her own jolt of reality. About six tables over and toward the back stood Theo, Corona in hand, alongside his cousin Victor. She shouldn't have been surprised to see him; he loved Reggae Sol as much as she. Star had to wave hello because they saw each other. She lifted a finger next to her flushed, hot face and bent it up and down. He returned the gesture with a polite wink.

She considered going over to say hello, but then the DJ's reggaeton jam ended, the lights went down—a sign that Reggae Sol would appear any second. Star, along with the rest of the partiers, including Chloe, Ofie, and Larry, crowded to the front of the dance floor.

The stage lights lifted to reveal a skinny bass player with a body like Bugs Bunny and a blond heavyset drummer who immediately broke into a thick reggae dub. The hypnotic sound made the audience roar and cheer for what was to come next.

It cast a spell over Star. Without thinking, she wormed her way over to Theo, grabbed his arm, and led him through the crowded dance floor, all the way to the front row. They made it, although they were smashed between two sweaty plus-sized fans in reggae tams, but that only made the experience livelier. Star closed her eyes and let the music radiate up through her feet, moving in rhythm with the drumbeat. She reached for Theo's arms from behind and placed them around her waist, so they could sway in unison to the groove. She loved that he used his thumb to stroke her stomach. She didn't feel one bit nervous or hesitant, and knew he didn't either. The two of them were a natural fit. No words, no games.

Next, the three-piece horn section jumped on the wave, followed by two percussionists, who infused an African Nyabingi beat. Chloe inched her way over to Star, and whistled through her teeth when the spotlight flicked on Gustavo's face. The audience roared as he stepped forward, dressed all in white like Rastafarian royalty, and moved to the beat with his guitar. His feet were planted firmly, but his body rocked in sync with the bass line as his dreads swooshed back and forth behind his head. The tune ceased abruptly so Gustavo could sing the first verses a cappella before the band kicked back in. He rarely took his eyes off Chloe. The man was a solid crooner, comparable to Michael Bublé or Harry Connick Jr.—if either of them hailed from Puerto Rico and sang reggae songs in Spanish.

For the first five cuts, Star and Theo danced facing the stage, singing to the air and cheering. The sixth song—a sexy island version of Bobby Caldwell's "What You Won't Do for Love"—inspired her to turn around, put her arms around Theo's neck, and press her body against his. She had missed his smell, and to close her eyes and breathe him in now almost stopped her heart. She moved closer to him. He welcomed her, and anchored his hips against hers, as they rocked back and forth to the melody.

Star couldn't help herself any longer. She reached up and kissed Theo with parted lips. A weird sense of peace mixed with excitement surged through her body, as though every shaky nerve from the past six months had been calmed.

He kissed her back lovingly, as if he too had been longing for this moment. And their kiss told the most romantic story ever, even without the melodramatic speech bubbles or racy illustrations like in the *El Solitario* novella.

Star let go first. "Are you really moving to Santa Fe?" she shouted over the music.

He drew her to him again. "Let's just enjoy the moment." He set his hands on her shoulders and steered her toward the bar.

"Cheers to old friends," Star said, holding up a Corona.

"To old friends," he repeated back.

She took a sip from her bottle and Theo bent his head down to gently kiss the moisture from her lips. Star wanted the moment to last forever.

An hour later, after saying goodbye to Chloe, Ofie, and Larry, Star and Theo headed outside, arm in arm, where Victor waited at Theo's '48 Chevy. The last time Star rode in it, it was a boring primer gray. Now it sparkled a metallic green.

Theo put Star's coat around her shoulders to shield her from the chilly late-night November air. "Estrella, Victor is driving us home before this gets out of hand. Give me your keys and I'll bring your car home in the morning."

"I don't want to wake my folks this late. At least, not after I've been drinking. Let's go to your place and sober up on coffee first. Please?"

Theo turned to Victor. "Okay, then. You heard her. My place."

36

Star snuggled up to Theo's chest in the backseat of his car, and heard the familiar sound of the tires pulling into his gravel driveway. He gently nudged her cheek to signal their arrival and she opened her eyes to see his smiling face nestled to hers. Victor unlocked the door and helped them out.

"Good to have you around again, Star," Victor said before making his own way home. Just like old times, Star thought. Crashing at Theo's after a night of too much fun. She inhaled the scent of the oleanders that encased the property, and looked up to see a full moon glowing in the black sky. She tightened her coat around her waist to guard against the chill, and followed Theo inside.

When she entered his home, she heaved as if a bucket of ice water had just been dumped on her head. Large moving boxes everywhere, filled and taped shut, were stacked along the walls. She did her best to hide her distress. After all, he did tell her about the move weeks ago. It just hadn't sunk in until now.

Star tossed her jacket, tugged off her boots, and climbed into her favorite chair, the leather La-Z-boy recliner, a gift from Theo's grandfather. She couldn't believe this was the same house she had visited so often. Theo had always had a slick way of decorating.

Hues of deep reds and greens, stark matted prints and, of course, lots of accessories Star had given him over the years. Now all were removed, leaving empty walls and vacant corners.

Cody, Theo's bear-sized mutt, pounced on her lap and licked her neck.

"Cody! Bad dog! Get down!" Theo yelled as Cody slobbered on Star's chest, neck, and face. She rolled around on the chair in a fit of giggles. Cody finally retreated, fell to the hardwood floor, and rested his heavy head on her feet. Star slapped the armrest, gripped her stomach, and rocked back and forth. "Oh, man...," she said through heavy breaths. "I miss that!"

"So what's up with the fireman?" Theo blurted. Star wondered how long he'd been wanting to ask her that.

"Nada," she assured him. "We're friends. It ended before it started. That's all." She felt no need to elaborate any further; she had her own probing to do.

"So you're really leaving. Excited?" She tried to sound upbeat, but it was a struggle. Still, she wouldn't let herself be selfish about this. Many blessings had come her way, and now Theo had the opportunity of a lifetime. Every night she prayed for him to be happy, and he deserved to be recognized on a national level.

"Yeah, tomorrow I take off." He sighed. "Frank is renting the house. Estrella, I'm really glad we got to hang out tonight. There is no one else I would have rather spent my last night in Phoenix with."

Star climbed off the chair to rub his back. "I'm glad too. Thank God for Reggae Sol, huh? They are like the bookends to our relationship."

"Yeah...I suppose they are." Theo leaned over, opened one of the boxes in the hallway, and grabbed a couple of sheets and a pillow. "You take my bed and I'll crash out here. If you need anything, tell me and I'll find it in the boxes."

They kissed for several minutes, and then slowly pulled apart and retreated to opposite corners of the house.

A noise from his studio out back woke Theo a few hours later. He rolled off the sheet and went to his bedroom. No Star. He shook his head in disappointment, thinking she had left, and was about to dive face-first into his bed when he heard the noise again. He walked to the window and saw her hourglass silhouette in the studio. Wearing only his boxers, he jogged outside through the cold air to see what she was up to.

He pushed open the creaky door to find patchouli incense burning, a candle lit, and Star sitting on a barstool in his favorite lucha libre silk-screened tee and his baggy paint sweats. She stroked a brush across a small canvas and winked when he entered.

"You're moving to Santa Fe to kick up your art career and you haven't even packed your supplies?"

"That's trip two," he answered. "It's three in the morning. What are you doing?"

"I can't sleep. I thought practicing painting would help. Come check it out." She flicked her fingers toward her as an invitation.

Theo moved to stand behind her. The more time they spent together tonight, the harder it would be to say goodbye tomorrow. But her spontaneity was too hard to resist. "You can't create without tunes," he said, reaching for the stereo remote. He fired up his favorite lowrider oldies to match the mood. Star didn't respond. She was too involved in blending a background on the canvas.

Finally, she spoke. "Thanks for the roses you sent for my art show. They brought me good luck."

"You don't need luck," he said. "You are the only person I

know who can score an exhibit without ever having made art, and then sell every piece in one night. That's my Estrella."

"I like to think it was Nana Esteban watching over me." Star rinsed her brush in a cup of water on the table. "By the way, I peeked at your new paintings. Why haven't you shown them? Are they for Santa Fe?"

He scooted to the edge of the red canvas sofa, where he sat and rested his elbows on his lap. "Painting, going to galleries, all of it—it's not exciting anymore. I can't explain it. But ... I did do one piece I like. Want to see?"

"Bring it on," Star replied, standing up to approach him.

He went to a cart by the wall, lifted out a canvas, and handed it over: A three-by-four-foot mixed-media painting of her. Black and blue curly locks of hair, which swirled around her head like tentacles underwater. A metallic gold arch floated above, like a gilded crown. Her chestnut eyes were outlined with ultra-fine green glitter and her Cupid's bow lips in pinkish red. All of it was immersed under a layer of thin opalescent wax, creating a shimmery, antique effect. Around the border of the painting were miniature illustrated mementos of their friendship: a piece of pan dulce, a matchbox from La Pachanga, a Spanish book, jars of paints, a boom box, and various versions of heart milagros.

Star put her hands on her cheeks and breathed heavier than she ever had before. She closed her eyes in disbelief and when she lifted her lids, she felt Theo's eyelashes on her temple.

"I miss you," he said, nuzzling close.

She didn't respond. She couldn't.

He smelled her hair. "I miss everything about you. Your smile. Your laugh. Your hair. Your clothes. Your crazy philosophies. Your bad Spanish. All of it."

Silence.

"Estrella? Please say something."

She took his hand and led him to the couch. She turned out the light, so only the candle illuminated the room.

"I miss you too," she whispered before covering his chest, neck, and face in what seemed like a million tiny kisses. He gripped her petite waist and moved her back just a little so he could return the favor. Then he pulled her close and took in the scent of her skin.

"Remember at Sangria when I said I regretted falling in love with you? I lied."

She rubbed his nose with hers. "I deserved it. I'm sorry again about your mural."

"I know a way you can make it up to me... ," he whispered into her ear. She kissed his nose, took his hand and they dashed through the backyard to his bedroom.

As they toppled down onto Theo's bed, Star felt a sense of peace and closure. This is where she wanted to be, with Theo. They kissed, touched, and tumbled like two rowdy puppies, twisting across the brown serape bedspread that had a blazing Aztec warrior in the center.

"I can't believe what I've been missing out on for so long," Theo said, amazed at his prize. His dark brown fingers traced her curves. "Your body... It's as fun as a set of monkey bars." He ran his nose up her forearm, and then kissed her bandida tattoo.

Star giggled, enjoying his playfulness.

"You're as tasty as a ripe peach. You're like a brand-new acoustic guitar, right out of the box. No, wait," he said as he slouched back and examined her from afar. "No, no, no... wait. I got it!" he said. "Your body? It's like Raquel Welch without her loincloth in *One Million Years B.C.*" He growled and teasingly bit her belly.

Star giggled louder and stroked his head with her hand. "Can you believe we're doing this again? I've fantasized about this night for months."

Theo looked up into Star's face. "But this is better than a fantasy. This—we—are real."

The next morning, Star and Theo cuddled under the blanket, with Cody snoring between them. She slipped out of bed, and not thinking, took the blanket with her.

"Hey, hey, hey, mujer! It's freezing!" Theo complained as he tugged on the corner with one hand and rubbed his leg with the other. She retreated and drew the blanket under her chin. "Sing me the song."

"What song?" he said as he curled up next to her, clasped her hands in his, and blew on them for warmth.

"The one you sang to me when you were drunk at Día de los Muertos. The Lola Beltran song. Please?"

Theo slapped the bed in embarrassment. "I knew you'd bring that up. I was in *pain* that night, girl. Pain!" He flopped to his back, clenched his heart, and bluffed an attack. He then sat up against the headboard. "Only if..."

Star rolled onto her stomach and propped her head up in her hands. "Anything."

"Move with me to Santa Fe. Today. Grab the basics and we'll start fresh in New Mexico. They've rented me a killer condo. You won't have to worry about anything."

For a second time in only a few short hours, Start was struck silent.

"I don't care if you don't have your life planned, or if you want to sing in a circus, or knit that Victims of Violence blanket, whatever. I just want you to be with me. We're both serious, right? We've come a long way since the summer."

She crawled up to him and rested her head on his bare stomach.

Why did this conversation have to come on the heels of such a perfect night? "I can't."

He let out a chuckle, as if she were joking. "Right! Are you trying to torture me some more?"

"I'm serious." She sat up, pulled the sheets up to cover her, and gathered her long tangled hair to one side. "First of all, I have the CraftOlympics in two weeks. Everyone is counting on me."

"What day does the event end? Come out after that. You can tell me the whole story on our road trip."

"There's more. You know the back house at La Pachanga?"

"The junk shed? What happened, you didn't spray paint that too, did you?" he teased. Eyes wide in mock shock.

She smacked his chest. "It's no longer a junk shed. It's my new crafts boutique; I'm buying the property from my parents. I'm going to be a business owner! I'm excited, Theo. I've made progress, progress you inspired. If I let all this go to move with you, it would be just another thing I started and didn't finish..." Star bit her bottom lip to keep it from trembling.

"Come here." He motioned for her to scoot over, then wrapped his arms around her tightly. "I get it. I know it's short notice."

"Don't worry," she said. "I love you. And I won't let anything come between us ever again. We'll make it work long distance. We have to."

37

The same hour, a day later, Chloe had something new in common with Star.

She had reconnected with her lost love as well.

Chloe rolled over to the other side of the bed, reached for a tissue and blotted her face to save the embarrassment of sniffling in front of Gustavo. She rarely bawled and wasn't about to begin now, even if she was happier than she'd ever been in her otherwise miserable life. She thanked Star under her breath. If Chloe had never reported on the mural, she would have never stopped at the coffeehouse. And she would have never met this tropical paradise of a man.

Gustavo exited the bathroom dressed in his drawstring pants from the evening before. He handed Chloe a bathrobe to slip on.

"Do you regret last night?" he asked. "I know it was... unexpected."

"No way. No regrets here," she assured wholeheartedly as she combed her fingers through her hair. "To think just a bit ago I planned to launch a new career, say goodbye to my friends, leave my home—all to move back to a place that never brought me any happiness. And now, here I am, lying in this luxurious honeymoon suite at the Venetian, married to a Puerto Rican–Jamaican reggae singer whom I met two nights before. I love Vegas! I love you."

"Months before," he corrected. "Don't forget about the coffee place. What did you order again? A double cup something…"

Chloe twirled one of his black dreads around her finger and replied in a sultry manner. "Triple Underwire Sugar-Free Vanilla Latte." She paused. "We haven't even discussed where we're going to live, or what you want to do now that the band is over and I've quit my job. We're both homeless. Just wait until my mother hears about this!" she joked.

"Easy," he said, lying down and using her lap as a pillow. "I'll move to Phoenix. I've always admired the desert. It has a healing quality to it. I'll buy us a house where we can raise our children. Your mother will adore them."

"Seriously?" Chloe asked, surprised. She gripped his face and turned it toward her.

"Yes. In my town, when I wasn't touring, I worked as a chef. It's my other passion besides music. Maybe I'll hook up with a restaurant or open my own. Know anybody looking for someone who makes great Puerto Rican or Caribbean food?"

"Actually, I do. Remember my friend Star? Her parents own La Pachanga and have been on the hunt for a new chef. I'm sure they'd love to spice up the menu."

For an instant, the old Chloe tried to appear. Thankfully, Gustavo didn't have kids or a previous wife, but she had just said "I do" to an unemployed musician. She couldn't count on Star's parents offering him a job and opening a restaurant most likely translated into her footing the bill *and* the house payment.

But the new Chloe didn't care. She loved this man in a way no teleprompter could spell out. They really could be homeless, and living in an alley, but as long as he stayed by her side, she'd be elated. As soon as she returned home, she would make a brand-new to-do list that involved a life they could create together. Maybe she would join a public relations firm or launch her own consulting business. Anything was possible, as long as it didn't involve television or crafts.

Gustavo sat up and leaned over to the Tuscan-inspired nightstand. He filled two drinking glasses with bottled water. "In case you're worried," he said, "I have some money stashed away."

"From the band?"

"My mother is an investment banker, and taught me how to save. I've made the most of every penny from Reggae Sol. We should have enough for both of our lifestyles." He handed her a glass, so they could clink them together.

Chloe let her body fall back on the cushy pillow. "Right now, I want to work on making those *children* you mentioned," she said, suddenly feeling frisky and oddly maternal at the same time. She set the glasses aside and slid under him, but before they could get rolling, the phone rang.

No one knew where they were or what they had done. However, Chloe had overheard Gustavo tell the band manager only to call him in case of an emergency.

Gustavo answered and after trying unsuccessfully to speak, handed the phone to Chloe.

"It's for you. Your friend Star. Everyone is wondering where you are."

38

"Just because you're married now doesn't mean you're excused from wearing the damn shirt! It's been two weeks, the honeymoon is over!"

Chloe replied with a sarcastic chuckle. "What does being married have to do with it? Nana Chata you don't understand," she challenged, standing in Ofie's newly reconstructed, more subdued, and clean-scented living room. "It's not about me being married. Those professional crafters will crucify me with embossing powder and a heat gun if I show my face at that convention. I've been banned...shut out...forbidden! I impersonated an expert—week after week. Year after year! In front of hundreds of thousands of viewers. I betrayed them." Chloe tried to reason with the stubborn matron. "I can't show my face! I'd much rather wear a SpongeBob SquarePants disguise."

"Sorry. This nana is not pickin' up what you're throwin' down," Nana Chata said, annoyed as she swiped her hand over her head and walked away.

It was the morning of the CraftOlympics and the group met to prepare and drive to the Phoenix Convention Center together. As soon as they arrived Larry walked in holding a large box. "I had T-shirts made for you!"

The black cotton jerseys were emblazoned with red glittered tattoo hearts and hot pink letters that read, "Craftista amigas para vida." Crafty friends for life. Even Benecio put one on under a black suit jacket.

In fear of being recognized at the high-profile event, Chloe refused. She had grown to enjoy cardmaking as a pastime and genuinely wanted to attend the conference for ideas. But she didn't want to draw attention to herself. So for the three days of the convention, she planned to Greta Garbo it in a Burberry trench, floppy hat, and a pair of oversized Chanel sunglasses.

Ofie, on the other hand, couldn't stop chatting about her speed crochet competition, and called every name in her phone book to inform them, including the exterminator, the plumber, and the cable guy. Ever since she signed up Ofie did nothing but practice, practice, practice. She still could only create squares or rectangles, but she worked it like Michael Phelps in the water.

Ofie churned out Christmas blankets, scarves, pot holders, pillows, and wristbands using different grades and weights of yarn. Twenty minutes before she conked out every night, she trained by crocheting with jute, for the same reason a baseball slugger warms up with bat weights. When she switched to yarn, her fingers flew faster than Superman on speed. Hours from now she would be on the main stage of the convention, battling it out, lucky hook in hand. In the meantime, Larry and Anjelica took turns massaging her wrists and timing her rows until Nana Chata shooed them away and requested a moment alone with her daughter-in-law.

Ofie didn't know what to expect from Nana Chata. After her breakdown she knew Larry had spoken with her, but didn't know the specifics. Whatever he said had worked. Nana Chata had sent Ofie a store-bought apology card and flowers. Twice. More important, she released the reins, allowing Ofie to reign as queen of La Casa Fuentes. Ofie knew she deserved that title, but deep inside she felt connected to Nana Chata. Aside from her African drumming group, the family was all she had.

It didn't take much for Ofie to forgive, and she and Nana Chata had been spending time together once or twice a week. Still, a weird, uncomfortable distance lingered between the two. Neither mentioned the subject of Nana Chata's scathing remarks on the phone that day, even though the words still haunted Ofie.

"Ofie, come here and sit," Nana Chata ordered in her usual fashion.

Ofie put aside her crocheting and sat next to her mother-in-law on the floral-patterned loveseat—a hand-me-down from Ofie's parents before they moved to Utah in the late nineties.

Wearing crisp new capri jeans, and her craftista shirt, Nana Chata sat like a boxing coach, legs spread apart. She put her hand on Ofie's head and looked sternly into her eyes. "I'm proud of you, m'ija."

Ofie felt birthday-party happy. She had lived for years feeling invisible and unworthy to Nana Chata. To hear these words made her want to break down and sob like she did every time she watched *The Joy Luck Club*. "Thank you! I hope I come through today. I really want to win the prizes for our family."

Nana Chata shook her head. "No, not the yarn stuff. I mean, yes for that, too, but mostly I'm proud of you for being a good wife to my son, and a good mother to my granddaughter. I'm sorry you heard me that day. I didn't mean it. Ay, menopause and all that...sometimes my meds are out of whack and I unleash. Ay, that didn't come out right...What I'm saying is...taking care of my family is what I know best. It's all I know and it's what I love to do most."

Ofie reached out and took Nana Chata's hand. "I owe you an apology too. You've done so much for us, and have never asked for anything in return. I needed to hear the truth. Even with the craftistas, you are always there to help and keep everyone on track. I don't know what we would do without you, Nana Chata. And I'm so happy you have your drumming group!"

Nana Chata tossed her head back, laughed, and patted Ofie on the knee. "I do. And I owe that to you. For making me go to La Pachanga. I didn't want to go to eat that day at all. I only went because I knew you *didn't* want me to go. Ha! Pero, I ended up liking it. And finding a boyfriend too!"

"What?" Ofie asked, not sure if she had heard Nana Chata correctly.

"Never mind. I'll save that for later. All I want to say is that I love you. I always have, and no matter what happens today, you are a champion. *The* champion. Got it, kiddo?"

Ofie threw her arms around her mother-in-law and hugged her so tightly, Nana Chata coughed. "I love you too, Nana Chata."

Anjelica ran into the room, with Larry right behind her.

"Mommy, Star is here. Look what she made you!" Anjelica held up a colorful glass prayer candle decorated in turquoise glitter, paint, sequins, and an illustrated image of Ofie. Across the top was a small banner that read "Santa Ofelia."

It was a gesture of good luck, although they all knew Ofie didn't need it.

39

The nineteenth annual CraftOlympics opened for business at the Phoenix Convention Center. A row of jumbo charter buses snaked from the front of the building all the way around to the side. As each set of transport doors opened, eager craft enthusiasts raced to the convention entrance, praying they would be first in line to win one of the top-dollar door prizes.

The eight-hundred-thousand-square-foot consumer show could be described as Fashion Week Meets ComicCon: Costumed mascots, cameras, speeches, demos, runway models, agents, movie stars, and editors. Everyone who attended was on a mission. Retail buyers from chain stores and craft boutiques hunted for cool, innovative merchandise that would fly off their store shelves and motivate shoppers to craft. More than four thousand vendors showcased all those new products, such as computerized silk-screen machines, glitter vacuums, yarn spun from soybeans, kits that allowed you to create custom colors, even decorate-your-own patron saints. Each business trotted out celebrity crafters from around the country to demonstrate glitters, glues, resins, varnishes, papers, and scissors.

Early in the day, Anjelica and Benecio visited a vendor and constructed a book from embossed cardboard and paper made from celery. They used it to collect autographs from the many craft-lebrities wandering about, each with their own superhero tagline: The Sublime Stitcher, the Impatient Beader, the Crafty Chica, the Craft Diva, the Mantastic Crafter, Sew Darn Jenny, Funky Shui, the Mad Cropper, the Knitty Gritty lady, Pattie Wack, the Scissor Seesters—and the most famous of them all—Betty Oh! from their hometown of Phoenix, Arizona.

Spread out across five halls, each carpeted aisle in the event buzzed with do-it-yourself conviction. Artists paraded samples of reconstructed clothing, stitched handbags, and plush toys. Some worked the endorsements and book deals. Domestic divas from across the nation flew out to meet with TV producers and to audition for upcoming cable network series.

To think this was the gig Chloe had prepared for all year—her chance for national fame. Nowadays, she'd rather read an old issue of *Cat Fancy*, and she didn't even like cats. Chloe wandered up and down the never-ending rows tiered with a multitude of hi-tech adhesives, ornate stencils, and luxurious scrapbook kits. She admired the experienced artists demo-ing in the exhibit booths, and daydreamed about what her life would have been like if she had tried to make her own crafts instead of using Frances'. Maybe then she could have truly been self-respecting Crafty Chloe. But no. Her tagline had become Phony Chloe—forced to act like a recluse at the most artful gathering in the nation. She decided to buy a glass of wine and hide out at the craftistas' booth.

When she arrived, Benecio Valencia Sr., Benecio's father, grinned while straightening the pamphlets on the table.

"Hi, Chloe, I'm Ben, Benecio's dad. I've heard so much about you."

Chloe removed her glasses and shook the gentleman's hand, confused. Last she heard, Benecio kept his design career on the double down low from his parents.

"I know you're wondering why I'm here… ," Ben began to explain. "I've…left my wife. Or I should say, she left me. For our summer intern."

Oooh, ouch! Chloe thought, astonished he would speak so openly about family affairs. Chloe had heard gossip at the station about Benecio's mom's reputation with the assistants, but didn't think she'd ever leave her husband for one. "I'm so sorry…I don't know what to say…"

"Don't worry. It's better for everyone, to tell you the truth. Listen, um…Benecio told me all about the craft group and the centerpieces last night. You must think we're awful parents, having no clue what our son is up to. Frankly, I'm embarrassed…" His polite expression turned stoic. Chloe rushed around the table to soothe him. Several months ago, Benecio and Chloe had had a heart-to-heart about neglectful parents—despite their age difference, it was a topic they shared and it pleased Chloe that Ben had seen the light. Hopefully Benecio wouldn't have to go through the pain she'd gone through all her life.

"Thank you for taking care of my boy," Ben said. "I'm so impressed by him—I really had no idea…Anyway, I'm going to be his business manager from now on…and an even better father."

Chloe patted his back. "Just be a good dad, show him you love him, listen to him, support him. That's all he needs." Then, bumping him with her arm, she said, "Now let's perk up and show off his hard work!"

"Excuse me," said a woman dressed as a gypsy, wearing a tiara wrapped in sequins. "Would you like a sample of Color-Your-Own Tarot Cards?"

On the oddity scale the gypsy didn't even rank. Chloe had already encountered a giant walking crayon, storm troopers, a human statue covered in glitter, models in dresses made from juice pouches, and a Scottish bagpipe troop.

"Sure!" Chloe answered cheerily as she and Ben accepted a pack. She tossed it in her tote, where it joined bladeless scissors, premade scrapbook pages, edible glitter, and invisible markers.

She checked her watch because she knew Ofie's Speed Crochet was coming up soon, and she wanted a front-row seat.

At that moment, Star, Maria Juana, Benecio, and Anjelica ran over, frenzied and out of breath.

"It's time! Speed crochet! Ofie! Stage A!" Star panted, gesturing for Chloe to follow. Benecio's dad stayed behind to watch the booth, while the others took Star's enthusiastic cue.

"Come on," Star said, busting through the mass of attendees. "Let's all walk together in a row, so we'll look like a bad-ass—but happy—crafty gang. Did you see the Craft Queens of New Orleans? Their shirts light up! I also saw the Austin Craft Mafia. They're wearing sharkskin suit dresses and pillbox hats—all made from fabric scraps. Look!" Star pointed and jumped. "It's the NYC Craft Bunnies! We need to invite them to La Pachanga tonight!"

"Star!" Chloe hollered. "Stop. You passed it! The main stage is over here. Hurry!"

Star did a U-ie to meet up with her crafty comadres, and then clung to Chloe's arm. "How is Mission Undercover going?"

"So far, so good," Chloe replied as she jerked her hat down to her brow line.

When they reached the fifty-foot stage, they all froze mid walk and gawked. Star covered Ofie's eyes.

"Oh dear alpaca. Larry! What did you get me into?" Ofie said, brushing Star's hands away.

Her visual inventory of the behemoth of a stage began with the multicolored theater lights that hung from the inside ceiling. Ofie then admired the ornate embroidered backdrop that draped and swagged across the back wall, and then the twelve giant spools of thread that doubled as chairs, which were lined up in the center of the floor. She thought the Hulk-sized scissors leaning against each wall for decoration were clever, and the four microphones frightening. Ofie's eyes traveled around the exterior of the structure, taking in the thousands of twinkling lights, capped off with front-facing JumboTrons on either side. If that wasn't intimidating enough, dozens of cameramen began to set up tripods.

"What? Is HGTV doing rock concerts now?" Star remarked as guests immediately filed in, taking up almost all the seats. She couldn't mask her surprise. "Wow, this really *is* a big event!"

"All speed crochet contestants in Heat Number One step up to the side of the stage," boomed a voice through the convention hall speakers.

"That's you, Mommy," Anjelica said.

"No, baby, I'm Heat Number Three," Ofie corrected just as a group of college-aged women surrounded her.

"Ofie Fuentes? Can we talk to you for a sec?"

Ofie turned to the six smiling women who surrounded her.

"Did I do something wrong? Am I'm disqualified? Can I at least stay to watch?"

They all chuckled, but one, a young lady with long curly blond hair and a cherub face, put her hand out to Ofie. "It's an honor to meet you. You inspire us!"

Ofie craned her head around to make sure they were talking to her. "Me?"

"Yes, you! I'm Emily Savoy from Bundle Up America. We received the blankets you sent for needy families—as well as your letter about how you came to make them."

"You really read it?" Ofie asked, pressing her hand against her chest. After finally clearing out her house she didn't want to clutter it again with her blankets. So she did a little research and found a way to put them to use. "I didn't mean to sound so whiny, but it's all true."

"We all read it," acknowledged another girl in a *Twilight* tee. "Your story is very moving and inspiring. You brought us all to tears. We even saw your video footage on YouTube!"

"Video footage?' Ofie asked, completely confused.

"Oh, I forgot to tell you, Mom," Anjelica confessed. "Remember the parking lot crochet race at Maker's Marketplace? Well... I kinda filmed you with my camera phone, and posted it online. It has thousands of hits!"

Ofie covered her mouth with her hand. "What?"

"We came all the way from the East Coast to cheer you on," Emily said before Ofie could respond to her Internet fame. "We want you to be the national spokesperson for our next campaign!"

Honored, and feeling like the Susan Boyle of yarn, Ofie happily agreed and then signed autographs until she heard "Heat Three, take the stage!" from the announcer.

Her instant fan club just about lifted her off the floor and funneled her toward the stage for her heat. At last, it seemed, the insecure cuckoo crafter had blossomed into a radiant artistic expert.

The group all whistled as Ofie gracefully walked to her battle station to greet large balls of worsted-weight yarns. Larry stood next to Anjelica, and they held up a glittery banner that read "Viva La Crochetinator!"

Chloe rushed the stage and handed Ofie a bottled water. "Consider me your personal assistant, my friend. Tell me whatever you need and I'll fetch it!" Ofie took the water and said thanks. The four opponents all mouthed the words "good luck" to one another.

Betty Oh! stepped up and the crowd yahooed, whistled, and applauded for the pretty national media personality.

"Are you ready for this?" she screamed into the red, white, and blue Bedazzled microphone.

The crowd roared back in response.

"Alrighty, it's time to get looped!" Betty yelled at the

contestants. "Here's the deal: You each have two rows of twenty stitches as your foundation. You have *three* minutes to crank out as many double stitches as you can. The person with the most wins and goes on to the finals. Got it, ladies?"

The women sat poised and agreed.

"Ready...goooooo!" Betty Oh! screamed.

The crowd cheered as hooks flew at a dizzying pace. When it ended, Ofie had won her heat with ease. Everyone expected her to cry, but she didn't. She fluffed her hair, cocked back her shoulders, and blew a kiss to the crowd as they howled for her.

Chloe and Star were the ones who wept like babies. They hugged and wiped away each other's tears of joy. Larry and Anjelica, however, rocked out as if it were Ozzy Osbourne on that stage. The father-and-daughter duo pumped their fists in the air and cheered.

Next up, the finals. Ofie's competitors were three-time champion Nina Sakumoto and...the infamous Scary Lady—as Anjelica and Ofie had affectionately named her. Ofie had whipped her butt at Maker's Marketplace, and knew she could do it again.

"Ready! Set! CROCHET!!!!" Betty howled again, this time jumping in the air like a possessed cheerleader.

Ofie, Nina, and Scary Lady twirled their hooks faster than the speed of sound. Or so it seemed to Star and Chloe, who screamed for their friend as if she were Oscar De La Hoya in the final minutes of a high-stakes bout.

"Hooks down!" Betty Oh! ordered after three minutes.

The ladies turned over their work to the judges and awaited the verdict with heightened anticipation. A minute later, Betty Oh! skipped over to Ofie, grabbed her wrist, and raised it high in the air. "We have a new Speed Crochet winner for the National! Craft! Olympics! At fourty double stitches a minute, Phoenix's own Ofie Fuentes!"

Ofie's friends jumped and screamed with the rest of the audience.

"What do you have to say, Ofie?" Betty Oh! asked, pogo-dancing around her. "You won! You won! You are the country's fastest crocheter!"

Ofie took the mic from Betty, confident as if she were a seasoned speaker.

"Hello, my fellow crafters! My name is Ofelia Fuentes and thank you for welcoming me to the nineteenth annual CraftOlympics!"

The crowd roared and chanted in her honor. Ofie bounced her hands in the air as a signal for them to quiet down.

"I wouldn't be up here today if it were not for my friend Benecio Javier Valencia II, who taught me to crochet; my husband, Larry, daughter, Anjelica, and mother-in-law, Chata, who encouraged me to enter this competition; and my dear friends, Chloe and Star. And to all of you out there who think you are not special? I'm here to prove you are! Even when all the world is against you, you have to have faith in yourself; otherwise you are no good to anyone. Find what you are good at and celebrate it. Even if you only know one crochet stitch like me—look how far you can go with it! So get out there and craft your life the way *you* want it!"

Tears glistened down Betty Oh!'s cheeks from Ofie's emotional speech. She hugged Ofie again and handed over the blender-sized trophy. Ofie, cradling her prize, invited Anjelica onto the stage. She then kissed her daughter and gave her the trophy. "This is for you," she said.

Anjelica sobbed, held it high above her head, and danced. Just like Cha Cha DiGregorio in *Grease* when she won the dance-off with Danny Zuko.

40

Even though the second day of the CraftOlympics couldn't quite live up to the excitement of Ofie's feat the day before, it came pretty damn close.

Ofie spent the day signing autographs, answering questions, and meeting with yarn companies about endorsement opportunities and even some guest TV spots. Right by her side stood Benecio's father, who agreed to act as her manager and agent. Thanks to his son's crochet lesson, Ofie's life, and that of her family's, would never be the same.

While Ofie repeated her meltdown-to-mogul story to the press, Star used the hours exclusively to sample and learn about as many craft products as possible for her new store. She played with inks, wands, beads, charms, wire, papers, cutters, tracers, nippers, erasers, scissors, slicers, hooks, and hairpins. Her head spun with ideas for workshops. She hadn't quite nailed down a theme for the shop, but knew she wanted it to involve glitter, graffiti, and mixed media as an ode to the chaos of the past fall. It had been the longest, toughest months of her life, but in the end, rewarding. She thought of a quote from Mohandas Gandhi that her father always told her growing up. He repeated it so much that she had blanked out the message. But today, as she pondered about her new journey, the words floated through her mind like a bird gliding through the air with a ribbon in its beak:

"Every worthwhile accomplishment, big or little, has its stages of drudgery and triumph; a beginning, a struggle, and a victory."

At 5:59 p.m. that Thursday evening, fifteen hundred hungry industry professionals waited outside the main banquet hall for the formal dinner and awards presentation. Finally, the servers slowly pulled the majestic gilded doors open to reveal the regal banquet hall. The mouths of the incoming guests gaped. They released a unified chorus of *"Oooooh!"* when greeted with millions of enchanting, sparkly glimmers of light all across the enormous dining room. The glass-glitter cactus garden centerpieces.

Ofie, Star, and Benecio watched the professional attendees marvel at the handiwork on each piece—and then rib each other over the silent auction sheet. They passed the paper back and forth across the table, each person scribbling a higher price to determine which lucky person would own the southwest collectable.

"Our job here is done," Star told Ofie, who put her arm around her friend and escorted her to their assigned table. Poor Chloe refused to attend the dinner, for fear of confrontation by her former crafty colleagues. She did, however, have a special package for Frances and hoped to encounter her before the convention ended.

By the end of the ceremony, every centerpiece had sold, raising almost twenty thousand dollars for local and national charities, more than any previous CraftOlympics event. When Betty Oh! revealed the figure during dinner, the crowd roared with applause, and Star, Ofie, and Benecio stood, waved, and bowed to show thanks. They knocked knuckles with one another and went back to eating their strawberry cheesecake. Despite the drama it took to complete the centerpieces, they agreed the ordeal was worth every drop of sweat and tears.

On Friday, the last morning of the CraftOlympics, Star taught a love shrine class arranged by her dad. She returned from the three-hour seminar glowing about how she helped a group from the women's shelter. During lunch with Chloe, Ofie, and Benecio, she went on about her students, who created shrines for inspiration and hope in dealing with everything from divorces and infertility to job hunting and returning to school. Star even talked to the director of the shelter, and volunteered to teach the class once a month. After the meal, Star made one more spin around the convention center to ensure she soaked everything up. She licked her thumb and ruffled through the pages in her embroidered notebook to check her list, and heard a group of young girls asking people to knit a stitch.

Star tucked her notepad in her embossed leather shoulder bag and took a look at their booth.

"Wow, that poncho is gorgeous. Did you make it?" asked one of the girls to Star.

"I wish! My grandmother made it for me when I was a teenager. It's two oversized Acapulco tourist scarves that she sewed together." Star lifted her locks and spun around to show off Nana Esteban's handiwork. "So what are you up to here? I must have missed this booth."

Two other girls stood up. One of them guided Star to a large cardboard chair and had her sit, while the other girl shoved knitting needles in her hands and a kamikaze-looking knitted blanket on her lap.

"Would you like to knit a stitch for our Victims of Violence blanket? It's okay if you don't know how to knit. We'll teach you."

Well, what do you know? Star thought. *Great minds think alike.*

"By any chance, was this awesome blanket knitted by all kinds of people united with a common goal of comfort and warmth to those who have been harmed by violence?" she asked.

The girls swapped stunned looks. "Yes! That is exactly what it is about! We've been working on it for two years. This blanket has traveled through Africa, Latin America, and India. After this show it goes to Japan. We're trying to make it the world's biggest blanket, knitted by the most people."

Wow, Star thought. They even one-upped her idea. "Well, I'm honored to have met you."

"What do you do? Are you an artist or a crafter?"

"Both. We all are both, don't you think?" Star asked. "So, are you based in Phoenix?"

"We are, but the national organization is in San Francisco. Why?"

Star pulled out her notebook again and wrote all of her contact information, ripped out the page, and handed it over. "I'm opening a local craft boutique soon and I would love to have you bring the blanket for people to see and learn about your cause. I can help you reel in more knitters, plus set up a donation drive too. In the meantime, I would love to add some stitches. Will you teach me?"

That afternoon Star returned home to work on her business plan for The Glittered Cactus. Chloe volunteered to work the booth, since Ofie had been asked to do a last-minute media satellite tour. The CraftOlympics executives were even talking about sending her to New York in March for a National Craft Month publicity road trip.

While Chloe manned the table in her ludicrous getup, her brain free of worries, she slouched back in her folding chair and crossed her Rockette-worthy legs. She examined her unpolished nails, which hadn't seen a mani in a month. Now unemployed, she'd have to cut back on a few splurges even though Gustavo had agreed to take over her loft payments until it sold. She couldn't wait until they found a place together so they could begin their new journey as a married couple. Chloe smirked just thinking about it. With both their savings, she didn't have to find a job for a while. For the first time since grade school, she could actually *relax*.

"I can't believe you had the nerve to show up. Who are you trying to scam now? I should report you to the CraftOlympic authorities."

Chloe didn't move, but flicked her eyes up. She removed her glasses. Just the person she wanted to see—Frances. Talk about a makeover! Frances showed off a tailored black business suit, no glasses, full makeup, and her hair stylishly piled and pinned on top of her head. Ezra was by her side, and they both glared at Chloe as if she had just drained the blood from their firstborn.

"Frances, you look beautiful! And I'm not here for me. I'm here to support my friends and, as you can see, I'm lying low."

"Right," Ezra said, rolling his eyes.

Ignoring him, Chloe looked at her former assistant. "Frances, I have something for you." Chloe bent over, retrieved a manila envelope from her briefcase, and offered it.

"What is this?" Frances asked, standing back as if she expected the package to explode.

"It's a letter of recommendation for you. Considering my situation, I'm not sure how much it will help, but I've also included my entire media contact list for you to use as you wish. I put ideas in there on how to pitch a new craft series. If you work hard, you can build it into something bigger. I've always said you were an outstanding designer, and anything I can do to make up for my past shortcomings, I'll do."

Frances pouted. "Why are you being so nice? I mean, th-thank you." She started to leave the booth, but then suddenly turned back. "I'm sorry I hurt you like that. All I ever wanted was for you to like me! I worked so hard to please you, but nothing was ever good enough for you."

In that moment, Chloe saw herself as her mother, and Frances as her. Chloe rose and looked Frances in the eye. "I apologize for being a horrible person. You deserved a better boss. Please call me if you ever need anything at all, okay? You are the real deal. Beautiful inside and out."

"Thank you, Ms. Chavez," Frances replied, dabbing a tear from the corner of her eye. "For once, I can really tell you are being sincere, and I appreciate it."

Ezra, feeling excluded from the sisterfriend circle, wandered onto the next exhibit area. Chloe took advantage of the opportunity to offer Frances a nugget of advice.

"If you don't mind me saying, Frances—unless you and Ezra are madly in love, you can do much better."

Frances nodded reassuringly, as if she already knew. The women shook hands with balanced respect, and wished one another the best of luck.

Maybe Chloe's father's dream of her spotlight moment wouldn't manifest after all, but he would be proud that she married Gustavo, a good man who loved her. And who could serenade her while he steamed up a killer curry stir-fry.

"Did you have a good show?" Chloe asked Benecio when he approached the booth an hour later. He came around to stand next to her and tugged at her glasses. "Those specs are hideous.

Big sunglasses are so 2008. I could have designed a better disguise than that!"

"Like I asked, did you have a good show?"

Benecio gave her a fast hug. "It was great. I got an endorsement from Ebony Leather, and two guest spots on some craft TV shows!"

"Congrats, I knew you'd kill it!" She softly punched him with her fist.

"Chloe, I made you a wedding gift. I don't think Gustavo will wear it, but I'll make him his own bag later in Rasta colors. Here's yours. I call it the Naughty Neapolitan bag because it's cream, hot pink, and light brown. I think it's time you end the taupe fixation, and move on to brighter colors. At least I gave you a longer strap, just how you like it."

"Aw, thanks. Hey, these days, I'm all about trying new things. Pink, brown, and cream it is. It's already my favorite," she said, tilting her head. "Hey, now, you're dad is waiting for you. Go home and be a teenager. No more talk about work!" she said, twisting him around by his shoulders to face his dad, who waited by the exit doors. Benecio waved and left the building.

Yes, the cosmos had sent Chloe a message: Step out of the spotlight so it could shine on others more deserving. She pushed the silly hat off her head, let her blond hair cascade to her shoulders, and swiped the glasses off her face. Who cared if anyone recognized her? She'd have to fess up to the crafting community eventually. Might as well be now. Bored, she unfastened her makeup compact and checked her teeth for lipstick smears. She heard a couple women snicker in her direction when they passed by the table. Maybe she wasn't ready for the backlash after all, she thought as she lunged for the hat.

"Chloe Chavez?" came an upbeat voice from behind.

Chloe inhaled, exhaled, and turned to answer. After being so mean to so many people, she braced to take some boomerang blows. "Yes...?" she replied with caution, ready to block any oncoming rotten tomatoes aimed at her face.

Chloe could have hyperventilated, but she didn't.

The voice belonged to Betty Oh! And alongside her stood a gentleman in a smooth black suit, briefcase in hand. "Hi, Chloe, I'm Betty O'Hara. I've heard so much about you, I wanted to come and introduce myself. It's so nice to meet you!"

Chloe let her hat fall to the floor so she could shake Betty Oh!'s famous hand. "The honor is all mine, Betty. You've been such an inspiration to me. I suppose you've heard about what happened, but I assure you, I'm a changed person. I didn't mean to disgrace the craft industry."

"Please, you don't have to explain anything to me. I've been there."

"You have?" Chloe asked.

"Sure! We've all had to go to extremes to reach our goals. The TV industry will do that to you. Do you know one time I posed as a belly dancer just to sneak into a media expo? I wore a scarf around my face, and shimmied and shook my hips. At the end of every performance I handed out little Betty Oh! CD-ROMS cut to the size of business cards." Betty laughed.

Her friend, visibly surprised, crossed his brows and half smiled. "You never told me that. Is that how you've come so far? Secret belly dances?"

Betty tossed her head back and let out another robust chuckle. "Oh gosh, I haven't thought of that in ages. I like to think of it as my *Charlie's Angels* undercover moment. I have always loved crafting so much that I wanted to make a living from it. I didn't want to be a journalist or a TV star. I used those avenues to launch my home arts career."

"Funny," Chloe replied, wrapping her arms around herself, "that is the opposite of my story."

"Well. It gets better." Betty continued. "You know the morning craft segments I did on KPDM? Originally when I asked to do them the executive producer said no. He thought it would lessen the credibility of the newscast. But I knew different. I crafted with women and kids in my spare time, and I knew they would love the feature. I couldn't convince him. So one day, I hid all the supplies under my suit jacket. Instead of sharing the Wednesday grocery ads, I pulled out the supplies and taught how to make a gift card book from cut-up cereal boxes. My boss stormed onto the set, furious! I almost lost my job. He sent me home early, suspended me for a day without pay. I cried my eyes out because I thought I had lost income for my family, all because of a self-indulgent delusion. But the viewers saved me, Chloe. They called in and demanded my return—and more crafty ideas! The rest is history."

"Oh my God, Betty, that is an amazing story," Chloe said. "I've followed every inch of your career and never knew that. I always thought these great gigs came your way out of luck."

Betty walked behind the table and relaxed on the closest chair. "The great gigs come from loving what you do. And you have to love it so much that you would do it for free. If my career ended tomorrow, I would still be at home cropping photos of my kids. And yes, some amount of luck—or as I call it, serendipitous timing—is involved. But we have to make our own luck, Chloe. And it can't be modeled after anyone else's. We have to pinpoint our best qualities and market them. And that is what brings me here to you."

"What?" Chloe asked, fascinated, as she smoothed her hair back. She wondered if she needed more lipstick.

"Chloe, I'd like you to meet a colleague of mine, Rene Cordova," Betty said.

Rene extended his arm and shook Chloe's shaky hand. "Hi, Chloe. I'm a senior casting director from Cosmopolitan Casa Productions. We produce high-quality Latino-themed shows for various networks. Betty has become a partner, and has shown me some of your clips. You're a natural. We're very impressed with you. We're here because we have some exciting opportunities that we'd like to run by you and your agent."

"I'm flattered. Thank you! But can I ask a question?"

"Of course," Rene said.

"Betty, would you ever consider visiting our craft group sometime?"

"As long as there is an outlet for my glue gun, I'll be the first to arrive!"

41

Ofie added the final touch of cream cheese frosting to the red velvet cake she had prepared for the evening's holiday craft up. She used brewed espresso instead of water for the mix, and chocolate fudge pudding for the inside filling. Because those were two new experimental techniques, Ofie taste-tested the concoction. She licked her lips, slid the knife into the cake, and trimmed off a one-inch strip down the shortest end. She scraped it into a small cereal bowl and quickly frosted up the raw side.

She had ten minutes to partake in this sinful, secretive delicacy, and she savored every moist and gooey chew. As she leaned against the fridge and ate, she replayed the last month's events.

Noticing the hour, she tossed the bowl in the sink. Time to fire up the heaters in the back room for the craftistas. They had all agreed to keep the group going every other Wednesday and bring whatever they wanted to work on. After cranking out two hundred identical centerpieces, freeform crafting seemed like the way to go. Ofie volunteered to host for the rest of December, and promised herself to save all her crafting for the meetings.

The hullabaloo over the CraftOlympics had simmered down in the week since the event, but Ofie's new persona trumped

Rachael Ray's on Thanksgiving Day. As winner of the Speed Crochet competition, Ofie not only scored prizes galore, but a book editor from a major trade publisher asked her to share her story. After thinking long and hard, Ofie came up with the title *Stitches for the Spirit: Crochet Your Way to Personal Glory*. In addition, Bundle Up America hired her to appear in magazine ads this winter, and Benecio's dad signed on as her agent. Even Anjelica got tapped to participate in a teen craft book.

Ofie set the clear plastic covering over the table and thought about how Benecio's life had turned a corner as well. His mom moved out shortly before the CraftOlympics, but Benecio and his father seemed closer than ever. His dad converted the guest room into his son's design studio, and stepped up as his manager. The beauty, Ofie thought, was that he agreed to accompany Benecio to the craft meetings—not for the sake of BJV's Design, but for friendship and conversation.

But Ofie was most thrilled with Nana Chata, who joined the group in order to scrapbook her memories with the Del Tambor Africana.

The Wednesday-night gathering was in full swing, but they all agreed it just wasn't the same without Star, who spent most of her time working on programs for her new shop, which she aimed to open in January. Her friends knew full well it was her way of dealing with Theo living five hundred miles away. Star said they talked by phone every night, but Ofie knew that didn't quite satisfy the itch.

"I'm so happy Star got drunk and spray painted happy faces all over Theo's mosaic mural," Ofie blurted while she passed around the cake slices. "Chloe, did you bring the coffee?"

"That's kind of random, Mom," Anjelica said.

"Me too," Chloe said, hiking up a box of freshly brewed java from the local bagel shop and setting it on the table. "Think about it. If it weren't for Star, we wouldn't have all come together.

I wouldn't have stopped at the Chi-Chi Coffee Cabana and met my husband."

"Hey," Benecio added. "You're right!"

"Right. I'm sure Star is real happy. Because of her mess, her soul mate is stuck in another state," Nana Chata stated. "You all made out like bandits, and that girl is all alone."

"Why don't we throw her a surprise party for her birthday? It's this Friday, December tenth! I can ask Al and Dori if we can use her new shop; it's still empty."

The group agreed and brainstormed the logistics before starting their projects in progress.

An hour later, Benecio and his dad halfheartedly worked on their lino print note card project. Ofie crocheted a skinny rainbow scarf for Anjelica, and Nana Chata painted a drum. Chloe just drank coffee, and told them about her new job hosting a home-improvement series for a new English-language Latino network. They didn't hire her for her crafting skills; they wanted her strictly for her talent as an upbeat, quick-thinking host. The show would take only six weeks out of the year to film, so she could still live in Phoenix and start a family with Gustavo.

The doorbell rang and everyone looked at one another, stumped as to whom it could be.

"Larry...please get that...," Ofie yelled. "I keep money in the jar on the bookshelf in case it is kids selling Christmas candy to earn a trip to Disneyland..."

"Aye, those are all scams, m'ija," Nana Chata said as she dipped her brush onto a paper plate filled with purple paint.

"Now, Nana Chata...," Ofie said.

Larry walked into the Arizona room with his hands in his pockets.

"Tyra mail?" Chloe asked.

"Better. You'll never believe who just arrived."

42

Lying on her antique iron-framed bed, wrapped tight like a butterfly inside of a cocoon, Star hugged her pillow and tried not to think about Theo falling in love with someone else in Santa Fe. Sure, they talked every night by phone, but how long could that last? His new art rep already had several swanky affairs booked in his honor, and they all fell on days when Star could not attend. Holiday season had settled in; her parents needed her back at La Pachanga full-time, on top of her press release clients and situating her new business.

Star squeezed her eyes shut at the thought of dying a spinster at her art desk, with a jar of German glass glitter in one hand and a bottle of dried-out varnish in the other.

This had to be the worst birthday in all her twenty-five years. Her parents and the craftistas took her to Matt's Big Breakfast in the morning, and it took every ounce of energy for Star to show appreciation. Ever since Theo left, nothing excited Star. As much as she cherished their last night together, it made the separation twice as hard than if they had never crossed paths. At least she had moved on and her skin had thickened. Now, here she sat, all alone on her birthday, wanting to scarf down every type of Warm Delight dessert invented.

As long as she channeled her energy into the shop, she'd be fine. She'd make it the hippest place to splash paint. She planned to devote every waking minute to setting it up, teaching classes, and scouring the universe for killer merchandise. Anything to keep her mind off Theo.

A little after six p.m., Star put on her pajamas and crawled back under two thick rainbow afghans that Ofie had made. Tonight's cinematic double feature fit with the mood: *Splendor in the Grass* and *Moulin Rouge*—two sappy tales about love that would never be. She had accomplished so much these past few months, she'd earned a night of wallowing. Pathetic, maybe. But at least it was a step up from the doomed love scene compilation DVD she'd made before. She reminded herself to post it on YouTube for other tortured women. The opening music for *Moulin Rouge*, a Rufus Wainwright ballad, had just started when her iPhone rang.

"Star, you need to come down to the restaurant, please!" her father pleaded. "The back house has been vandalized. Put some nice clothes on this time. Hurry!"

Star hung up, and groaned. Her dad wouldn't win any Academy Awards with that kind of acting. She had predicted all along they would throw her a surprise party. She even fake-coughed all day so they'd think she was sick, but obviously it didn't work.

Oh, who was she kidding. Star loved surprise parties, especially when they were for her. And this would be just what she needed to lift her mood.

Over at La Pachanga, to prepare for the night, Ofie had rounded up Star's parents, Benecio, his dad, Chloe, Gustavo, Maria Juana, all of Las Bandidas del Fuego, Nana Chata, Anjelica, and Larry. This would be the gang's biggest crafty project yet.

The group worked all day Friday transforming Star's shop into an artful atmosphere. Of course, more details needed to be added, but at least it was off to a good beginning.

When the magic hour came, Dori cranked up the holiday spirit by playing Los Kumbia Kings, Ozomatli, Selena, Girl in a Coma, Manu Chao, and Star's favorite—Yerba Buena—from the jukebox while they set the stage for Star's surprise party. Larry and Gustavo hung two dozen red Sacred Heart papel picado banners from the ceiling, while Nana Chata and Dori worked in the kitchen to prepare an enchanting Mexican feast of molé, rice, beans, and churros drizzled with chocolate sauce.

Benecio, his dad, and Maria Juana cut and sprinkled silver Mylar squares all over the ornate stenciled floor while Ofie whipped up a set of red and purple place mats. Chloe took up Frances' idea of covering a lampshade with poinsettia petals. The mood, the lighting, the food—everything had to be just right.

"Okay, let's run through the list. Are all of these done? Birthday cake, mariachis, dinner, decorations, party favors...," Ofie demanded with the determination of a head nun at the annual church craft fair.

They all agreed in unison.

"Has anyone heard from our subject? Where is she?" Chloe asked.

"On her way," Al confirmed. "We should assume our positions."

Star parked her Chevy Bel Air as the gang hid behind the bushes and watched. With her hair pinned up, she stepped out in a flirty gold satin cocktail dress, strappy heels, and a long sparkly red sweater—all that an Arizona winter required.

She walked briskly through La Pachanga, and greeted all the customers who waved at her. As she passed through the back door of the restaurant, she saw her soon-to-be craft shop dark and abandoned.

When she opened the door, she was stunned. Though totally void of party guests, the room looked as if Colin Cowie himself had lit every candle and arranged every flower. Small café tables filled the space, partnered with glittery emerald vinyl chairs. The only other fixture was a bar table in the center of the room with a hot-pink gift box on top. The always-inquisitive Star approached it, read her name on the stamped tag, and picked it up. She wondered if there were cameras rolling, if this was some sort of prank. Cautiously she removed the lid.

For a moment, everything stopped: Her thoughts, her breath, even her heartbeat.

Nestled inside a bed of paper shredding was the first, and most personal, love shrine she'd ever made—the shrine for Theo. She raised it and noticed it had been refurbished. Suddenly the back door of the shop opened and the next moment played out like a Mexican soap opera. Theo sauntered inside.

She craved him like a BBQ dinner on an empty stomach. He looked so tasty and garnished just right: His dark hair combed back, clean-shaven face, charcoal-gray sweater, black slacks, and shiny black dress shoes. She had never seen his body more cut. Star felt her chest rise and fall, half because she didn't want to cry, and half because she was so thrilled to be near him.

A mariachi trio stepped out and began to play *"Paloma Negra"* by Lola Beltran—the song Theo sang to her on Día de los Muertos.

There in the middle of The Glittered Cactus, he greeted her with a deep and devoted kiss.

"How in the world did you get this?" Star asked, pointing to the shrine. She couldn't contain her joy and her hands began to tremble.

A broad smile spread across his face, showcasing his irresistible dimples. "Chloe had it all this time. She'll have to tell you the details. I wish I had kept it the night you tried to give it to me—"

"Theo, wait," she cut him off. "Why are you here. You have your first show tonight."

"I wanted to be here for your birthday. No show is worth missing that."

The idea of him chancing his new lifestyle just for her was touching, but didn't sit well. She didn't want to be the one who caused him to lose his new high-profile sales rep.

"You can't do this. Oh my God, all those people are there waiting for you!" Star began to pace around the room, until she plopped down in one of the chairs.

"Hey, I was kinda expecting a warmer welcome, Estrella. Give a guy a break. I knew you weren't going to come see me anytime soon."

"Are you trying to make me feel bad? I need some fresh air…" She swung her arms and left swiftly through the front door.

Nana Chata's head emerged from the top of the hedges that lined the entrance of the property. "Star, get back in there! He has good news!"

Everyone else popped their heads up one at a time over the hedge too and hollered in agreement.

Star paused with a pensive look on her face. She grinned and shook her finger at her conspirators. "You guys are too much," she said and laughed before returning inside. She barely crossed the doorway when Theo slid his hands around her waist.

"I'm moving back, and I have my agent's blessing. I had no motivation out there. *You* are my motivation. They saw the painting I made of you and want more of that style. They told me they would rather have me live in Phoenix and make art I enjoy than be in Santa Fe and be blocked."

Star's legs felt limper than cooked spaghetti. "Are you saying what I think you're saying?" she asked, needing verbal confirmation before she considered a triple-happy back tuck.

Outside, Nana Chata scrunched down and excitedly signaled Anjelica over with a whistle. "Mi reina, take this quarter, run in there, and put it in the jukebox. Press E-seventeen and then run back over here. Andale!"

Anjelica sprinted in, her sneakers squeaking along the tile floor as she made her way to the jukebox Al had installed that week. She dropped in the coin, pressed the buttons, dashed back outside, and ducked along with the onlookers below the hedge.

Theo and Star squinted at each other, almost wanting to smile at the scheme they just witnessed. Star knew her girlfriends were crafty, but she never expected over-the-top corniness like this. Good thing Star had a weak spot for corny.

E17 loaded and began to play. It was Rose Royce's falsetto love ballad, "Wishing on a Star."

Theo danced with her for a minute and then led her out back. They walked to the edge of the property, and floodlights lit up along the wall of the studio. He had painted a mural over the fuchsia base coat she had painted. It was a wedding cake topper with a dark-haired couple. Above it was an outline of a ribbon banner held up by a pretty bluebird on each side. Inside the ribbon read in perfect script: "Estrella, will you marry me?—Te amo, Theo."

"Wow, your artistic vandalism sure beats mine—"

Theo didn't let her finish her sentence. He put his hands on her cheeks, and kissed her hard, so intensely she lifted a foot and balanced on the other, just like in the movies. He broke his lips away from hers. "Do you still mean it? The shrine you made me?"

Star couldn't say yes fast enough. "Every bit of it, and more."

He put his hands at the small of her back, and they swayed to the classic lowrider oldie that had since been cranked up a few notches in volume.

I feel it's time we should make up, baby.
I feel it's time for us to get back together.

He hugged her head, and leaned in to her ear and sucked in, sending a chill across her already-shivering body. "I love you, Estrella. Will you answer my question on the mural?"

"Do you even have to ask?"

"I want to hear it from your juicy lips."

"We all want to hear it from your juicy lips!" Benecio shouted. Everyone started to whistle and howl.

"YES!" Star threw her arms in the air. "I want to be your wife! I can't wait! Especially for the honeymoon," she said with a naughty nod. At last, Star had her love shine moment, just like her mom hoped she would.

"We can take care of that tonight... ," he said, pecking up and down her shoulder. "Want to hear something funny?"

"Go for it."

"You were right about the wedding brochures. I had too much pride to say so before, but I really did plan to ask you to marry me that night."

"Want to hear something funny, too?" Star asked.

"Go for it."

"I had planned to spray paint 'I love you, Theo' on the wall, but chickened out, and did happy faces instead."

"Hey, you two," Al interrupted. "Now that your business is all straightened out, can I change the subject? I found something while setting up I don't understand. What's this about three hundred and fifty pounds of glitter?"

Ofie led him away to fill him in and give him a sample. The others came out of hiding and a few new guests arrived.

"Star, I want to introduce you to my former remote cameraman from KPDM," Chloe said. "I bumped into him in the restaurant tonight and he has something he wants to tell you."

The burly Ving Rhames lookalike Star remembered from her

mural TV segment stepped in and nudged her elbow. "I want you to know, I learned to knit thanks to you!"

They all gathered around him and howled with laughter as he reenacted Star's actions from that day.

After a few more rounds of hugs and "I'm so happy for you!" conversations, Theo and Star coerced everyone inside to escape the cold. Gustavo began to play a samba-tinged version of Bob Marley's "Waiting in Vain," which made all the guests stand up and dance. Even the mariachis played along while Las Bandidas del Fuego rolled around on their skates and boogied.

The lights dimmed, and a disco ball sparkled all over the walls.

Star walked to the center of the dance floor and watched her friends and family sway to the tunes. She opened her arms over her head, twirled, and let the light's reflections dance on her skin. This was it. The love shine.

And no amount of glitter in the world could top it.

Glossary

Waking Up in the Land of Glitter has Spanish (and Spanglish) terms sprinkled throughout the book. Many of these words have multiple meanings that vary by region. However, this glossary features the translations as presented by the characters in the book.

amigas: female friends
ay, pobrecito: aw, poor thing
barrio: neighborhood
borincano: Puerto Rican man
borracha: drunken girl
cabrón: brat
café con leche: coffee with milk
cajita: small box
cariño: endearing affection
casita: small house
cerveza: beer
champurrado: Mexican hot chocolate
chicle: gum
chiquita: little girl
chola: A tough chick who represents her barrio. Usually wears a lot of makeup—thick liquid eyeliner, dark brown or red lipstick, and arched eyebrows drawn on really thin.

chonies: underwear

cojones: courage

corazón: heart

craftista: female crafter, as in *artista* (female artist)

Día de los Muertos: Day of the Dead

egotista: egotistical

El Solitario: Jinete Sin Fronteras: The Solo One: Rider Without Borders

esa: homegirl

estrella: star

familia: family

flauta: corn tortilla rolled up like a flute, filled with beef or chicken and then deep fried

gracias: thank you

grito: a hearty shout

hombre: man

huevos: the nerve; the balls or guts

la cocina fina: the fine kitchen

La Isla del Encanto: The Charmed Island

la pachanga: the party

Las Banditas del Fuego: The (female) Bandits of Fire

loca: crazy

lucha libre: Mexican wrestler

mamacita: little mama

menudo: Mexican soup made with hominy and beef tripe

mi hija: my daughter, often written as a contraction, *m'ija*

mi hijo: my son, often written as a contraction, *m'ijo*

mi loca artista: my crazy artist

mi tierra: my land

mota: marijuana

muchacha: little girl

mucho: very much

mujer: woman

nada: nothing

nalgas: butt cheeks

novia: girlfriend

ofrenda de amor: offering of love

pan dulce: sweet bread, Mexican pastries

pasión: passion

pero: but

pinche pendejo: crude way of saying "stupid idiot"

por favor: please

prima: cousin

puta: hootchie

que linda: how beautiful

qué pasa: what's up?

quinceañera: celebration for a girl who turns fifteen

si: yes

ruco: boyfriend

siéntese: sit down

talavera: a type of pottery painted with vivid colors

te amo: I love you

uno mas: one more

vato: dude

veté: go!—as in "Get out of here!"

Acknowledgments

Warning—excessive exclamation points ahead!

I owe 350 pounds (times a million!) of imported green glass glitter to my husband, Patrick Murillo, for his love and patience with me while I wrote this book. Every time I doubted myself, he made me push on. My kids, DeAngelo and Maya too! Some of my favorite memories are of all of them sitting on the bed while I read my chapters aloud. They offered so much insight, quips, and great tips—this book is theirs as well as mine!

Many prayers to my dad and grandparents in heaven for being my guardian angels. A tray of homemade cupcakes goes to my mom, Norma Cano, and my Nana Jauregui, for being so supportive. To my mother-in-law, Susie Murillo, for helping me with the house, kids, cooking, and chores so I could meet my book deadlines! Much love to the Cano, Hadley, Hidalgo, Christensen, Jauregui, and Garcia families for always asking for status updates with my writing.

I would also like to thank my friends who listened to me go on and on about the outline, plot, title, cover, and everything else involved: Valerie Marderosian, Alyson Dias, Lauren Binci, Cheryl Ball, Debbie Hines, Lindy Selnick, Jennifer Perkins, Alexa Westerfield, Margot Potter, Laurie Notaro, Michelle Savoy, Carrie Wheeler, Randy Cordova, Sarah Hodsdon, Nancy Marmolejo, and the Phoenix Fridas. Special gracias goes to my early readers, Kathya Hildalgo, Yoli Manzo, Belén Rodriguez, and Deborah Muller. A jar of sequins to everyone in the chica lit genre for paving the way for Latina writers! Thank you to Vickie Howell and Lisa Gentry for help with my speed crochet facts. Gracias to Terri Oulette and The Craft and Hubby Association.

A double-deluxe group hug to my agents, Erin Malone, Scott Wachs, and Bethany Dick at the William Morris Agency. Triple-thick thanks to Selina McLemore, my superhero editor, who coached me through the process and didn't get too upset when I had "Ofie" moments of my own! And to Latoya Smith and the staff at Grand Central Publishing—thank you for making my dream come true!

Glitter glue to Natalie, Jenny, and Rachel, and the crew at CraftZine.com for all the love.

A huge shout-out goes to the craft community and the Crafty Chica Cruises. I have met so many wonderful people in workshops, book signings, meet-ups, craft fairs, online networks, at conventions and other gatherings. Thank you for being just as *loca* for paint, paper, glitter, and glue and fabric as I am!

And a hand-over-my-heart thanks to YOU for reading this book. I hope it inspires you to live an artful life, or at least get crafty now and then. Remember—

Life is art.

Art is love!

Make a Love Shrine!

You know what kind of magic Star's shrine worked on Theo; now it's time for you to break out the glitter and glue and make one too!

This type of art is called assemblage. It's all about arranging objects in a random yet balanced manner. Because of this, no two shrines will ever look the same. Your masterpiece will be one-of-a-kind!

A shrine can be used for a variety of purposes. Create one to dress up a corner in your home, your desk at work, or give it as a gift to a friend or loved one. Theme it toward something you adore or hope to do—like a travel adventure, a wild date, or anything else that triggers happy emotions. If you have a loved one who passed on, make one in honor of them.

Here is what you'll need:

Music! Background music helps set the mood. Why not check out some of the artists mentioned in the book? Foreign movie soundtracks, Yerba Buena, Manu Chao, Amy Winehouse, Rufus Wainwright, Dusty Springfield, Girl in a Coma, Lola Beltran, The Pinker Tones, Rose Royce, and Ozomatli are great discs to start with.

A shallow box or container. Cigar boxes (Star's favorite), matchboxes, cake pans, dresser drawers, suitcases, and jewelry boxes work great. And don't worry—you don't need to have a bad habit to make art. You can find cigar boxes at any smoke shop.

A focal point. Star used an image from a Mexican comic, but you can use a family snapshot, a postcard, a small painting—anything that visually anchors the theme.

Decorative papers. Visit the scrapbook section of the craft store to find a treasure trove of options. You can also use vintage newsprint for an antique look.

Embellishments. Sequins, crystals, glitter, mini mirrors, stickers, old jewelry pieces—anything small that will give your box character.

Ribbons and trims. These are great for livening up the sides of your box and can be readily found at any craft, gift, or drug store.

Letter beads. Use these to spell out a name for your love shrine. Most craft stores carry a great variety.

Thick white craft glue (a glue stick or a hot-glue gun will work also), **scissors,** and **dimensional squeeze paint** (found at your favorite craft shop or any art supply store.)

Here's how to make it:

1. Line the inside and outside of your container with the decorative paper by using the white craft glue, a glue stick, or hot-glue gun.
2. Arrange your objects in the box. Start with the focal point image, and then build out. Don't glue anything

yet! Move the items around until you like the layout and then glue it all in place.

3. Affix any small embellishments, like ribbon, glitter, sequins, and crystals, along the sides of the box.

4. Using the letter beads, glue the title of your happiness shrine on the top border of the box. Let everything dry. Step back and take a look to see if you need to add anything else.

5. Once you're happy with how your shrine looks, glue a piece of paper on the back of the box. Use a pen to write about what inspired you to make the shrine. And don't forget to sign your name. All fabulous artists do!

Grow a Glittered Cactus Garden!

After reading so much about these marvelous centerpieces, how about making your own?

Here's what you'll need:

- **1 plastic prickly pear cactus, 8" tall** (you can look for these at craft stores or find them online)
- **1 medium-sized terra-cotta pot**
- **1 chunk of floral foam**
- **1 bag of faux moss**
- **Decoupage medium** (this is better than traditional glue and can be found at craft and art supply stores)
- **Crafty Chica Glamour Queen Green Glitter**
- **Brushes**
- **Hot glue**
- **Purple and red water-based acrylic paints** (colors optional, of course, but this is what Star and the craftistas use in the book for the desert feel)
- **Water-based brush-on varnish**

Here's how to make it:

1. Paint the base of the pot purple and the rim red and allow to dry completely.

2. Working over a sheet of paper, brush on the cactus a coat of decoupage medium and pour the glitter over it. Tap away the excess and set aside to dry. Pour excess glitter back in jar.

3. Insert the floral foam in the pot. Poke your finger into the middle of the foam, pushing down from the top, to create a hole. Add a dollop of hot glue onto the bottom of the cactus and insert it into the hole. Hold in place until glue cools and cactus does not move.

4. Add hot glue around the top of the foam and press on the faux moss until it looks nice and even.

Trivia!

Love Shine: Love Shine is an actual store in New York City. It is one of my all-time favorite boutiques because it specializes in crazy cool Mexicana pop art, like lucha libre coin purses, oil-cloth messenger bags, and glow-in-the-dark Virgin of Guadalupe statues. See for yourself! Love Shine is located at 543½ East 6th Street NY, NY 10009 or www.loveshinenyc.com.

Star's movie collection: Movies are a big part of Star's personality. She even sometimes dresses like her favorite characters. This is probably because movies are a big part of my life too. I used to get paid to interview actors and write about their film projects. Whenever I craft, I always have a movie on at the same time. The movies listed in this book make for great background noise while crafting. Romantic comedies are perfect for small projects because they are about ninety minutes, and epics are ideal for glitter marathons.

Ofie-isms: Ofie had an inspiring quote to fit any situation, but she had a little help coming up with them. She was a loyal reader of *The Ultimate Guide to the Perfect Word*, by Linda LaTourelle. This handy book is a must-have for any artist and/or crafter. It includes hundreds of sayings, quotes, and phrases for dozens of topics. You can use them in journaling, cardmaking, scrapbooking, rubber stamping, painting, and more.

Chloe's local TV crafting segments: While you may not come across anyone like Crafty Chloe or Frances, you'll be happy to know that craft segments do exist. Check out your local morning newscasts, and offer to be a guest crafter. Call the station to find out the name of the producer and send a sample or picture of your project, along with a short bio about yourself. You might just end up on television!

Grand Avenue: This is a street in Phoenix that stretches diagonally across the valley. Around the downtown area, Grand Avenue is lined with dozens of art galleries, shops, eateries, and boutiques—all very edgy, with an indie vibe. The best time to go is on "First Fridays"—the first Friday of every month during the evening. All the galleries are open and there are art receptions, live music, firewalkers, dancers, and many other surprises. There are other popular streets on the Phoenix First Fridays route too—Roosevelt St., 7th Avenue to 7th Street. Take the free shuttle and hop around!

Start a craft group: Maybe you don't have two hundred centerpieces to make, but you can still form a craft collective. Follow Ofie's idea and hang flyers in places that fit your personality. You can also look online for people in your area.

Speed crochet: Yes, this is an actual event that is held every year! Google the term to see for yourself!

La Pachanga and Maker's Marketplace: My fantasy landmarks.

Reading Group Guide

1. How do you think the title of this book, *Waking Up in the Land of Glitter*, relates to each character? What is your perception of "the land of glitter?"

2. From her clothes to her music and, more important, her life choices, Star is all over the map. Do you think she is hardwired that way, or is it more because of the way she was raised by her parents? Why do you think she was so flighty and indecisive in the beginning of the book? Or do you think that is an unfair description?

3. What do you think it was that made Star get serious? Do you think she wanted to make up for the mistakes she made at her parents' expense, or prove she could be a responsible adult? Do you think she made the changes for other people or for herself?

4. Star found a good friend in Harrison, but for some reason, things didn't click. Do you think it was because she was still in love with Theo, or because Harrison just wasn't her type?

5. All of Ofie's family and friends love her so much that they hide the truth about her lack of talent because they don't want to hurt her feelings. Do you think this was the correct way to handle the situation? What do you think would have happened to Ofie if they continued

the lie? Do you think it is more important to always tell the truth, or to let a person enjoy doing what she loves?

6. What role does crafting play in each woman's life? Did the experience of knowing and working with one another change their original perception of what crafting is all about? Did their stories change your perception of crafting?

7. Chloe went to many extremes for the sake of her career. Why was it so important to her? Can you think of a time when you almost lost yourself in trying to achieve a goal? When is it time to stop?

8. Do you think being apart from each other helped Star and Theo's relationship? In what ways? If she had never spray painted his mural in August, do you think they would have ended up engaged by December?

9. Can you identify what each woman subconsciously yearned for in their lives and if they attained it? For example, what void did Gustavo fill in Chloe's heart? After being so precise and strategic with her decisions, what made her elope with a man she barely knew? Do you think their relationship has a chance to survive?

10. Do you think Chloe deserved what Frances served her, or was Frances being unfair?

11. Did culture play a part in how you perceived these characters? Did their heritage make you feel more connected or less connected?

12. Which character do you feel most in touch with and why? Which one would you like to spend the day with and chat?

13. What is your take on art vs. craft?

14. Have you ever been in a craft group? What were the dynamics between the members?

Questions for the Author

1. **You are known for writing instructional craft books. How did the novel come about?**

   My two favorite pastimes have always been crafting and writing. I dreamed of writing a novel that combined the two, but the task seemed too huge to even consider. All along, I had been blogging about living an artful life. I had two editors from publishing houses write me and ask if I had ever considered writing a novel based on my adventures. On the outside, I said, "Yeah, right." But inside I knew I wanted to try it! I wrote an outline, but still couldn't write that first page. But then I learned about National Novel Writing Month. I signed up and wrote the first draft! It was quite a journey to reach this point, but I never gave up faith.

2. **Is being crafty really as drama-filled as it is portrayed in the book?**

   Yes, it can be. Especially if you are very passionate about it. Crafting isn't just a hobby to many people, it is a lifestyle. And there is not just one type of crafter. Everyone has a different motivation. Some people, like Star, separate art from craft; others, like Chloe, see only the monetary value of a career in the industry. And then there are those like Ofie, who are addicted to making things as an expression of love. When I developed the plot, I wondered what it would be like to force these three types of crafters together in a group. I knew the glitter would fly!

3. **Are your characters based on real people?**

   Chloe, Star, and Ofie—all of them have a little bit of me from different phases in my life. At the same time, Al,

Gustavo, and Larry are inspired by my dad, David Cano, and my husband, Patrick. As for the other characters, in my first draft, I did have specific people in mind, but as I went through dozens of rewrites, the characters bloomed in their own way. They didn't want to reenact my experiences; they had their own stories to tell. As soon as I gave in to that, everything clicked into place.

4. **How does fiction writing compare to crafting?**

They are very much alike! With crafting, I have to decide on a concept, make a sketch, and choose colors. With fiction writing, I nail down a plot, develop characters, and draft an outline. With writing, the words and sentences are the paints and glitter.

5. **What is the deal with glitter, and why did you give it such an important role in the book?**

To me, glitter is a metaphor for life. It catches your eye and the sparkle makes you forget all your worries because it is so beautiful. I love it because it is so shiny and indulgent, yet calorie-free!

6. **Have you ever had Star, Ofie, or Chloe moments?**

Oh sure! My Star moment: Once when I worked at the newspaper, I thought I could multitask on making my crafts. I went outside to the smoking lounge to spray varnish on my project. All the smokers got mad because I stunk up their area and they kicked me out! My Chloe moment: One time, just a few minutes before my live-TV segment, one of the news anchors came to my craft table and took a bite out of my demo project! (It was a Rice Krispies chocolate tree.) And I have Ofie moments every day of my life!

7. **Years later, what do you want people to remember about this book?**

   I want them to feel like there is always hope. Even when you hit rock bottom, as long as you have a good heart, and a strong spirit, you can overcome. I also want them to try to express themselves through some sort of art form. I hope it inspires people to meet with their friends and get crafty!

8. **How do you fit writing into your busy schedule?**

   When I love something, I will find time to do it. For this book, I wrote every night after my family went to sleep. I had zero interruptions—it was perfect. During editing, I swore off all TV shows for three months. I tell myself, "No one will make this happen except you—so do it!"

9. **Is Phoenix really as artful as it sounds?**

   Yes, it sure is! We have First Fridays that bring out thousands of art lovers. It is very much how it is described in the book. There are many fun coffee houses and bars, dance clubs and concert venues. It's very active!

Guía de Lectura

1. ¿Cómo relaciona el título del libro, *Waking Up in the Land of Glitter*, con cada carácter? ¿Cuál es su percepción del mudo de purpurina?

2. De su ropa a su música, y más importante de sus elecciones en la vida, Estrella no sigue ningún estilo de vida. ¿Cree usted que ella fue nació así, o es mejor a cause del modo en que sus padres la criaron? ¿Por qué era Estrella tan veleidosa e indecisa al principio de la novela? O, ¿cree usted que esta descripción no es justa?

3. ¿Qué cree usted que causó el cambio en Estrella a hacerse seria? ¿Cree usted que ella quería recobrar las faltas que ella había hecho contra sus padres? ¿O cree usted que ella quería enseñar que ahorra era una persona responsable? ¿Cree usted que hizo los cambios para otras personas, o para si misma?

4. Estrella encontró un buen amigo en Harrison, pero por alguna razón, no hubo química romántica. ¿Cree usted que el problema fue que Estrella todavía estaba enamorada de Theo, o simplemente que Harrison no era su tipo?

5. La familia y las amigas de Ofie la aman tanto que esconden la verdad—que ella no tiene talento artístico— porque no quieren hacerle daño. ¿Cree usted que ésto fue el mejor moda de ayudarle? ¿Qué le hubiera pasado

a Ofie si las mintiras hubieran seguido? ¿Qué cree usted que es más importante: siempre decir la verdad, o permitir a una persona haciendo lo que ama?

6. ¿Qué papel tiene la artesanía en las vidas de Estrella, Ofie y Chloe? ¿Cambiaron sus ideas de lo que es el arte porque se conocieron y trabajaron juntas? ¿Cambió usted sus ideas de la artesanía después de leer sus cuentos?

7. Chloe hizo muchas cosas extremas para ganar éxito en su trabajo. ¿Por qué era tan importante para ella tener éxito? ¿Tiene usted un ejemplo en su vida cuando casi perdió todo tratando de realizar una meta? ¿A qué punto debe parar?

8. ¿Cree usted que la separación de Estrella y Theo ayudó la relación de ellos? ¿Cómo sí o cómo no? ¿Si Estrella no hubiera pintado el mural en agosto, hubieran estado comprometidos en diciembre?

9. ¿Puede usted identificar lo que cada mujer deseaba en su vida, y decir si lo realizaron? Por ejemplo, qué vaciedad llenó Gustavo en el corazón de Chloe? Después de ser tan precisa y tan estratégica con todas sus decisiones, ¿por qué se fugó con un hombre que casi no conocía? ¿Cree usted que esta relación puede sobrevivir?

10. ¿Cree usted que Chloe mereció lo que Frances le hizo? ¿O fue injusta Frances?

11. ¿Influyó su cultura en como notó usted las caracteres? ¿Sintió usted una conexión con ellas a cause de su patrimonio?

12. ¿Con cuál carácter conecta usted más y por qué? ¿Con cuál le gustaría usted pasar el día?

13. ¿Qué es su opinión del arte versus la artesanía?

14. ¿Ha estado usted en un grupo para hacer la artesanía? Si sí, ¿cómo funcionaron los miembros? ¿Todos se llevaron bien?

Preguntas para la autora

1. **Eres conocida por tus libros instructivos de la artesanía. ¿Cómo decidiste escribir una novela?**

   Mis dos pasatiempos favoritos siempre han sido hacer la artesanía y escribir. Soñaba de escribir un libro que combinaría los dos, pero me parecía imposible. Escribía un blog de vivir una vida artística. Eventualmente, dos editoras de dos casas editoriales diferentes me llamaron para preguntar si yo estaba interesada en escribir un cuento basado en mi vida. Al principio dije, "No hay como"—bromeando. ¡Pero sabía que quería tratarlo! Escribí un sinopsis, pero todavía no podía escribir la primera página. Entonces aprendí de "National Novel Writing Month." ¡Me matriculé y escribí la primera versión! Ha sido un gran viaje a este punto, pero nunca perdía la fe.

2. **¿Hay tanto drama en la vida de una artista real como hay en el libro?**

   Sí, es posible que lo hay. Particularmente cuando una artista es muy apasionada. Para muchas personas, la artesanía no es solo un pasatiempo, sino un estilo de vida. Y no es solo un tipo de persona que hace la artesanía. Cada persona tiene una motivación diferente. Algunas, como Estrella, separan el arte de la artesanía; otras, como Chloe, solo ven el valor financiero de una profesión en la industria. Y también hay las otras como Ofie, que están adictivas de hacer cosas para mostrar su amor. Cuando escribí el libro, pensaba en que pasaría si estos tres tipos de personas tuvieran que trabajar juntos. ¡Sabía que las purpurinas volarían!

3. ¿Están fundidos sus caracteres en personas reales?

Estrella, Ofie, y Chloe—todas tiene un poquito de mí, en tiempos diferentes en mi vida. Y Al, Gustavo, y Larry tienen algo de mi padre, David Cano, y mi marido, Patrick. En mi primera versión pensé en personas específicas, pero poco a poco los caracteres empezaron a tener unas vidas propias. No querían contar mis experiencias; tenían sus propios cuentos. Tan pronto como me rendí a eso, todo pasó bien.

4. ¿Cómo comparas escribir una novela con hacer la artesanía?

¡Son muy similares! Con la artesanía, tengo que decidir en una idea, hacer un esbozo, y escoger los colores. Cuando escribo una novela, tengo que formar un trama, crear mis caracteres, y hacer un bosquejo. Con el escribiendo, las palabras y las frases son las pinturas y la purpurina.

5. ¿Por qué le das a la purpurina un papel tan importante en el libro?

Para mí, la purpurina es una metáfora para la vida. Cuando coge su ojo y brilla, se olvida todos sus problemas, porque es tan bella. ¡Me encanta la purpurina porque es brillante e indulgente, pero sin calorías!

6. ¿Has tenido momentos como Estrella, Ofie, o Chloe?

¡Claro! Mi momento Estrella: Cuando trabajaba para el periódico, quería hace mi arte al mismo tiempo. Por eso, un día fui a dónde la gente fumaba para pulverizar barniz en mi proyecto. Todos los fumadores se enojaron porque el barniz olió muy mal. ¡Me expulsaron!

Mi momento Chloe: Una vez, algunos minutos antes de mi segmento vivo en la televisión, uno de los presentadores vino a mi mesa y tomó una mordida grande de mi proyecto. (Era un árbol de chocolate hecho de Rice Krispies.) ¡Y tengo momentos Ofie cada día de mi vida!

7. **En el futuro, ¿Qué quieres que otras personas recuerden de tu libro?**

Quiero que sientan que siempre hay esperanza. No importa que mal la situación parezca; si tienes un corazón bueno y un espíritu fuerte, puedes sobrevivir. También, espero que traten de expresarse con algún tipo de arte. ¡Espero que el libro inspire a otras a reunirse con sus amigos y hacerse artísticos!

8. **¿Cómo hallas tiempo para escribir en tu horario tan lleno?**

Cuando amo algo, encuentro el tiempo para hacerlo. Con este libro, escribía cada noche después de que mi familia se retiraba a cama. No tenía ningunas molestas—era perfecto. Durante el proceso editorial, rendí la televisión por tres meses. Me dije, "Nadie va a hacerlo para ti—solamente tú lo puedes hacer."

9. **¿Es tan artística Phoenix como aparece?**

¡Absolutamente! Tenemos "First Fridays"—una celebración en el primer viernes de cada mes que atrae miles de aficionados del arte. Es muy similar a la descripción del libro. Hay muchos cafés, bars, clubs, y lugares para oír música. ¡Es muy vigoroso!

About the Author

With a life motto of "Crafts! Drama! Glitter!" Crafty Chica
KATHY CANO-MURILLO is a creative force of nature. A former
syndicated columnist for *The Arizona Republic,* she is the founder
of the award-winning Web site, CraftyChica.com and the author
of seven nonfiction craft books and a Web series on LifetimeTV
.com. Kathy has a Crafty Chica line of art supplies that are sold
nationwide. She also has been featured in numerous media out-
lets such as *The New York Times Magazine,* NPR's Weekend
Edition, *USA Today, Bust,* and *Latina* magazine. She has shared
her crafty ideas on local television, as well as on Sí TV, HGTV,
and DIY network. She has been writing stories longer than she
has been crafting. Inspired by Judy Blume and Erma Bombeck,
she caught the literary bug in grade school, where she used to
draw a picture and then write a colorful story to go with it. It's a
creativity exercise she still practices to this day! Kathy lives in
Phoenix, Arizona, with her husband, two kids, and five Chihuahuas. This is her first novel.

CRAFTY CHICA™

Hey there all you future craftistas!

Thanks for reading *Waking Up in the Land of Glitter*. I hope you had as much fun reading it as I did writing it! Are you wondering where ladies like Star, Ofie, and Chloe go for creative new project ideas? Then check out my Web site, www.craftychica.com. It's loaded with pictures, products, projects, and the inside scoop on what's hot right now. You can read my blog and sign up for my newsletter, so you'll be the first to know all the latest, breaking news—like when my next novel will be out!

Here is the best part —you can even pick out a special gift from me! Here's how: Complete the contact form on my Web site, mention the code word "GLITTER" — and don't forget your name and mailing address. One per person (while supplies last, of course!).

Check out www.craftychica.com and find everything you need to unleash your inner craft goddess!

Peace, love, and glitter!

Kathy

IF YOU ENJOYED *WAKING UP IN THE LAND OF GLITTER,* THEN YOU'RE SURE TO LIKE THESE AS WELL—

Now available from Grand Central Publishing:

"This book is a delightful feast for the reader."
—Susan Wiggs, *New York Times* bestselling author of *Just Breathe*

A secret journal threatens to destroy a young woman as she uncovers the truth about her deceased mother's past in this stunning debut novel.

"Zepeda is a master wordsmith."
—Alisa Valdes-Rodriguez, *New York Times* bestselling author of *The Dirty Girls Social Club*